Dying to Know

A Detective Inspector Berenice Killick Mystery

Alison Joseph

© Alison Joseph 2013

Alison Joseph has asserted her rights under the Copyright, Design and Patents Act, 1988, to be identified as the author of this work.

First published 2013 by Endeavour Press Ltd.

Chapter One
Falling

It is the end of the story.

She imagined him on the beach, pacing out the last moments of his life. She thought about him climbing, somewhere high up, up on the cliffs along the coast. Standing, on the top, gazing out to sea. Breathing. Jumping. Falling. One, two, three seconds. And then you hit the water.

After that…

Water in the lungs, they're saying.

Which means, still breathing. For a while, anyway.

And now, here, washed up, a silent twisted heap in the midst of noise, the wind across the beach, the crackle of police radios, the flap of blue and white tape in the breeze.

'Berenice. What you thinking, Boss?'

She blinked. 'Oh. Mary.' She looked across the shingle that sparkled in the sunlight. 'I was thinking…'

'About death, was it?'

'Do you think he fell by accident? Do you think he jumped?'

'Usually it's the high points near Folkestone that wash up this way.'

'But wanting to die…'

'You always ask those questions.'

Berenice gave a brief smile. 'Do we know who he is?'

DS Mary Ashcroft shook her head.

'Someone will have missed him,' Berenice said.

'He's been in the water at least twenty four hours, they reckon,' Mary said. 'He's what, forty odd? Well dressed, at least he was till those crabs fancied a bite of Harris Tweed…'

'No one just disappears these days.' Berenice said. She held out her hands in their blue latex gloves. 'The SOCO gave me these. He said, seeing as I was the investigating officer…'

'Of course you're the investigating officer,' Mary said. 'Detective Inspector Berenice Killick…'

'Look.' Berenice held a see-through plastic envelope up to the light. 'Stuff from his pockets.'

'No ID?' Mary took the envelope.

Berenice shook her head. 'We should get back to HQ.'

'"… whence is it that the sun and planets gravitate towards one another without dense matter between them?"'

'What?'

Mary was peering at the envelope. 'That's what it says here. Writings.'

'You're making it up.'

'I'm not. Look.'

Berenice stared, read the words. 'Clever bloke, then. It's always the brainy ones. Do you remember that poor man in

Wetherby? Wrote out a ground-breaking formula for a new TB drug and then blew out his brains?'

'We were still Yorkshire-women then.' Mary turned towards the cars.

'Perhaps we are still.' Berenice fell into step beside her.

'You mean, you can take the girl out of Yorkshire…' Mary smiled.

'Something like that.' The pebbles shifted under their feet. The sea had withdrawn into quiet, distant waves, as if to declare itself incapable of killing.

Further inland, beside the pale ribbon of the Hythe road, stands a haphazard arrangement of concrete buildings, which make up the East Kent Lepton Research Institute. Here, in a swish of automatic doors, Liam Phelps, physicist, walks into the control room.

'Elizabeth. You called?' In the wide, bright room there were banks of screens. At one of them sat a woman, in crisp shirt and trousers, her pale brown hair tied back.

'Where is he?' She looked up from her screen. 'It's not like him to disappear.'

'Murdo? Perhaps he went for one of his walks.'

'He can't have done. Not today. Have you seen this?'

He leaned on the nearest desk, one arm on her chair. She sat, smart, upright and nervous. He stared at the data in front of him. Two lines, one red, one blue. 'Full beam – ' he began to say.

'No, Liam, look. Look at the chart for the last half hour.'

He stared some more. 'But these can't be B-mesons…'

'Exactly. It's the same thing again.'

'The same as yesterday?'

'And the day before,' she said. 'Something weird's going on. That new pattern - these collisions…'

He leaned towards the screen. 'Did you check luminosity – what about charge errors?'

'We've checked. Look.' She pulled up a screen, scrolled down it. 'Everything's clear. We've checked and checked. The results don't make sense.' Her voice was soft, with a trace of an American accent.

Liam looked at her. 'And Murdo's missing.'

'It's too weird. This is his experiment – '

He turned to go. 'We'd better call a meeting about these results. Just us five. And the director. OK?'

She reached up and touched his sleeve. 'Liam – what about Murdo? It's not like him to disappear.'

'Maguire? I'll keep trying his mobile,' he said. 'Unless you want to?'

She shook her head. 'No,' she said. 'Not me.'

The screens murmured their gentle beeping, and her gaze travelled back to the graphs in front of her. 'Perhaps we should phone the police,' she said.

'I'm not sure it's part of their brief to worry about changes in the make-up of the universe - '

She gave a thin smile. 'I meant, Murdo.'

'I know,' he said.

'Although I guess they're tired of hearing from us.'

'A broken window is different from a missing man,' he said. 'Even if it was a deliberate attack on this building.'

'Just bored kids.'

'Three nights running? And what about the hate mail?' he said.

'Superstition. Or Sci Fi heads. Anyway, Richard has got security guys at both entrances now.'

He glanced down at her. 'I'll be back,' he said. He turned back to her. 'No one else must know about this. Only the team. Understood?'

She nodded, her gaze fixed on the screen.

She got out her phone, called up his number. Murdo Maguire. Her finger hesitated over the name. She clicked it off. In front of her the red and blue lines lurched upwards, crashed downwards.

DI Berenice Killick splashed water on her face. Her face in the mirror stared back. She ran a finger through her long black hair extensions.

It is my case, she thought. A man washed up on the beach, with no ID but his pockets full of weird writings about gravity. I should be in charge.

Had she imagined it, she wondered. That sneer from the SIO on their return, Detective Chief Inspector Stuart Coles, 'Well, Miss Killick, there's no point asking me where he might have fallen from… of course, a little local knowledge might come in very handy at this point…'

Something about the word 'local'. A tone of voice…

The door creaked open. 'Thought I'd find you here,' Mary said. 'We've had a call from Hythe. Missing person. Physicist, works at the lab there. Murdo Maguire, aged 43, white, grey-haired, blue eyes, not been seen for a couple of days. Not out of character, they said, but they were worried about him. He's got a wife up the coast here.'

'That's our man, isn't it?'

'His car's been found too,' Mary said, 'abandoned on the Hythe Road, right by that old lighthouse there. Looks like he drove there with the intent of climbing that tower.'

'And jumping off?'

Mary shrugged. 'Who knows. Anyway, Stuart said, as we know who it is, you and I can go back on the warehouse raid case for now. He wants us to follow up the number-plate sightings.'

'Doesn't that need local knowledge too?'

Mary looked at her. 'Oh, God.'

'I didn't just imagine it, then?' Berenice sighed. 'Is it the Yorkshire bit he doesn't like? Or the women bit? Like he would prefer it if everyone was Kentish, male and white?'

'You don't regret the move, do you?' Mary glanced at herself in the mirror. She was wearing a neutral navy suit, and bright red shoes.

Berenice shook her head. 'You know my reasons for coming south.' She took a lip-gloss out of her bag. 'Physicist?' she said. 'Explains that stuff in his pocket about matter and thing. Funny the fish didn't eat that too.'

'Nah, too clever for fish.'

Berenice studied her reflection. Mary met her eyes in the mirror. 'You're thinking about Him, aren't you? Talking of reasons for leaving Yorkshire. Like, how would his wife react if some DC turned up on her doorstep in Leeds – '

'I wasn't actually.' Her voice was sharp. 'I was thinking about these extensions? I mean, really honestly, I know you said you liked them but maybe a short Afro is best for a new DI.'

'Berenice, would I lie to you?'

'– Like, I look like I'm doing an Alicia Keys cover on the X Factor–'

'Listen, Boss, I had blonde extensions all last year and I didn't look like white trash, did I?'

'I never said trash.' Berenice turned away from the mirror. 'And as far as "Him" is concerned, drowning's too good for him.'

'You know the physicist's wife didn't report him missing. Weird eh? He'd been gone two days and a night.'

Berenice shrugged. 'As far as I'm concerned, nothing's weird between man and wife. Come on. Let's go and talk to that villain about the warehouse stuff. While we've got time.'

'What do you mean?'

'Well, there's a dead physicist in the fridge. God knows what that's going to do to the universe.'

'What is there in places almost empty of matter, and whence is it that the sun and planets gravitate towards one another without dense matter between them?'

Virginia Maguire sat in the shadows of her cottage, the book on her lap. She ran her finger along the parchment-thick paper.

'Whence is it that nature doth nothing in vain; and whence arises all that order and beauty that we see in the world? What hinders the fixed stars from falling upon one another?'

She tutted loudly, her lips tight with disapproval.

'For if Nature be simple and pretty conformable to herself, causes will operate in the same kind of way with all phenomena, so that the motions of smaller bodies depend upon certain smaller forces, just as the motions of larger bodies are ruled by the greater force of gravity…'

She held the book in her lap. Perhaps I should throw it in the fire, she thought. She looked at the fireplace at her side, its dusty black surfaces, the cold ash in the grate.

And what would he think, my husband, to find I've thrown his precious book into the fire…'

She picked it up and read some more.

'The Imprint of the origin of the universe can, in the right hands, be detected in its ancient chemistry. It is a creation of infinite duration, and yet, the question we must ask is, how did

matter become matter? Who, or what, set this universe in motion? It is this that we are working to uncover – '

'Hah.' She spoke out loud. She turned to the very first page, and ran her finger along the line where her husband had written, in pencil, his own name. 'Murdo Maguire.'

Her finger, roughened through age and hard work, brushed against the words. '*We have the authority of those the oldest and most celebrated philosophers of Greece and Phoenicia, who made a vacuum, and atoms, and the gravity of atoms, the first principles of their philosophy…*' She slammed the book shut.

The thick window panes let in a dusky daylight which picked out the grain of the wide oak window sills, the faded whitewash on the old stone walls.

There was a knock at the door. She stared at it. Another knock. She got to her feet and went to open the door.

A uniformed policewoman was standing there, with a police officer next to her, a man. He gave his name, Detective Sergeant something or other, but she felt only weariness at the sight of them, standing there on her doorstep.

'Mrs. Maguire?' they said. 'Mrs. Virginia Maguire?'

'Yes,' she said. 'Do come in.' But she knew, as she showed them in, as she went to the kitchen to put on the kettle, she knew as they told her about the body found on the beach, a man, drowned, that the moment she had always dreaded, had thought of as inevitable, had come.

She would show no emotion. Like the quiet hiss of the kettle as it sat on the stove, as she listened to their words, 'body found on the beach... initial identification suggests... we're very sorry, Mrs. Maguire...' her feelings would stay hushed, simmering quietly. There would be no rage. Even when the kettle came to the boil, even when its whistle shrieked through the air around her, she would sit there, quiet and pale, her head on one side, listening politely.

Alone at her desk, Elizabeth Merletti, physicist, sat by her computer. Her gaze was fixed on the screen as she clicked between images. Click: multi-colour lines emanating outwards from the chaos. Click: two lines, one red, one blue, intersecting where the beams collide. Click, a graph, a sharp upward black line. Click: a photo; him, standing, in sunshine, by water, head turned towards her, smiling. The blue of the lake, the blue of his shirt, the sun on his hair, the warmth of his smile...

And now gone.

Beneath her feet, sixty metres under the ground, there is a tunnel of ice-cold nothingness and infinite collidings, its giant, glinting engineering conjuring the figures on to the screen in front of her.

But all she sees is a blue and blonde picture of life itself. Her eyes shine, perhaps with tears.

She murmurs to herself, one word. It sounds like 'cheated'.

Tyres sliding into mud. Engines silenced. The flash of head lights on the black bare branches of the trees. Berenice Killick opened her car door. DS Mary Ashcroft did the same.

They surveyed the scene before them. One ancient white van, one caravan, their wheels mired in mud.

'That's the van all right.' Berenice nodded towards it. Mary took a photo of the number-plate.

Silence. Grey afternoon light, grey of the concrete wall behind the caravan. They knocked on the door.

Still silence. They peered through the windows. There were sleeping bags heaped on the seats, empty beer cans on the table.

Berenice stepped back on to the mud.

'So what's that, then, over the wall there?'

Mary looked at the high concrete, the barbed wire on top. 'That's the lab. The physics place, where they're smashing atoms.'

'So that's where he worked, our drowned man?'

'Secret of the universe in there, Boss. Keeping the whole show turning.'

'Shame it can't stop just long enough for us to find our villain at home - ' She stopped, short. There was a flick of curtain in the window of the caravan. 'There's someone there.'

Berenice knocked loudly. 'Or do you want us to break this door down – '

The door swung open. Standing there slouched a girl, in a huge red sweatshirt and tattered leggings.

'Who are you?' Berenice said.

'I'm Lisa.'

'Police,' Berenice said, as Mary flashed a badge.

'Yeah yeah, I know.' The voice had a teenage weariness.

'D I Killick and DS Ashcroft. We're looking for Clem Voake. Is he your dad?'

The girl laughed. 'My dad?' She shook her head. 'Look at me, blad. He's a white man, innit.'

Berenice had her foot in the door. 'My dad's a white man too.'

Lisa eyed her. 'You saying you black like me?'

'That's exactly what I'm saying.'

'Black you may be, but you're gavvers all the same.'

'Do you know where he is, Clem Voake?'

The girl met her eyes. 'Don't know. Don't care. Berenice turned to go.

'He's at a funeral,' the girl said.

Berenice turned back. 'Thought you didn't know where he was.'

'Just remembered.'

'Whose funeral?'

She shrugged. 'Dunno. Shall I tell him you called?' She gave an empty laugh.

Berenice faced her. 'Yes,' she said. 'And tell him we'll call again.'

At the car, Berenice handed Mary the keys. She sank into the passenger seat, as the wheels span in the mud before skidding out on the track.

'Did you see those marks on her arms? If we don't get him for the warehouse raid, we can get him for child abuse.'

'Child?'

'I reckon she's about fifteen.'

'Do you think she's related to him?' Mary accelerated onto the main road. The rain had begun again.

'Why else is she there?'

'I can think of many reasons, and none of them good.'

Berenice yawned. 'Gavvers,' she said.

'Makes a change from Filth, I suppose. Or Scum.'

The radio crackled against the to and fro of the windscreen wipers.

Berenice's phone rang, loudly. She answered, listened, then clicked it off.

'Well, well. The drowned physicist. They've stopped the Post Mortem. Called in the Home Office. Bruising to the head. Fractured cheekbone. Suggests he was assaulted before he hit the water.'

'Not suicide…' Mary stared at her.

'Unlawful killing. Maybe.'

'Maybe Stuart'll need us after all.'

Berenice looked at her. 'He might need you…'

Mary sighed, shook her head. 'Far be it from me to deny your radar where that kind of thing is concerned,' she said.

'Good.' Berenice yawned, again, settled back in her seat. She watched the drizzle in the windscreen wipers. She thought about the physicist, his last moments, his fractured cheekbone. A fight of some kind, a scuffle on the tower. The wind, the tide high, the sea… Then falling.

Falling.

'Maybe he was pushed,' Mary said.

Chapter Two

The Reverend Chad Meyrick walked along the beach, his collar buttoned against the cold sea wind. He'd been telephoned by the police, that community constable, he'd met him a couple of times now, the last time was that business with the sign outside the village hall. At the time they'd found it amusing, he and Helen, how in his previous parish he'd been comforting the bereaved mothers of gang members and now here he was, having to describe a stolen parish notice board - but the policeman, PC Andrews, he was called, said, no, this time it's quite serious, 'You know they found a body on the beach?'

A body. Helen had told him that morning at breakfast that they'd identified the drowned man that they'd found further up the coast.

'Yes,' Chad had said to PC Andrews, 'I had heard.'

'Well, the widow has asked if you'd visit her, as she's one of your flock, you know how it is, Sir…'

My flock…

A pebble caught his eye. A fine, smooth, pink quartz. He stooped to pick it up, held it in his hand.

I hardly know the woman. She's probably set foot in church a handful of times. She did arrive with those flowers once, arranged them in a dingy vase by the porch, said it was a memorial. I should have pried, I suppose, I should have made it my business to find out more…'

Privacy, though. My flock should have their privacy from me, just as I should from them.

They'd not got on well, the policeman had said. But it's still a shock for the widow, don't you think, Sir…

He'd agreed, yes, of course, yes he'd visit her…

And now it felt like prying. Just as it felt like prying when he faced his congregation. All those questions in their eyes, why doesn't his wife come to church, I've heard she's a dancer, you know what they're like, never was a respectable profession, and as for them not having children, it's not as if they're young enough to put it off…

Perhaps I'm imagining it. Perhaps they respect me. As the sheep respect their shepherd… no, that didn't seem quite right.

He dropped the pebble, watched it bounce against the others. "To any action," – the words came to his mind - "there is always an opposite and equal reaction. If anyone presses a stone with a finger, the finger is also pressed by the stone…"

He headed up the beach, away from the sea, wondering what had made him think of Newton, wondering how to include Newton in a sermon, imagining the faces of his congregation as he tried to explain the role of the Creator in Newton's universe. There would be blank stares, shuffling feet, glances exchanged, the almost audible thoughts, what a shame dear old Robinson died, you knew where you were with Robinson…

He took the path away from the beach, towards the sandy track that led to the village. He noticed, once again, how the sound of the sea made an upward, rushing note, like a song.

The cottage was a low, two-storey building. Two old stone flowerpots stood either side of the door. From their damp earth projected some barren twigs and a few weeds. He knocked on the heavy wooden door, checked the directions on the scrap of paper that PC Andrews had given him, knocked again.

The woman who opened the door seemed very small, as if she'd been designed to fit the scale of the cottage. She had hair that he thought was a kind of silver colour, but it might have been blonde. Her grey eyes considered him with a blank look.

'Mrs. Maguire?'

Her gaze scanned him, up and down. Her expression didn't change. 'Oh,' she said. 'They sent you.'

'They – they said you'd asked for me. Parish priest, you know…'

'Their idea, not mine. Well, you'd better come in.' She turned, abruptly, and led him into the house. Inside he was aware of warmth, the afternoon light filtering through the windows. There was a sofa, draped with a knitted patchwork blanket, a shabby leather armchair next to it, on which was curled a tabby cat.

He sat on the sofa. 'He – he was your husband,' he began.

She filled the kettle with water from the tap, placed it on the kitchen range. She turned to him, wiping her hands on her apron. 'They've told you nothing, it's clear,' she said.

'I can go if you like.' He hadn't meant to sound so sharp, but he felt like an intruder. He'd expected to be comforting a grief-stricken widow, and this calm, expressionless response was disconcerting.

She considered him. He felt suddenly self-conscious, as if his jacket was hanging badly, or his dog collar was dirty, or his brown brogues were muddy. He smoothed down his hair (dark brown, greying at the temples), checked his trousers, which still looked clean in spite of the walk along the sand. Something seemed to pass muster, because she softened.

'It's a relief, actually,' she said, as if it had just occurred to her. 'To have someone who doesn't know the whole story.'

And what is the story, he was about to ask, but the whistling of the kettle drew her away from him. 'Tea?' she said. 'Otherwise I've only got instant.'

'Tea, then. Please.' The cat stirred, stretched and looked at him. He reached out a hand towards it.

'I'd be wary of her if I were you.' She was setting out cups, a jug of milk. 'As soon bite you as look at you, that one. Her sister was nicer-natured, but she's long gone.'

He withdrew his hand, noticed on the table next to him a leather-bound volume. He picked it up. It showed signs of antiquity; the calf-skin cover, the thick creamy paper, the neat brown ink of the writing inside.

"We have the authority of those the oldest and most celebrated philosophers of Greece and Phoenicia, who made a vacuum, and atoms, and the gravity of atoms, the first principles – "

'That's enough of that,' she said. Her voice was loud. She turned back to the kitchen range.

Her tone had surprised him. 'Newton,' he said.

She didn't reply, spooning sugar from a bag into a bowl.

'It must be,' he went on. 'Greece and Phoenicia, the gravity of atoms…'

'Nothing but trouble, that book,' she said.

She brought the tray to the table, arranged cups and saucers.

'Someone's copied it out, by hand,' he pursued, 'some years ago, by the look of it.'

'How do you know it's Newton?'

He met her eyes. 'Or someone imitating him, perhaps,' he said. 'But the language is familiar.' He shrugged. 'I studied all that. A long time ago. I'm no expert.' He turned to the first page. Two names were written there. The first, in curled archaic ink, said, 'Johann van Mielen'; underneath, in neat pencil, 'Murdo Maguire'.

'Milk?'

'Just a splash.'

'The sugar's there.'

She settled opposite him, and the cat jumped down from the sofa and took up a position on the arm of her chair. She murmured at it, petted its neck.

He waited for a moment, then said, 'They said – that your husband was based at the lab for some years.'

She nodded at him. 'What else did they tell you?'

'Nothing else. Only that I should visit you. Which was it seems, unnecessary.'

'I wouldn't say that.' She reached forward to her teacup. 'I call myself a Christian, at least.'

'I'm glad to hear it,' he said. It sounded forced, and he wished he hadn't said it.

'Well, it's your job, isn't it,' she said. 'Although, your God, claims to be a God of love, can't say there's any place for that in my life now.'

The cat yawned, then jumped down from the chair, sauntered out to the kitchen, and sat by the back door, peering out through the cat-flap.

'He worked in physics,' she said. 'My husband. Worked at the East Kent Centre. Research, particle physics, neutrinos… might not mean anything to you - '

'Mass-less particles,' he said. 'Sub-atomic.'

She almost smiled. 'Sort of, yes.' She took a sip of tea. 'I have called myself his wife for seventeen years, and for twelve of those we were happy.' She looked up at him. 'Are you married?'

'Yes,' he said.

She looked surprised. 'Children?' she said.

He shook his head.

'But you'd like them?'

He breathed in, then out. 'Yes,' he said. 'Yes, I would.'

'Your wife – '

'My wife used to be a dancer. Well, she still is…'

'Don't leave it too late,' she said. 'For children, I mean.'

He opened his mouth to speak, closed it again. He had a sudden urge to confide in her, this odd, blank, tightly-sealed person. To tell her all about it, the miscarriage, two years ago, the silences, the sense of loss, of being culpable, of being the one to blame for their continued infertility. There – that word. To say it out loud –

But she was speaking. 'Drowned,' he heard.

'Who?'

'Such an odd balance,' she said. 'First our boy, and now here he is. Choosing water.' She looked up at him. 'A watery grave.' She almost smiled, but he could see, for the first time, the hint of tears in her eyes. 'Oh, heavens, see, I'm so used to people knowing, and there you are, uncomprehending…' She slapped her hands on her aproned lap. 'Though I'm surprised no one's gossiped to you about it. How many months have you been living up there now?'

'Five,' he said. 'Nearly six.'

'Hmmm,' she said. 'Well, it was like this. Five years ago, our son, who was eight, they went fishing, you see, out on a boat, not here, not the sea, no, a lake, further up the coast, inland,

Daneswater, it's called. And...' Her voice cracked. 'And he didn't come back. Our boy. An accident, of course, capsizing, the water very cold, not a strong swimmer, you see...' She put one hand across her eyes. She sat silent, unmoving.

'I'm sorry,' he said.

'Never forgave himself.' She straightened up, met his gaze. 'Or perhaps it was me.'

'What do you mean?'

She shrugged. 'He'd say to me, you will never forgive me, never. What could I say to him? How could I help him? I'd say to him, it's not a matter of forgiveness. It's about how we live our lives now, how we carry on at all, given that what I wanted to do was join my son where he was, wherever that was, and I think perhaps Murdo wanted to too, and perhaps now...' Her words faltered. 'Perhaps now he has,' she said.

She looked different. No longer that closed-in, empty look, her eyes now bright with tears, her face open, younger, even. He reached across and laid his hand on hers. The gesture took him by surprise, and perhaps her too, but she didn't move, sitting still with his hand on hers, while the sea sang louder outside the window.

'Blame,' he said. 'Culpability.'

She nodded, not looking at him. 'He talked of leaving, going to Geneva. But there's no escape. Not until you do what he's done. I envy him, perhaps. Or perhaps not.'

The sea was a roar in the silence now, but there was another sound too, the phut-phut of an engine, a motorbike, growing louder and louder, then stuttering to a stop.

She took her hand away, as if waking from a dream, smoothed her apron, rubbed her eyes. 'That'll be Tom,' she said, getting to her feet.

The door of the cottage swung open. A tall young man stood framed by the dark wood, the sunlight a glare behind him. He blinked in the dim interior. 'Auntie.' He nodded towards her, then turned to Chad, screwing up his eyes. 'Who's he?' He pointed, his arm outstretched.

'Tobias, dear, this is Reverend Meyrick.'

'Ah.' He nodded, as if with great wisdom. 'The vicar. I've heard all about you,' he said to him. He fixed Chad with a clear blue gaze.

'Tobias,' she said, 'but we call him Tom. Don't we dear? Back from work already?' She cleared the cups onto the tray, carried them out to the sink.

He flopped onto the sofa, his eyes still fixed on Chad, combing his fingers through his thick blond hair. 'Why is he here? Is it about Uncle Murdo?'

'Sort of.' She came and stood next to him, smoothed his hair with thin pale fingers. He brushed her touch away. 'God, is it?' He still stared at him. 'What good can that do?'

'Well, that's a good question,' Chad began, but she interrupted him. 'He's always like this,' she said, as if in apology.

Tobias stood up, and paced out to the kitchen with an awkward gait, then paced back. He stood, towering over them. 'Auntie Ginny, if you drown, is it like breathing water in the end? Roger at work said it was like breathing water.'

'That's what people say,' she said.

'He said it wasn't horrible at all in the end. But how can he know? He hasn't drowned, has he? And what if it wasn't like that for Uncle Murdo?' He began to pace again, circling the room. 'Can I have chips?' He stopped again. 'Can I have money to buy chips out on the corner? I wanted chips with Lisa but she had no money.'

'Lisa?' Her eyes narrowed. 'I didn't know you'd seen her.'

'And she had no ketchup,' he went on. 'Nothing. Nothing in that caravan fridge. That's why she's thin, I think.' He stood next to Virginia, his arm held out, palm upwards. She bent to her handbag, fished out some coins, placed them in his hand. 'Not too much, now, Tom, remember?'

'I know,' he said. 'But ketchup too. I'm allowed ketchup.' He was gone, lurching out of the door, striding down the path.

The room seemed smaller without him.

'He's not quite…' she began. 'Twenty-four, he is. He came to live with us when…' She bent to plump the cushions on the sofa. 'I say he's my nephew, actually he's my cousin's son, but it's easier. She died, poor Jenny, breast cancer. There was no one else to look after him.' She glanced up. 'Best thing that ever happened to us, it turned out. We all adored him. And it was company for me, for us, after…' She lowered herself onto the sofa, as if suddenly exhausted. 'He works at the lab, where my husband worked. Just a jobbing assistant sort of thing, nothing technical. They found it for him at the Job Centre, but it's wrong for him, he's usually such a calm boy, but these days he comes back full of worries, you saw him just then. Odd friends too, eating chips with the Voake girl, probably the only meal she ever gets…' She stopped, breathed, continued. 'Of course, this news makes it harder, not related to my husband at all, but close, they were, close, on top of all his other losses. He's taken to…' She paused, breathed, continued, '…things about the work there, they worry him, atoms and things, the idea of smashing them. And the machines are huge, they frighten him. He's always asking questions, and of course, I can't answer him.' She reached absently for the diary, put it back down. 'I'm trying to get him something else. He had some work experience at the DIY shop in town for a few weeks, he loved it there, but they couldn't afford to keep him. Something like that, though, he's happier with simple things.'

She glanced across at him. He met her gaze, then looked away. His eye fell on the book on the table, and he repressed the urge to pick it up again. Instead, he reached for his coat which was draped over the sofa behind him. 'Well, Mrs. Maguire,' he began.

'Virginia,' she said.

He felt that a concession had been made. 'Virginia,' he repeated, getting to his feet. Again their eyes met. He struggled into his coat, tied his scarf around his neck. He hesitated, trying to find the right words. 'I won't pretend I can offer you any help at all,' he said. 'But please don't hesitate to ask. I'm in the office in the church, or at the vicarage, you can always find me there…' He stopped, disconcerted by her unflinching gaze.

She nodded. 'Thank you,' she said.

They heard the scrunch of heavy footsteps, and the door swung open.

'Mayonnaise too, is that all right Auntie?' Tobias was smiling at them from the doorway.

She smiled back at him. 'Yes, love. That's all right.'

'You're wearing your coat.' Tobias spoke through a mouthful, waving a chip at him. His fingers were smeared with ketchup.

'Reverend Meyrick is just going,' she said.

'Do call me Chad,' he said.

'Chad,' Tobias repeated. 'Charlie Chad.' He waved another chip in his direction. 'Do you speak to God, then?' His tone was conversational.

'Well,' Chad began. 'Yes. I suppose I do.'

'And does he say anything back?' Tobias placed his paper bundle of chips on the table. 'When I've tried, I've listened and listened but I've never heard anything at all.'

Chad smiled at him. 'It is a bit like that, talking to God.'

'Mostly I give up.' Tobias sat down and took another chip. His gaze fell on the diary. 'What's this doing here?' His hand went towards it. Chad saw the sticky, greasy fingers and dived for the book. He straightened up, holding it, embarrassed.

'I'm sorry,' he began, looking at Virginia. 'It's just – ' he gestured towards Tobias, who now had a chip in each hand. 'It's such a beautiful thing. The idea that it might – '

'The World can't arise out of Chaos by the Laws of Nature,' Tobias intoned. 'That's what he says in there. He says that blind Fate could never make all the Planets move in the same way. He calls it "Orbs concentrick", with a "k". That's because it's old.' He dipped a chip in a puddle of ketchup. 'And then he goes on about God. And then the other writing at the end says that she's very unhappy and she wants to die, but that's not about the atoms and the orbs and the planets, that's about her husband who's not nice to her. Amelia, she's called. It's difficult to read because of how they wrote in those days.' He stopped, breathing. He smiled at Virginia. 'We think he's right, don't we, Auntie? There can't be nothing, can there? Everything is stuff. Even what they call a vacuum, it's just a different kind of stuff. That's what I tell the people at work, and they argue with me and then I get upset and I have to sit in the fridge thing until I feel calm again.'

'The fridge thing?' Her voice was tight.

'It has a nice hum,' he said.

She glanced at Chad. The only sound was Tobias finishing his chips.

Chad held out the book to Virginia. 'I'd better be getting back,' he said.

She looked down at the book in his hand, then looked up at him. 'Keep it,' she said.

'Keep it?' He stared at her.

'It's trouble, that book. We don't want it, do we Tom?'

Tobias looked across at the book. 'Doesn't matter to me,' he said. 'I know it all in my head. I use it for my mixtures.'

'It belongs to my husband,' she said. 'Belonged,' she corrected herself.

'So – ' Chad looked at her. 'Don't you want to… I mean, surely…'

'No.' Her lips were set in a thin line. 'Nothing but trouble, that book.'

'Well, as a loan,' Chad began. He felt the smooth leather between his fingers.

'If you want to see it that way…' She took a step towards the door. He placed the book in his coat pocket, turned to Tobias. 'It's nice to meet you,' he said.

Tobias gazed up at him. 'Why?'

'It just is,' Charles said.

Tobias nodded. He dabbed at some salt, then licked his finger.

The sun was low in the sky, and the clouds were gathering. In the doorway he held out his hand to her. 'Thank you for agreeing to see me,' he said.

She heard the warmth in his voice. 'Thank you for coming to see me,' she said.

He took a step on to the path. She was standing behind him.

'What you said,' she said. 'About blame. Always blaming yourself. Do you think it will be over now he's dead?' And as he turned back to her the tears fell. 'Or will it be worse,' she was saying, 'knowing that they're both gone, knowing that wherever our boy is, Murdo is there with him, if there is such a place?' She dashed her hand against her eyes. 'And I'm left here.' She felt in her pocket for a tissue. 'For a long time I thought I simply couldn't live without him, without my son. And then I realized that that was how it was going to be. You can't will your own death. Unless you do it yourself. And I was a coward about all that.' She dabbed at her eyes, then looked at him. 'Does that make Murdo a coward? Or does that make him brave, to fling himself off that tower at high tide and wait for death?'

Her face was luminous, her eyes dark with feeling. He wanted to wrap his arms around her, to give her hope, but he knew he had none to give. He shook his head. 'Virginia – I don't know.'

'No,' she said. 'I don't know either.' She was staring at the floor.

'What was his name?' he said. 'Your boy.'

She looked up at him. 'Jacob,' she said. 'I don't say it very often. Not out loud, anyway.' She gave a sob, turned away. 'I must go in,' she said.

He touched her arm. 'I'll see you again,' he said. She said something in reply, but her hand was across her face and he couldn't catch the words. He watched the door close behind her.

'I feel sick.' Mary dabbed at her nose with a paper handkerchief. 'That smell… My sixth one, and they get me every time.'

The mortuary coffee bar was warm and noisy. They sat by the wide, sunlit window.

Berenice stared out at the car park. 'I still don't get why he drove there. Did he know someone was waiting for him? And the records show there were threats to the lab too, hate mail kind of things… but then why that lighthouse, what's it called…'

'Hank's Tower,' Mary said. 'It was never used as a lighthouse, they say. Out on the flats there. No one knows what it was for.'

Berenice sipped her coffee. 'Someone's going to have to talk to the wife again. Don't you think?'

DS Mary Ashcroft shrugged. 'All I'm thinking is, I wish I hadn't splashed my best perfume all over this handkerchief. Now I'll always associate Stella McCartney with the smell of that poor bastard half eaten by fish.'

Berenice smiled.

'And you've got your work cut out,' Mary went on. 'Unlawful killing now. And there's the Chief going on about how he's relying on you to head up the team.'

'Yeah. In spite of my "lack of local knowledge"… Perhaps he's waiting for me to fail.'

'You'll just have to prove him wrong, then, won't you?'

Berenice drained her mug. 'Yes,' she said. 'That's what I usually do.'

Clem Voake walked unsteadily up the steps of his caravan, leaning heavily on the flimsy rail. He spent some minutes fiddling with the door handle, until the door opened in front of him.

'Oh,' he said.

'Dad. Where were you?'

'I'm OK, girl. I'm OK.'

'Drinking again.' She turned and went inside.

'Only a bit. Got to give the dead a good send-off, eh?'

She curled up on the seats, gathering a thick blanket around her. 'No gas either,' she said.

He seemed not to hear. He sat down heavily at the small table.

'Where were you last night, then?' she said.

He shook his head.

She looked at him. He was tanned and muscular, with a shock of black hair, a growth of black stubble, a shabby checked shirt. His bright eyes settled on her. 'What you staring at, girl?' He smiled.

'You.' Her face softened.

'Peas in a pod, you and me. They might say you're just like your mother, but you and me… peas in a pod.' He yawned. 'Anything to eat?'

'Nothing.'

'It's freezing in here.'

'Like I said. No gas.'

'Enough for a cup of tea?'

She shrugged. 'Maybe. Then that's it. We'll have to drive to the retail park.' She got to her feet, lit the small hob.

'You're a good girl, Lisa,' he said. 'I'll make sure you don't come to any harm.'

'Gavvers were here,' she said.

'Hmm?'

'Feds. Cops. You know.'

He blinked. 'Feds? Here?'

'Yeah.'

'What did you tell them?' There was an edge to his voice.

'I told them you weren't here. Cos you weren't.'

He was punching his fists together. 'Bastard cops. How did they know… Did they say what they wanted?'

'Oh, yeah, like to invite us to tea? Course they didn't.'

He stared at her, blank-eyed. Then he stumbled to the tiny fridge. 'Nothing to drink,' he said.

'Told you. No money, innit.' She smoothed down her jumper. 'Just tea.'

'Tea,' he said. He flung himself back down on the seat. 'Tea. That's all they bleeding gave us.'

'At the church?'

'Weren't a church. Crema – Crema thing. You know.' He fished in his pockets. 'No fucking fags neither.' He looked at her. 'Who else was here?'

'No one.'

His eyes narrowed in his thin, leathery face. He surveyed her.

She looked at him, thought how it was just like him to wear a red checked shirt to his cousin's funeral.

'What?' He stared her out. 'You got a problem?'

'No, Dad. No problem.'

The kettle's whistle broke the silence. She poured water into two mugs.

'What I want to know is, what did that cow think, sending you over to me? She knows I can't claim for you?'

'It weren't like that, Dad.' She stirred sugar into his tea, passed it across to him.

'You're a good girl,' he said, again.

She sipped her tea in silence. Then she said, 'Hank's Tower, was it? Last night?'

He shrugged.

'Don't know what it is with that place,' she said. 'Tobias is always going down there too. His experiments, he says. Far as I can see all he does is stand at the top and throw stuff off it.

Stones and that. And it's dangerous, innit, there's signs up there saying keep out, I'm always warning him...'

'Dangerous,' he repeated. He seemed not to have heard her.

'And anyway,' she said, 'it weren't like that with Mum and you know it. She didn't send me here so you could get benefits. It was me who wanted to come here – '

'Yeah, and it leaves her free to live at my expense with her fucking pimp too – '

'Dad – '

'She's always got her own way, that one. They tried to warn me – '

'Dad – I came here because – '

'Selfish bitch. Always was. Always will be. I should have listened...'

'I came here because I wanted to be with you.' Her last word was a sob.

He looked up at her. She stood there, under the low roof, with tears in her eyes.

'Baby girl...' he tried to say.

She turned away. 'Don't matter,' she said.

'Babes...' he tried. He watched her for a moment. Then he drained his tea, noisily. 'I'll go and get gas,' he said. He got to his feet. 'Did the feds ask about the van?'

She still had her back to him. 'No,' she said.

'I'll take the car just in case,' he said. 'I'll get us some chips too, eh? You'd like that, baby, wouldn't you?'

She shrugged. 'Sure,' she said.

'I haven't eaten for hours.' He pulled on his coat. 'Those van fucking Mielens,' he was saying, 'and they're still too mean to give Digby a decent send-off. Still, all that will change now, eh Baby? You and me, we'll have money now, won't we?'

She sniffed, dabbing at her cheeks with her fingers.

'Won't be long, babes.'

The caravan door rattled as he shut it behind him.

She waited until the roar of his car engine had faded. She went outside, stood by the tow bar of the caravan. She rested one hand on the tow bar. In her mind, the first few bars of piano music. In her mind, she was wearing pink, like Miss Helen at the Centre, with her hair pinned up and shoes with points and everything. And third position. And point, and close, and point…

It was quiet outside the caravan. Soon she'd hear the return of his car. But for now there was calm, and light, and the thought of satin shoes.

Chapter Three

The sea is a soft background sound in the wide, light room.

My studio, Helen thought, looking at herself in the mirror, her right arm balanced on the barre. My ballet studio.

Once there was a real studio, a real ballet company, and me, a part of it, and the mirrors reflected us layered in cardigans and leg warmers and our feet in pink.

Now there is just me. Alone. Silent. Silent, that is, apart from the sea.

She placed her hand on the barre. And *plié en seconde*. And rise, and down. And fifth, *plié*, rise -

She stopped and crossed the room to the CD player.

And all because I followed my husband, she thought. All because I said, yes, to Chad, yes of course we can move from here, leave the city, take up a new parish on the coast, if that's what they want you to do. If that's what you want to do.

She pressed a button on the CD player. A few sparse piano notes filled the air. She returned to the barre. It had been a condition of the move that one of the huge empty reception rooms in the vicarage would be converted into a room for her, with a floor and barre and mirrors…

Battement tendu. And point, and close…

Her arms were fluid in their movement, her face fixed in concentration. Questions hovered, several questions, in fact, that she might have asked herself. Was it, in the end, what Chad had wanted to do? She hoped he was happier here. In the nearly six months since they had moved, it was difficult to tell.

He gave no indication of being unhappy, she thought, turning to face the other way, placing her feet in first position. He seemed busy in his work as the new priest in this quiet parish by the sea, no less busy than he had been back in the inner city with its noise and life.

She wanted him to be happy. Six years ago, he'd asked her to marry him, standing in the rain outside his church in Hackney, at the end of an evening which had started with a broken-down bus which meant they didn't get to the film they'd planned to see, a French new wave thing, she remembered now, they'd always meant to get the DVD but never had. And then dinner in a Thai restaurant, in which he'd confessed to never having eaten crab before, ever, or lobster for that matter, or squid. She'd laughed. Mussels? Oysters? He'd shaken his head. 'Why?' she'd asked him, laughing still. 'I think my mother thought they were fancy foreign things,' he said. 'Something to do with the French. And the war. Like rare steak. Or fresh cream cakes. And my father thought they were unclean,' he'd said, and blushed.

'Unclean?' she'd asked him, 'like, not kosher? But you're not Jewish.'

In answer, he'd described his father. A man of strong and rather selective Biblical beliefs, who married late and not very happily, produced two sons of which he was probably, quietly, very proud but never showed it. An upright Christian man, for whom God was more the vengeful God of wars and smiting than the God of love and forgiveness. A man who sent his sons to boarding school rather than admit that his own schooling had been torment...

'And was it torment for you too?' she'd asked.

'Yes,' he'd said. 'But probably not as bad as it had been for Father.'

She'd heard herself ask, 'How did you keep your faith?'

'I don't know,' he'd said.

There had been a silence, and then the conversation had drifted back to the shallows; his first taste of prawn, (he wasn't sure if he didn't agree with his mother after all), the next film they ought to see, should the Number Thirty-Eight bus be working after all, the dance show that she was about to open in, a modern ballet set to a minimalist score...

'You know,' he'd said, 'before I met you, I knew nothing about dance. Or minimalism.'

'Or prawns,' she'd said.

He'd reached across the table and grasped her hand.

Leaning on the barre, now, with the piano notes falling softly around her, she remembered how he'd turned to her, later that evening, standing at the gate of his church. He'd said to her that all through his childhood, somehow, in the face of his father's diminished and mean-minded God, he had always had a sense of another way of thinking about it all, a way of love and beauty and warmth and generosity, and that even with no evidence, it was enough to hope that the world might turn on such things. And that through her he'd come to see that it was true. And that what he hoped more than anything was that she might agree to spend her life with him.

'You're asking me to marry you?' she'd said. Incredulous first, then pleased, delighted - 'Yes,' she'd said. 'Yes, I will.'

She stepped away from the barre and stood in the middle of the room.

And we were happy. For a long time, we were happy. But now...

Was she happy teaching dance rather than performing it, her classes of little girls at Miss Dorothy's School of Dance during the week, with the occasional boy, or the haphazard collection of teenagers at the Community Centre at weekends?

And why, every day, without fail, was she to be found in her studio, practicing her barre work, when a glance in the mirror would show you a woman in her late thirties, chin-length blonde hair already touched slightly with grey, her once-lean dancer's body beginning to fill, to curve...

She looked away from the mirror. This was a question she refused to ask, refused to hear in the silence of the room, in the whisper of the distant sea. She crossed the room, turned up the music, allowed the piano notes to fill the space, and point, and close, and point, and close, *en seconde*, and close…

She rose up on *pointe*, balanced, poised, her hand barely touching the barre.

The tide was going out, and the daylight was fading into evening. Chad walked back towards the town.

Above him, the canopy of sky, pricked with the first faint stars. He felt the book in his pocket. He wondered how that odd woman in the tiny cottage had come to possess it. He wondered why she was so keen to part with it. Pages of handwritten natural philosophy, quoting Newton. Some kind of debate or disagreement, from what Tobias had said, about the nature of matter and the existence of the vacuum. Written by a man called Johann van Mielen.

To one side, the sea, as dark as the evening. At his feet, the pebbles, worn smooth by the waves' to-and-fro, over years, over centuries.

And all this exists, he thought. All this is here, when it could so easily not be. Determined by chance? Or by God, the God that doesn't answer when you call, as Tobias so rightly pointed out. The fact that matter comes into being, and goes out of being, and yet, quite randomly, there is all this, the waves of the sea, the stones at my feet, the breeze against my face…

It was odd, he thought, that Virginia's husband, a physicist himself, should have treasured this book. Or perhaps it wasn't odd at all – perhaps questions of gravity, of atoms, of nothingness, are the same whether they're from the nineteenth century or from the twenty-first.

In his mind he saw her, again, standing on her doorstep, raw with loss. How could I help her? What is there to say about the death of a child? A real, living child. All I know is the loss of the chance of a child. We have no howls of pain, Helen and I. Only the silence, filling the gaps between us.

"…It is very unlikely, Mr and Mrs Meyrick, I would say, impossible, that you could ever conceive again…" The consultant's words, again. "There are, of course, all sorts of treatment paths we could pursue… I leave it to you both to discuss it… my door is always open…"

IVF. DI. ICSI…

'But I'm only thirty-five,' is all Helen would say, then thirty-six, thirty-seven… And somehow, the subject was closed.

The lights of the town shone damp and yellow. He took the path away from the beach. The seafront was loud with cars and strolling boys, clusters of girls smoking and laughing by the derelict pier, its broken lines black against the charcoal sky.

Helen poured herself a glass of red wine and sat down at the kitchen table. It seemed to be night outside, and she wondered when her husband would be back. She got up and crossed the room, hearing the echo of her steps in the empty house.

The vicarage, she thought, not for the first time. I live in a vicarage. 'A vicar's wife?' her friends had shrieked, when she'd told them she was engaged to Chadwick. 'Helen, a vicar's wife? Who'd have thought?'

Oh, the merriment. She wandered into the lounge. The two sofas brooded in the darkened room, like slumbering giants. She switched on the lights, put down her glass. She looked at the pale gold walls, she'd chosen the paint herself, stripped out the heavy green-striped wallpaper which was there before. She looked at their Patrick Caulfield print, which seemed brighter and bolder than it ever had in their rather dingy Hackney sitting room. There was a bureau in the corner, one of their few bits of decent furniture, Georgian, handed down from an aunt.

I give it two years, her friend Anton had said. 'You're a dancer, babe. Dancer into vicar's wife, it just ain't going to go.'

Had she thought then he was right?

But I love him, she must have said. I love Chad and I want to marry him.

There was more I could have said. I could have said that the first time he put his arms around me, it felt like coming home. I could have talked about his shyness, his awkward tenderness, his concern for me that was almost paternal. I could have told them that after all the years I'd spent being a free spirit, Chad had prevented me floating away altogether, had tethered me to earth. What I would never have told them, though, was about the desire, the rightness of it all, the private, physical spaces that freed him to be so urgently, powerfully male, that allowed me to be so fully a woman…

She took a sip of wine, went over to the window. The curtains were still open, their heavy drapes tied back with silken ropes, and she could see the line of sea against the sky.

Yes, I said to them, I shall be a vicar's wife.

A vicar's wife. A warm house, a cosy fire, a welcoming table, a smile for my husband in our noisy, family home, our children running to and fro…

Not this. Not this echoing shell, these well-appointed rooms in which there is only silence and the tap of my footsteps on the polished floors.

She found herself back in the kitchen again. She heard her husband's key in the lock. She bent to the oven and retrieved the casserole for supper.

Chapter Four

At twelve noon, on the thirtieth of July 1922, Amelia Voake paused, breathless and shy, at the door of her husband's workshop.

'Gabriel?'

She lifted her long skirts, muddy from the garden, took a step over the threshold. The laboratory, he called it.

'Gabriel?' she called again, but there was no answer. Only the hum in the silence, in the heavy dark shadows of the panelled walls.

On the oak bench sat the machine, giving off its sour green light. Rays, she thought, gazing at it, something to do with the aether, is that what it was, or was that something else? Dangerous, anyway, he was always saying so, not to come too near, not to let their child anywhere near.

She wondered where he was. The rain beat against the windows. She stared at the tangle of wires, the light beaming from the lens.

She'd forgotten, now, what errand had brought her here, a question from Cook, wasn't it, something about sharpening a knife for the pheasant…

Above the hum, another sound. She jumped. The machine seemed the same, the flickering light unchanged.

Again, the sound, like a cry. A human cry, a howl of pain. But where…

There it was. Out of the corner of her eye, a movement, white in the green light.

She felt faint, sick with dread. Not this, not this again. Last time, she thought, it was my own imaginings, it was I who'd brought it into being. Last time her husband was there, talking, explaining in his dry voice and dry words the working of the experiment, 'You see, Amelia, with this modification, the movement of the optical components interferes as little as possible with the actual beam…'

She'd feigned comprehension, as usual, but behind him, in the thin light, she'd seen a shape, a man's face, translucent, the bench visible through the human form, the pale hair, the rough white linen of his shirt.

'…and here you see the counter-rotating beams…'

'Gabriel – ' she'd interrupted him. 'Did you see?'

'What, my dear?' His voice was tight with irritation.

'There – ' She had turned back, pointing.

'Your nerves, Amelia. Playing tricks again.'

Pointing, staring into the shadows. Seeing nothing.

And now – now, here alone in the laboratory, she'd seen it again. She turned, breathing, ready to face it, whatever it was. A young man, limping, she thought, even in that one glimpse, the military coat, the torn white shirt…

She saw only the dark wood walls, the grey daylight beyond. No man. No coat, no shirt.

The noise of the machine was louder, and the light seemed to pulse more fiercely, as if on the brink of change, throwing fractured colour across the bench, across the wiring and the sheaves of papers.

Her husband's writings. A series of numbers, Greek lettering, arithmetic. Phrases, 'decreased density, thermal expansion…'

"What is there in places almost empty of matter,' she read. 'And whence is it that the sun and planets gravitate towards one another without dense matter between them?"

'Gravitate towards one another…' She spoke aloud, holding the page in her hand, hearing footsteps, hearing a gentle rattle at the door, as the light from the beam faded and a shaft of sunlight crossed the windows. She remembered it was Thursday, breathed with relief, putting down the page, hearing her own daughter's voice, 'I wondered where you were, Mama,' and as the child came, laughing, into the room, she laughed too and said, 'It's Thursday. Papa has gone to collect the logs, darling.' She gathered her child into her arms, and they left, because 'Papa doesn't like people being in the laboratarry, does he, Mama…'

She felt her daughter's soft arms around her neck. As they crossed the kitchen garden in the sunlight she noticed the lettuces were ready for eating.

The click of her heels echoed along the corridor. Berenice glanced down at her new black boots. Investigating Officer's boots, she thought. Much too warm, of course, Mary warned me that Maidstone always has the heating on, but stilettos aren't going to work in a Major Incident Room, and my old shoes are too dowdy…

She pushed the door open in front of her. 'Morning everyone.'

'Ma'am,' came the murmured answer from the assembled team.

'For those of you who haven't met me,' she began, surveying the room – paper coffee cups, open notepads, lap-tops, phone-things, several pairs of eyes fixed on her – 'I'm DI Berenice Killick. Thanks for being here. Shall we start?'

Dutiful nods of heads in front of her. She glanced at DC Mary Ashcroft, who flashed her a quick grin.

'OK. You know the background. You've got the SOC team reports there?' More dutiful nods. 'Murdo Maguire. Physicist. Worked at the lab on the edge of town. The East Kent Lepton Research Institute. Initial reports suggest drowning subsequent to a fall from the old lighthouse. However…' She paused, scanned the faces. 'Forensics are showing injuries prior to the fall into the sea. Bruising to the skull, brain bleeding too. Brian?'

A middle-aged man with thin silvery hair nodded behind his thin silvery spectacles. 'We're waiting for the final X rays,' he said. 'But everything we've seen so far suggests he was struck, perhaps with a fist. He either fell or was thrown. Cause of death was drowning, there's significant water in the lungs.'

There was a scratch of pens on notepads, a flurry of typing onto keyboards.

Berenice had been standing, but now she perched on a chair. 'Other things you need to know. There'd been threats to the lab. Couple of incidents of broken windows. Nothing stolen. And hate-mail. The odd note delivered, and a spate of e-mails too, accusing them of interfering with the order of the universe, that kind of thing. As you know, they've got a particle collider down there, smashing things… The chaps that work there take this for granted, apparently, that the lunatic fringe get upset about black holes and stuff, the universe imploding, the end of the world and it's all their fault…' She smoothed her jacket, waited for the note-takers to catch up. She noticed that Mary wasn't taking any notes at all, sitting there all cool, sipping from her paper cup.

'The threats might be connected to a family of low-lifes who are parked on the edge of the site. Caravan dwellers, though not travellers as such. DC Ashcroft, do you want to fill us in?'

Mary put down her cup. 'A family called Voake. When I say family, it's one kid, a daughter of about fifteen, and a father. No apparent mother. The father, Clem Voake, may be connected to a warehouse raid last week at the docks at Dover, but we're drawing blanks at the moment. And why he's living rough when that kind of villainy seems to be worth a bob or two, we don't know. It's probably unconnected, but it seems odd he's on the edge of the lab when they've had all this trouble. He's got previous, too, did a stretch for robbery over in Herne Bay six years ago.'

'Murdo Maguire,' Berenice began again. 'He was forty-three. Very well thought of in his field. He's published papers on these meson things. Muons, neutrinos...' She avoided Mary's gaze. 'He'd been with this lab for years. Family – one wife, she lives locally. According to one of his colleagues, it wasn't a happy marriage. Estranged, he said, but still sharing the same house. No siblings. He grew up in Aberdeen. Parents deceased. The wife – ' she scanned the room. 'Who did the visit?'

A young DS raised his hand. 'With DC Cowling,' he said. 'We told her we were waiting for more tests.'

'So she thinks he flung himself into the sea. Listen, Ben, as soon as the results come through, you need to see her again. The rest of you, the schedule is up on the wall. The car's secured, but it can be towed now. The tower site is secured. I want an assessment of the tower, I want CCTV of the seafront, and there's a team on the victimology. It's all up here. Any questions?'

The room was hot and airless. She clicked off the power point, told them, once again, that she'd be in her office – 'And if anything – Anything – comes to light, anything you want to say, however small… I'm here. Got it?'

And then the room was empty. She went over to the windows, reached up and opened a tiny, high-up pane. The door clicked behind her.

'Thought you'd need a coffee, Boss.'

'Mary – '

'Thanks aren't needed.'

'Thanks anyway.'

DC Mary Ashcroft gave a smile.

Berenice went back to her seat and sipped at the paper cup. 'The seaside's not for wimps, is it?'

Mary laughed. 'You never took this job for an easy life. Though, it's true, you don't get drownings in inner city Leeds.'

Berenice dabbed white foam from her upper lip with a finger. 'There was always the canal.'

They sat in silence. Outside there was birdsong and the occasional rev of an engine.

'Estranged,' Berenice said.

'You what?'

'I was thinking about that word. This dude washed up on the beach – they were estranged, someone said. But still sharing a house.'

'And?'

'It's kind of weird. What do we know about the wife?'

Mary shrugged. 'Ben said you can never tell when you're bringing that kind of news. She was very quiet, he said.'

'He's right. You can never tell.'

'Biscuit? There are two in here and I should only eat one.' Mary passed her a chocolate digestive. 'Well, I shouldn't be eating any really.'

'You're not dieting again?'

Mary nodded. She pulled at her sweater, which was fluffy and turquoise. 'We're like a comedy double-act. DI Killick and DS Ashcroft, the thin black one and the fat white one…'

Berenice laughed. 'You're not fat.'

'It's all right for you. You don't eat. I'd say it was heart-break, but you didn't eat in Leeds either.'

Berenice looked at her. 'No,' she said. 'Not heart-break. Not over him.'

'You don't even drink.'

'Apart from alcohol,' Berenice said.

'And you wonder why you get cystitis.'

Berenice shook her head. 'That's just stress, that is.'

'You don't need to prove yourself.' Mary got to her feet. 'Remember that. You were a great copper in Leeds, and you'll be a great copper here.'

A brief squeeze of her shoulder, then the door closed behind her.

Alone, Berenice picked up her phone. 'Hi, yes, it's DI Killick. DIO on the Hythe drowning. Can we get those fibres over to the lab asap? Thank you.'

She rang off. She stared at her computer screen. A great copper, she thought. One day, maybe, I'll believe it.

'And the Lord God said, 'The man has now become like one of us, knowing good and evil. He must not be allowed to reach out his hand and take also from the tree of life and eat, and live forever.' So the Lord God banished him from the Garden of Eden to work the ground from which he had been taken…'

Chadwick looked out across a sea of heads to the thick wooden beams above them. The morning sun shone through the stained glass of the East window behind him, throwing patches of colour on to the plain white walls.

'This is the word of the Lord,' he finished.

The congregation murmured the response. The organ played the opening notes of the Psalm, the choir began to sing. Chad took his seat again.

"The voice of the Lord is upon the waters; the God of Glory thunders…"

In his mind he began to rehearse his Sunday sermon. He had prepared a homily about Adam and Eve, about exile from the Garden of Eden, and how we must remember that, even if we have left God, he hasn't left us, and that in our suffering he is by our side.

From his seat he could see Virginia, sitting in the shadows at the back of the church, her head bowed. As he looked at her, the words in his head seemed to lose all their meaning. That God is by our side, he thought. An empty hope.

The reader was now reaching the ending of the Epistle. It would be time to read the Gospel and then to give the sermon. Chadwick stood up. In his mind he heard the words, 'The man has now become like one of us, knowing good and evil. He must not be allowed to live forever…'

He stuttered through the Gospel, Matthew, Chapter Four, Jesus tempted by the Devil. There was an expectant hush in the church. He glanced at his notes, saw nothing there of any help, and began to speak.

'We are the fallen,' he said. 'It is a necessary part of our humanity that we have fallen from Grace. To be human, we cannot be otherwise…'

He saw Virginia lift her head. Her eyes met his. He took a deep breath and continued to speak.

'Man, I'm not having all this ballet shit, you get me?'

Helen glanced at the rest of the class, then back at the boy who was standing in front of her. He was tall and muscular, in T-shirt and leggings, his feet in their black ballet shoes placed firmly on the floor, his hands on his hips. His blue-grey eyes shone from his face, which glowed dark with sweat. Behind him the class took a break, leaning on the barre, sipping water, stretching legs, watching with interest.

'Finn, it's a ballet class.' Helen faced him.

'You told me dance, man. Dance to me, it's the beat, right? Like, living the music. Not this…' He waved his arm around the studio.

'It's all dance, Finn.'

'And the music's shit too.'

'You don't have to do it, then, blad.' One of the girls approached. She had straightened Afro hair pinned back, and was dressed in a scarlet T shirt with matching leggings. 'We don't need you here, you get me?'

'Wha' else me going to do?'

She tutted, turned to Helen. 'Sorry about him, Miss, he's just like this, y'know?'

Helen smiled at her. 'It's OK.' She turned to him. 'It's up to you, Finn.'

He shrugged.

'You're good, you know?' she went on.

He slouched in front of her, staring at the floor.

'Really, you are.'

He raised his eyes. 'I ain't no good at all this shit. All them words, don't know what they mean or nothing.'

'You don't have to know what they mean. You just have to dance them.'

The girl in red tugged at his sleeve. 'You wasting our time, bruv.'

'Leave it, Lisa.' He shook her off. He walked over to the corner of the studio and sat on the floor.

Helen started the music CD again, and the class gathered into lines.

'Adage,' Helen began. 'Chassé forward on the left, *port de bras*...' She was aware of Finn watching the class. She was also aware that the energy had faded from the group and was now concentrated sullenly in his corner of the room.

Chapter Five

Chad stood at the church door, greeting the departing congregation, shaking hands, smiling, asking after absent parishioners, 'How is Joan now? Out of hospital this week? Oh, good, I am glad…' 'The cat, yes, I know, all very sad, I heard… Lovely flower arrangement in the Lady Chapel, Mrs. Lynch…'

There was no sign of Virginia. He watched them go, the tap of sticks on the old paved path, the sunshine silvering the gravestones.

He went back into church. A relief, to find it empty. He would just finish the last few tasks, and then home for lunch.

She was still sitting in the pew at the back. She turned as the door clicked behind him.

'Oh,' he said.

'Didn't mean to scare you,' she said.

'Not at all. I didn't expect to see you in church today, that's all.' He sat down next to her. The altar candles were still alight, and he found himself worrying about the wax dropping on to the altar cloth.

'I thought of them all,' she said, 'all what they'd say, there's Ginny Maguire, fancy her showing her face after all this time, and then I thought, let them. Let them gossip all they want.

There's been enough said about me in the past, and there'll be enough said about me in the weeks to come.'

He nodded his support, watching the flicker of the candles.

'Your sermon,' she said.

'Hmmm?' he said.

'It wasn't what I expected.'

He turned to face her. 'I – I have no idea what I said, I'm afraid.'

The hint of a smile lifted the corners of her mouth.

'Did it seem like that?' he asked her.

'Depends what they're used to, I suppose,' she said.

'I – ' he hesitated. 'I didn't want to offer you empty hope,' he said.

She met his eyes. 'That's very kind of you,' she said. 'The thing is – we had bad news this morning, Tobias and me. The police came again. It – it wasn't suicide.'

He looked at her hands clasped tight together in her lap. 'Not suicide?'

'Type of injuries, they said, brain injury, bruising… suggests he was already unconscious when… when he hit the water.'

He looked up at her. 'But how…?'

'Killed,' she said. 'By person or persons unknown.'

'But – who? Why…?'

She opened her hands, palms upward. 'I can't help them, can I? He goes to the lab. He comes home for tea. He talks to Tobias. We watch the television. I can't help them…'

A shouting outside, a hammering on the door of the church. Chad jumped to his feet, swung the door open. 'Tobias,' he said.

He loomed in the church doorway, dishevelled and tearful. 'Can I... ' he sniffed. 'Is she here?'

'I'm here, love.' Virginia spoke from her pew. Tobias screwed up his eyes in the dim light, stumbled towards her, sank down next to her. She put her arm around him.

'I woke up and you weren't there,' Tobias said, his face half-buried in Virginia's shoulder.

'It's all right, love, I'm here now.' She looked up at Chad. 'It's been awful for our Tom.'

'Uncle Murdo,' Tobias said. 'I keep thinking about him and who would do that to him, who would do it? I asked that woman from the police, why? I asked her, why do people do that to other people? She didn't say anything, did she Auntie? She couldn't tell me.'

Chad walked to the altar and blew out the candles. He gathered up the pages from the lectern.

Tobias had followed him. He stood next to him. The white altar cloth was splashed with colour from the stained glass window. Tobias circled a patch of red with a finger. 'No one should do that to someone else, should they?' he said.

'No,' Chad agreed. His gaze fell on Virginia, where she sat, cold and still, at the back of the church. He took a step towards her, wanting to help, wanting to offer her warmth, kindness. 'Come to the vicarage,' he said. 'Come for lunch.'

'He's the most talented of the whole class, and he spent most of it sitting on the floor.' Helen tucked the phone under her chin, slipped off one ballet shoe and then another.

'Babe, if he don't want to do it, he don't want to do it.' The soft drawl of his voice down the phone. 'I'd tell him you don't need him.'

She smiled, stretched herself along the sofa. 'The problem is, Anton – '

He interrupted her. 'The problem is, babes, you *do* need him. What's the day job? Working with Miss Doris – '

'Dorothy,' she corrected him –

'Coaching all the Maisies and Evies through Grade Three – '

'Two of them are on Grade Eight – '

'It's always been the hand-picked rude-boys where your heart resides. Nothing's changed, even by the sea.'

She laughed.

'I'm tempted to join you there,' he said. 'I'm sitting in a Starbucks in Soho, on my own because a certain gorgeous man is late as usual, and it's pouring with rain. How is it where you are?'

She looked out at the slate grey sky. 'Well, it's not raining,' she said. 'But Chad will be back from church in a minute, and I've got nowhere with lunch.'

'What kind of vicar's wife are you?'

She laughed again, at his fake-scandalized tone. 'A very bad one, as you knew I would be.'

There was a brief pause. 'Babe – how is it really? Apart from recalcitrant rude-boys and the lack of lunch?'

She breathed a deep breath. 'Whatever is wrong with my life here,' she began, hearing footsteps outside, voices too, 'it would have been just as wrong in London.'

'Well, I guess that's one way of looking at it.'

'Anton – I've got to go. Chad's back, and he's got people with him, from the sound of it.'

'Needy parishioners,' Anton said. 'Rather you than me. Speak soon, Hon.'

She clicked off her phone, unfurled herself from the sofa and went to see what was happening.

Two people were standing in her kitchen next to Chad. One was a small blonde-ish woman of indeterminate age in a neat navy raincoat. The other was a huge young man, or perhaps a giant child, his fists clenched at his side, his eyes blinking as if he was about to burst into tears.

'Helen – ' Chad glanced at her nervously. 'This is Virginia – Mrs. Maguire. And this is her nephew, Tobias. They've had some rather bad news. I don't suppose there's any, um… '

Helen was aware of the woman looking at her. She felt suddenly exposed in her layers of pink dancewear. 'Lunch,' she said, brightly. 'Yes, of course. Nothing special, but I'm sure we can find something.'

Twenty minutes later the casserole from the night before was bubbling gently on the hob, having been extended with various chopped vegetables, and there were potatoes roasting in the oven. Helen, now in jeans and cashmere jumper, put her head round the door of the lounge. 'Drinks, anyone?'

Tobias looked up from the large armchair. 'I like Coca Cola,' he said, 'but I'm not allowed it, am I Auntie?'

'I don't think we have any,' Helen said. 'How's orange juice?'

'I don't like orange juice,' Tobias said.

'Just water is fine for us both,' Virginia said.

As Helen stood in the kitchen pouring glasses of water, she wondered at her husband's life. How had he not told her about this tiny sad-faced woman who sat on one corner of the sofa as if she didn't deserve to be there, and this large man-boy who filled the huge armchair as if he belonged in this house made for giants.

She returned to the lounge, and all four sat and sipped water. She felt as if she'd silenced a conversation. On the coffee table there was a book, a beautiful leather-bound, honey-coloured thing. She reached across and picked it up.

'What's this?'

Chad seemed to blush. 'A loan,' he said, glancing at the sofa. 'Virginia lent it to me.'

'Gave it,' Virginia said, with a harsh rasp.

Helen looked up at her. 'A gift? Why?'

'Because I don't want it,' she said. 'And because he's interested in it,' she added, with a tilt of her head towards Chad.

Helen tried not to stare, fascinated by her sharp tone. She flicked through the book instead. 'What is it?'

'Careful,' Chad said.

She glanced at him. 'It's only a book,' she said.

'It's quite old,' he said. 'Late nineteenth century. It's a kind of diary, someone's copied out loads of natural philosophy, ideas about gravity and atoms, Newton and people, and then at the end there's another writer, a woman, taking issue with it all, heart-felt arguments about the aether, absolutely fascinating, all hand-written…'

'Is that what you were reading last night,' she said, 'when you wouldn't come to bed?'

A look from Virginia made her feel she'd said too much.

'It does that,' Virginia said. 'Takes you over.'

'It's ours,' Tobias said.

Chad looked across at him. 'I'm only borrowing it, remember?' he said.

'It's all in my head anyway.' Tobias breathed out. He picked up his glass of water and drained it in one gulp.

'"If we are to say that there can be nothing, that matter can support the absence of itself, then we are lost,"' Helen began to read. '"For nothingness is a gap that must be filled, if not by good, then by evil –"'

'Then by evil,' Tobias repeated. 'That's why you can't have nothing – ' he was almost shouting. 'When you smash particles together, there can't be nothingness, that's what's wrong with it all –'

'Hush, hush…' Virginia reached across and laid her hand on his shoulder. 'Tom, dear, it's all right…'

He quietened.

Helen looked from Tobias to her husband. Chad was staring down, his hands gripping his knees. She turned a page of the book. '"He is an uniform Being,"' she read, '"void of Organs, Members or Parts, and they are his Creatures subordinate to him, and subservient to his Will; and he is no more the Soul of them, than the Soul of a Man is the Soul of the Species of Things carried through the Organs of Sense into the place of its Sensation – "'

'Newton,' Chad said, a false brightness in his voice. 'That's what's so fascinating about the book. Great chunks of people copied out, references to all sorts, even alchemy, mercuries, all higgledy-piggledy.'

'The Prof says you can have nothingness.' Tobias was calmer now. He addressed Chad directly. 'And I tell him he's wrong. But he's not a nice man, is he, Auntie?'

Virginia shook her head. 'Prof Moffatt. He runs the lab. My husband didn't like him either.'

'He says that some of the bits are mass-less and I say what about gravity, then, and he just laughs at me as if I'm stupid, I don't like him.' Tobias stopped, breathing fast.

'He's a difficult man. Brilliant, everyone agrees,' Virginia said. 'But not to be trusted. Murdo always said he'd steal your research and take the credit for himself.'

'Perhaps he killed him, Auntie,' Tobias said, with an odd equanimity.

She shook her head. 'He might be difficult, but I wouldn't go that far.'

'Well someone did,' Tobias said.

'Yes,' Virginia said. She looked even smaller, sunk in her corner of the sofa. 'Someone did.'

Helen looked from one to the other. She wondered if anyone was going to explain.

Tobias met her eyes. 'They hit him on the head,' he said. 'They pushed him from Hank's Tower into the sea, that's what the police told Auntie.'

Helen glanced across at her husband, waiting for him to step in, to explain, to take control. He didn't look up.

Tobias got to his feet, and began to roam the room, running his fingers along the edge of the bookshelves. Helen stood up too. 'The potatoes will be done, I expect.'

'Ballet shoes.' Tobias was standing by the window, framed by the heavy gold curtains. He was holding up her shoes, one in each hand.

She blinked at him. 'Yes. They're mine.'

'I did that, didn't I, Auntie? Dancing. I used to do it at school.'

'He loved it,' Virginia said.

Helen looked at him, standing in the window's light. She tried to see a dancer in this huge figure, his hands dangling at his sides, his feet at odd angles as if they were so far away he'd forgotten all about them. But then he raised his arms to shoulder height, one shoe still grasped in each hand, and turned a perfect double pirouette. He stood and faced her, perfectly still.

'Pirouette *en-dedans*,' she said.

'And this one's *en-dehors*,' he said, and did another perfect turn.

It was as if the proportions of the room had been restored, she thought, watching this tall boy-man suddenly graceful in the golden light.

'Where did you learn that?' she said.

'His school…' Virginia's voice was weary. 'He had five years at an excellent school. While his Mum was still alive. It closed…'

'She danced too.' Tobias was standing poised, balanced. 'My mum. She was a dancer too.' He placed the shoes back on the floor.

There was a brief silence. 'Well,' Chad said. 'Lunch, I think.'

Tobias shifted from his ballet posture, and immediately seemed to forget his feet again, as he lumbered towards the door.

Virginia followed him. Chad glanced at Helen as she joined him in the doorway, and briefly squeezed her arm.

'Nice boots, Ma'am,' Detective Sergeant Ben Conway said, as he sat down.

'Thank you.' Berenice nodded a smile at him. Well-turned-out too, she thought, crisp checked shirt, and those jeans look brand new.

They sat alone in the airless office. 'How was she?' she said.

He settled into his seat. 'We followed the rules,' he said. 'But how do you tell someone that her husband was hit on the head and then thrown from that lighthouse thing…'

'Estranged husband,' Berenice said.

'There is that,' he agreed. 'No tears. No – hist… what's the word? Cowling always has these posh words – '

'Histrionics?'

'Yeah.' He gave a quick smile. 'But – she said this weird thing. She said, "So he didn't even have the courage to kill himself". Weird, eh?'

Berenice reached for a notebook and wrote down the words. 'Weird,' she agreed.

'Guess that means she didn't do it,' Ben said, as footsteps approached and the door opened.

'You can never tell with wives,' Berenice said.

Mary stood in the doorway. 'Don't get the Boss started on marriage,' she said. She handed a series of photographs to Berenice. 'CCTV,' she said.

'Any good?' Berenice spread them out on the desk.

'I'd say not.' Mary took a seat. 'A couple of number-plates they're following up. There's this guy here…' She pointed. 'And he's here again, along the seafront, but we're nowhere further on until they confirm time of death.'

'What about the physics lab?' Berenice flicked through the photos in front of her.

'They're obviously a tight team – more tearful than the wife, I'd say.' Mary glanced at Ben, then opened her laptop, clicked on a few keys. 'There's Liam Phelps, nice chap. We met a colleague of the dead man's, Iain Hendrickson. He said they had a controversial experiment that was Murdo's own, he said they were at a loss as to how to carry on. The rest of the team, we didn't meet them but I got their names. Roger Newbold, he's a physicist. The director's called Alan Moffatt, he wasn't in. And there's a woman on Murdo's team, Elizabeth Merletti. Merletti's her married name. Used to be known as Elizabeth van Mielen.' She closed her laptop.

'Can you get those names to Ben here?' Berenice stacked the photographs and tucked them into her file. 'Well, thanks, both of you. You might as well go back to Sunday lunch.'

Ben got to his feet. 'Cool. Mum's doing chicken specially.' He gave a sort-of bow, and left.

Berenice stared at the door. 'How old *is* he?'

Mary laughed.

'What I need to know is…' Berenice picked up her phone, and glanced at it. 'What changed in this man's life? It all seems so stable. Whoever wanted to kill him, it must have been triggered by something.'

'The wife?'

Berenice gave her a look.

'OK, not the wife. The physics,' Mary said. 'This groundbreaking experiment?'

'They all sound tight-knit.'

'They've had death threats.'

'We need to look into that.'

'They don't take them very seriously,' Mary said.

'That's the seaside for you.' Berenice put her phone into her bag. 'Any talent?'

'Talent? We're talking scientists.'

'Some of them must be OK.'

'I think my radar went dead as soon as I came South,' Mary said. 'It ain't quite party city out there.' She got to her feet. 'Am I allowed to go home to Mum too?'

'What, seriously?'

Mary looked down at her. 'Mum is three hundred miles up the M1, as is yours. No roast chicken for me.'

'Nor me.'

Mary passed Berenice her jacket. 'How about the pub, then? Steak and chips? Or are you going home?'

Home, Berenice thought. Cold white rented formica and a shabby floral carpet. 'Steak and chips sounds great,' she said.

They walked along the corridor together. 'Boots not too warm, then,' Mary said.

'There was rain forecast,' Berenice said, as they walked out into the sunny afternoon.

Chapter Six

Liam Phelps leaned back against the scruffy common-room armchair, crossed his legs awkwardly in front of him.

'It's just not the same,' he said.

'Without Murdo, you mean?' Elizabeth set two mugs of coffee down in front of them.

He tapped on the edge of his packet of cigarettes. 'It was his experiment. And now it's all going weird, and I keep thinking, if he was here, he'd have an explanation. As it is, every time I look at the results I just feel…' He pulled out a cigarette and looked at it.

'You know you're not allowed,' she said.

'I know.' He put the cigarette back into the packet. 'I mean, one would expect B-mesons – '

'They can't be.' She sipped at her mug of coffee. 'Though, I don't know what else they are.'

'If it's true, it means that we've – '

' – we've made anti-matter that survives for seconds. Minutes, even.' She shook her head. 'Except, we haven't.'

'No, of course we haven't.'

'And if this shows an axion pattern…' she began.

'That doesn't make sense either.'

'No,' she agreed.'

They sat in silence.

'It must be weird for you,' he said.

She looked up at him. 'Yes,' she said. 'It is.'

'You'd only just come back…'

'Not to him.' Her voice seemed loud. 'I'd come back to the lab. Not to him.'

Liam shifted his long legs. 'It's not for me to intrude…' he began.

'I mean even if there is a funeral…' She seemed not to hear him. 'What's to stop her just excluding me? I don't think I can bear it.' She passed her hand across her eyes, shook her head.

The door opened and they both looked up.

'Sorry, I'm…' Iain Hendrickson was standing in the doorway. 'I wasn't sure if you…'

'It's fine - ' Liam indicated the seat next to him.

Iain was in denim, as usual. Liam wondered whether he'd ever seen him in anything else. It gave him a boy-ish, student-y look, in spite of his seniority, the touch of grey in his hair. He looked weary, sleepless, he thought, though probably we all look dreadful…

'These charges,' Iain was saying. 'The whole standard model turned on its bloody head. We ought to be delighted, I suppose.' He spoke with a soft Scottish accent. 'Ground-breaking results. Those boys in Geneva being kept on their toes…' He sat down next to Liam. 'But of course, what we want as scientists, is to add to knowledge. We don't want to take the whole damn rug out from under everyone's feet so we all have to start again. And have you seen this?' He pulled a piece of paper out of his pocket. 'Another in the green ink correspondence, though not green. And ramped up, I'd say.'

He passed it to Liam.

Liam scanned the crumpled, lined paper. He looked up at Iain. 'One down?'

'It means Murdo. "That will show you all you bastards."' Iain took the letter back. 'Our friend seems to think that Murdo's death is our fault for interfering with the rules of nature.'

'We should show the police.' Elizabeth reached out for the letter.'

Iain passed it to her. 'Are you OK?' he said.

'What do you think?'

Liam got to his feet, knocking the table as he did so. 'Sorry… Um…'

'Don't leave on our account,' Iain said. 'What shall we do about this?' He pointed at the letter, which Elizabeth was holding between two red-polished finger-nails.

'We're supposed to be rational,' Liam said. 'Scientists. Not people who panic at the first sign of superstitious nonsense.'

'Like the ghost, you mean?' Elizabeth looked up at him.

He smiled. 'Like the ghost. One minute trying to pin down the fundamental laws of the universe, the next claiming that a wounded soldier is walking the corridors like something from Dickens…'

'Neil was convinced,' Iain said.

'Neil swore blind he saw him,' Elizabeth said.

Liam shrugged.

'It's not like Neil to be superstitious,' Iain said.

'I think we have to tell the police.' Elizabeth handed the letter to Liam. 'Do you want to?'

'OK.' He put it in his pocket, headed for the door. 'I'll check with Moffatt first. I've got to sort out this Tobias situation with him as it is. It's not fair on the lad, to keep him doing lab work. Particularly not now.'

Liam closed the door behind him. As he left, Elizabeth gave a weary sigh and rested her head on Iain's shoulder.

'One down.' Clem Voake gave a hoarse laugh.

'He's really gone?'

'You heard. Pushed off Hank's Tower.'

'Not the right one.'

'Don't care. If it puts the wind up them, it's good enough for me.'

Lisa sat outside the caravan, her back pressed up against the damp wall. Next to her, Finn passed her a cigarette. Above them, the voices drifted out of the open window.

Finn produced a lighter, and she leaned into him, drew on her cigarette.

'You get him up there first. Tell him you've got to have a little chat with him. Then, thwack, over the edge, death by drowning, all evidence gone.'

'Seem to know a lot about it.' The other voice was male, older, with a Kentish burr like Clem's.

'Yeah, well, I've thought about it, see.'

'Only thought about it?'

Clem gave another harsh laugh. 'Thinking. Doing. What's the difference? Another of those?'

Outside Finn whispered to Lisa. 'You telling me you're going to stay here?'

'Only home I've got,' she whispered back.

'Come with me,' he said. 'I've got a place at the Archway. They'll let you in.'

'They'll send me back home. That's even worse.'

'It can't be worse than a freezing car and him going on about all his enemies.'

'He's my dad.'

He looked up at her tone. 'So?'

She pulled at a thread in her jeans.

'You really telling me he cares about you?'

She met his eyes. 'He says he does. And in any case, I ain't going back to my Mum.'

The laughter from the window was louder now. 'That would be the prize, Clem, my friend. Wouldn't it. Then you could stop skulking out here in this dump.'

'Suits me, this,' Clem said. 'People come, people go, no one to ask them where they've been, no one to ask them where they're going.'

'And the kid?'

'Lisa? She's OK. She's a great kid. She's come home to her Dad and she ain't going nowhere else.'

'Scared of you, is she, like everyone else?'

Clem's voice was sharp. 'Not her. I love that kid. You hear me? Wouldn't hurt a hair of her fucking head.'

Under the window, Lisa blew rings of cigarette smoke.

There was a silence. Then Clem's voice again. 'It'll all change now. I'll give my little girl anything she wants. I'll send her to that school on the other side of town, you know the one where they wear them hats with the orange…'

'You sound very sure.'

'I stood by that graveside yesterday, and I thought, we're family we are.'

'You hardly knew him.'

'He was still family. A cousin. That's family.'

'I'd heard there weren't nothing left to leave.'

'You winding me up, Manny?'

'Wish I was, son. Wish I was.'

'You're wrong, Manny boy, you're wrong.'

The voices were loud and slurred. There was the sound of more cans being opened.

'Last of that line. That's what my Mum used to tell me, God rest her soul.'

There was a laugh. 'You and God? That's a good one.'

'Yesterday, right, I stood by my cousin's grave, and I looked up to Heaven, and I said to Mum, you kept your promise and now I'm going to keep mine.'

'And if I didn't know you better, Clem Voake, I'd bet there were tears in your eyes…'

'There were, Manny, there were.'

'I'm amazed they didn't lock you up.'

There was laughter, then more words, louder, incoherent. Finn got to his feet, took Lisa by the arm. They moved away from the caravan into the trees, settled on a tree stump.

They smoked in silence.

'Tobias was up Hank's Tower again,' Finn said.

Lisa shrugged. 'He loves it up there.'

'Doing his science, he calls it. He takes all those bottles of stuff up there, and he watches the tide, he says. Going in, going out.' He turned to her. 'He ain't right, y'know.'

Lisa met his eyes. 'He's OK.'

'No, I mean, he's got things on his mind. Bad things.'

'He has?'

'Talks about death. Talks about how we're all falling through space. Goes on about particles and colliding and gravity. And then he goes up Hank's Tower with his little glass jars, and hangs them from their strings until the tide carries them away, and then he just stands there, staring.'

'Listen, bruv...' Lisa took a last drag from her cigarette. 'You should start worrying more about your own life and less about everyone else's. Like, you've got to stop trashing any chance that's come your way.'

'Yeah?' He faced her.

'Yeah. Like at ballet, sitting in the corner. That's what you do, sitting in the corner of your life.'

He watched her as she ground her cigarette stub into the earth. 'I just don't think you should go back there,' he said.

She got to her feet. 'You tell me where else I can go, I mean like in real life, not in your head.'

He stood up, rubbing his legs. He could see the lights of the caravan through the trees.

'See?' she said. 'There's no way out.'

He followed her back to the caravan. At the steps she leaned towards him. 'Give us another fag.'

He passed her his last cigarette. She patted his arm. 'Laters, yeah?'

The stairs wobbled as she walked up them.

It was the end of the day. Finn's feet were silent on the damp grass. The sky was dark blue, through the silhouetted trees.

Chapter Seven

Helen could hear her husband outside as he said goodbye to the departing guests, their murmured thanks and fading footsteps on the drive. Now he reappeared in the kitchen, switched on the lights.

She was standing by the fridge.

'A whole Sunday lunch with only water to drink,' she said. 'There's a half bottle of that rosé in here somewhere.'

'That would be nice,' he said.

There was the clink of the glasses as she placed them on the table, the gurgle of the wine as she poured. She handed him a glass. He watched the condensation, a mist against the pink.

She appeared to be waiting for him to speak.

'I suppose…' he began, but she was already speaking.

'An explanation,' she said. 'That would be nice. How do you know her so well? How long have you known this whole story about the dead husband?'

'Hardly any time at all,' he said.

She didn't reply.

'You managed very well,' he said.

'I had no choice.' She circled her glass on the kitchen table, along the floral swirls of the PVC tablecloth.

'What are you thinking?' she said, and he didn't dare say that he was thinking that the table would look better without those abstract pink flowers, the plain wood underneath would be so much better, oak, he seemed to remember it was, unvarnished…

She was waiting, again.

He met her eyes. 'I don't know what to say. If you want apologies, I can apologise. They're just parishioners, you heard about it on the news, her husband, and now they're saying he was killed – '

'Yes,' she said. 'That's all she talked about. What I don't get…' she leaned back in her chair, her glass in her hand… 'What I don't understand is, why she cares. It's quite clear from what she was saying at lunch that she never liked him, that they were living separate lives– '

'That's not true.' His voice sounded loud.

'It isn't?' She took a sip of wine, watching him.

'She told me she loved him very much. Until – '

'Until what?'

'Something changed, she said. Six years ago.'

'They had a son.' Helen's eyes were fixed on him. 'She said at lunch. She mentioned him.'

'Yes.'

'Well?' Helen's voice was sharp.

He looked up at her. 'Their son died. Drowned. Six years ago. He was eight.'

She was sitting straight-backed, waiting. Chad said nothing more. 'Are you going to tell me the rest?' she said. 'Drowned sons, drowned husbands, some kind of foul play, this weird connection with the research lab…'

'There's really very little…' he began.

' – or do you want me not to know? Do I just serve out lunch, the proper vicar's wife, and sit quietly, and smile when appropriate, and look sympathetic and not ask any questions, even when it's quite clear from the way she looks at you…'

Now it was his turn to sit upright, his gaze fierce. 'What?' he said. 'What's quite clear?'

Helen stood up. She went over to the sink, found a tea-towel, began to dry the glasses.

'I don't know how you can even begin to think that,' he said.

'I'm not thinking anything,' she said.

'She's a very unfortunate woman.' He picked up his empty glass, turned it in his hand.

'Clearly.' Helen reached over and took the glass from him, and immersed it in the soapy water in the sink. 'And why did she give you that book?'

'Book?'

'That old book there, the one about atoms. Why you?'

He glanced towards the book where it sat on the edge of the table. 'I'm not sure. I expressed interest and then she said I could have it.'

'Your kind of thing, I suppose.'

'Yes,' he agreed. He raised his eyes towards her, but she was washing up, taut and silent, her back to him. 'It is my job,' he said. 'I'm their priest. Her husband's been killed, thrown off a tower, after all their other troubles, she has to care for Tom as well…'

He waited for a response, but there was only the splash of her hands in the soapy water. 'How was your work?' he said.

'Fine,' she said.

'Did Finn behave?'

Her hands ceased their movement. 'Do you care?' she said.

'Yes,' he said. 'Of course I care.'

'Well…' She turned, dried her hands. 'Finn didn't behave, no. Which is a shame, as he and Lisa are the two most talented dancers in the group. It's all very well Anton saying I should tell him I don't need him, but the problem is, I do.' She perched on the edge of a chair.

'Anton? When did you speak to him?'

'After class.'

'Ah.'

'Is there any reason I shouldn't speak to my old friends?'

'None at all.' He shifted on his chair. 'None at all,' he repeated. 'How is he?'

'Fine.' Her eyes were still fixed on him. He waited, wondering what she was about to say. But then she stood up and left the room.

He stared at the door, noticing the chips in the turquoise paint. He wondered whether the parish would extend to redecorating. He wondered whether he should finish the washing up. He wondered how it was that the only woman he had ever loved was lost to him. How had it come to this, he thought, to see her turned away from him, as if there was glass between them and he could see her speaking but not hear?

He reached towards the old leather, turned the creamy pages between his fingers.

"… *spiritum quondam infinitum,*' he read, "*spatia omnia pervadere et mundum universum…*"

There was a line scored through the Latin. Underneath, in the same ink handwriting, he saw the words, "A certain infinite spirit pervades all space and contains and vivifies the whole world." Underneath that, and underlined, were the words, "Therefore that force by which the moon is kept in its orbit is the very one that we generally call gravity." The last word was underlined three times.

Chad flicked through the pages. He wondered who he was, this Edwardian diarist who had gone to all the trouble to transcribe these words, at least some of which were Newton's, he was sure of it, to translate them from the Latin, to annotate them. It seemed to be a labour of love, a reflection of the transcriber's own views.

He turned to the inside cover, and saw in the same handwriting, the same brown ink, the name, 'Johann Van Mielen'. He ran his finger under the name, turned the pages to the end of the book.

"…an empty space into which will see the seeping of evil, an evil kept at bay by our Lord. And the Lord knows how I pray to him to keep me safe, for my husband with his prism and his rays is risking all…"

Chad turned the page. The writing was different, he realised, the loops more rounded, the ink a different colour, more black than brown. He read some more.

"I fear for our souls, and for that of our dear child. My husband chases the missing force, the aether, that unites gravity with light, that allows the being of all matter, from the smallest particle to the greatest star. He sees neither me, nor our daughter any more…"

Chad turned the page. The rounded handwriting continued. "The death of my dear brother haunts us all. Last night I slept alone. My husband inhabits a world wherein I cannot join him. He sits at his bench long into the night, with his lenses and rays and beams. Last night I watched our dear child in her cradle, and I prayed to the Lord to keep us from this Heavyness, this Darkness. When I awoke this morning I ventured to my husband's room and found him sleeping there, a makeshift mattress on the floor. He is like a shadow to me now, this man whom once I loved, and my heart does bleed. Where once was joy and laughter, now there are tears, and Silence."

The next page was blank. Chad turned back, and read the woman's words again. Then he closed the book.

The kitchen was quiet. The lamp above him shed a pool of light. He could hear distant piano notes coming from Helen's studio.

Last night she had slept there. Venturing in this morning he'd found her sleeping, wrapped in blankets, a makeshift bed on the couch.

A shadow to me now.

The words echoed in his mind.

This woman whom once I loved. Now there are tears. And silence.

Chapter Eight

I didn't mean to sleep in the studio, Helen thought, as she folded blankets, lifted the blinds to let in the morning sun. It just kind of happened.

Last night, there we were, sitting side by side on the sofa, watching television, I can't even remember what it was, a game show? A kind of competition thing involving food, that's what it was. I remember pouring wine, probably too much. I remember asking him, again, about that weird lunch yesterday, that Virginia woman. Why are you involved, I said, when what she needs is the police? And he just said what he'd said before, about being her priest… and so after that I got up and came in here, I told him I needed to tidy up before the week's lessons. And then I sorted out some CDs and then I thought I should work through the Grade 8 *barre* music, and I put on the CD player.

And for some reason the Board have chosen a long piece of Chopin for the *Adage*, the *Lente con Gran Espressione*, and it's the music we had at that show, the first one where I ever had a real solo, Oh that crimson costume, and Xavier the director claimed to have fallen madly in love with Anton, even though it turned out he was living with someone else all along, that Welsh boy who worked in the zoo and knew all about lizards…

Another life.

Chad came to the first night. It was in those weeks before our wedding. I was so nervous, almost sick before I went on… And afterwards, he said, did it go OK? And I remember thinking, what an odd question, how could he not tell how well it had gone, how as soon as I took my first steps I had forgotten to be nervous, and the feeling in the music had led me…

It had been jagged layers of dark red silk, the costume deliberately torn. It floated around me, as I did a turn, like that, a pirouette, arabesque…

Chad had said, afterwards, I don't know anything about it, you see. But –

But what? I'd said.

You were very beautiful, he'd said. 'Graceful.' And then he'd stood there, twisting his fingers together like he did when he was shy, still does sometimes, and talking about the word Grace, 'like the word in the scriptures,' he'd said, 'a state of Grace, you see, a completeness with things, and that's what it was like watching you dance…'

She had looked up at him, at his awkwardness, his hesitancy. She had taken hold of his hands to still them, and her eyes had filled with tears.

'What's the matter?' he'd asked her, concerned, and she hadn't been able to reply, hadn't found the words to say that it was the greatest praise she'd ever had. Instead, she'd smiled, and said, 'I'm so glad I'm marrying you.'

A *jetee*, *pas de bouree*. The feeling of the floating silk around her.

And now, here I am. The same steps. The same tears in my eyes.

She stopped, motionless in the sunlit studio.

Chad's gone out now. I don't know where he's gone.

She switched off the music, opened the studio windows, huge sheets of glass with a view of the sea, she'd had them fitted specially. She pulled on her leggings, her pink leg-warmers, Anton always laughs at these, she thought, so very eighties… She pressed Play on the CD player, and resting one hand on the *barre* she began, and point and close and point and close and *en seconde* and close…

We were full of hope, then, Chad and me. He seemed so strong, so capable. When my mother insisted, as she always did, that I visit without him, our first Christmas, 'it'll be back to normal, dear, just you and your sister,' Chad had said, firmly, that they would have Christmas at home, in London, 'we can invite your mother to visit us instead, the sights of Hackney will be a nice change from Wiltshire…'

En cinquieme… and point and close, and point…

When did that desert him, that strength? When did he cease to be dependable? When we lost the baby, what made him shrink and furl away, so that instead of being there with the right words, the right touch, a reassuring hug, he was absent, somehow, nowhere to be seen?

Chad must have gone out early this morning, she thought. There was no sign of him at breakfast, although coffee had been made and there was a plate in the dishwasher…

And *demi-detourné*, and point and close…

A ring on the doorbell.

Perhaps he went for a walk.

Another ring.

He must have keys.

The bark of a dog.

A dog?

She went to the CD player, pressed STOP, hurried to the front door.

A man was standing there. He had floppy blond hair, a well-cut beige raincoat. Beside him sat a dog, similarly coloured, the two of them giving a general impression of smiling sandy-hairedness.

'Hello,' he said. 'You must be his wife.'

She stood there, aware of her leggings and leotard, and wondered what to say.

'I mean, of course, shouldn't assume,' he went on, 'please forget I said that…' He ran his fingers through his hair. 'Terribly rude of me, I always do it, no manners at all…' He held out his hand. 'Phelps,' he said. 'Liam Phelps. From the lab. Hoping to see your old man about poor old Tobias, gather he's stepped in rather…'

His head was on one side, and the dog, too, had one ear tilted. She smiled at the dog, then at the man, then shook the offered hand. 'Helen,' she said. 'My husband's out, but I don't expect he'll be long.'

She led them into the kitchen, picking up her old cashmere cardigan from the back of a chair, throwing it round her shoulders. He sat down at the table with an expectant air, which was echoed, again, by the dog.

She glanced down at him. 'Does he… I mean, is he…?'

'Just some water if you've got anything suitable, bowl or something, you know. We've had rather a long walk this morning, haven't we Jonas-boy?'

The dog gazed up at him and thumped his tail on the tiled floor.

'A collie?' she said.

'Cross,' he said. 'Mongrel, really. But something Collie-ish in there. Rescue dog. Got fed up with living alone, thought I'd share my damage with someone similar.' He laughed.

The kitchen seemed brighter, somehow, warmer.

'What about you?' she asked him.

He blinked at her. 'What about me?'

'I meant, coffee? A drink?'

'Oh.' He laughed again, and she laughed too. 'Yes,' he said. 'Coffee. If it's not too much trouble.'

As she turned to fill the kettle, she saw that he had blushed pink. She wondered whether she had too.

'Chopin,' he said.

She turned back to him. 'Sorry?'

'Your music. Just now. Back there…' He tilted his head towards the studio.

'Oh. Yes.' She switched on the kettle, reached for two mugs.

'The *Gran Espressione*. I've always liked it. Used to play a bit, when I was young.'

'You're still young,' she said, turning back to face him, meeting his eyes.

For a moment his gaze was fixed on hers. Then he shrugged, and she laughed, and turned away to find the cafetiere, ground coffee, milk from the fridge.

'Awful cheek,' he said, 'turning up like this, asking for your old man, and now making myself at home, sitting at your table, drinking your coffee… it's really very kind of you…'

She pushed down the plunger of the cafetiere.

'It's Tobias, you see,' he said. 'I didn't mean to get involved, but Murdo was a good friend of mine, a great colleague at the lab… and now this awful business, it's a shock for all of us, and Tobias is taking it badly, the job was wrong for him at the best of times, but – I don't know if you've met Tobias?'

'Yes,' she said. 'I have.' She found a plastic dish, poured water into it, placed it on the floor. The dog ignored it.

'Well, you'll know what I mean. He's a swell chap, but – fragile. You know. And the work is distressing to him. And Virginia said that your husband had offered to help find him something else, and I suggested to her that we pop over there this morning, and she agreed. And given how bloody difficult she is at the best of times, I thought it was best to seize the moment, as it were…'

'He was here yesterday. Tobias. They both were.' She passed him a mug of coffee, pushed the milk across to him, sat down opposite him.

'Here?'

'My husband invited them to lunch.'

'Oh.' He glanced at her, then down at his mug. 'Brave man.'

'Tobias was talking about Nothingness,' she said, 'and gravity. He seemed very exercised by it. He said he argued with someone at the lab about it…' She raised her eyes to him. 'That wasn't you, was it?'

He shook his head. 'No, that's the Prof. Not me. I'm an underling.' He smiled at her.

'He didn't seem very happy about this man.'

'No. Alan is not the most, shall we say, empathetic of men. He makes no allowances.' He took a sip of coffee. 'The sooner we find Tobias something else to do, the better.'

'He danced. Yesterday.'

He frowned. 'Who? Who danced?'

'Tobias. He seems to know ballet.'

'Ballet – you mean, a dancer like you?'

'Yes.' She met his eyes. 'Like me.'

His eyes were still on hers. She looked away, fiddled with her mug. 'He's quite good. You wouldn't think so to look at him.'

'No.'

There was a silence. Liam stirred a spoon around in his coffee and she wondered whether she should have offered sugar.

'And then there was a row,' she said, 'well, kind of, about that stupid old book.'

'What book?'

'Oh,' she sighed. 'Virginia gave it to us. I wish she hadn't. It's here somewhere…' She stood up, lifted the book from the corner of the dresser, passed it to him.

He leafed through the pages. She watched how he held it with care, how delicate his fingers were, more like an artist than a scientist, she was thinking, more like a dancer than someone who smashes atoms or whatever it was he did…'

'What?' He looked up.

'I was just wondering whether smashing atoms takes brute force.'

He laughed. 'No,' he said. 'It means staring at screens. A lot. That's all. That, and doing sums.' He handed her the book. 'It looks extremely interesting. It quotes Newton.'

'Yes, that's what Chad says. That's why he's so obsessed with it. I don't know why Virginia gave it to him.'

'Virginia – Virginia Maguire?' His gaze was intense.

'It belonged to her husband. She didn't want it anymore.'

'Murdo?'

'It's almost as if she knew that it was very him. I mean, my husband.'

'Very him? And him a clergyman?'

'Yes. These things are complicated.'

'Clearly.' He leaned back in his chair. 'Of course, the quest to shed light on the workings of the universe might be seen to be religious. As Newton saw it. And a lot of his contemporaries.'

'That's what Chad says.'

'Even now,' he said. 'Like Higgs Boson being called the God particle. Not that we call it that,' he added.

'And what is there to find now?'

He hesitated. 'Well, our work. Super-symmetry, you see. Dark matter, CP violation…' He glanced up at her. 'There's a balance, between matter, and anti-matter. And for every particle that's matter, there is its opposite. And the whole thing is held in balance. But – ' he said the word emphatically - 'the odd thing is, there is a tendency towards matter rather than anti-matter. Otherwise there might just as well be nothing. But there isn't nothing. There's Something. So, yes, it does raise questions of why matter should "be" rather than "not be". However, personally, as a physicist, I don't think you need God as a cause for it all.'

'You explain it very well.'

He gave a nod of his head. 'Thank you.'

'I think, for my husband,' she began, then stopped.

'Different ball game, isn't it?' He glanced at her. 'I mean, sometimes, I suppose, I'm looking at the graphs and thinking, is this it, then? Is this how it looks, the One-ness of it all, the Hum of the Universe, the Great Vibration in the Silence that contains us all, even us tiny dots on a small planet at the edge of a minor galaxy…' He was smiling now, a warm brown smile.

'Go on,' she said.

'And then, I look at the graphs some more and I think, my job is to explain how, not why.'

She sighed. 'Whereas for Chad…'

'Much more complicated for him, I'd say.' He met her eyes. 'I only have to do the maths.' He picked up his mug and stared into it, then put it down. 'Funny that Murdo had that book,' he said. 'Perhaps your husband understands it better, though.'

'I don't know where he is,' she said.

There was a silence in the room. Jonas the dog opened one eye, then closed it again.

'Do you want more coffee?' She stood up.

'No, really, it's fine.'

She sat down again. She was aware of his eyes upon her as she gathered the mugs towards her. She could hear the rumble of the boiler as it clicked into life. Then a car, approaching, stopping, the bang of the car door, footsteps to the back door.

'Here he is – ' she began. Jonas sprang up and went to the door, glancing back at his master.

'Ah – ' came a voice. The door swung open, and Chad stood there. 'There you are,' he said. 'And – '

'This is Mr. Phelps.' She got to her feet. 'Doctor Phelps – Professor - ?' Her eyes were on Liam.

He smiled. 'Liam,' he said. He was standing up, his arm outstretched towards Chad. 'I said I'd come to talk about Tobias.'

'Ah, yes, of course.' Chad shook his hand, then bent to stroke the dog, who wagged his tail and then went to drink from the dish of water.

'I'm already running late…' Liam began. 'I don't want to drag you away, but – '

'That's fine, that's fine.' Chad readjusted his coat, ready to go out again. 'I had a meeting with the Archdeacon, went on a bit. Shall we go?'

Chad glanced at Helen. She moved towards him, reached up to his collar, smoothed the lapels of his coat. It was a gesture that took them both by surprise.

'We'll go in my car,' Liam said. 'That way I can leave old Jonas in there. I've learnt from past experience not to bring him anywhere near Mrs. Maguire.'

Helen bent to pat the dog. Chad took a step towards the door.

'I have an idea,' Liam was saying. 'There's a do at the lab this evening. A drinks thing. A sort of welcome to the new researchers. Why don't you both come? Bit of a funny atmosphere there at the moment, of course…' He stared at his feet. 'Apart from this awful event, we seem to be a focus for hostility at the moment, and then there's been some odd results, shall we say, all hush-hush at the moment…' He looked up at them. 'But we didn't want to cancel it.'

Chad glanced at Helen. She turned to Liam. 'Thank you. We'd like to,' she said.

'Six-ish,' he said, backing towards the door, his dog at his legs. 'I'll give your husband the details.'

Chad squeezed her hand, then followed him out of the door. She heard their feet on the gravel path as they walked round the house to Liam's car.

She put the mugs in the dishwasher. She put the milk in the fridge.

We never go to drinks 'do's, she thought.

She touched her hand, where Chad's had been.

Something has changed, she thought.

In her mind, she heard Liam's voice. 'Chopin,' he'd said. 'A dancer, like you.'

She thought about the wide studio windows, the top one open, through which the music would have floated.

He must have seen me at the *barre*. Before he rang the doorbell, he must have passed the studio.

She sat down at the table. She placed her cool hands on her warm cheeks. Then she reached for Virginia's book and began to read.

In the cottage, Virginia waited. An odd sort of clergyman, she thought. But Tobias took to him. Didn't even mind him taking that book away.

Glad to get rid of it, she thought. That poor woman, mired in a web of particles and hauntings and grief.

Not that anything is lighter now.

I will not cry, she thought. All these years, I barely shed a tear. Not now.

She stood up, rubbing her back, aware of a distant hum of a car engine.

15th August, 1922

'*Still writing in your book? You're just like your father.*' Gabriel picked up his fork. '*I hope you're not writing about the same things.*'

'*No, dear. Just thoughts.*' Amelia passed him the dish of potatoes.

'*Your father with his Newton and his Mercuries. And his need for a Creator too…*'

Amelia poured gravy onto her meat.

'*Guy used to say he was out of his time, your father.*'

'*Some of us still believe.*' She spoke quietly.

He looked up. She saw his deep blue eyes, his shock of black hair, "Welsh looks," Guy used to say, she was never sure what he meant, the Voakes had been a Kentish family for years…

'*You can believe if you want. If it helps.*'

'*It does help,*' she said.

'*I'd rather have truth.*' He began to cut his meat into slices.

'Guy used to say - ' she began.

'Guy? Don't try to link your brother with your so-called faith.'

His knife was sharp, tearing at the meat. The noise of the blade against the plate was loud. She wanted to put her hands over her ears.

'It's not so-called.'

He looked up. 'What?'

'My faith,' she said. 'It's not so-called. It's real.'

'If you say so.'

'I do say so. And Guy believed too. He was baptized, confirmed, just as I was, we made our promises together…'

'Oh, and he's in Heaven now, is he?'

She bit her lip. 'Yes,' she said. 'I believe that he is with our Lord.'

The noise of his knife resumed, tearing the meat to strips under savage blows.

'Well, you're wrong,' he said.

'How can you – '

'How can I be so sure? I'll tell you how. In those last hours, did he cry to your God? No, he did not. In those last hours, lying in the mud, the life draining out of him, surrounded by the wreckage of battle, the screams of the dying, the stench of flesh… ' The knife clattered on the plate. 'Where was your God then? An empty promise of Heaven when we were all in Hell.'

'Hush, Gabriel, please…'

'What do you know of it? Were you there, when we called for help and no one came? The light going out of his eyes, and I'm pleading with him to stay with us, stay with me…'

'Gabriel, please dear…'

'Where was your God then?' His eyes flashed with rage.

'Hush, please, think of Grace - ' she could hear the light footsteps of their daughter in the hall.

'Grace - ' His face was blank.

She knew these times, when his mind was elsewhere, attending to other sights, other places.

'Guy,' he said.

'Guy is my brother.' Was, she corrected herself.

His eyes stared at her unseeing. He frowned, appeared to focus, nodded. 'Yes,' he said. 'Your brother.'

The door opened, the handle tugged down with difficulty by small fingers. 'Naddle said you'd have finished I could come now, can I mummy, can I?'

Amelia wrapped her arms around her daughter, lifted her onto her lap, buried her lips in the blonde curls.

Opposite her, Gabriel sat, frozen, staring still at unseen horror.

Chapter Nine

Chad stooped to get through the door, as Virginia stood to one side to let both men in.

'I thought you weren't coming,' she said. She was in black, black skirt, black jumper.

They followed her into the living room.

'The Archdeacon,' Liam said. 'The Reverend was delayed.' He smiled, but her face remained expressionless. 'Is Tobias here?' he asked.

She shook her head.

'Shame,' Liam said. 'I like to catch up with him when I get the chance.'

'He's off with his tutor,' she said. 'Once a week, I can still afford it while he's earning. After that…' She shook her head. She turned to Chad, and reached her arm out towards him. 'Can I take that?'

Chad was standing in the middle of the room, his coat slung over his arm. He looked down at her as she took the coat, watched her as she went to hang it up. She seemed dwarfed by her clothes, her sleeves hanging over her fingertips. She sat on the edge of an armchair.

He felt his way to the sofa and took one end of it. Liam took the other.

To the surprise of both men, Virginia burst into tears. 'They've been here again,' she said. She put her hands up to her face. 'Coppers. Can't bear them…' Her words were swallowed up in sobbing.

Neither man moved. They sat, side by side on the sofa, their hands on their laps.

'I can't answer them, can I?' Virginia looked up. 'Anyone would think it was me who'd killed him, the way they go on.' She sniffed, dabbed at her cheeks with her fingers. 'That detective sergeant, the one who came the first time, saying his name was Ben as if we're best friends… He had a different girl with him, Ashcroft or something, she was just as bad.' She fiddled in her pocket and produced a handkerchief. 'And now they're saying they want me to come in, they kept asking me about Jacob, it was years ago now, why did they have to bring that up, it's not as if I don't think about him all the time, I loved that boy more than my own life…' Her eyes welled with tears again, and she dabbed at them with her handkerchief.

'Why – ' Chad glanced at Liam, then went on, 'why do they want to question you?'

'The police?' She looked up at him. 'I've no idea. The cheek of it, that policeman asking me about the state of my marriage, I told him it was none of their business. That's when he said I might have to come in for questioning. Then I said, why are wasting your time with me, why aren't you out there looking for a real murderer, if murdered he was?'

'What did they say?' Liam's voice was soft from his corner of the sofa.

'The girl said they wanted to help. As if that's helping. Then she told me about his injuries, a blow over the head at the top of the tower there, and then whoever did it pushed and he fell. They're up there now, looking for fingerprints or whatever they do these days. And she said her boss wants me to come in tomorrow, in the morning, that's why I wanted you two here, it's going to upset him so much, he needs us all on his side, he's not himself at the moment as it is, and seeing me carted off by the Law isn't going to help.'

'No one's going to cart you off,' Chad said. 'They want to interview you, that's all. It'll be quite straight-forward, they'll just need a statement – '

'So I told them you'd be with me, tomorrow,' she said. 'I said, I'm bringing my priest.'

A look passed between them. 'OK,' Chad said.

There was a silence. 'They'll be wanting to talk to us at the lab too,' Liam said.

'And that's another thing.' She addressed Liam. 'I told them, they're not to go near Tom, he's got nothing to do with this and he's upset enough as it, I'm worried I'm going to lose him altogether…'

'I've been meaning to say this.' Liam leaned towards her. 'I think he should leave that job. I don't think it's doing him any good. I'm going to talk to the Prof about finding him something more appropriate. He shouldn't be near the experiments.'

'But the money – '

'The library need someone to sort out the journals, he could do that.'

'He'd like that,' Virginia said.

There was a clatter of the cat flap from the kitchen.

'Ooh, that new moon.' Virginia turned to greet her. 'You're in and out all the time today, aren't you poppet?' The cat eyed her, then went to sniff at her food bowls.

'I miss him.' Liam spoke abruptly. 'Murdo. I can't believe he's gone. On research trips there's e-mail, skype… but this… It's so final, isn't it.'

'And yet it's only just begun,' Chad said.

Virginia sat, poised and motionless on the arm of the chair. The sunlight fell across the faded upholstery, touching the worn roses briefly into life. The cat approached, and Virginia bent and gathered her on to her lap.

Helen flicked through the thick, yellowing pages.

"What we know, is that Gravity, whatever it may be, is not innate to matter. The actions that we describe as Gravity, must be caused by an agent acting according to certain laws. If the word for such an agent is God, then so be it. After the devastation of

War, we are ready for a new story, a story of light and truth and courage, where the Beginnings of All shall be accounted for and the Stuff of Matter truly described. It is in Chaos that order is restored. We who have survived, we must face the Chaos in order to reveal the truth…"

Helen closed the book. She ran her finger over the worn leather edges of the cover, over the name, Johann Van Mielen. She put the book down, picked up her wrap from the back of her chair and gathered it around her.

Chad must have read these same words, she thought.

She went to the dishwasher, filled it with stray mugs. Irish, she thought. Liam's hint of an accent. Southern Irish, she thought. Not Belfast. I must ask him next time.

Later today.

She felt her body clench in anticipation. She wondered what to wear. She wondered whether her black crepe dress was too smart. She wondered what physicists usually wore at drinks dos. She imagined them in cardigans, patched corduroy.

This strange, nervous feeling. Familiar, and yet so long since she'd last felt it. Enjoyable, and yet…

The black crepe dress it would be. Flat shoes maybe, rather than heels. A concession to the dowdy physicists.

There was a loud knocking at the front door. She slipped her feet into her slippers and went to answer it.

At first she didn't recognize him, away from the noise and bare plaster of the Centre.

'Finn,' she said, at last.

He gave her a wide smile. 'Didn't know who I was, did you?' He wore a large striped woollen hat, low-slung jeans.

She stepped aside, and he walked into her hallway.

He'd been here before. On the way, he'd almost turned back, reluctant to step back into those dark, wood-panelled corners, that smell of damp. But she was right, Lisa was, he couldn't keep hiding. He'd walked along the sea front, thinking about her stuck with her Dad, it's like what Matthew at the Archway says, live each day like it's your last, or some shit like that, because it ain't my last, not if I can help it…

And now he was here, being led into a room with light and colour and paintings and she was gesturing to him to sit down.

'You've changed it,' he said.

'You know it? The vicarage?'

He nodded. 'One of the things my Mum tried. Didn't work though.'

He sprawled on a chair. 'Lise said it was like what I always do, trash any chance that comes my way. So I was thinking, and that's why I'm here.'

Helen smiled at him. 'She said that?'

He folded his arms across his chest. 'Yeah. It's like ballet, right?' he said. 'Like when you first see it, you think what is this shit, know what I mean, but then when you watch it close you can see them all muscle-y, even the girls, and, man, that control what he has, like that bit when he does all them jumps right round the stage, and he lands just where he wants to land, like on his tip-toe…' He flashed her a smile. 'And that's how it started, cos Lise said if I'm going to spent all my days watching it I might as well be dancing it, innit.'

'Watching it where?'

'Just on the net, you know. YouTube and thing.'

'Finn,' Helen said. 'You're very welcome in my class. But as a dancer. Not as someone sitting in the corner.'

He nodded. 'That's what Lise said. About me sitting in the corner of my life.' He smiled at her. 'Have you got anything to eat?'

She appeared with a plate of biscuits. He took one, then said, 'Tobias were here, weren't he?'

'Tobias?' She nodded. 'Yes. He was.'

'With his aunt.'

'Yes,' she said.

'I see him up Hanks Tower. I say to him, All right? And he say, All right. And then we talk. I seen him last night up there, and he tells me he was here. He said you were safe, you and your old man. Told me all what you had for dinner too.' He laughed.

She reached for a biscuit and broke off a small piece. 'Did Tobias tell you he did ballet?'

'He did? Him do ballet? Like what, he had to play the Giant or something?'

She smiled. 'They did it at his school. He learned it then. And he said his mother was a dancer.'

Finn frowned at the biscuit plate. Then he looked up. 'He weren't right, you know? Tobias. He was chatting stuff, about falling from the tower. And I said, what, like jumping off, you don't want to try that Tom, I said to him, them of us that ain't Angels, how we going to fly - like a joke, right? And he said, you could kill someone from up here, he said. Like really serious, you know? Went on about gravity. Went on about pushing someone off the tower, and all the forces that would make someone fall from there.'

Helen broke off another piece of biscuit and began to eat it.

Finn watched her. 'The guy they found. On the beach. Tom's step-dad, sort of, isn't he? That's what it is with him, with Tom. Reckon he know something about all that. And it gnawing away at him. I told him, don't go thinking about that shit. Just because there's death walking the streets out there, don't mean those of us what's alive have to go and walk with him too. Know what I'm saying, Miss?'

'My name's Helen.'

He met her eyes. He nodded. 'Helen,' he said.

'What do you know of death?' she said.

He shrugged. 'This and that.' He sighed. 'People I know, them die young.'

'You've lost friends?'

He shrugged.

Helen broke off another piece of biscuit.

'Lisa, right?' He scratched at his head. 'Didn't know who to ask.'

'What about her?'

'Her Mum kicked her out 'cos her new boyfriend don't like her, innit. He says Lisa is trouble, which she is, but that ain't no reason to come between a mother and her daughter, know what I'm saying? So that's why I've come. Cos Lise said I had to sort out my life before I sort out anyone else's, even though there she is stuck with her dad and he's weird, right? She said no one could help, and last night I was out all night, walking and thinking, that's what I do, I go up the Canterbury Road and I walk and think and what came into my mind was you.'

'I don't know what I can do,' she said.

'Yeah?'

'I mean, I could ask Social Services, I suppose…'

He began to laugh. 'Yeah, right.'

'We haven't been here long, we don't know…'

'Funny, isn't it.' He got to his feet. 'All this.' He waved his arm around the room. 'All yellow and light and stuff, but it might just as well be the same old place I came to with my Mum all them years ago.'

He was heading out to the hall, and she followed him.

'Finn – I'm just a dance teacher.'

He stood on the doorstep. 'Well, you think about it. That's the deal. I'll stop sitting in the corner, and you think about it. OK?'

'OK,' she said.

He held out his hand. 'See you in class next week, yeah?'

'See you then,' she said, taking his hand.

She watched him saunter away from her out onto the road. He didn't look back.

The black crepe dress was laid out on the large double bed. Helen moved around the room, gathering up a scarf here, a necklace there. She reached her dressing table, settled in front of the mirror.

Face cream, foundation, powder compact. She felt a sudden weariness as she picked up her eye pencil. Her reflection stared back at her. Who is this for, she wondered. For him? For me?

Words brushed against her mind, her mother's voice, sniping away in the background… 'Once you're a wife, it's all about making an effort, and even then you can't count on him taking the blindest bit of notice…'

Helen drew a firm line of black against her eyelid.

She wondered where Chad had got to. She was aware, as she painted the other eye, of an image of Virginia, so pale, and fretful, and vulnerable, holding out that book to him, and then, as he reached out to the soft leather and the gold leaf, she would reel him in, Helen thought, and he, lost in the delight of the dusty pages, wouldn't even see…

She brushed mascara onto her eye-lashes.

All nonsense, of course. She isn't the type.

And now this. Finn, coming here, asking for… for what, exactly? This glimpse of another life beyond the confines of the vicarage, beyond Chad's straggling congregation of old ladies. Finn, of no fixed abode, Lisa, trapped with her weird father. And, Tobias… If what Finn says is true, we have to talk to Virginia about it. If Tobias really knows more about Murdo's death, people must be told…

Virginia hovered, pale and predatory.

She picked up her favourite lipstick, film-star red. She turned it in her hands, thinking about patched corduroy. Perhaps just a subtle neutral lip gloss…

She thought of Liam in his linen shirt, his careless, thrown-together look, sipping coffee at her kitchen table, talking about the One-ness, the Hum of the Universe, the pictures on the graphs, matter and anti-matter, so clever, so warm, so alive…

In an hour I'll see him.

Downstairs, the door slammed, Chad's voice called her name.

'I'm here, love,' she called back. 'Just getting ready.'

She put down the red lipstick, applied a thin coat of lip gloss. She slipped her feet into her flat, black shoes.

We will go together, Chad and I. A married couple, as one out in the world. We will go together.

Chapter Ten

The wind buffeted the bricks around her. Berenice pulled her scarf tighter around her neck as she ascended the last few steps of the tower.

'Afternoon, Ma'am…'

Berenice nodded a greeting at the Scene of Crime Officer, tried to remember his name, a detective constable, wasn't he…

'DC Dexter Jones,' the young man said.

'Yes, of course. How's it going?'

He gestured around him, as if the gathering clouds and the waves crashing beneath somehow held the truth.

'Does the tide come high up?' she asked him.

He shook his head. 'This is as high as it gets.'

She peered over the cracked bricks. 'What's it for, then, this tower?'

He shrugged. 'No one knows. It's old,' he said.

'I can see that.'

'Not safe,' he added.

He came and stood next to her. He looked younger close-up, with his shorn afro hair, his wide, trainer-clad feet.

'What you looking at?' He turned to her.

'Nothing.' She gazed out to sea again.

'I can wear trainers if I want,' he said.

'Of course you can,' she said.

'You mean, a black man joining the Job, got to be more careful than a white man?'

She met his eyes. 'I'd say so, yes.'

'So what made you sign up?'

'It's the only thing I've ever wanted to do,' she said.

'No regrets?' He smiled at her.

'Not so far,' she replied. 'Shall we get to work?'

'Sure thing, Ma'am. Though the lads have taken most of it to HQ.'

'I know.' She pulled out her file, leafed through the papers. 'So, this gap in the fence…?'

He crossed to the other side of the tower. 'Here…' He pointed. She saw a curve of chicken wire, roughly pulled apart. 'We think the deceased must have climbed up the stairs, and then come through this gap to stand where you're standing now.'

She nodded, reading the file. 'The fibres…'

'Here.' He pointed at the wall. 'And here. And the blood spots here…'

On the flagstones, brown dots, a tiny trail leading to the brick wall. 'Of course, nothing to say it's his,' Dexter was saying.

'Well, we'll know when we get the lab results,' she said. The horizon was tinged pink with the thickening cloud. Further up the beach she could see Murdo's car, where he'd left it. 'We need to get that towed,' she said.

'Sure,' he said.

'Anything else?'

'Just one thing,' he said. 'I found it earlier on, on the staircase.' He fished in his pocket, and held something out to her.

It looked like a toy, a small plastic lion, painted green.

'I bagged it just in case,' he said. 'Might be nothing.'

She took the plastic bag, stared at the lion. 'Thank you,' she said.

Liam circulated, greeting people. There was a flight of steps down into the reception area, polished wood with spindly black railings. He glanced up.

She was there, under the beam of a spotlight. He saw her hair, blonde, pinned up. He saw her black dress, shiny black shoes. More than that, it was the way she glided down the steps, her head bent shyly downwards. She turned to her husband, said a few words to him, and then they were there, beside him.

'Liam.' She smiled up at him.

Chad was scanning the room, distracted.

Liam turned to her. 'A drink?' he said.

He shepherded them both over to the drinks table. 'Red or white, I'm afraid. Or orange juice. This place isn't known for its niceties. The white's slightly more drinkable, I reckon. French, at least.'

'White, then,' she said.

He handed her a glass. She met his eyes, looked away.

Chad was gazing at the wall. There was a canvas, rough painted blocks of orange and red. He turned back to Liam. 'Oh. Er, yes. White. Thanks.' He took the glass Liam handed to him, waved his spare hand towards the wall. 'Art, is it?'

Liam smiled. 'Art,' he agreed.

A booming voice came from behind them. 'Phelps – there you are. Keeping the most charming guest to yourself, as usual…'

Liam seemed to flinch. He turned. 'Professor – '

'Alan Moffatt. Director.' He held out his hand towards Helen. He was square-jawed, bespectacled, with thick grey hair. His jacket seemed too big for him, despite his large frame.

'This is the Reverend Chad Meyrick,' Liam said, 'and his wife, Helen.'

Alan took Helen's hand. His eyes behind the wire frames were pale, almost blank. 'Mrs. Meyrick.' His smile showed teeth that were somehow too white. 'And a Reverend,' he said. He relinquished his grip on her hand, and turned to her husband. 'Not often we get a man of the cloth in here,' he said. 'They tend to steer well clear of what we're up to here.'

Chad let go of his hand. 'Oh? And why is that?'

Alan threw him an affable smile. 'Similar territory, isn't it? Big Bang, beginnings of the Universe. Only we're coming up with a different explanation from yours, don't you know.' He gave a gruff laugh.

'I'm not sure ours is an explanation at all,' Chad said. 'I wouldn't say we're in any kind of competition for that.'

'But the Biblical account – ' Alan began.

'The Biblical account is an entirely different discourse,' Chad said.

'Soon to be overridden altogether, old chap. Now it looks like we've pinned down the Higgs mechanism, and I have to say, the data is looking very promising, then we'll have the whole story…'

They began to move away. Alan was animated, smiling. Chad quieter, but waving his wine glass as he spoke.

Helen rubbed her hand where Alan had gripped it. She looked up at Liam. 'How's Jonas?' she said.

His gaze passed from the Professor back to her, and he smiled. 'Chasing rabbits, unfortunately.'

'It's just normal,' she said.

'Not when the rabbit is called Daisy and belongs to the little girl next door. Then it's criminal behaviour.'

She smiled up at him.

'I'm sorry about just then,' he said.

'What?'

'You became Mrs. Meyrick.'

'Oh,' she said. 'That's OK.'

'Do you have a surname?'

'I used to,' she said.

'Used to?'

'When I was a dancer,' she said.

'But you still dance,' he said.

She remembered his visit yesterday. 'I teach,' she said.

'Does teaching not need a surname?' he said.

She met his eyes. She felt too warm, and wondered if it showed.

'I'm sorry I borrowed your husband,' he said. 'Earlier on. Virginia was insistent…'

'Yes.'

'It's awful there. Did Chad tell you?'

'No,' she said. 'Not much.'

'We're very worried about Tobias.'

'Yes,' she said. 'One of my students came to see me. He's a friend of his, apparently. They hang out together.'

He glanced down at her. 'Your glass is empty,' he said. He crossed to the table, reappeared with a bottle, refilled both their glasses. 'How does a ballet student know Tobias?'

'He's not your usual ballet student. I do a class at the Ridge Centre.'

'Ah.'

'He's called Finn. Finn Brady.'

'My sister might know him. She knows the Ridge.'

'Your sister?'

'You'll find this is a very small world after London,' he said. 'My sister Sinead works in social services.'

'Oh. I wonder if she knows Lisa Voake.'

'Voake?'

'She comes to class too. Finn made me promise to help her. She's stuck between warring parents by the sound of it.'

'Well I can ask Sinead…'

'When I mentioned Social Services he laughed.'

Liam nodded. 'I can imagine.'

'According to the Ridge people, Finn lives at a residential centre. His real name is Felix but he never uses it. Although it is plastered in spray paint under the railway arches – at least, I assume that's him.'

He smiled down at her.

'He's hard work,' she said.

'I can imagine.'

'But a very talented dancer,' she added.

He said something that she didn't quite hear, as the Professor's booming voice approached again. 'There's superstition…' he was saying. 'And then there's reason.'

'That's not a divide I accept.' Chad was flushed, his voice raised, as they came to stand near the drinks table again. 'If one wants to address the big questions-'

' – then it's important to look at the evidence,' Alan interrupted. 'The way I see it, we can be rational, we can ask questions and then attempt to answer them based on experimentation and investigation and research – OR, we can tell ourselves fairy stories and wish that they were true. I know which I prefer.'

'Newton was religious,' Chad said. 'All his investigations were in the name of God. Are you going to tell me he was just dealing in fairy stories?'

'Poor old Newton lived in his time,' Alan said. 'And, thank goodness, I live in mine. And by the way, Phelps – ' he turned to Liam, as if Chad was now dismissed, 'talking of superstition, we need to do something about the Maguire boy.'

'Tobias?' Liam seemed to flinch again as he faced the professor.

'Downright hostile to me this morning. Sackable behaviour, I'd say.'

'You have to take into account, Professor, that he's had terrible news. We all have…'

Alan seemed pulled up short. 'Yes,' he said, quieter now. 'We all have.' He looked towards Helen, and gave a small bow. 'Madam, forgive me.' He turned back to Liam. 'Whatever the cause of his behaviour, that boy should not be here. Calling me all sorts of names, he was. Very disturbing. We can't take the risk. I don't mind for me, but some of the more retiring members of staff find it very disconcerting.'

'What do you want me to do?'

'I want you to tell him he's out. You know him better than I do, it'll be better coming from you.'

'He likes it here – ' Liam began. 'I thought we could give him something to do in the library – '

'We're not here to provide day care for the mentally disturbed, Phelps.' His eyes wandered towards the crowd in the room, then focused back on Liam. 'I'm relying on you to get rid of him, is that clear?' He turned to Helen and took her hand again. 'Lovely to meet you, Mrs…' He turned to Chad, but Chad was standing some way off, talking to someone else, an awkward young man whose clothes seemed too short for his height.

'A parishioner,' Helen said. 'I recognize him.'

'Hmm.' Alan nodded at Liam, then ambled away.

Liam's eyes followed him. 'I can't bear the man,' he said, his voice quiet. 'And neither could Murdo. He's not really a scientist. He's good with funding, that's all. These weird results are lost on him – Good Heavens, I didn't think she'd turn up.' He was watching the stairs.

Helen turned to see. There was a woman standing there. She was scanning the room, pinch-faced and nervous. She wore a beige raincoat and heeled boots, her light hair tied roughly back, and as she approached, Helen could see how pale she was, her skin scrubbed clean. The boots were in worn brown leather, expensive, Helen thought, but old.

'I wasn't going to come.' Her words, in a soft American accent, were addressed to Liam.

'I was surprised to see you,' he said.

'But then I thought, why should he win? I thought, it's better to face him out, pretend nothing's wrong.' Her grey-green eyes were fixed on Liam's.

'He's watching you now,' Liam said.

'I'll bet he is.'

Helen glanced towards Alan. Sure enough, he was staring towards them. Aware of her gaze, he looked away.

'Sorry – ' Liam was speaking to her now. 'I didn't introduce you. This is Elizabeth Merletti, one of our physicists.'

'Pleased to meet you.' Elizabeth held out a shy hand towards her, and Helen took it.

'Helen… um…' Liam began, then smiled at her. 'She doesn't have a surname.'

Helen laughed. 'It rather got lost when I married,' she said to Elizabeth.'

'Oh, I know that one.' Elizabeth nodded at her. 'Is he a physicist, your husband?'

She shook her head. 'A priest,' she said. 'Anglican.'

'Even worse.' Elizabeth threw her a smile. 'Or maybe, better. What do I know?'

Liam was watching the crowd. 'He's leaving,' he said. 'You've won.'

Elizabeth breathed out. 'Thank God for that.'

Liam turned to Helen. 'Elizabeth has been the hapless victim of Alan's paranoia.'

'We take it in turns here.' She smiled at Helen.

'There've been threats to the lab,' Liam went on. 'Weird notes stuck to the building, pushed under doors. For some reason Moffatt thinks she's involved.'

'It passes from one to another here,' she said. 'Poor old Iain got it for a while.'

'Is that why he's not here?' Liam scanned the room.

She shrugged. 'There are many reasons why Iain's not here. The main one being grief.'

'Poor man.' Liam turned to Helen. 'Iain was Murdo's teammate on the experiment - '

'Best friend,' Elizabeth added. 'He couldn't face it. Everyone trying to be jolly. When what we all feel is…' Her voice tailed off. She looked at Liam. 'His research… His results… and now he's not here to see it. It was Iain who persuaded him to join the team. Iain said no one could do what he did. He was right, but…' She stared at the floor.

'Poor Helen,' Liam said. 'You're not seeing us at our best.'

Helen was about to speak, when Elizabeth said, 'Ah. Good. Here's Neil…'

Liam glanced across to the stairs. 'Neil. More trouble.'

'Neil's not trouble,' Elizabeth said, turning to greet him. 'Not if you know how to treat him.'

'What was that?' A large, red-faced man with a chaotic moustache was approaching.

'She said you needed careful handling,' Liam said. 'Can I get you a drink as we seem to be the bartenders here?'

'Another glass of red would be just the thing.' He spoke breathlessly, as if the effort of crossing the room had been a little too much.

Neil kissed Elizabeth on both cheeks. 'Nice to see you dear. How's the family?'

'Which family?' Helen noticed how her face looked blank.

'The Van Mielen's, of course.'

'Oh.' Elizabeth breathed out. 'The American family. They're fine, thanks for asking. Dad's bought another parcel of land at the back of the ranch. He's talking of growing spelt, although I reckon the pets'll take it over before he can plant it.'

'Pets?'

'The cows. Ponies. Cavies too. My step-mom is just so soft-hearted…'

Neil laughed. 'Typical Kentish farmers.'

'In Wisconsin?'

Neil laughed again.

'We're not even van Mielens,' Elizabeth turned to Liam. 'It was my grandmother's name. It just amuses him to pretend I'm local.'

Neil patted her arm, turned to Liam, took the glass of wine that Liam was holding out to him. 'Any more news on the experiment?'

'No beam strength today.' Liam spoke quietly. 'So, no more significant reactions.'

Neil nodded at him. 'We've got a target luminosity of eleven hundred,' he said. 'Nowhere near that at the moment.'

'Us too – Ah, look Helen – ' Liam's eyes were on the crowd again. 'Here's your husband. So,' he said, turning to Chad, 'you managed to survive your brush with science?'

'Science?' Chad frowned at him. 'Oh. Yes. I think it's going to take more than one of these Boson things –' He looked up at them. 'Has anyone seen Tobias?'

'Tobias?' Liam glanced across the room. 'I didn't know he was here.'

'I saw him a while ago, out in the lobby. He was very upset, he was looking for you. I thought perhaps he'd found you.'

'I haven't seen him.' Liam's face was concerned.

'He was ranting about the Professor. Very upset. Tearful, pacing about…'

'Come on – ' Liam began to head for the lobby. The others followed.

They heard Tobias before they saw him, a stream of words, a shouted muddle, 'They'll come for him, they'll stop him, he shouldn't have done that to me…'

He was striding around in circles in the lobby, the thin light from the fluorescent tube above him, the windows dark navy.

'They'll put a stop to him,' Tobias was saying.

Liam called to him. He stopped still, staring at the floor, his hands still winding around each other.

'Tobias,' Liam said again.

He looked up, saw Liam, then saw the others standing behind him. He put one hand up to shield his eyes. Liam took a step towards him. 'Tom,' he said. 'What's happened?'

Tobias shook his head, biting his lips.

'Is it the Professor?' Liam stood close to him, his voice low.

'He's done a wrong thing,' Tobias said.

'Have you just seen him?'

'He was there – ' Tobias pointed towards the door. 'And I was coming in, and he said "There's no place for you here young man." His voice cracked with tears. 'He said I didn't work here anymore, and I said, but what about the collisions and the aether, and he said he can't have me wasting time looking into all that anymore and he'd get someone who knew about things properly and not nonsense…' He began to sob, big wet tears.

Liam laid his hand gently on his arm.

'And he asked for the Book,' Tobias said.

'What book?' Liam said.

'The Book about the atoms and the Green Lion and the Nothingness,' Tobias said, 'and I told him we didn't have it any more, and he got very angry, very very angry, and he said we shouldn't have got rid of it…' Tobias was gasping between sobs. 'He said there's a kind of knowledge which is dangerous in the wrong hands. And Murdo's not here to tell him…' Tobias bent and buried his face in Liam's neck.

Liam murmured, patting his back.

Helen stepped forward with a tissue. Liam tucked a finger under Tobias's chin and dabbed at his wet cheeks.

'We should get you home,' Liam said. 'Is Virginia back there?'

Tobias nodded, through sniffs. He allowed Liam to take his arm and steer him out of the door into the car park. The small party followed awkwardly.

Chapter Eleven

The night air was cool and fresh. Elizabeth smoothed down her coat. 'I guess I'll leave you to it, Liam. Neil and I…'

Neil was nodding at them. 'Not wanted on voyage, I'd say. Let's go back inside.'

Chad was swaying from foot to foot. 'Perhaps I might be… I mean, we – '

'Sure. We'll go in my car.'

Helen found herself getting into the back of Liam's car, sitting next to her husband amongst paper cups and half-empty bottles of water.

Liam steered Tobias in next to her, and Chad sat in the front.

Helen watched the road, the hedgerows ghostly white in the headlamps. Tobias sat next to her. He was screwing up and unscrewing a lid on one of the water bottles, tipping it to and fro, watching it in his hands.

No one spoke.

They pulled up outside the cottage.

The door opened sharply. Virginia stood there, white-faced. 'Thank God,' she said. 'I thought something had happened.'

Tobias stumbled towards her, then past her and into the house. Helen watched as Liam briefly explained to her what had happened. She saw Virginia's face harden at the name.

'Moffatt? What did he say to Tom to upset him so?'

Liam helped her to a chair. 'Something about there not being a place for him anymore.' He spoke quietly, but Tobias overheard, coming back into the room. 'He said I shouldn't be looking at it on the screen, the beam, the collisions. But Bizzie showed me how to do it, I need to know about it, I told him, and that's when he said I shouldn't work there anymore.'

There was a silence in the room. Chad sat down on an armchair, Helen perched on the arm next to him. It was Virginia who spoke first. 'Bizzie?' she said.

'That's what I call her,' Tobias said. 'She's kind. She helps me.'

Virginia looked across at Liam. 'Elizabeth?'

He nodded.

Virginia held his gaze for a brief moment, then turned to Tobias. 'It's kind of her to help you,' she said.

Tobias thumped himself down on the sofa next to Chad, punching the cushions either side of him.

Chad said, 'Alan wanted the book.'

Virginia met his eyes. 'The Book?'

'He was cross with poor Tobias here, for not having it anymore.' He sighed. 'I'm saying again, if you want it back… I don't want to cause more trouble by hanging on to it…'

'It's nothing to me.' Virginia's expression had hardened. 'And God knows what Moffatt wants with it. Murdo must have talked about it.' She crossed to the sofa, placed a hand on Tobias's shoulders. 'You should try and rest, dear. We can talk tomorrow about finding you another kind of work.'

He turned away from her and shook his head.

'There are other things you can do.'

Another shake of the head.

She sat next to him, took his hand. 'Do you want some hot chocolate?'

He turned slightly towards her.

'You can make it yourself, if you like.'

'Two sugars?' He faced her now.

'If you like.'

'Three?'

She smiled. 'As a special treat.' She squeezed his hand.

He got up from the sofa, murmuring 'Three sugars' in a sing-song voice. He went out to the kitchen and they heard the clatter of pans.

Liam sat on the sofa, next to Virginia. He looked from Chad, to Helen. 'This book? The same one that – '

Virginia shook her head. 'It's nothing. It's an old thing of Murdo's, a text from the early twenties. Tobias loves it, but we don't need it anymore.' She turned to Chad, as if to change the subject. 'Tomorrow,' she said. 'Can you be here at half past nine?'

'If you're sure…' he began.

'You're my priest, aren't you?'

'But you don't believe…'

'They don't know that.' She gave a harsh laugh.

Helen thought about the losses in her life, the mark they'd left in the lines around her eyes. She saw how Virginia's face softened as she looked towards Chad, and how Chad returned her gaze. 'OK, then' Chad said. 'But I can't imagine they'll let me in with you.'

There was a clatter from the kitchen, the sound of a smash of a mug, a shriek of pain – 'I've dropped it' – followed by loud sobbing. 'I've dropped the milk.'

Liam jumped to his feet, followed by Virginia.

'It hurts on my hand,' Helen could hear, followed by Virginia's soothing voice, then Liam's asking for cold water, 'you'll be OK,' he was saying…

Helen looked at Chad.' We're not needed,' she said, quietly.

'But – ' he was half on his feet. From the kitchen doorway, Virginia turned towards him.

'We're in the way,' Helen said. She stood up. 'We should go,' she said, her voice loud.

Virginia turned back to Tobias. Helen could hear water running. Liam was squatting on the floor, picking up broken bits of mug.

Helen went to the door. 'Come on,' she said.

'We ought to tell them we're leaving,' Chad said, looking back towards the kitchen.

'Come on.' She was almost shouting now. Chad hesitated, then followed her through the door.

Much later, as she lay next to him in bed, the events of the day played through her mind. She wondered whether Tobias was badly scalded. She remembered how calm Liam had been. She remembered the lab, how Liam had reached up and dried Tobias's tears. She remembered his warmth, his grace.

She saw in her mind the glances cast between Virginia and her husband. 'You're my priest,' the woman had said, staring straight at him. As if that gives her the right, Helen thought, to have him on her arm at the police station tomorrow… and the way he'd agreed, too, so quickly, not a moment's hesitation, agreed to give up his morning to her, I can't think why…

He'd been silent on the walk home from Virginia's. The moon had been high in the sky, almost full, and they'd walked along the sea front. The tide had been a long way out, a murmuring blackness in the distance. The pebbles on the beach shone in the moonlight, the railings sparkled at their side.

She could have raised it then. It's nice of you, she'd have said, this visit to the police station.

But he'd only have repeated the same excuse about being her priest.

And you're my husband, she wanted to say, now, lying next to him.

She wasn't sure whether he was asleep or not.

'Are you awake?' she murmured to him.

'Hmmm?' He shifted, his back still turned towards her.

'The name in the book,' she said to him. 'It's Van Mielen.'

She waited, but he didn't reply, and a few moments later she heard him snoring.

*

The phone was ringing, sharp through grey daylight. Helen, instantly awake, blinking, stumbling down to the landline in the study, aware of the drizzling dawn against the windows.

'Hello?'

' – the vicarage?' the voice said, a man, and Helen realized it was Liam.

'Yes. Hello. It's me.'

'Oh, Helen, thank God....'

'What? What's happened?'

'I didn't know who to tell,' he was saying. 'Virginia just called me, terrible state, it's Alan, you see, they've found him… He's dead, Helen. He fell from Hanks Tower.'

'Alan – '

'Yes, the Professor. Anyway, the God-awful thing is, Tobias is missing. No one's seen him since last night, Virginia swears he went to bed, but this morning, no sign of him, bed not even slept in, he must have crept out during the night…'

Helen listened, the phone held tightly to her ear. Outside the guttering dripped, its rhythm making rivulets against the window's edge.

Chapter Twelve

'Look.' Berenice slid the photograph across the desk.

Mary picked it up. 'That man…'

'Clem Voake.' She snatched the image back. 'Bad-boy Dad of Lisa Voake.'

'Where's that taken?'

Berenice handed her the image again. 'CCTV from the back of the industrial estate on the Faversham Road. There are lock-ups there. The boys reckon that whatever was stolen from the warehouse raid is being stored in them. They think it's weaponry, sawn-off shot guns.'

'Maybe it's the kid,' Mary said. 'Maybe she's an expert in overseas armaments markets.'

Berenice shook her head. 'Nah. Not her.'

Mary sighed.

'There's no need to look like that.' Berenice smoothed a hand over her hair. 'I'm right about this.'

'You weren't right last time. That butter-wouldn't-melt blonde kid from Pudsey, and there you are seeing him as a child in need, talking to social services, and all the time he's coining it…'

' - He was still damaged.'

'Putting his own mother on the game. In the end it was the mother who needed the social worker…'

'I want this Lisa away from that man. And I want that man brought in for questioning.'

'We need more than just feeling sorry for his kid.'

'We'll get it. We're watching the lock ups now – Enter,' she added, as there was a knock at the door.

'Ma'am.' DS Ben Conway stood there. 'Another death, on the beach…' He was pink-cheeked with nerves. 'Thing is, it's the Prof. From the lab. Dead. Same as the other one. His car at the tower, just the same. The tide was lower, he hasn't been in the water so long.'

'Two – two physicists?' Mary stared at him.

He nodded.

'Bloody Nora.' Berenice whizzed her office chair across to her desk.

'Antimatter,' Ben said.

She looked up from her computer. 'Yeah?'

He pulled at his earlobe. 'What I mean is, both the deceased were working on it.'

'I'm only a copper, not bleeding Stephen Hawking.' Berenice eyed him. 'And now you're going to tell me it's not rocket science, is it?'

Ben seemed to relax. 'Rocket Science is quite easy, actually.'

She looked at him. 'Studied it, have you?'

'Just a bit. In the first year.'

Mary was trying not to smile.

'Bloody graduates.' Berenice shuffled the papers on her desk. 'Still, for once having a physicist on the team might be helpful. For the first and last time in my career, I reckon.'

'I didn't finish my degree, Ma'am,' he said, still blushing. 'Once I decided I wanted to join the Job – '

'Very wise,' she said. She took the papers he handed her, riffled through them.

'Threats to the lab,' he said.

'Have they had any more?'

'There's one there addressed to Prof Moffatt.'

Berenice held the plastic folder up. 'So there is.'

'There was a lot of hostility to the lab round here. Talked about in pubs, you know.'

Berenice narrowed her eyes. 'The pubs I go to, DC Conway, no one discusses particle physics. Mostly we're watching the football.'

Mary laughed. Ben laughed too, nervously.

'And what about the other one? Was there a direct threat to Maguire before he washed up on the beach?'

'That's what we're trying to find out, Ma'am.'

She leaned back in her chair. 'Good,' she said. She looked at her watch. 'I want everyone in the conference room. Five minutes. Make that ten.'

'Same old trouble?' Mary said, as Ben left the room.

Berenice stood up. 'If they can find anti-matter, they can bloody well find a cure for cystitis.'

'They'll blame me.' Virginia stared straight ahead, watching the to and fro of the windscreen wipers.

'They can't blame you.' Chad braked as the lights ahead turned to red.

'Murdo dead, Moffatt dead, and Tobias missing. I'm the only person at the centre of all that.'

The lights changed. Chad joined the line of traffic heading into the town centre.

'It doesn't make you a suspect. Just tell them what you know.'

'I can't do that.'

There was an odd certainty about her tone. He glanced at her. 'Why ever not?' he said.

'Because it will make it all worse.' She folded her hands together in her lap.

Another set of lights on red. The windscreen wipers tick-tocked against the rain.

'Do you want to tell me more?' he said.

They set off again, stop-start in the morning traffic.

'It would have been all right if she hadn't come back. That woman. If she'd left us alone…'

'Which woman…' but he knew the answer.

'… She'd just come to the lab from Geneva. And then everything goes wrong, everything…' She glanced up at the window, ran a finger through the condensation. 'She's a minx that Elizabeth,' she said. 'Worming her way into Tom's affections now too, I wish she'd never come back...' She stopped, her lips pressed tight together.

'It's her name in the book,' Chad said, then wondered if he'd dreamt it, his wife telling him so last night, murmured words in the silent darkness.

'Van Mielen,' Virginia said.

'Yes.'

Virginia sighed. 'I'm not telling them a thing, you hear me? It'll make it all much much worse.'

Chad pulled the car up in a parking space. The police station loomed ahead of them, muted in the rain. He switched off the engine and turned to face her. 'Virginia…'

She turned towards him. He saw her face, lined with pain. He saw a life lived in the shadows. Her eyes met his. He lifted a hand towards her, brushed her fingers with his own. 'Even if you don't tell them…' he began.

'What?' Her hand went back to her lap.

'Will you tell me?'

She gazed into his eyes. 'That depends,' she said.

'On what?'

'On whether you can keep a secret,' she said.

'I've never tried,' he said.

She threw him a thin smile. 'Never? You've never had to lie?'

'No,' he said. 'Not that I can remember. Maybe as a child…'

'You've had a charmed life,' she said. The warmth in her eyes faded. 'Don't let me spoil it.'

Once again, the urge to take her in his arms. Instead, he looked at his watch. 'We should go in,' he said, reaching behind him for his umbrella.

They crossed the car park in the rain. He held the umbrella over her head.

'Two physicists. Murdo Maguire and now Alan Moffatt. Both hit over the head and pushed from Hank's Tower.'

Berenice surveyed the room. 'And the sort-of step-son of one is missing. What have we got? How's imaging going? Ray?'

A crumpled man with thin grey hair got to his feet. 'As of this morning, we think we've got the kid. If I may, Ma'am?'

She gestured to the screen by her side.

'Here – ' Click. On the screen, a fuzzy black and white image. 'The sea front. You can just see the old lighthouse in the background…' Click. 'There. There's someone, you can see him, approaching the old Scallop Tower.'

There was laughter. 'Showing your age, Ray,' someone said.

'Hank's Tower,' Ray said, tight-lipped. Click. 'There.'

The figure was visible. Male, tall, slightly stooped. 'Answers the description. You can see the lettering on his sweatshirt.'

'And the timing?' Berenice leaned in to see the screen.

'This is 9.04 pm.'

Berenice looked across the room. 'Claire?'

A brisk, white-shirted woman stood up. 'Time of death is between 8 pm and anything up to about 4 am. The seawater doesn't help, I'm afraid. But he was on the way out when he hit the water, that's all we know. Bleeding from a severe blow to the head. It was low tide, his injuries are clearer than in the previous deceased. We're doing more tests.' She gave a brief nod, sat down again.

Berenice returned to the screen. 'So, this kid here. If it is the sort-of nephew, step-son, whatever. DS Ashcroft?'

'Tobias.' Mary spoke. 'He worked at the lab. From what we can gather he was told last night that he was no longer needed and now he's gone missing.'

'Whose nephew?' someone asked.

'Well,' Mary clasped her hands together, 'technically not a nephew. He's the son of a cousin of Virginia, wife of Murdo Maguire, but the cousin died when Tobias was in his early teens, and Virginia took him in and raised him. He has some kind of learning difficulty, but seemed happy working at the lab, and from what we've gathered so far was very upset last night when Professor Moffatt told him he was no longer required. And this morning he'd gone.'

She turned back to the photo. 'And could this be him? Sighted by the tower?'

Ray nodded. 'Fits the description, yes.'

She looked up at him. 'I want every sighting you've got.'

'He's often at Hank's Tower,' Mary said. 'According to one of the kids there, it's a favourite haunt of his. He does something he calls experiments there.'

'I want timings.' Berenice said. 'To the second. Is that clear?'

He turned to her. 'Yes. Ma'am.'

Berenice was on her feet. 'Who's got the ground plan of the lab? I want round-the-clock on the lab from now on. Ben?'

Ben Conway stood up. 'Two main entrances, and there's a side entrance, garage thing.'

'I want it watched. All of it. Is that clear? I don't want the natural order of the universe to be upset any further.'

There was a scrape of chairs, a piling up of paper cups in the bin. The room emptied.

'Not sure they got the joke, Boss.' Mary drank the last of her coffee.

'Not sure it was a joke, DS Ashcroft.' Berenice looked at her watch. 'Mrs. Maguire. When she's due?'

'Any minute.' Mary looked at her watch.

'I want to be there.'

'We'd better wait for you. Ten minutes? Twenty?'

'Ho ho.' Berenice opened the door.

'There's a thing you can get from the chemist that really works,' Mary said, as they headed down the corridor.

She lay curled on the sofa. She arched her bare feet, watching the pink of her toe-nails against the yellow fabric. She listened to the hammering of the rain on the window sills.

Next to her, on the coffee table, lay the book. She reached out for it, picked it up, turned the pages. She stared at the cover for a long moment.

She could hear the landline ringing. She rose, wearily, a parishioner, the archdeacon, someone for Chad, that woman about the flowers, "ah, the vicar's wife," she'll say. Her hand on the handset –

'Is that Helen?'

Liam. Of course.

'Just wondered if there was any news,' he was saying.

'No,' she said. 'Chad's with Virginia now.'

'Right,' he said.

There was a silence.

'Can't settle to anything here,' he said. 'Thought I'd go and see Mrs. Maguire, but as your husband's there – '

'They've gone to the police,' she said.

'Oh. Right.' Another silence. 'I feel I'm – '

'You could wait here – '

' – to blame,' he finished. 'Oh,' he said. 'That would be… I mean, if you're sure that's all right…'

'Of course it's all right.

'Right,' he said. 'I'll just sort a few things out here.'

'OK.'

He was still on the phone. 'Can I ask you one thing,' he said.

'What?'

'Am I allowed sugar with my coffee this time?'

'I want him back.' Virginia faced them both, the Detective Inspector, a black woman, she wasn't expecting that, next to her another girl, white this time, one she'd seen before, only with bright red shoes. 'Tobias,' Virginia said. 'Find him.'

'Mrs. Maguire…' It was the red shoes that spoke. 'We've invited you here because we believe you can help us….'

'And why's that thing on?' Virginia pointed at the tape recorder.

Berenice leaned forward across the table. 'It's to help you,' she said. 'It's to help us all.' She indicated a seat. 'Won't you sit down?'

Virginia didn't move. 'Why have you left him outside? He's my priest,' she said.

'The Reverend Meyrick,' Berenice said.

'I asked him to help,' Virginia said.

'Are you religious?'

Virginia eyed her. 'What's that got to do with it?'

'Won't you sit down?' Berenice said, again.

Virginia lowered herself on to the edge of the plastic chair. It was thin and worn, like the paintwork of the walls, on the frame of the high window that seemed to let in no light at all.

'So,' Berenice said, 'let's begin, shall we?'

Chapter Thirteen

There was the making of coffee, coffee that neither of them really wanted, but it gave them both something to do. Liam was looking brighter now, or perhaps it was just the sunlight after the rain. When he'd appeared on her doorstep, Jonah in tow - 'Hope you don't mind, he's used to being with me'- he looked like he hadn't slept all night.

A bowl of water for Jonah. Sugar for the coffee, yet more biscuits, which they left untouched on the plate as they sat at an unnatural distance from each other in the living room. She was wearing a wrap-around skirt and a cashmere sweater, both navy blue. The skirt clung against her legs as she crossed them in front of her.

'I knew he was in distress,' Liam said.

'It's not your fault,' she said.

'Perhaps he's turned up.'

'Perhaps he has.' She sipped at her coffee.

'Your husband - he'd have called you, wouldn't he? If they'd found him?'

'He's with Virginia,' she said. Even to her, it was an odd answer. Through the window she could see the sea, a distant ribbon of blue in the sunlight.

'The book,' he said, picking it up from the coffee table. He flicked through it.'"… The truth resides in the most noble and subtle particle of all"' he read. '"Yet is that particle hidden from us. It is my view, and that of the great teachers who have come before me, that the truth waits to be revealed by He who made it, in His time alone."' He looked up. 'When was this written?'

'There's no date. Chad thinks it's late nineteenth century. The writings at the back have a date, 1922, but they're more recent than the stuff at the front.'

He flicked to the back of the diary. '"My father writes from faith,"' he read. '"But the oneness, the indivisible particle, how can that bring back my brother from the dead?' Who's this? He said.

'Amelia. She seems to be the daughter of the author of the science stuff at the front.'

'If you can call it science,' he said.

'Van Mielen,' Helen said. The author of the front of the book. Johann van Mielen. And his daughter is Amelia.'

'"My husband talks about rotation, about the whirling of the aether."' Liam read, out loud. '"He has his beams and his lenses, and he talks of the speed of light."' Liam looked up. 'That sounds more like science. Who's her husband then?'

'She seems to have married someone called Gabriel Voake.'

'Voake. I suppose the name goes back years. "If only it were to afford him some solace…"' he read.

'They don't seem very happy.'

'No.' He put the book down on the table.

'So, Elizabeth?' she said.

He looked at her.

'Elizabeth van Mielen,' she said.

'Oh. Yes.' He leaned back against the cushions. 'She always said her family came from here, way back, but her father's an American. Farming lot. Settled over there before the Great War. Must be a distant relation. Neil's always teasing her about her Kentish roots, but she always denies it.'

At his feet Johan stirred, snuffled, looked around, settled down again, one paw across his eyes.

'And Murdo's wife gave this to you?' he said.

Helen got up and went to the table where the tray of coffee things sat. 'It was odd. She seemed very keen to get rid of it. Chad offered it back to her the other night, as Tobias seemed to have a sense of loss about it, and the Professor was asking for it too, as you know. But Virginia wouldn't touch it.'

'Weird,' Liam said.

In the silence she poured them both more coffee, carried his cup over to him where he sat on the sofa. She bent to hand him the coffee. She was aware of his gaze holding hers. 'Sugar?' she said. He laughed, spooning two large spoonfuls into the cup, and she laughed too.

'Maybe I should ask Elizabeth,' he said, as she returned to her place on the sofa. 'Although…'

She glanced at him. 'Although what?'

He shook his head. 'Perhaps all labs have secrets. All workplaces…' He stirred his spoon around in his cup. 'There were rumours – ' he glanced up. 'An affair,' he said. 'Between Elizabeth and Murdo.'

'When?'

'Some years ago. Then she left for Italy. But they were only rumours.'

'Do you think they were true?' Helen tucked her legs under her.

He sighed. 'Murdo was a friend. And Elizabeth…' He hesitated. 'She's a difficult woman. Her version of events is not always to be trusted, let's say. And anyway, it was before my time at the lab.'

'But if this book – ' Helen reached over and placed her cup on the table. 'If this book is so significant, why has Virginia only just now got rid of it? If my husband was given a love-token from a rival of mine, I'd throw it out at once…' Helen stared at the book lying on the table in front of her.

Thoughts flickered through his mind - the phone call, the relief to hear she was alone, tumbling into his car, almost jumping red lights to get here…

'I watched you dancing,' he said.

She met his eyes. 'I know.'

'You're good.'

She smiled. 'How can you tell?'

'I know about these things,' he said.

'You do?'

'Not as a practitioner,' he said. 'Just audience, you know….'

'Do you like ballet?'

'Yes,' he said. 'I do. Does that surprise you?'

She frowned, thinking. 'Only, perhaps, with the physics…'

'So ballet and physics don't mix?'

She smiled. 'Ballet and lots of things don't mix. My husband…'

He waited. 'Your husband?' he said.

She shook her head. 'Oh, I don't know,' she said.

'Surely he likes ballet,' he said. 'To have met you, to have married you…'

She raised her eyes to his. There was so much to say, she realized, and she didn't know where to start, about the giving up of things, the loneliness, the new life by the sea that seemed to have put such a distance between herself and Chad, and now here he was, this man sitting opposite her, waiting for her reply, his gaze so intense - and what could she say?

She felt her eyes fill with tears.

'I'm sorry…' It was Liam who broke the silence.

'It's fine, really…'

'I didn't mean to upset you…'

'You didn't upset me,' she said.

'I've never been married, I don't know anything about it, seem to have managed to avoid any kind of commitment…'

'Apart from the dog,' she said, dabbing at her eyes.

He glanced down at Jonah. 'The dog,' he said. 'The dog seems to be commitment enough for me.'

'Married to your work, perhaps?' she said.

He nodded. 'That's what I'm always being told.'

She smiled at him.

'Perhaps we need more coffee,' he said.

DS Ashcroft placed two cups of instant coffee on the desk in front of her. 'Milk, no sugar,' she said to Virginia.

Virginia reached across and picked up the cup.

'So,' Berenice said, picking up her cup, glancing across, 'How far have we got?'

Mary Ashcroft pulled her notepad towards her. 'The young man has gone missing before. On this occasion, however, he was very distressed and angry – '

'Not angry.' Virginia put down her cup. 'Distressed I'll have. Not angry.'

'He'd just been told they didn't need him anymore,' Mary said.

'Distressed,' Virginia repeated. 'As you would be if they threw you out of your job.' She fixed her eyes on Mary.

Berenice turned to her. 'Mrs. Maguire – have you seen this before?' She pushed the plastic bag towards her, in which was visible the green-painted plastic lion.

Virginia stared at it. 'Where was it? He's been looking for that.' She reached towards it.

'It was at the top of Hank's Tower.'

Virginia met her eyes. 'And?'

'Can you confirm it belongs to Tobias?'

Virginia nodded. 'Yes,' she said. 'I can. Now are you going to find him?'

Mary put the lion back in its file and returned to her notebook. 'He went missing at some point between midnight and early morning. His bed wasn't slept in.'

Virginia picked up her cup of coffee.

Berenice sighed. 'Mrs. Maguire. We want to find Tobias as much as you do.'

Virginia flashed her a glance. 'But for very different reasons,' she said.

Helen held the kettle over the Aga, aware of Liam standing behind her.

'So, did she come back because of Murdo, Elizabeth?' she said, as she filled the cafetiere.

'I've no idea. She was married to a fellow physicist in Geneva, a few years ago. But it didn't last, and then she was offered the research post here.'

'And his marriage?' She picked up the tray, led the way back towards the lounge.

'No one knows.' He followed her out of the kitchen. 'They seem bound together, Murdo and his wife. They had a child who died,' he said. 'Everyone said they were happy, before that. The little boy was a lovely boy, apparently.'

'And Elizabeth?'

'Her marriage was over,' he said. 'And she's working on B-D asymmetry, and she wanted to join Manfred's team here.'

'And the van Mielen name?'

'It was her maiden name, but she always used Eduardo's name once she was married. Merletti, I mean, his surname…'

'But she inherited the book. And then gave it to Murdo.' She bent to place the tray on the coffee table.

'You could ask Neil about that book,' he said. 'If you're interested. Neil Parrish. His family go back years here. Local history is rather his thing.'

'Why not just ask Elizabeth?' Helen met his eyes.

'You could.'

'But - ' she prompted.

'With Elizabeth, there's no relying on a straight answer.'

She smiled up at him.

They stood in the middle of the room.

'I'm sorry…' he began.

'For what?'

'Back then… I didn't mean to pry…'

'You touched a nerve, I suppose, that's all.'

He was silent, so she went on. 'In London, I danced. For a living. On stage. The Coliseum, Sadlers Wells. Touring, too, France, the States… When Chad suggested we move here, I tried to explain to him what I'd lose. And he was right, of course, I was tiring of it, too many injuries, I did want a new start, I'd been saying so for ages, children, even, but what I tried to explain to him was that something had to put back what I'd lose, there had to be something else here, and he just said, we'll find that something. He's a man of faith, you see…' She looked up at Liam, aware that they were standing very close together. 'Yes,' she went on, 'Faith. He always thinks everything's going to be all right.'

'God's will?' Liam was gazing into her eyes.

'Not exactly. It's more intelligent than that. I don't mean to make him sound like a carefree optimist because he's not, and in fact these last few months he's been as weighed down as I am, we've barely communicated at all and I really don't know what to do about it. I don't know how to help him, and every time I try to reach out I seem to say the wrong thing and it just makes it all worse and I do love him, really I do, but there are times at the moment when I think about how he used to be, and I look across the table and there just seems to be a gap between the man I married and the man he is now…' She stopped, breathing hard.

She was aware of two things. One was that she had never, ever, put these feelings into words until now. The other was that Liam's gaze was burning into her and she could feel the closeness of him, standing there in the middle of the room, the carpet warm under her bare feet. So that as he reached out to her, took her in his arms, pressed his lips to hers, it didn't seem to be surprising or unusual in any way at all, but rather, as she responded to his kiss, the most natural thing in the world.

Being on the run, Tobias thought. That's what they call it. On the run. On the run from the Law, he thought, playing with the words in his mind. On the run from the Cops.

Law's better than Cops.

Except, I'm not running. I'm not even walking. I'm just standing here with the stones between my toes, the waves licking the beach in front of me.

He wondered if it was because he'd run out of anywhere to run to. He thought about Virginia, and how she'd be worried. But she'll know, he thought. She'll understand why I've gone. Once they find the Prof in the tower, they'll understand why I had to run away.

The Prof, he thought. An image of him lumbering across the stone floor, the yelling of his voice, loud in the darkness. Scary, he thought. It was scary, how he shouted at me, coming towards me like that, so tall and angry…

Tobias held up his two hands in front of him, palms outward. Like that, he thought, both my hands up like that and then, Push, get him out of the way, put a stop to it, to the shouting and the anger.

It was because he knows. Entelechia, he said, and then I knew that he knew about the writings in the Book, asking me how much I knew about the Red Lion and the Green, the Aether and the Irreducible Particle. Where is it, he was saying, where is it, and I didn't want to tell him about Auntie Ginny giving it away and he was talking about the tunnel, not the big shiny fridge one, the old warm dark one, and I didn't like him then, I didn't like him knowing all my things because they're private things, just me and Lisa, it's safe there so I said Stop to him, Stop Stop Stop…

There would be a big splash if someone fell from Hank's Tower when the sea was up like that. When Uncle Murdo did it there was a big splash. The Prof is a bigger man than Uncle Murdo. That's what it would sound like, a big big splash…

He stared out at the flat grey sea.

'We've tried Hank's Tower.' Chad turned off the car engine, leaned back wearily in the driver's seat. 'We've tried the caves. We've tried all the places you claim to be his usual places…'

'It's because he's frightened.' Virginia's voice was thin. 'He must have found a new place. If that police woman had let me go sooner we'd have had more chance of tracking him down.'

'She was just doing her job.' Chad glanced towards the clock on the dashboard.

'Treating me like a criminal, is that her job?'

'It's a murder investigation.' One fifteen, the clock said. Helen will be wondering where I am, he thought. Helen. How odd to think of her now. There was a worry about this, but Virginia was speaking to him.

'There's another place,' she was saying. 'It's further along the coast. He went there once, before we'd noticed he'd gone, it's quite a way but if he kept walking he'd be there by now…' Her voice was shaking.

Chad started the car again. He pulled out into the line of traffic.

'You take the Canterbury Road from here,' she was saying, 'but then at the roundabout you turn off towards the coast.'

In his mind, Chad saw the vicarage kitchen. Would she be sitting down to lunch? Would she have given up on him? Would she even have noticed how long he'd been away?

The mobile had only rung twice this morning, both parish matters. No missed calls from her. No messages.

We used to text each other all the time, he thought. Silly messages. Jokes, endearments…

'… it's this road, here – ' Virginia was pointing. She was pale, tearful, sitting tense beside him. 'We must find him,' she said.

He wondered how this had happened. How was it, that he was driving along the coastal road with a woman he hardly knew in search of a man with learning difficulties who was quite seriously implicated in the murder of a physicist. That DI, Berenice Killick, made it very plain. A man was thrown from Hank's Tower to his death, and the only witness, backed up by CCTV, was Tobias, now on the run.

As they'd left the police station, Berenice had taken his arm. A smart woman, he'd thought, tall, bright, nicely dressed. 'You're the vicar?' she'd said, and he'd nodded. 'Keep an eye on her. I don't think it's sunk in just how serious this is. Two killings,' she'd said. 'Two men dead.' She'd patted his arm, slipped him her card. 'Look after her,' she'd said. 'And call me if you hear anything.'

And now here he was, looking after her. Or rather, driving along the coast, watching storm clouds gather, with Virginia at his side, wraith-like and motionless.

'We'll find him,' he said. 'Don't worry. We'll find him.'

He'd gone, now. He'd held her tight, there'd been another kiss, several… And now he'd gone, and she was sitting at her kitchen table wondering whether it had happened at all.

Extraordinary, she thought.

In front of her two cups and saucers, coffee-stained.

It was all true.

She remembered fragments. The feeling of his soft sandy hair. His murmured words, something about not ever doing anything like this before… She remembered her hand flat against his shirt, her mumbled explanations of marriage and morality as she took a step away from him. He'd gathered himself, apologized, 'No,' she'd said, 'no need for that, no one's fault…'

He'd kissed her again and then he'd gone.

And now the house was still, and she was left with only the washing up. That, and the thrill throughout her body, an ache of need for him, a deep awakening desire. So new and so familiar. It made her want to dance. It made her want to weep for what she'd had with Chad that seemed to have so thoroughly deserted her.

She stood up, wandered through the house, into the lounge. She tidied cushions, straightened curtains, checked that everything was neat again. Then, in the middle of the room, she danced.

Tobias heard the car before he saw it, pondered what it meant, this approaching drone of engine noise. Someone after me, he thought. The Prof, come back for revenge. The Cops, the Law, but they won't find me here.

He ducked down behind a rock. Above him, on the beach road, the car drew nearer, stopped. Doors opening, slamming, his name being called, a man's voice.

Tobias shrank further down.

But – that was her voice. Auntie's voice. He leaned to the edge of the rock, peered out.

'Tom…' he heard her call.

A wave of relief, as he got to his feet, stumbled out from the rock, along the beach, 'I'm here,' he cried, shouting, 'I'm here…'

Virginia met him at the steps, wrapped her arms around his waist, felt his hug around her neck. 'Thank God,' she was saying. 'Thank God.'

'Entelechia,' Tobias said, into her hair.

'It's all right, love,' she said.

'It wasn't my fault,' he said.

'Of course it wasn't.' She took his arm, began to lead him back to the car. 'You're safe now.'

Tobias stopped still. 'But – him?' He pointed at Chad, who was standing next to the car, leaning on its open door. 'Not with him. He'll take me back to them.'

'It's all right, love,' Virginia was saying. 'Isn't it?' she said to Chad.

'Don't take me back to them,' Tobias said.

Virginia turned to him, placed her hand on his arm. 'Nothing's going to happen, love,' she said.

'It's the two Lions,' he said. 'The Green Lion and the Red. If the Red Lion wins then it's the end, the noble particle turns to lead instead of gold, and the waters will rise up…'

His voice was loud in his distress. Virginia hushed him. 'It's all right, love. We're going home.' She faced Chad, her eyes steel-bright.

He could think of no answer. He held the door for Tobias as he curled himself into the back seat.

'Philalethes faced the Dragon and won,' Tobias said.

Chad started the engine, turned the car round on the narrow lane.

But afterwards, having dropped them back at the cottage, he couldn't help but wonder. That police inspector would want to see Tobias. Two men killed. One of them, his sort-of-father. But the other…. At least the poor boy should clear his name.

Chad turned off the coastal road, drove towards the town centre.

We know he's innocent.

His words circled in his mind. He tried to dismiss the doubt that shadowed them.

Chapter Fourteen

15th August, 1922

'*Entelechia?*' Gabriel faced his wife. 'This is all nonsense, Amelia.' He handed the book back to her.

'My father writes about it. Completeness,' she said. 'What Aristotle called the perfection of matter – '

Gabriel was shaking his head.

'My brother believed – 'she began.

'Your brother?' He reached for the bottle of claret.

'Gabriel – it's only luncheon…'

'Your brother was a scientist.' His voice was harsh. 'As I am.'

'And my father too.'

'Your father was wrong.' He splashed wine into his glass. 'Your father never lived to see the work that men are doing now. Our work, our machine, is about seeing the universe as it really is. Your father was content with faith, not proof. Our detector will help us see the truth, the quintessence, the tiniest particles that show us the whole. We don't need Aristotle.'

She was watching him, waiting for the signs of rage, of madness, but he seemed calm. He turned to her. 'It's like this. If I'm walking on the beach, and it's raining, and I look at the pattern made by raindrops in the sand – I think I see something. The particles that Guy and I are seeking, they're as elusive as that.' He smiled at her. 'Your father was content with the gaps. Where he saw an emptiness, a space between the particles, he called it God. Fairy tales, you see. Mere fairy stories.' He patted her hand. 'In the end, Guy and I knew better.'

She smiled up at him, breathing with relief.

He reached for the fruit bowl. 'The last of the peaches,' he said.

'The end of the summer,' she agreed.

He cut the peach into quarters.

She watched him eat it. She wanted to clasp this to her, this moment of peace between the two of them, a married couple finishing their lunch with the late summer sunshine falling across the windows, their daughter sleeping in the nursery…

She reached for her father's book.

'That can be thrown into the fire,' he said.

She hesitated. 'I would rather keep it,' she said.

'A museum piece,' he said. 'What place is there for all that now?'

'But you must agree,' she began, 'that the new physics still follows Newton - '

'When I speak of gravity, I am describing a force within the universe. That's all. I have no interest in divining the workings of some God or other. Do you really think we are put on this earth because of some benign force?'

'But Guy always said – '

'What do you know of what Guy believed?'

The flash of rage in his voice. I should not have spoken, she thought. 'You forget, Gabriel, dear, that Guy and I were educated by our father – '

'Your brother came to know better. If he ever once believed that there was an order in the universe, a controlling force – such beliefs were trampled to death in the mud of France.' The table shook as he got to his feet. 'Only I know how it was.' His voice was loud.

'Hush – dear - '

'If I don't tell the truth, there is no one left to tell it.' He brushed past her, seized hold of the door handle.

'Grace will be waking from her rest,' she said.

'And I shall take my walk.'

She heard his hurried steps upon the flagstones. When he'd gone, she tiptoed up the staircase to the nursery, blinking back tears.

The tide was up. Waves the colour of earth crashed against the stones. Gabriel stared at the shingle beach. He could almost see it, the rough geometry between the gaps, the smaller and ever smaller parts that vibrate in their invisibility.

All this is here, he thought. It might just as well not be here, but it is here. It sustains itself in being here.

His hand went to his jacket pocket, fingered the silver chain.

There is the before, and there is now.

There is a gap between them. A gap that cannot be repaired.

He drew the chain out of his pocket, watched the silver crucifix swinging in the sharp sea air.

This was once his.

When first I met him, me, the son of the blacksmith, hearing the clatter of hooves in the yard, coming out into the sunshine, wiping blackened hands on my leather apron… And he stood there, smiling, his hands holding the reins of a snorting, stamping gray mare, 'D'you think you can do anything for this poor old lady? Dropped a shoe out with the hounds this morning, limping now, though she's always one to be dramatic…'

Was it then that I first saw this silver chain? Did this catch the sunlight, as we agreed a price for the shoe? I fancy now that it did. Certainly, it became familiar to me. So that, when, as he lay in the mud, his trembling arm reached to his neck, his shivering fingers dropped it into my hand - 'Take this, Gabe. And my watch. Keep them – ' I knew, then, that it was the end.

'For your sister?' I said, but he shook his head. 'For you, silly.'

He had closed his eyes, then.

Gabriel saw it still. Guy's face, shadowed like a skull against the khaki green, rivulets of brown slashed dark with blood.

He had clutched the silver cross so hard it had made marks in the palm of his hand.

There was moaning, screaming, the pounding of artillery. But at his side the halting breath was louder still.

And then it stopped.

Gabriel found he'd walked as far as the Scallop Tower. He stepped along the jetty, climbed the ruined stairs, wondering, not for the first time, who it was who'd thought to build a lighthouse on this flat shore. A folly then, and a folly now.

He reached the top. He crossed the circular platform, leaned on the low wall, looked out to sea.

They had come home by ship. Herds of soldiers, wounded, sick, blank-eyed, crazed.

They called us Heroes. But all I could think was, he is still there. His headstone, there, across the sea, one among the hundreds in their serried ranks.

It was that, as much as anything, that broke his father's heart.

The gulls circled above him, their song rising and falling with their swooping path.

And Amelia, he thought. If only I could make her see. In those last hours we talked, two men of science, half-drowning in the swamp of war. We both came to see, then, that the search for meaning is as foolish as this tower. There is no meaning, no redemption. But there is science. There is investigation, evidence, knowledge. There is matter, atoms, particles, subject to the force of gravity. But there is no divine will. Were I to fall, now, from this tower, it would be because of Gravity, not because of God.

He straightened up, smoothed a lock of hair from his face.

I promised him then, to continue the work we started. And I know that he is with me.

He looked at the crucifix between his fingers. He saw that he'd been clutching it so tight it had left marks in the palm of his hand.

He crossed the stone platform and descended the lighthouse stairs. He picked his way along the brickwork jetty, the waves splashing at his feet.

"It is not that we are the fallen. It is nearer to the truth, to say that we are still falling." Amelia turned the page of her father's book. "For if gravity can be said to be the force that acts upon all matter, we must assert that it is put in motion by the Lord…"

She paused, the book in her hands. She thought about her husband, even now pacing the marshlands. His walk always took him back along the ocean's edge, past the Scallop Tower. Soon he will return, she thought, to lock himself away in his laboratory, to emerge, as usual, at dinner, taciturn, despairing, even hostile.

We were happy once, us three. Guy, Gabriel and me. Our father used to tease us about finding our friends amongst farmhands and blacksmiths, but he knew as well as we did how quickly Gabriel became one of us. He was brilliant, charming, always questioning, always seeking after truth.

We all loved him.

When he returned from the Front, so thin, yellow-skinned and haunted, my father began to live again, a little. He lived long enough to see Gabriel make me his wife, to witness our wedding in the village church, a simple white dress, a posy of pink roses…

I was happy.

And now…

From the hall came the sound of a door slamming shut. Amelia got up from her seat. Grace had only just gone with Cook to pick raspberries, how odd they should be back so soon…

She went out to the hall.

'Gracie?'

The house was silent.

A draught of air blew through the hall. She followed it, down the dark corridor that led to the kitchen.

'Oh – ' She wasn't sure if she'd spoken, or even screamed, the silence was so thick – but there he was, his sunken face and torn white shirt, staring, staring at her through the choking cold of the corridor.

And then he'd gone.

'Guy?' She took a step towards him, towards where he'd been. 'Guy?' Another step. 'Why?' she said, out loud. 'Why here? What do you mean by it? Why can't you rest in peace?'

She had reached the kitchen door. Through the glass she could see her daughter, skipping in the sunlight, holding her skirts with *one hand, a basket of raspberries in the other, laughing as she came towards the house.*

"It is not that we are the fallen. It is nearer to the truth, to say that we are still falling. For if gravity can be said to be the force that acts upon all matter, we must assert that it is put in motion by the Lord…"

Helen turned the page, just as her mobile rang, loudly. She jumped, almost dropped the book, Liam, she wondered -

'It's me.' Her husband's voice.

'Chad.'

'I'm on my way back. We found Tobias,' he said.

'Oh. Good.' She felt a wave of relief.

'I'll pop into the office,' he said. 'See you after that. Tea time ish.'

'Sure. I'll be here.'

'I… ' he began.

'Are you all right?' she said.

'Yes.' His voice was distant now. 'All a bit upsetting, that's all. I'll see you later.'

He'd gone. She placed her phone on the table.

I love you. Was that what he was about to say?

We used to, she thought. Both of us. Just part of the ebbs and flows of normal married life, endearments, jokes…

Normal married life. It seemed so far away.

She went into her ballet studio, switched on lights against the gathering clouds, began to flick through books of piano music for Barbara to play for the Grade Threes tomorrow.

The girders of blue steel rose high above his head. The wide windows flashed with the low sunlight. Liam walked towards his office.

It's as if there's a gap, he thought. If we've fixed the luminosity, and if the charge is at its limits, it still doesn't explain why that's a negative charge and not a positive. Yes, a gap, he thought. A B-meson, if that's what it is, having a negative charge but behaving as if it has positive charge. It makes no sense.

The quiet swish of a glass door. He was on the staircase, climbing back towards his office. Through the windows, the low roofs of the lab complex. Beyond that, the lush green of the fields.

It'll rain later, he thought. He thought, she is out there somewhere. He wondered whether she too was thinking it might rain.

'Liam – '

He looked up. Iain was on the landing above him.

'They've found Tobias,' Iain said.

'Thank God for that. Was he OK?'

'Seems to be. Though there's a finger of suspicion…' Iain held the door open.

'What, just because he got upset with Moffatt?'

'It makes no sense. No sense at all.' They reached Iain's office. Liam noticed his pallor, the shadows round his eyes.

'I mean, why Moffatt?' Iain flung himself into a chair.

'Why what?'

'Dead, I mean.' He drummed his fingers on the desk, absently, gazing unseeing at his computer.

Liam sat down on the other chair.

'I miss him.' Iain looked up. His eyes were bleary. 'Murdo. Don't know how I'll manage…'

'Can you take a break?' Liam watched the twitch of his fingers.

'A break?' He spoke loudly. 'We're right at the crunch point, aren't we? These charges are all wrong, Murdo would have known….' His voice cracked.

'Family? Someone you can visit?'

Iain met his eyes. 'My mother is in a home in Morningside and doesn't know who I am.'

'But back in Edinburgh…' Liam remembered there was someone, some story, he couldn't quite recall, a girl, certainly, a *grand amour*, maybe, a microbiologist, was it, Penelope –

Iain shifted in his seat. 'I'm better off here,' he said.

'Wasn't there someone – ?'

Iain gave a brief bark of laughter. 'Penny's the last person I want to see at the moment,' Iain said.

'Of course,' Liam murmured, feeling foolish.

A flock of geese crossed the sky, black triangles against the now thunderous clouds. 'Do you think we're worse than most?' Liam said.

'What?'

'Physicists. All dysfunctional. No families, no connections, all wedded to our work…'

Iain gave a dry smile. 'Not worse. Just more committed. Anyway, you'll be OK. Someone will sweep you off your feet, you'll be married with two kids and a dog to walk on the beach – '

'Maybe…' I'd like that, Liam was about to say -

'Haunted.' Iain spoke suddenly. His fingers assumed their tapping 'Ghosts, walking the corridors. I was here last night…'

'Ghosts?' Liam looked up.

'Murdo. That soldier. God knows. Definitely someone, over by the workshops, disappeared before my eyes…'

'Iain, mate – '

'By the wall there.' Iain went on. 'You know where the old house is, on the other side. You know, where Moffatt was buying the land.'

'The famous expansion.' Liam smiled.

'Don't suppose it'll happen now.'

'We could never have afforded it. To rebuild the tunnel now. Although the new results are going to get us noticed…'

Iain picked up a pencil from his desk, gazed at it for a long moment. He seemed to be elsewhere, edgy, anxious. 'Do you think that's why Moffatt was picking on Lizzie? Because of her family connection with the land there?'

Liam shrugged. 'Doubt it. Don't you just think it was her turn? He didn't like people being cleverer than him.'

'Even though everyone is. Was,' Iain corrected himself.

'There's a book,' Liam said. 'From the van Mielen's.'

Iain focused again.

'Newtonian stuff. The vicar's got it, from Mrs. Maguire – '

'She gave it to him?' Iain's voice was loud.

'You know about it?'

'Sure. Lizzie had it. From her family. And when she and Murdo…' He picked up the pencil again. 'Murdo wanted it, she didn't.'

'Alan was bullying Tobias to give it to him.'

'Alan?' Iain's eyes narrowed. 'Why?'

'No idea.'

Iain shrugged. 'Alan bullies everyone.'

'He was bullying you – ' Liam began.

'No, not really. Only because I thought I might buy the old house.'

'There was that shouting match – the two of you…'

Iain narrowed his eyes. 'He hates competition, that's all. And anyway, I gave up on the Voake house in the end. Left the field free for him.'

'Perhaps that's why he wanted the book. Some old connection…'

Iain shrugged. 'Oh well. Now it's with the vicar. Funny old world.' He turned to his computer, pulled up a screen. 'Back to work, eh?'

'Sure.' Liam got to his feet. 'What's that?' On Iain's desk there was a crumpled sheet of lined paper.

'This?' Iain picked it up. 'Oh, this.'

'Another one?'

''Fraid so.' He handed it to Liam. 'Pinned to the main gate last night.'

'"Dont think it's finished."' Liam read. '"The flood will come and our sins will be washed clean."' It was written in pencil, in capitals. 'We should show the police.'

Iain nodded. 'Aye. That was my intention.'

'The police have promised some kind of guard.' Liam looked down at him.

'Do you think it'll help?

Of course, Liam was about to say, but Iain was speaking again.

'What if the threat is from within?' He stared out of the window at the heavy sky.

'Iain – '

Iain waved him away. 'Do you think – ' he turned back to Liam. 'The ghost. He was bleeding. Red blood, you could see it. Or was I imagining it, do you think? The mind playing tricks…' His voice was a whisper, almost to himself. 'Torn shirt, you could see it, white shirt…'

'Iain, you should talk to HR. Sort out a break from here…'

Iain shook his head. 'Murdo's gone. The experiment is critical. And anyway, I've got nowhere else to go.' Another wave to indicate the door.

Liam leaned over and patted his shoulder, then left.

'Lisa Voake,' Berenice read. 'Aged fifteen. Mother, Nina Carey. Father, Clem Voake. Family known to Social Services…' There followed a record of interviews, incidents, visits from social workers, various concerns noted, various actions indicated.

And she's ended up in a caravan by the lab with a villain for a father.

Whatever you might say about my mother, Berenice thought, she would never have let me end up like that.

Mind you, she seemed sparky enough that kid. Maybe she'll survive too.

Footsteps, the door opened. Mary was standing there.

'Here you are, Boss.' She slapped a file down on the desk in front of her. 'The boys have been following up leads on this Voake character. Someone answering his description tried to off-load a doctored shot-gun. The guy in the shop, told us, reluctantly, that it had been altered. He wasn't happy about it. Wouldn't take it. The guy, if it was Voake, threatened him vaguely, then said there'd be plenty of people who would take it, and it was his loss not to get a bargain. It's that little shop on the Dover Road. Dodgy bloke, though he was helpful, the boys said.

He said it wasn't the first time this Clem guy had been in. He said he must be storing them somewhere.'

'Any thoughts where?'

'We've checked the field again, round the caravan. The Chief has told the lads to go back to the disused airfield. He said someone's shipping stuff that way.'

Berenice looked at her. 'The Chief? What's he doing on a minor case?'

Mary fiddled with the edge of the file. 'Dunno. Guess he's keeping an eye on the case.'

'Not on the case. On me.'

Mary threw her a look. 'Surely you're not suggesting…'

'That a senior male copper might not be up to speed on feminist and multi-ethnic issues?'

Mary smiled. 'Didn't think you were.'

Berenice shrugged. She picked up the file. 'So, what do we do about Voake? Is he adapting rural shot guns and selling them on to gangs?'

'That's what our friend in the gun shop suggested.'

Berenice yawned. 'He can't be that good at it, if he's slumming it in that caravan. And his daughter is in rags.'

'Saving up, maybe?'

'Yeah, right.'

Mary was about to answer, when the desk phone rang. Berenice picked it up, nodded, said Yes, twice, rang off.

'Another shout. They've found the suspect boy who was at the tower.'

'Tobias?'

'That's the one. We're going to have to call him in. Now. Get someone to pay a call to his stepmother or whoever she is.'

'Will do.' At the door, Mary paused. 'One other thing. That physicist dropped by. Hate notes. Wanted us to see them.'

She passed a plastic bag across to Berenice.

Berenice picked it up, peered through at the enclosed papers. She passed it back to Mary. 'Get the fingerprint boys onto it.' She clicked her computer into life. 'And I thought it would just be cattle rustling out here.'

Mary smiled. 'Don't chat breeze, Boss. You never wanted no quiet life.'

'Don't suppose I did,' Berenice said, as Mary went out of the door.

I could go home, Chad thought. He stared out of the windows at the late afternoon.

Nothing to keep me here. The stationery order is done. The readers' rota is e-mailed out. And Phyllis has sorted out the church hall bookings.

The office was attached rather as an afterthought to the side of the church. It had a small dark window, a bright strip light which made a whining noise. His study at home was book-lined, comfortable, with a lamp on his desk and a broad window which gave on to the rose garden.

I should go home. Helen will be... waiting for me? No, he thought. Helen will be in her studio, as if hiding. I'll breeze in, pop my head round the door, suggest a cup of tea... There will be a distance, a frostiness, as if I've interrupted something private.

It was not like this in London.

In London, I would go home. Home to my wife. Not home to rattle around a huge vicarage in a weird kind of solitude.

He bent to the computer keyboard, pulled up his sermon document. He flicked through the reference texts he'd printed out. He picked up Johann's book, and flicked through that.

'The truth is not that we are the Fallen. It is that we fall still, continuously, in this world now. The force of Gravity is exerted upon Everything, and upon Everyone...'

He wondered about these words as a start for a sermon. Man's Fall From Grace, he thought, picking up his Bible, scanning the Old Testament for references. How simple it was for van Mielen, to tie his faith to his physics. Enviable, really -

The ring of the ugly grey phone on the ugly grey desk.

'Hello – '

'It's Virginia. It's not over...' Her voice was faint and shaky. 'They want to see him, tomorrow, Tobias, I tried to refuse but they talked of arresting him...' A choke in her voice, then she carried on. 'Can you – can you come too? Tomorrow? Solicitor there and everything… Oh, it's all so impossible, why won't they leave us alone? Tomorrow at ten o'clock, we have to be there…'

'Yes,' he said. 'I'll be there.'

An out-breath of relief. 'Thank you,' she said.

'I'll come to you and we can go on from there,' he said.

There were more thanks, and then she'd gone.

Chad replaced the phone receiver.

He returned to his screen, scrolled through his notes. 'Fall,' he saw he'd typed. 'Gravity. Emptiness.'

It had come on to rain.

Emptiness, he read, again.

He saved the document, folded up the papers into his briefcase, and left for home.

The name was still visible. Voake. Carved into the old post box on the edge of the path.

Clem ran his finger along it. He turned towards the house. In the twilight, in the rain, the old walls loomed in front of him. He reached the front door, pushed against the rotten wood, which gave at once. He was inside.

He twitched his nose at the smell. Animal, fox, perhaps. Wood smoke too, though the grate when he touched it was cold and damp. Rain dripped through gaps in the ceiling, edged through the broken windows.

He tried to remember how it was, all those years ago, when his mother had brought him here. He was six, seven, perhaps. A visit to her Uncle Voake, she'd said. An old man, sitting by this very fire. He remembered warmth, and light. He remembered the pattern on the carpet, dark red with curled green leaves, long since rotten under foot. Uncle Voake had been vague and kind and whiskery. 'Are you looking after your Mother, boy?' he'd asked him.

Clem hadn't known what to reply.

How? he'd wanted to say. My father is so much bigger than me. When he goes for her, there's nothing I can do.

'I did try once – ' he'd begun to say, but his mother had flashed him a warning glance. She knew how that had turned out, and she didn't want him telling anyone.

And then there'd been a woman bringing in cake and lemonade, not his mother's aunt, a paid woman. And they'd sat by the fire and eaten, and he'd wondered, is this how life is for other boys? This feeling, of warmth, and safety and kindness.

He put his finger through a hole in the glass window. I wouldn't have called it those words, but those are what I meant. And those are what I mean now, now that Digby's gone and this house can be mine, and I can make a home for Lisa and me and it will be warm and safe like it was when it was just Mum and me…

A clap of thunder broke overhead. A gust of wind threw raindrops down the chimney.

Three years later, Mum was dead. Cancer. And I was left with Dad. Not that I stayed around much after that.

He stepped across the kitchen into the hall. There was the cellar entrance, its door swinging half off its hinges. He put one foot on the wooden steps, then another.

What do you hope to find? Manny had asked him. Poking around in the old house? Then Voakes would have left nothing behind.

At the last step he tripped. His foot twisted, and he found himself sitting on the cellar floor in two inches of rainwater. He bashed his fists on the ground either side of him. He wanted to howl with rage, at the step, at the rain, at the doubters, the ones who said nothing would come to him, he didn't deserve any of it, he didn't deserve to raise his own child, the ones like his dad who said he'd brought it on himself, the ones like his Mum…

Not that memory. Not that one. He'd remember her as she'd been here, in a pink dress, floating in the sunlight, sipping tea with her whiskery uncle. Not how she was later, when they got home, and he was trying to say but I didn't say nothing, Mum, I didn't tell him nothing, and then later, curled into the corner, his hands over his ears, and her screaming at him, like she always did, about him heading for a beating again, 'you never learn do you, you stupid or something, am I going to have to learn you all over again?…'

He could remember the smell of the wall, the bare plaster damp and cold against his cheek.

He sat in the puddles of the cellar and looked around him. Then he got up and began to search.

Chapter Fifteen

Helen placed the breakfast things in the dishwasher. She sat at the kitchen table with a second cup of tea.

Tobias. It seemed too terrible to think of, that that boy could be accused of such an awful thing.

At least Chad has gone with them, she thought. He'll make everything OK. He'll be there, quiet but forceful, good in a crisis.

Virginia will be glad he's there with her.

There was a flurry of birdsong from the eaves outside, next-door's cat aggressing the house martins, again. It had rained overnight and the garden was green and damp in the morning sunlight.

The book was on the table in front of her. She opened it at random.

"… of Water does each Thing have its Beginning," she read. "It is Prime Matter, the Abyss of Darkness, the Residence of Behemoth…"

She thought about Liam's hands on these pages.

She wondered what Chad was doing now.

At breakfast, they'd hardly spoken. He'd been packing papers into a briefcase, murmured something about notes for his sermon. Should I have asked him, she wondered now. Is that what a vicar's wife should do, express interest in what her husband wants to tell the faithful on a Sunday morning?

She stared into her cold tea. It was her mother who'd put it into words, all those years ago, and of course she'd ignored her. 'But surely, darling, if you can't even share his beliefs…?'

There was no point even trying to tell my mother. There was the time we'd talked, me and Chad, about the rare moment in a dance when one simply *is* the dance, when one's self merges into the role, into the physical being of the role… and Chad had said, 'that's what I mean by God.' She'd never forgotten it, the way he took her hand, the deep undertow of shared belief.

She got up, poured her cold tea down the sink. She stood at the window, watching the flickering sunlight.

It had gone, that shared delight. And now all I can think is that perhaps Chad should have married someone who was capable of believing in the same God as his.

Chad stared up at the window, which was high in the gloss-painted wall, and grimy with neglect. He looked back to Virginia. She was standing by the coffee machine, prodding hopelessly at its buttons.

'I think it needs money,' he said.

They had been ushered into this room, 'relatives' room,' the desk sergeant had said, and were now left alone. There was a sporadic loud hum from further down the corridor, a vacuum cleaner, perhaps.

'You'd think they'd let me in there with him,' she said. 'What does that solicitor know about any of it?'

Chad fiddled with the machine. 'Fifty pence,' he said. 'Do you want any?'

She shook her head. She met his eyes, briefly, looked back to the carpet, which, like the chair she now settled on, was a faded orangey-brown.

Outside the hum seemed to draw near, then faded away again. Chad sat opposite her. 'Murdo,' he said. 'And the Professor. And the Book…'

She gazed at him. 'What about them?' she said.

'What has brought them to this?' he said. 'What is the connection that has proved so dangerous?'

She shook her head, but he went on, 'It was you who said it. About secrets. When I mentioned Elizabeth – '

She gave a harsh laugh. 'Oh yes,' she said. 'There's secrets enough where that one's concerned.'

'Well?' He sat upright, his gaze fixed on hers. Confessional mode, Helen always called it. She reckoned he could get anyone to divulge anything when he took up his Confessor's pose. She claimed he'd try it with her, he never knew what she meant, but it used to make her laugh.

Used to.

He wondered when he'd last heard that laugh of hers, so bright and full of life, her eyes dark with joy, with desire…

Weeks. Months. She has been absent from me all this time.

He felt a sudden, overwhelming, wave of loss.

'Are you all right?' Virginia's voice sounded loud in the sparse room.

He blinked, tried to smile.

'It's not your fault we're here,' she said.

'No,' he agreed.

'You asked me about secrets,' she said. 'The big secret, the one I can't fathom, is what he saw in her.'

'Elizabeth?'

'Who else? Who else came prancing and smirking into my life like that?'

'Did – Did they have an affair…?'

'An affair?' Virginia gave a harsh laugh, her eyes fixed on his. Then she said, 'Murdo always denied it. Always. The fact that Iain was after her, everyone knew that. But the rumours about my husband… they wouldn't go away. It was demeaning – ' she spat the last word. 'Every time I walked into the lab, the glances, the women exchanging looks…' Her words faded away. 'Still, now she can be happy with Hendrickson after all.'

'Both of them, you're saying?' Chad stared at her. 'Iain and Murdo, both of them involved with her?'

She seemed to wilt in the chair opposite him. 'I'll never know. Not now. He always denied it. But there was something…' She raised her eyes to his. 'You can tell when someone's lying, can't you?'

'Me?'

'I mean, generally. When someone's holding something back, it always betrays itself somehow.'

Chad considered this. 'I suppose so,' he said.

The hum outside started up again, now much nearer.

'So – what happened?' Chad asked.

She sighed. 'It was so long ago. I'll never know really. I would see her from time to time, flaunting herself with Iain. And then Murdo was so odd at home. They were very good friends, Iain and Murdo,' she said. 'Iain must be suffering too.' She gathered herself, went on, 'And then suddenly, it was all over. She took the job in Italy. Next thing we heard she was married. Murdo never mentioned her again. Life went on. Until…' She sat straight-backed, drumming her fingers on the seat beside her.

'Until your child died…?'

She nodded.

'And what brought her back now, do you think?'

She looked so weary, he began to regret his questioning. 'Who knows? Her marriage seems to be over. And a job came up here. She's ruthless, you know? Whatever she wants, she gets…'

'And Professor Moffatt?'

She blinked at him. 'What about him?'

'I just wondered if he, too, was anything to do with…'

'With Elizabeth? Why would he be?'

'I just mean, as he's now dead too…'

'Oh. Yes.' She gazed at him, blank-eyed. 'I can't understand… it makes no sense,' she said.

'No,' he agreed.

She sighed. 'Well, Iain's welcome to her now.'

'Her maiden name,' he said. 'Van Mielen.'

'What about it?' She was looking at him sharply.

'It's in that book. The book you gave me, the physics one – '

'She gave it to my husband. It's from her family.'

'How is it from her family?'

She shrugged. 'A long story, and a dull one, actually. One of her ancestors was a cousin of the author. It ended up with the American side. Murdo's friend Neil Parrish at the lab, he told me. There was a local branch of the family, but her lot went to America before the Great War. That's what he said. Anyway, it amused her that Murdo was so interested in it. That's all.' She shifted on her chair. 'Now you can see why I was glad to give it to you.'

'Yes,' he said.

He felt she was about to say more, but instead she looked down at her lap, at her hands clasped tight together there. A thin shaft of sunlight caught the edge of her hair, her face, her clear, freckled skin. She raised her eyes to his, and he saw their pale clarity, and thought how odd it was, that beauty could shine through pain.

In the distance a door slammed. There were footsteps along the corridor. A uniformed officer put her head around the door. 'D.I. Killick will see you now,' she said.

"My work has been a quest for the smallest, the purest, the most true particle of all, and my methods have been honed through the trials of the laboratory…'

Helen turned the page.

'…and the test of my own soul. It has come the time to set these words to the page, for darkness hovers above the surface of the world, and I fear for my dear wife and children…

She put the book down.

Darkness, she thought. Was Johann seeing the signs of war?

She went over to the window. Outside clouds had gathered, and the sea was flecked with white.

I wonder if Chad thinks that way. 'My dear wife…'

If he does think that way, he doesn't show it. 'My dear wife and children…'

Perhaps you need both. Wife, and children.

It was a constant pall, a background heaviness which drained the colour out of life. Every month the hope was raised, every month dashed, until gradually they made the choice, without ever speaking of it, to avoid it altogether.

All that was left was the hollow sense of loss, and the knowledge that whenever she looked at Chad she saw it echoed in his eyes.

My dear wife and children…

She wondered what it was that Johann had found to be the test of his own soul.

Berenice stood with her back to the window, her hands flat against the radiator.

'Mrs. Maguire – Your nephew admits he was present at the old lighthouse tower at the same time that Professor Moffatt met his death.'

Martin, the duty solicitor, sat at one side, scribbling notes.

'Where is he now?' Virginia's voice was sharp with anxiety. She was in a chair in front of Berenice, with Chad next to her.

'He's with one of my officers.' Berenice left the window and came and sat down opposite them. 'Let me repeat, Mrs. Maguire, this is not an official questioning. We want to help. But everything indicates that Tobias was there at the time that the Professor fell. And, unfortunately, Tobias's response, whenever we mention the Professor's name, is one of rage.'

'Well, I'm not surprised.' Virginia clasped her hands together in her lap.

'He holds him responsible for the loss of his job. He also says that there were secrets that they held in common, but he won't say what they were.'

'It's that blasted book.' Virginia turned to Chad. 'That's why I wanted it out of my house. I don't know why the Prof was interested, but it did Tom no good at all.'

'Book?' Berenice looked towards Chad.

Chad glanced at Virginia, then spoke. 'It's a funny old thing, early twentieth century, a kind of rewriting of Einsteinian physics, with Newton, some other people, an obsession with gravity...' He was aware of her blank expression. 'It was in their family...'

'Perhaps I should see it.' Berenice looked at Virginia.

'Ask him.' Virginia lifted a thumb towards Chad. 'I got rid of it. It caused too much trouble. It's his now.'

'It belonged to – ' he began.

'No it didn't.' Virginia spoke loudly. 'It didn't,' she repeated. 'It was ours.'

Chad glanced up at Berenice. He nodded. 'In their family, you see,' he said.

Berenice got up. She gazed outside. The window was steel-framed, double-glazed, but you could still hear the comings and goings down below, the vehicle sirens, bits of conversation, the patter of the rain. She turned to face them. 'The evidence so far is circumstantial. Tobias is free to leave, but with some conditions. We will need to question him again. You have to understand, he's in a very serious position.'

Virginia clapped her hand to her mouth.

'There's no way he could have done it,' Chad said. 'And anyway, he's disabled, you can't just apply your normal rules...'

'All the evidence places him at a crime scene.'

'And my husband?' Virginia's voice was loud. 'Two of them are dead, not just one. And Tom wouldn't have harmed Murdo. Did you ask him about Murdo?'

'We did, yes.' Berenice faced her. 'As you say, he says he wouldn't harm him. He became upset at the suggestion.' She went to the door and opened it for them. Martin the duty solicitor got to his feet too.

'His friends,' Berenice said. 'Lisa Voake.'

'What about Lisa Voake?' Virginia faced her.

'We'll be talking to her, too.'

'You can talk to who you like,' Virginia said, tight-lipped with rage.

Chad led her to the doorway, his hand gripping her elbow. In the doorway, Berenice turned to him. 'I mean it, about that book,' she said.

"… And yet my husband spends his days in his laboratory, as if somehow that will bring about peace for him, for me, for us." Helen lay on her sofa, the book in her hands. She turned a page. "I pray that one day he will see, that our dear child needs him as her father. He tells me that the work he began with my brother, before they went away to battle, must continue, that he owes it to the memory of Guy to do so, and although I too wish my brother's memory to be kept alive, yet do I also yearn for the return of the peace and happiness we shared before…"

Helen wondered how it was that Amelia had placed these pages in her father's book. Presumably it was without his knowledge, a record of her feelings.

Helen shifted on the sofa cushions. Bright sunlight broke through the rainclouds. She checked her watch, thought about the trip to the supermarket, Chad had asked her to get some more biscuits for the church tin…

She looked at her feet on the cushions. Dancer's feet, Anton used to say. Born to be dancer's feet, he'd say, 'not pushed and pummeled and reshaped like the rest of us poor saps…'

She heard Chad's key in the door, looked up as he came into the room. He was grey and weary, and he sank onto an armchair.

'How- ?' she began.

'They've let him go for now. On various conditions. They can see that there's nothing that implicates him in Murdo's death.'

'And Moffatt's?'

'It looks bad for him. He was there, around that timescale, when Alan fell from the tower. Caught on CCTV and everything.'

'What does he say?'

Chad shook his head. 'He's not helping. He was very angry with Alan, and he won't say otherwise. Virginia says he's one of the most honest people she's ever known, but it's not helping him now. And he went on about that book – ' he glanced at it where it lay on the table next to her.

Helen shifted to sit upright on the sofa. 'What did he say about the book?'

Chad sighed. 'He's been going on about the secrets in the book, and how Alan was after them. All that gravity stuff in there…' He met her eyes. 'You've been reading it too.'

'The wife is very angry,' she said.

'Wife?' He frowned at her.

'Amelia, wife of Gabriel Voake. Daughter of Johann van Mielen. There are pages from her at the back.'

'There are?'

'Didn't you see them? They're loose, folded in. She must have added them in later.'

'Elizabeth is a distant descendant of them. Virginia told me.'

'Right.'

He glanced up at her tone. 'Elizabeth ended up with it, for some reason.'

Helen leaned back on the cushions. 'It's all very odd. It all seems to centre around the lab.'

'That's why the police want to see it.'

'Police?' Her hand went towards the book.

'I said I'd give it to the Detective Inspector woman.'

'Oh.' She picked it up, weighed it in her hands.

'If it helps Tobias…'

'Yes,' she said. 'I can see that.'

They sat in silence, listening to the birdsong outside.

'Poor Virginia,' he said.

She looked up at him.

'She's beside herself with worry.'

'I can imagine she is,' Helen said.

'But – ' he threw her a glance. 'Surely you can understand…'

'Understand what?' She unfurled herself from the sofa, placed her feet in their sheepskin slippers.

'She's a very vulnerable person,' he said.

'So I gather.' Helen picked up the book.

'Helen – ' He reached an arm towards her, let it fall to his side.

'What?' She stood, looking at him.

'I'm her parish priest,' he began. 'She's alone in all this. She and Murdo adopted Tobias, they've cared for him. And now this, her husband's death, in these circumstances. It's too much for anyone to bear, isn't it?' He shook his head. 'Tobias is the only person left in her life.'

Helen headed for the door.

'They had a child who died,' he said.

She turned to him. 'And is that better or worse than having no child at all?'

Her eyes flashed rage. He could think of nothing to say.

Chapter Sixteen

A burst of sunlight brightened the concrete of Police HQ, sharpened the signage to angular blue, before the next shower muted it all to grey again. In the trees, the gossip of the starlings rose and fell, between the sudden lurch of sirens and wet tyres.

'I need to talk to them,' Berenice had said to Mary the night before. 'All of them,' she said.

'All of who?' Mary had looked at her blankly.

'Starting in the morning. Those clever scientists. And not just them, everyone. Secretaries. Porters. Cleaners, if they have them.'

'I'm sure they have them – '

'… hoovering up that particle thingie by mistake. Always a risk, isn't it?'

Mary had laughed, then worried that Berenice wasn't joking. Sometimes, she thought, scanning Berenice's unsmiling face, it was difficult to tell.

Now it was Thursday morning, and inside, the desk sergeant was all courtesy. 'Of course, Madam, do wait here, the DCI will be down to see you shortly, we've had a lot of you lab people in this morning… Yes, Sir, if you don't mind waiting a second, DCI's instructions, although what she thinks she's doing dragging you all away from the secrets of the universe, I read in the paper that you're very near finding the last bit, ain't that so?… There is a drinks machine, Madam, though I wouldn't recommend it myself… Terrible weather for the time of year, Sir, dear me, look at it now, hope you brought an umbrella, they may give you a lift down here but once you're out those doors you're on your own, guvnor…'

Upstairs, in rooms marked Occupied, questions were asked, notes were taken, 'Were you aware of any hostility towards the Professor within the laboratory? Or to Dr. Maguire?' 'These threats to the lab that have been mentioned, can you tell me a bit about them?' 'Were they taken seriously at the time?' 'Can you think of any connection between Dr. Macguire and Professor Moffatt that might lead to their deaths?'

And, as the morning gave way to lunchtime, and Berenice sat at her desk ignoring a chicken sandwich at her elbow, the reports piled up in front of her. 'Interview with Roger Newbold, technician at CLEAR', 'Interview with Gwyneth Wilcox, administrative assistant at CLEAR', 'Liam Phelps, research physicist', 'Richard Moraes, deputy director', 'Neil Parrish, Physicist', 'Elizabeth Merletti, physicist'…

She read about the threats to the lab, 'There was a note pushed under my door once, must have been an insider with security as tight as it is. What did it say? Oh, something stupid about how the lab is endangering humanity. I reckon it was a contract person, unhinged. They stopped after a while. Oh, and by the way – ' Berenice checked the name. Roger Newbold, interviewed by DC Ashcroft. '… where Tobias is concerned, he's done nothing wrong, that kid, is that clear? I want that on the record. Heart of gold that boy.'

Berenice yawned, picked up the next report. 'Gwyneth Wilcox. "Well, yes, you could say there was bad feeling, I suppose, but they're all like that, aren't they? And the women are worse, although luckily we don't have many women in the department, just as well if you ask me. To kill someone? Oh, no, I don't suppose it went as far as that. I mean, people get very furtive over their results, don't they, and some of the more senior men are very competitive and secretive, but I can't imagine any of them coming to blows over a few numbers here and there…"'

She yawned again. The sandwich at her side was looking tired too. 'Neil Parrish,' she read. 'I won't have any nonsense about people not getting on. We're all a team, can't do physics without it. Between you and me, Ma'am, there's a big announcement due, ground breaking stuff, though don't go telling the world, eh? Hate mail? Some nutter. Best ignored that stuff. I've lived round here all my life. 'Fraid we're like that, us Kentish men, don't get me started… Clem Voake? Case in point. The way that family has gone – you know that big house over the wall from the lab? The derelict one? That was their family home, two, three generations ago, and now here they are, living on dodgy dealings at the back of the old airfield. Apart from old Dot, she's Clem's aunt, she has a second-hand furniture shop on the Faversham

Road, probably the straightest of the lot though that's not saying much. Our Moffatt here had his eye on the old house, wanted to expand the lab. I suppose now old Digby's died, might have raised a few issues. But it's up to Digby who he sold that house to, he don't owe Clem anything, if anything it's the other way round….'

Berenice scribbled a note. 'Old House. Lab. Moffatt. Neil Parrish.' She turned a page.

'Interview with Iain Hendrickson. Senior team member. "It makes no sense. No sense at all. Why us? Why target the lab like this? What did you say? Is there anything I can think of to explain it? Nothing. Murdo… I mean, Murdo Maguire of all people. One of the best men you could hope to meet. Key part of the team. And Moffatt? I don't understand it. I just don't."

Berenice picked up her phone. 'Any chance of a coffee in here?' she said. She replaced the receiver, rubbed her forehead.

The next report read, 'Liam Phelps. Interviewer DC Ashcroft. "I can't believe he's gone. Murdo was a good man. Very good physicist too. The Prof? Well, I wouldn't say I was as close to him, no. And it's an open secret that his work was pretty thin. Shouldn't speak ill and all that, but even so. We've been getting some interesting results on super symmetry, bumps on the curve, you know, talking to our colleagues at CERN a lot, and there he is, posturing away, claiming it as his research, when everyone knows it's a team effort, the CP violation stuff is all very well, but… sorry? Have I lost you? All I'd say is, I have no idea who would want Murdo dead. He's a great loss to us all…" [silence while he wipes tear from his eye]'. Berenice looked up and smiled at her sandwich. She took a bite from it, admiring Mary Ashcroft's attention to detail. She thought about this physicist having a quiet weep at the death of his colleague.

'Why did he leave? No one turns down the opportunity he had. The Higgs mechanism confirms the Standard Model, you see, but raises questions of asymmetry… Have I lost you again? And Murdo was never the same, after they lost their child, him and Virginia. Talked of going to CERN. We were glad he stayed with us, though.'

Berenice read on, picking up a cleaner's report, 'Bessie Wallace: "All I'll say is, Ma'am, people get mighty superstitious when it comes to atoms, don't they? And them notes put under them people's doors, that's what they were saying. That if you mess with the Lord's creation, who knows what might happen? All this smashing them tiny particles, all that nothingness, you're asking for trouble, isn't it? Opening up them empty spaces, who knows what might get in the gaps in between?"'

Berenice replaced the paper on the pile. She found that she'd eaten all her sandwich without noticing.

Helen dabbed at a scratch in the smooth polish of the bureau. Escritoire, perhaps it should be called, she thought, looking at the fine mahogany finish. Stacked on the surface were the loose pages of the book that she'd carefully unfolded and removed, and it occurred to her that the desk had been made long before poor Amelia had written the words in front of her.

"I fear for our souls, and for that of our dear child. Where my father had the Lord, my husband will have Aether, and Atoms, and Gravity. I ask him why Gravity, why is it so mysterious, and he tells me it's about the measurement of it, to see how it comes to bear on particles. He said, that he and Guy had set out to measure it, and he will do so still. He speaks much about my brother, about their work together, about honouring his memory. Then he takes my hand, and tells me we are falling, falling through space, through time, even. I remain silent, for to say any word at all is to risk his wrath…'

She turned the page.

"The death of my dear brother haunts us all. Last night I slept alone. My husband inhabits a world wherein I cannot join him. He sits at his bench long into the night, with his lenses and rays and beams. Last night I watched our dear child in her cradle, and I prayed to the Lord to keep us from this Heavyness, this Darkness. When I awoke this morning I ventured to my husband's room and found him sleeping there, a makeshift mattress on the floor. He is like a shadow to me now, this man whom once I loved, and my heart does bleed. Where once was joy and laughter, now there are tears, and Silence."

Helen slipped the pages into their folder. She'd bought it earlier today, a cardboard file, a designer one, covered in white roses. It seemed to suit Amelia, she thought, why she wasn't sure. Loss, perhaps; a husband who once had loved her, now turned away.

She got up, went to the window. The glass was dotted with drops of rain. Beyond that, the strip of sea was a threatening grey. Somewhere in the house her phone trilled, a text message coming in, and at once she thought, it'll be Liam, he'll be telling me –

Telling me what?

Chad had phoned earlier, to say that the police were interviewing everyone in the lab now. He'd dropped off the book at the front desk, felt a bit of a fool, he'd go straight from the office to evening service, they could eat together after that…

She wandered out to the kitchen, picked up her phone, found a message from Anton saying that one of their former colleagues was reviewed in the papers that day, 'Glowing, darling, glowing – and richly deserved, of course, dear Tanya…'

Anton, of course. Not Liam. She smiled at the message, at its Anton-ness. He'd always say to anyone who'd listen that Tanya was an "also ran". She told herself that Liam would have nothing to say to her, police investigation or not. She went back to the bureau, finished hiding away Amelia's writings.

Liam collected Jonas from the Duty Sergeant, with effusive thanks on his side and admiring comments from the Sergeant, 'Good as gold, he was, and you can't say that for all of them, tetchy breed, collies, aren't they…'

He left Police HQ in the rain, putting up his umbrella, gathering up Jonas's lead, checking his phone for messages…

He found himself hoping that Helen had texted him, ridiculous thought… Then he thought he might text her, or even call her, he could tell her… What? What was this urge to confide in her?

An amusement, he thought. That's what my sister always says. Another way of wasting your life, that was how she put it last time, you always manage to find the perfect distraction, Liam, they're either married, or they don't want you, what was the last one, oh, yes, she was just about to emigrate, wasn't she, always someone who isn't going to make any demands…

Sinead's voice in my ears. Perhaps she's right, he thought. Maybe Helen's a distraction. What is it to her anyway, Murdo and Elizabeth and poor Virginia…

I played it down, just then, with that nice policewoman, didn't want to besmirch Murdo's good name… Perhaps I should have said more. Perhaps it's more relevant than I think. Helen would know, I could ask her what she thinks…

'What would you do, Jonas boy?' he stopped, adjusting the umbrella. Jonas shook raindrops from his neck and looked up at him.

'You'd ring her, would you? Mind you,' he said, as they set off again, 'you've always been an incisive kind of chap. Always one to seize the moment, eh, boy?'

The dog lifted one ear, trotting at his side.

Liam stopped again, reached out his phone and dialled Helen's number.

Particles, Berenice thought, weighing the book in her hand. Gravity. Nothingness.

It was beautifully made, bound in soft leather, with thick creamy pages.

She opened it at random. Was it really dangerous, as the cleaner said, if you open up those empty gaps?

"… a most subtle spirit," she read, "which pervades all particles, by the force and action of which spirit all particles attract one another…"

She flicked to another page. "It is in the Chaos that order is restored. And we must face the Chaos in order that the Truth be revealed…"

And what was this to do with two murders? So, she thought, they happened to be scientists. So, they both fell from the old lighthouse. So, there was a certain amount of bad feeling, but only normal workplace stuff, they should try HQ here… And there's a thread of a dispute with this villain and some claim on the old house next door.

She held the book in her fingers.

From the sound of it, Virginia was keen to get rid of it, now her husband's dead. And the lad Tobias claims it carries some kind of secret, that Moffatt was after.

In my experience, she thought, murder is always human. Born of ordinary, human feelings. Like jealousy. Or greed. Or revenge. If we're looking for secrets in all this science here, this aether and nothingness and particles - we're looking in the wrong direction.

She glanced up as the door opened and Mary appeared with a mug of coffee for her.

'I didn't mean that *you* should bring it,' Berenice said. 'One of those lads out there, sitting on his arse-'

'I think you should join me,' Mary said. 'Elizabeth Merletti. Reckons she'd had an affair with the deceased. Before she was married. When she was Elizabeth Van Mielen.'

Berenice put the book down. 'Van Mielen, yeah? Now we're getting somewhere.' She stood up, gathered up her jacket. 'Like I always say. Not science at all. Just human feeling. Extreme, maybe. But, in the end, human.'

Chapter Seventeen

'I'm sick and tired of that blasted book.' Elizabeth Merletti flicked back a loose lock of hair. 'I wish the Kent lot had kept it.'

Berenice, having shown her the book, withdrew it, stacking it back on the desk with her papers.

'It's your name in it,' she said.

'Not my name,' Elizabeth said. 'Some ancestor. My grandfather's cousin.' She sighed, shifted on her chair, glanced up at the narrow window which was dark with the late afternoon rain. She was still in her raincoat, which she'd refused to remove – 'It's not as if I'm staying,' she'd said, in that cool, even voice with its very slight accent. Berenice wondered whether she put it on for effect, a kind of all-purpose continental sophistication. It certainly worked, she thought, or perhaps it was just the long sweep of hair, the well-cut clothes, the low-heeled but elegant black patent shoes.

'It's your maiden name,' Berenice said. She glanced at Mary, who sat, head bent, writing notes. 'Van Mielen,' she went on.

Elizabeth sighed.

'You must admit, it's rather odd…'

'Is it?' Elizabeth fixed her with her clear, grey-green eyes. 'My father's family were from round here.'

'You know its history, then?'

'Neil knows more about it than I do. Neil Parrish. He's the local history freak. It was he who told me about it. Frankly, I really wasn't that interested. We're from a different branch, you see. The American lot. I knew nothing about this eccentric ancestor until I mentioned the book to Neil.'

'So you gave it away?' Berenice watched her.

She yawned, but it seemed fake. 'Yes,' she said. 'I gave it away.'

'To Murdo,' Berenice said.

Once more that fixed, determined look. 'Which is what we're here to talk about, isn't it? Not some silly old book.'

Mary exchanged a glance with Berenice, then went back to her note-writing.

'Yes,' Berenice agreed. She took a sip of cold coffee. 'That's what we're here to talk about. You and Murdo Maguire.'

The room quietened. Berenice could hear the slam of distant doors, the revving of car engines as people began to head for home. For a moment she envied them, until she thought of what passed for her own home, a characterless rented terraced house where even the furniture didn't feel like her own…

'I loved him.' Elizabeth's words cut through her thoughts. 'Murdo. I loved him for years,' she said. 'And he loved me.' For the first time, there was a tremor in her voice. She looked across at Berenice. 'I don't particularly want to tell you all this,' she said, 'but I figured you'd find out anyway, and I don't want to "impede the course of justice" or whatever it's called, and anyway…' Again, the shake in her voice. 'And anyway,' she said, 'I owe it to Murdo.'

'Mrs. Merletti.' Berenice crossed and uncrossed her legs. 'Do you have any idea who might have wanted to kill Dr. Maguire?'

Elizabeth shook her head, with an expert swish of hair.

'People have mentioned bad feeling in the lab,' Berenice went on. 'Hatemail stuffed under doors. We've seen a few of them.'

She shrugged. 'People can get silly about scientific truth.'

'You'd only recently come here. From Italy.'

'Yes,' Elizabeth said.

'What brought you back here?'

The grey eyes fixed on hers. 'I got the job here. My marriage in Italy was over, and this experiment here, it's very exciting.'

'When was this?'

She gazed at the ceiling, calculating. 'About seven, no, eight months ago, it must be.

'And did you see much of him?'

She met her eyes. 'Here, yes. Of course. We were on the same team.'

'As colleagues?'

'Of course. As colleagues.' The voice was firm.

'And in any other sense?' Berenice's voice, too, was firm.

'I consider that intrusive, but I shall answer it anyway. You have to understand, Mrs. – ' she stopped, thwarted in her perfect manners.

'Detective Inspector.' Mary's voice was sharp. 'Not Mrs.'

'You have to understand – ' Elizabeth spoke as if Mary wasn't there. 'It was a meeting of minds. A perfect love affair. At the time, maybe, I didn't see how perfect. It was only afterwards… Later, when I met my husband, I thought I could just slough it off, like an animal changes their skin, just start again. But it wasn't like that. Oh no,' she said, 'it wasn't like that at all.'

The composure had returned.

A meeting of minds, Berenice thought. Two scientists as one, in the pursuit of knowledge. She looked at the well-fitted cashmere sweater and wondered whether Elizabeth was entirely right about that one. From what I know of men, Berenice thought, it wouldn't be her mind that kept him coming back. But then, she thought, maybe it's me who's wrong, what do I know of physicists, clever men like that, not stupid, stupid, moronic bastard journalists – She realized Elizabeth was speaking again.

'… and that drooping, self-pitying wife of his, keeping him for herself, she knew he'd had a chance of happiness and she made sure he turned away from it, made sure he tiptoed back into his grey, love-less existence.'

Ah yes, Berenice thought, the wife. I must have thought that too, told myself that I was all he wanted, I was the only one who could make him happy, until I found out that not only was she keeping him financially but they had a fab sex-life too –

'They'd fallen out of love long before he met me,' Elizabeth said. 'It's not as if I stole him from her.'

My words exactly, Berenice thought. Word for word. I used to say exactly that -

'Did you say something?' Elizabeth was looking at her, and Mary shot her a glance.

'No. Nothing. Do go on. What I want to know is, the timescale.' Berenice adjusted her voice to business-like. 'When was this affair? When did he go back to his wife? When did you leave?'

'Your assistant here has all the dates.' Elizabeth waved vaguely towards Mary.

'Detective Constable.' Berenice's voice was sharp. 'Not Assistant.' She caught a twitch of a smile on Mary's face. 'Tell me – ' Berenice leaned forward. 'Would you say there was any bad feeling in the lab? Between the Professor, say, and Dr. Maguire?'

There was a moment of hesitation, then Elizabeth shook her head. 'No,' she said. 'We're a team. Differences, maybe, but nothing that would lead to… to this.'

There was more, sitting in that stuffy room as the afternoon wore on and the rain eased. Mary's pen scratched away, taking notes, yes, Elizabeth supposed, the hate mail might be significant. And yes, she conceded, the Professor was more of a manager than a scientist. Was it a mistake to sack Tobias? Certainly it was, and as for you charging him, I will not hear a word against that poor boy, I can't believe you're even thinking of it, so what if he was spotted on those camera things? He likes

Hank's Tower, it's a known fact about him, he does what he calls his experiments up there, completely harmless... Someone else, someone with a grudge against both men? It's possible, yes, like you say, we've had these threats. Do I feel that I'm in danger? At this, she'd shrugged. 'Not any more than usual,' she'd said, and Mary had written it down.

At the end of the interview, Elizabeth turned her pale face to Berenice. 'There will be a funeral, won't there? You don't keep them in fridges forever, do you?'

'We try not to,' Berenice said, gently.

'I'd like to... at least, if I couldn't be there when he...'

'Yes, of course.' Berenice got to her feet, and Elizabeth followed.

At the main entrance, Elizabeth turned to her. 'If Murdo was in danger, he'd have told me. You have to know that, Detective Inspector. If anything was going on in his life, I'd have known.' Her eyes welled with tears. She stood in the doorway, newly vulnerable.

Berenice offered her hand. 'Thanks for coming in, Dr. Merletti,' she said. 'I appreciate it's difficult.'

'I want to help,' she said, wearily, returning the handshake. 'Anything you want to know, just ask.'

Berenice watched her go, clicking her way along the rainy, light-splashed pavement.

Funerals, she thought, turning back inside the building. I hadn't reckoned on that. If he dies, will I be there, lurking in the crowd, hiding from his wife?

Yet another hold he has over me. Bastard.

'Penny for them?' Mary was waiting in the corridor.

'I wish you wouldn't keep saying that,' Berenice said.

'Him again?' Mary nodded sympathetically. 'Time's a great healer, you know.'

Chad bent his head against the rain, which was falling with renewed zeal.

…of Water does each Thing have its Beginning… What was it that Van Mielen had said, about water as Prime Matter? The Abyss, where Behemoth lives…

He rounded the corner into St. Mary's Street. The church spire at the end of the road loomed darkly, blurred by rain. There'll be about four people there, he thought. Six if I'm lucky, if Mrs. Benfield comes with her sister. Mind you, they'll be exchanging glances if there's anything too fancy about the readings. They like their religion plain round here.

The gravel of the church drive crunched under his feet. The rhododendron bushes shuddered with rain.

Like my father, he thought. He liked a no-nonsense God, a sensible kind of chap who rewarded the good as long as they didn't get above themselves and sent his Son to keep an eye on things.

He remembered the chapel he'd go to as a boy, its blank walls, narrow pews, outsized and angular pulpit that seemed to be preparing to lecture its audience before the minister even stepped up to it.

I am no longer like my father, he thought. My faith is coloured red and gold, draped with altar cloths and incense, candles and flowers. My God is unknowable, his Son is Love incarnate. There is nothing no-nonsense about a faith that turns wine to blood.

He unlocked the church door, pushed at the heavy iron handle, walked through the darkness, switched on the lights. He found himself standing beneath the painting on the north aisle.

It was a modern painting of the crucifixion; the cross painted as a tree, in almost photographic detail, the bloodstained male form, the nails through the hands and feet.

He thought about the Green Man of Van Mielen's book, the first Adam and the last, the tree of life and the tree of knowledge.

And now, he thought, there's a new, Godless creation story, where the universe explodes into life, a story of fiery collidings told in mathematical equations. The beginning of matter itself.

As it was in the beginning, he thought. Is now and shall be forever, world without end…

He wondered if the physicists believed in a world without end. He wondered what his father would make of the lab's work, then thought that probably there was, even in the maths, even in these curves and signs and patterns, too much wonder for a man such as he.

He went to the Lady Chapel. Mrs. Lynch's flower arrangement drooped on its pedestal, wilted and yellowing.

He began to light the candles, listening to the rain hammering against the roof.

Helen too, was listening, standing by the sitting-room window. Was that it, that low rumble, his car approaching through the rain? But then the sound faded away, to leave just the ticking of the old clock, the dripping of the guttering.

Half an hour earlier, her phone had rung.

'Hi, it's me,' he'd said.

His voice on the phone.

She could hardly breathe. I know, she wanted to say, but he was still speaking. 'It's just, the police, they've been asking me questions, and I didn't tell them everything, and it's on my mind, I'm so worried about Tobias… Hello? Helen? Are you there?'

'Yes,' she'd said, 'I'm here.'

There'd been a silence, then, until he'd said, 'I could come over. If you want…'

'Yes,' she'd said. 'Come over.'

Now she was standing by the windows, un-looping the heavy curtain cords, blocking out the rain and the darkness, as a car drew up, and she heard a knock at the back door.

He was damp-haired and dishevelled, and she smiled up at him. 'No dog?'

He shook his head. 'I think he'd disapprove,' he said.

'Of what?'

He stood, looking down at her. 'Oh God. Of this. Of us.'

'He's not the only one,' she managed to say.

'You look fantastic,' he said.

She wondered, briefly, what it was about her jeans, her navy sweater, simple stud earrings, no make-up… She thought, briefly, that it was a long time since she'd been admired. But then he put his arms around her, and once again there was that feeling of completeness, of his lips against hers, and it was only the clock chiming the half hour, reminding her that Chad would be back from church, that made her take a step away from him, shaking her head, brushing her hair back from her face…

He was pink-faced, breathing hard.

'I'll make us some tea,' she said, and the words sounded ridiculous.

He followed her into the kitchen, sat down at the kitchen table, watched her doing things with mugs and spoons. 'Tobias,' he said. 'That's why I came. Although, if I'm honest… it was you, of course.'

She turned to face him. 'Liam… it can't be – '

'No,' he agreed. 'No. It can't.'

There was a silence. He glanced at the day's paper on the table, flicked at its pages. He looked up at her. 'Everything points to

Tobias being there when Moffatt was killed, and it can't be true. I'm a scientist, I deal with the evidence, that's what I said to that policewoman today, but in this case, just because the CCTV images show Tobias, that doesn't make him a murderer, does it? It makes him someone who likes being up at Hank's Tower, that's all.'

The kettle whistled loudly on the Aga. She stood with her back to him, pouring hot water.

'I tried to call Virginia today,' he went on, 'but she wouldn't speak to me, and then I thought, perhaps your husband could talk to her, she trusts him, doesn't she. What I've been thinking is, just because the evidence puts Tobias in the frame for Moffatt's killing, it doesn't connect him with Murdo's, and anyway, Tobias loved Murdo, he wouldn't wish him harm, and it's far more likely that the two deaths are connected, something to do with the lab, I reckon. Something to do with Moffatt wanting to expand the lab into the neighbouring land.'

Helen placed two mugs of tea on the table, then sat down opposite him. 'These threats to the lab, you mean?' she said.

He shook his head. 'I think it goes back before that. Neil Parrish was talking about it, you remember him, you met him at the lab, red-faced, jolly type. Anyway, he says Moffatt was trying to buy the land over the wall, where the old house is. Neil thinks he'd actually completed the sale just before all this happened. And then I was telling Neil about the book, and he said the old house was owned by the van Mielens before one of them married one of the Voake family, and then it became derelict. He reckoned Moffatt got it for next to nothing, even though Iain was after it too.'

'Why wouldn't Virginia speak to you?'

He tipped some milk into his mug. 'I asked her about the book. Neil said that Moffatt had confided in Murdo about the sale, I thought maybe she'd know, and it might take the heat off Tobias… She said, "If it's about that van Mielen house, I don't care." Then she practically hung up on me.'

Helen frowned into her tea.

'She said the book was with the police,' he went on, and that she hoped they locked it away for good. And then she put the phone down.'

'How very odd,' she said.

'Which is a shame,' he said. 'As I'd like to see it again. I think it could be a clue, in some way, part of the evidence, and it could save Tobias from being charged with anything. I tried to say this to Virginia too, but she wouldn't have it.' He looked up at her, hesitated, then said, 'Am I allowed sugar this time?'

She smiled, got to her feet, fished in cupboards.

'Sugar,' she said, putting a packet down in front of him.

'Thank you,' he said.

She was standing at his elbow. He looked up at her.

'Tea,' she said. 'You and me.' She shook her head. 'It's crazy.'

He placed his hand briefly over hers. 'I know,' he said.

'Wait here,' she said, and left the room. He sat and waited, wondering what she was going to do, reappear in different clothes, perhaps, there'd been that girl he'd met once, in London, he'd gone back to her flat with that muon researcher from Imperial, Steve, wasn't it, and then somehow much later he'd been left alone with her, what was her name, a loud and clumsy kind of girl, and she'd done this number of leaving the room and then coming back in wearing some ghastly kind of see-through lacy thing… He tensed with embarrassment at the memory, horrible it was, and he didn't even fancy her, and as he'd left she'd called him a typical bloody physicist, shouted it down the stairs behind him…

He heard footsteps, and Helen came back into the kitchen. Her clothes, as far as he could tell, were unaltered. 'Here,' she said. 'Not all the book is with the police.'

She passed a pink file across the table to him. He saw the pages from the book, neatly stashed inside it. He drew one out, glanced through it, looked up at her. 'How did you -?'

'It's Amelia,' she said. 'It's Johann's daughter. She's trying to keep his work safe from her husband, and I felt I should look after her.'

'"…My husband will have Aether,"' he read, out loud, '" and Atoms, and this Gravity, that holds the chaos at bay. My father will have God, who brings forth Light from Darkness, and the Earth from the Oceans, and who sent Satan away to exile…"' He looked up at Helen. 'Gravity,' he said. 'The force that makes the moon heavy...' He frowned, read the next page. 'It's very like – ' He met her eyes. 'It's like the threat letters we've been sent. This idea of Satan in exile. They seem to think that we're in danger of starting the whole process again, with some kind of primeval battle between Satan and God...' He glanced at it again. 'And what's this about a ghost?'

'She talks about seeing her brother's ghost. He died in the First World War.' Helen looked up at him. 'Are you all right?'

'Me?' He gave a narrow smile. 'Sure. Why wouldn't I be?'

'I just thought – '

'We have one. The lab. A ghost.' His gaze held hers.

'Is this a joke?'

'I'm a scientist. I don't believe in ghosts. But...'

'But what?' she prompted.

He shook his head. 'There've been odd reports. A man walking the corridors. Torn shirt, bleeding, military dress...' Again, the thin smile. 'Then again, we've had two of our number killed in as many weeks. People are bound to be frightened. If your Amelia here was talking of seeing a ghost, perhaps she had the same fears.'

'I don't think she's frightened about that,' she said, and her voice was thick with feeling. 'I think she just wants her husband back.'

She was flushed, with a stray lock of hair across her face, and he found himself imagining her coming back into the room in a thin lacy thing.

'What are you thinking?' she said.

'Oh, um - I was just thinking about being a typical bloody physicist,' he said. 'Only – only, with you, I'm not, you see…'

There was a long silence. Her gaze seemed to burn through him. 'These writings,' he said at last. 'What should we do with them?'

'I don't know,' she said.

'I wonder if Neil Parrish knows about this bit.' He picked up his mug, put it down again.

There was another silence. He met her eyes across the table. 'So, Amelia,' he said. 'She wants her husband back.'

'It's like that…' Helen stared at the table in front of her. 'When the man you love goes away from you, when you see him every day, when he shares your house, your meals, but nothing you say can reach him, and what he believes is so far away from anything that makes sense, and he only believes all this stuff about God the Father because his own father was so disappointed in him, or at least that's how I see it…' Her words tailed away. The room was quiet, and it occurred to them both that the rain had stopped.

'When you came here,' Liam said. 'Your husband said it would all be OK.'

She nodded, sniffed.

'The thing that your husband said would be OK, if you came here… Was that having a baby?'

She met his eyes. 'There was no baby.'

He waited.

'We had a miscarriage,' she said. 'Since then, nothing…'

In her mind she saw herself breaking down, here, just like this, with us sitting at this table, with Liam there, looking at me like that, and I'd start to howl and be unable to stop…

They sat, motionless, in the room.

He reached out his hand and took hold of hers.

'You're very beautiful,' he said.

A loud hammering on the vicarage door shattered the air around them. Helen paled, jumped up, her hand clutching the neck of her jumper.

'Chad?' He got to his feet.

'He's got keys.' She ran to the hall.

'Be careful – ' He was behind her as she opened the door.

Finn was standing on her doorstep, breathless and sweating. Leaning heavily on him, there was a girl. She was bleeding from a head wound, one eye half closed, her jaw swollen. She was wearing a scarlet leather jacket.

Helen stared into the blank eyes. 'Lisa? What the hell has happened?'

The girl swayed, shivering with shock.

Helen stood aside to let them pass into the vicarage. Behind them the night sky was seared red with the last of the day.

Chapter Eighteen

'Do we need an ambulance?' Liam half-carried Lisa into the kitchen.

'No – ' It was the first word she'd spoken, indistinct through her swollen mouth.

'No ambulance,' Finn said. 'He'll kill her.'

Lisa sat heavily on the kitchen floor, then lay down, curled into a ball, and closed her eyes.

'Blankets,' Liam said. 'Warm water.'

Helen did as she was told. Liam eased Lisa's jacket from her, bathed the cuts to her face, kept up a quiet stream of questions – 'Does this hurt? Can you move this? Can you wriggle your fingers… your toes…' He checked her pulse, her pupils, washed the blood from her hair.

'What happened?' Helen pushed a mug of hot sweet tea across the table to Finn.

'Her dad went for her.'

'Why?'

Finn glanced at Lisa, who moaned something.

'It's her dog. Tazer. Lisa's dad went for the dog.'

'Why?' Helen and Liam spoke in unison.

'Cos he's a bastard, that's why. Reckons he won't hurt a hair of his little girl's head, and then goes for her dog.'

Lisa murmured something that sounded like 'Not me.'

'Why did he go for the dog?' Helen asked.

Finn glanced at Lisa. 'Promise you won't tell no one,' he said.

Helen looked at Liam. 'That depends.'

'Then I can't tell you,' Finn said.

It was Liam who spoke. 'Do you want us to help you or not?'

Finn sighed, put down his mug. 'The tower, right? Hank's tower. Lisa's dad is doing trading there. Storing stuff. The gavvers were on to his lock-up. And he said Tobias was telling the gavvers, else why else was he hanging around there, and that Moffatt who died, he was in on it, because Moffatt wanted the house that Lisa's dad should have, right?'

Helen nodded at him. Liam was listening intently.

'So, Lisa's dad was going to go to the feds and say that he knew that Tobias had done it, and so Lisa starts to argue with him, right, and then Lisa says she knows what he's up to, and then Tazer's growling at him, and then he starts on the dog, and she jumps in front of him…' His voice faltered. 'I've never seen him go for anyone like that. I was like on my way there, heard her screaming, legged it up there, shoved on the door… I yelled at him to stop, shouted at him…' He wrapped his fingers round the mug. 'Thought he was going to go for me then.'

'What happened then?' Helen asked.

'Dunno. Clem kind of pushed me, legged it out of the door, ran off. Lisa was on the floor. All that blood… I didn't know what to do.'

'Did she black out?' Liam asked.

'Don't think so. She was talking and thing. I just thought I need someone to help her and I couldn't think of anyone, her mum's miles away and anyway she'd just say it was her fault, her mum would… so I came here.'

'I'm glad you did.' Helen reached out and touched his hand.

'I thought with him being a vicar, like…' Finn tilted his head towards Liam.

'Oh. That's not my husband.' It was all so strange, Helen wanted to laugh. 'This is Dr. Phelps,' she said. 'He's a physicist, he worked with the two men who died. His sister is Sinead, a social worker,' she added.

Finn stared at him. 'Sinead Foster?'

'You know her?' Liam smiled.

'Sure. She's cool.'

Liam leaned close to Lisa. 'How are you feeling? Do you want some tea?'

'Tea?' she mumbled. 'Brandy more like.'

'Tea will have to do,' he said.

'What are you, a bleeding doctor?' Lisa sat up, wrapping the blanket around her.

At that moment, the door opened. Chad stood there. At his ankles a dog cowered, black and white and scruffy.

Chad looked at Finn, and Lisa. He looked at Helen, and then, finally, slowly, at Liam.

'Oh,' he said. 'Didn't expect this. Didn't expect this at all.'

He'd left the church, after the Eucharist. Joyce Benfield had come, all set to read the lesson, and had brought her sister, so the Lady Chapel had felt quite full. Mrs. Lynch had asked him about the flowers, 'I know they're fading fast, apart from the carnations, they do something strange to them in the shops these days I reckon, they're like plastic, but what I wanted to say, vicar, was, we'll just have to manage until next week, unless I dig the artificials out of the store cupboard, there are some dahlias that would match, but I'd much rather not…'

Yes, of course, that's fine, Chad had said to her. Whatever you need to do. He'd wanted to add that he rather liked them fading, wilting. 'A meditation on decay,' he'd have said, but there would have been the now familiar twitch of disapproval, the implication that dear old Robinson, faced with a meditation on decay, would have reached for his plastic dahlias…

He'd walked back along the sea front, the sky a translucent grey, streaked pink with the sunset.

In his mind he saw the wilting flowers, the fallen petals lying on the old stone floor.

Decay, he thought.

'The body that is sown is perishable…' He heard once more the words echoing through the chapel in Mrs. Benfield's wavery voice. 'It is sown a natural body, it is raised a spiritual body… So will it be with the resurrection of the dead,' Mrs. Benfield had declaimed, with great certainty. Chad wondered whether she really thought that. He wondered, as he picked his way along the shingle, whether he really believed it too.

Certainly, Johann thought there was a life beyond this one. For him, it all seemed to make sense, that life on earth will turn out to be a particular way, to mean a particular thing. Chad thought of him, writing in his book, putting down his account of how it happened, his explanation for how it all came to be. He thought about the lab, all those crisp young men with their glasses of white wine, doing the same. This universe, this set of rules, these particles, this mechanism. This, is how it turned out.

He reached his house, feeling in his pocket for his keys.

And, he thought, if we have a child, Helen and I, then that's how it will have turned out. And if we don't… He'd turned the key in the lock, preparing himself, once more, for the silence of the vicarage, for Helen hiding away in her studio.

But there had been lights, and noise, a dog, and a slouching young man sitting at his kitchen table, and on the floor, an injured young woman. And Liam Phelps.

Liam jumped to his feet, arm outstretched. 'Chad,' he said. 'Just the man.' He waved towards the sofa. 'Finn Brady. And Lisa. They've escaped a horrible event. No need for police or anything,' he added.

Chad, standing by the table, lowered himself on to a chair, still in his coat. He wondered why Liam seemed to be in charge, as the physicist continued to explain that everything was under control. '… surface injuries only, I'm sure your wife can lend her a change of clothes…'

Helen was sitting mutely at Liam's side, and it seemed to Chad that he had become a guest in his own house, and that Liam was the host.

But then Helen caught his eye, and whatever she saw there roused her to action. She got to her feet. 'I think we need to eat,' she said. 'Chad, dear, you're still in your coat.' She laughed, went to him. 'Let's fix everyone some food.'

In the hall, he took off his coat, hung it on its peg. Too many questions, he thought, hearing her taking plates from shelves, opening the fridge, the clink of a bottle of wine. Who was that girl? Who had injured her so badly? And that dog, now nuzzling her elbow, licking her hand. How did they get here, these people, sitting there in my lounge? Who brought whom? Did Helen just find them on the doorstep?

Later he would ask her, did Liam bring them?

She'll hear him ask the question. She'll hear, underneath his words, something unasked, something waiting to be asked. She'll find that she can't lie. No, she'll say. Liam was already here, she'll say to Chad, knowing that in these words she's sowing seeds of doubt, unable to protect him by untruths.

But, for now, they stand in the kitchen, side by side, stirring soup on the hob, cutting bread, pouring drinks, helping Lisa sit at the table, helping her manage a spoon in her good hand, breathing again as, wincing through pain, Lisa eats, and laughs.

'The Green Man...?' Berenice wondered if she'd spoken out loud. She took a sip of red wine, turned back to the book.

'As did the Green Man himself once emerge from the Tree of Life, only to Merge once more into leafy desuetude, so does this knowledge risk falling on stony ground unheeded, and will go unnoticed by generations to come. In the wrong hands it brings terrible dangers, as witnessed once already; so do I commit these notes, the only true account of my findings, to these pages, in hope that by these rays of truth we may see more clearly.'

She took another sip of wine, turned the page.

'In the time of the Ark, when the world convulsed and the floods broke forth, they said it was to cleanse mankind of sin. And yet, what I say now, is that the world is made clean by the tears shed by mankind himself, as we bury our dead, as we commit our children to the earth, until the next flood comes again.'

Berenice rolled some spaghetti on to her fork. She closed the book and placed it on the far side of the table, don't want that vicar complaining about tomato sauce stains…

Terrible dangers, witnessed once already.

She wondered what they were. And children, committed to the earth, and people shedding tears.

Stories, she thought. The truth is always there, in the stories people tell themselves. All you have to do, is listen.

She swirled more spaghetti around her fork.

Dead children. Murdo and his wife had a child who died.

It takes less than that to kill a marriage.

And there's that Dr. Merletti with her passionate declaration of love, the mistress's manifesto, always the same, I could have written it myself.

Stories, she thought. It's time to talk to Virginia again.

20th September, 1922

The hum of the machine seemed to fill the room, so loud, that at first Gabriel didn't hear the click of the door. Then, aware of a shadow across the bench, he turned, sharply.

'Amelia,' he said.

'Were you hoping I was someone else?' She brushed her fingers along the edge of the bench.

'What news?'

'The doctor's here. He says it's a fever. He says she may be over the worse. Nanny Roberts is with her now.'

'Has she managed to eat?'

'A little soup, that's all.'

She watched him as he went to his switches, pulled them across. The hum faded. Outside, the sky was pink with the last of the day.

'I have been praying - ' she began, but he interrupted, appearing not to hear.

'No more.' His voice was rough. 'We have laid your father in his final resting place, and your brother. There will be no more loss…'

'I hope that you are right, my dear.' She laid her hand briefly on his arm.

He went to the bench, fiddled a wire into place. There was a fizz, a spark.

'We will be a family, you and me and our dear child,' she said, but he was concentrating on a dial. 'And the shadow of our loss…' she said.

'Oh, such a dark, dark shadow.' He seemed to be speaking to his dials. 'A gap that cannot be filled…'

She saw that his eyes had filled with tears. He blinked, dabbed at the corners of his eyes with a finger. He turned towards the bench, flicked another switch.

From the house she heard the maid calling her.

'Doctor Fitzgerald is about to leave,' she said. 'I must go to him. I'll see you at dinner.'

He gave a brief nod. She shut the door behind her.

Chapter Nineteen

Brightness after the rain. From the window of the spare bedroom, Helen could see the strip of sea, rippled with morning sunlight.

Lisa lay in the bed, fast asleep, breathing gently, her dog at her shoulder. The bruising around her eye looked darker, but the swelling seemed to have diminished, and the cut looked clean where Liam had washed and dressed it.

Helen gazed down on her sleeping form. Tazer stirred, watched her.

She ought to see a doctor, she thought. Or the police. Or someone.

I don't know what to do.

The room had pale blue walls. The curtains had a blotchy, abstract pattern in mauve and pink.

Our child would have slept here. Chad had let that slip, once, during the move, the nursery he'd called it, carrying a box of books.

The box was still there in the corner of the room, gathering dust.

And what about Clem? Was he going to pursue his daughter? Are we all somehow in danger now?

She thought of Liam, how cool he was, how calm and in charge. The sense of danger retreated at the thought.

She left Lisa sleeping, her dog too, snoring quietly.

She went back to her bedroom. She drew the curtains, funny old things, she'd been determined to replace them when she and Chad had first moved in, pale grey with abstract floral whorls in yellow.

She looked out at the shining slate roofs. From downstairs came the smell of coffee, the clatter of the dishwasher.

They'd overslept, woken to sunshine, blinked at each other, at the lateness of the hour, at, more than anything, finding themselves together, in their bed, facing each other in the unexpected sunlight.

He had put his arms around her, kissed her forehead, murmured about that poor girl in the spare room, was she going to be all right? And she'd answered something about how she couldn't go back to that awful father, and he'd agreed, they must think about it, he didn't have much time today, something about a session with the churchwardens and then a meeting about a funeral, yet another, it would be nice to have a marriage, or a baptism or two but such is the dear old C of E, he supposed…

Helen sat on the unmade bed. Last night he had come home, expecting silence, finding us all there. She remembered his flicker of surprise at seeing Liam, the questions, unasked, in his eyes.

She put on her slippers.

Downstairs Chad was pouring coffee. He held up her cup, and she said, 'Yes, please.'

They sat opposite each other.

'How is she?' he asked.

'Fast asleep. Very bruised still.'

'Perhaps we should call a doctor, he said.

'They're so scared of her father,' she said.

'Should we tell the police?' he looked at her.

'She won't let us.'

He spread butter on a piece of toast.

'A funeral, you said,' she said to him.

'What? Oh, yes. Nice chap from over the other side of town is coming to see me, his mum was in a nursing home up the hill, you know the one, it looks like an old convent or something, little stone arched doorway, anyway, finally she's died, ninety-four or something, so the niceties have to be done. She used to worship with us, apparently.'

'With dear old Robinson?' Helen asked.

He smiled at her across the table. 'No doubt,' he said. He reached for the marmalade. 'And then, I'll probably call in on Virginia.'

'Will you?' Helen watched him.

He continued to spread his toast. 'She left a message on the answering machine, she's feeling very shaky as you can imagine…'

'Oh, yes, I can imagine – '

' - Tobias is just hiding away waiting for the knock at the door. The first thing is to help her find a lawyer, he needs to feel that someone, other than us, is on his side.' The toast sat untouched on his plate.

'I'm sure he does.' She stood up, placed the kettle on the stove. 'Someone other than us,' she repeated.

'Did you say something?' He was looking at her now.

'Us,' she said again.

He picked up his toast and took a large bite.

'You can ask your Virginia,' Helen went on, 'what Clem Voake has got to do with Tobias, that when his daughter tries to defend the boy, her father goes for her.'

'I can, can I? And in turn, will you explain why that man was in my house?'

'I don't know what you mean.' She stood, looking down at him, and it was as if she had become much taller, and he had somehow shrunk. How had this happened, that in a few seconds they'd gone from amicable fondness to this bristling hostility.

'That man,' he was saying, 'that man from the lab, sitting in my house, next to my wife, bringing chaos into my kitchen, danger, even, introducing me to people I'd never seen before in my life, in my own house…' The last few words were almost shouted. He took another large bite of toast.

She listened to the loud crunching in the silence of the room. Not only hostility, but these odd, clichéd sentences.

'Did you invite him here?' her husband was saying. He was holding his piece of toast in front of his face.

'If we're going to argue, at least put that down,' she said.

'I can eat toast, can't I?'

In a minute, she thought, I'll burst out laughing, and so will he, and none of this will have been real, as if a script had been put in front of us and we started reading it off before we realized that it wasn't ours, we were just a married couple having breakfast together before we went to our day's work…

But there was no laughter. Instead, he got to his feet, looking at his watch. 'I must go, I'm late,' he said, 'Robbie will be wondering where I've got to, always prompt, that man…'

He walked out of the room without looking back. She heard his coat taken from its peg, the jangle of keys, the slam of the front door.

How had this happened?

The question circled in her mind.

What was he running away from? The poor girl upstairs? The threat of her father coming after her? The need to make decisions about her care?

It was more than that. We're both running away, she thought.

She wandered into the living room, drew back the curtains, went to the shelves, picked out the notebook into which she'd placed the pages of Amelia's writings.

"There was a time when we lived in peace, my husband and I, when we had hope of a future lived in joy. All that is gone now, squandered between the rays and beams, the light of our love dying away to darkness…"

She folded the page away.

These deaths, the lab, the book. Virginia living in the shadows of the past…

Footsteps behind her. Lisa stood in the doorway. Helen's borrowed shirt drooped on her slight form.

'Lisa – '

'I'm starving.' She slumped at the table. The bruising seemed worse, one eye half-closed, one side of her face swollen.

'Sure. Breakfast? What would you like?'

'Don't care.'

Helen threw her a look.

'Have you got a fag?' Lisa said.

'We don't smoke.' Helen said.

'I'll have whatever there is. And then I'm going home.'

'Home? But – '

'But what?' Lisa faced her.

'The state you were in last night – '

'What do you know about it?' Her voice was hoarse.

In silence, Helen poured tea, made toast, put butter on the table. She wondered what to do, who to tell about this troubled girl returning to certain danger, who to confide in about the criss-cross marks across her arms, savage red lines glimpsed through the thin fabric of her borrowed shirt.

"The spirit endeavours, in the virtue of its magnetick nature, to mix itself with the corporeal planets, until at last they arrive to the highest degrees…"

'It's rubbish, this,' Berenice said, putting the book down on her desk. 'I don't know why I asked that vicar to bring it in.'

Mary looked up from a pile of papers. 'He didn't seem that keen to part with it, either.'

Berenice turned the book over in her hands. 'And yet that poor sap thinks it'll tell him something, and the Professor seemed to think it had something too.'

'That poor sap – ' the morning sun glinted on her pen, as Mary made notes on a form. 'He may not be the best guide of what we need as evidence.'

Berenice smiled. 'Yeah. You're right.' She flicked through a few pages, then read out loud, '"And though we may be separated from our true nature, from our paradisiacal nature, though we are fallen, living in exile from Eden, yet we know that the Green Lion resides in Eden still, and with this purification can we be made whole so that our eyes may once more see the Garden of our true souls…"' She looked at Mary. 'It sounds just like my nan in church,' she said. 'Almost word for word, I'd say.'

Mary laughed.

'There's all this stuff about the lighthouse,' Berenice said.

'Hank's Tower?'

Berenice nodded. 'The author here, Johann, he's obsessed with it. He does experiments there. Calls it the Scallop Tower, but the vicar said that was the old name for it.'

Berenice closed the book and placed it on her desk. 'It would be more use if it helped me find a killer.'

'The Chief Super was asking about Clem Voake.'

'He was?'

'Yes.' Mary stared at her pile of papers.

'Why doesn't he talk to me?'

'He said, if we've scared the bastard off it's going to make his job twice as hard.'

'If we've scared him off? And what makes him think I've got anything to do with - '

The click of the door silenced her. Ben stood there. 'There's another one downstairs, asking for you.'

'Another what?'

'Another physicist. He wants to talk to you in confidence, he said.'

'About the universe?'

'About the case. I think. I hope, anyway.'

'Which physicist?' Berenice asked.

'Iain Hendrickson.' Ben consulted a bit of paper. 'Shall I send him up?'

'Sure. I might ask him about the luminiferous aether while I'm about it.'

Liam gazed at his computer screen, clicked the mouse, typed a bit. 'Fossil relics of the Big Bang,' he said. He clicked some more. 'Spin half particles,' he said. He leaned back in his chair and looked down at his dog. 'Three generations of spin half particles, eh, Jonas? And we don't know why.' He ruffled Jonas's head. 'Or perhaps you do, old dog. Here we are, replicating the conditions in the universe when it was less than a trillionth of a second old. It should all be plain to see – ' he waved at his screen. Jonas looked at the screen too, then back at Liam, one ear cocked.

Liam scrolled through the data. 'None of this makes sense,' he said, to his dog. 'Iain thinks that we're seeing axions, but I don't see how that would produce these charges. And anyway, whatever we're seeing is some kind of muon, surely…'

He looked at the dog. 'All I know is, we're going to have tell the world at some point. Results like this, we can't keep them to ourselves.' He leaned back in his chair. 'It used to be fun, Jonas. Of course, you didn't know me in my student days, discovering more and more about this stuff, knowing that this was all I wanted to do. I loved it. But now…' He glanced back at his screen. 'I never thought it would be dangerous. Something's up, that's for sure. But none of us knows what it is.' He patted his dog's head again. 'And that book of Helen's, what does he say? He says, that whatever it is, this thing called Gravity, all we know is that it explains the phenomena of the heavens and of our sea, and yet we do not know its cause. We're no further on than that.' He looked back at his screen. 'We're no further on than some Edwardian madman.'

He watched the live feed from the beam, studied the curves of data. He yawned, thought about coffee, wondered when to go into the lab.

'Too much to think about, Jonas,' he said. Last night he'd driven into Faversham, dropped that boy Finn off at some kind of hostel, 'sure you'll be OK, don't like the look of those lads,' and Finn had laughed, they're safe they are, he'd said. And he'd made Liam promise, don't let Lisa go back to her dad. Whatever she says, OK? And second promise - don't tell the feds. It'll make it so much worse for her if he knows she's grassed him up.' And Liam, exhausted, had promised.

And that was on his mind. But more than that, was the expression on the face of Helen's husband as he'd walked in the door. And then, ten minutes later, he and Helen are serving out soup as if they'd both invited him to tea…

He sighed, looked down at his dog. 'Out of my depth again, eh, Jonas?'

And what is she anyway, he thought. A lonely vicar's wife who wants to be pregnant. Hardly an option for anything long term…

He found he couldn't quite remember what she looked like. He leaned back, his hands behind his head.

Is that it, then? An amusement? Just another way of wasting time –

The mobile at his side rang.

'Phelps,' he said.

'Hi. It's Helen.'

And at her voice, there's a tumble of images, a rush of desire.

'Oh,' he breathes. 'Helen.'

She's speaking now, something about Lisa, 'she's gone, Liam, she's just walked out of the door, still wearing my shirt, dog at her heel…'

'Gone?'

'I couldn't stop her. Short of violence.'

'No. I can see that.'

'Liam, I don't know what to do. She's self-harming, too, her arms are in a terrible state.'

'What did she say?'

'She said I don't know anything about it. Which is true, of course. I don't know who to tell. The police – '

'Finn made me promise,' he said. 'Last night.'

'Oh God.'

His screen flashed in front of him, luminosity at one nine seven two bunches –

'Are you there?' she said.

'Yes,' he said.

'Well?'

He took a deep breath. 'Come to the lab,' he said. 'Lunchtime. If you can get through the police cordon… We'll have a think.'

'Oh.' There was a silence. 'OK. See you then.'

He clicked off his phone.

Jonas was staring up at him. 'Don't you start,' he said. 'It's bad enough with Sinead's voice in my head.' He ruffled Jonas's ears. The dog rolled his eyes in disapproval.

Helen sat at her kitchen table, staring at her phone.

Maternal feelings? she wondered. Perhaps this ache is just that, a sense of loss at finding that Lisa had gone.

I don't know what to do. I can't let that poor girl go back to whatever she fled from.

I'll have to tell Chad, she thought. He knows the police better than I do, he can talk to them.

She thought about lunchtime. She wondered what to wear.

Iain sat down as if the chair itself were unreliable.

'Dr Hendrickson.' Berenice tried her warm smile. 'Thanks for coming in.'

'I had to.' He looked around him, as if the walls themselves were hostile in some way. 'Two deaths….' He began.

'Yes,' she agreed. She gestured to the corner of the room. 'This is DS Mary Ashcroft. She's recording our session today. I hope that's OK with you…'

'Yes,' he said. 'Of course. I just want to help.'

He was dressed as if he'd made an effort. A well-cut grey suit, his blonde hair neatly brushed.

'You've brought another threatening note,' she said.

He nodded.

'How did it get to you?'

He shrugged. 'It was pinned to the outer gates of the lab. We're all tired of it. It was OK before anything bad happened, we all thought it was some random nutter, harmless, you know… and then there was Murdo…' There was a choke in his voice. 'And then Moffatt…'

Berenice tried her warm tone of voice. 'And what's made you come in today, Dr. Hendrickson?'

'It's the land dispute. It can't be anything else. Digby Voake has just died, you see, Neil Parrish was telling me about it. And he owned the old house, old Mr Voake did, the derelict one over the wall, it's been in their family for years. Anyway, Professor Moffatt had put in an offer on the land, and it had been accepted, and completion had already happened before Digby died. So the land, and the old house, now belong to Moffatt. And none of the Voakes realized this. Neil says it would have pleased Digby no end, to spite the rest of them.'

Berenice nodded. 'Go on.'

'Clem Voake has parked his caravan just across the wall, near the old house. He's furious with us. With Moffatt, but with the whole lab, really. Anyway, here's the next note. I'm sure it's from Clem…'

Berenice picked it up by one corner. "Don't think it's finished," she read. "The first tunnel brought the curse, and the second one will bring the flood." 'It's like all the others,' she said.

Iain nodded.

'Do you know anything else about Clem Voake?' she asked.

'You know Hank's Tower? Well, there's a rumour that he's storing weaponry there. For sale, you know.'

Berenice flashed a quick glance at Mary. 'Anything else?'

He glanced around him, again, as if fearful. Then he looked at her. 'You have the book,' he said. 'The van Mielen book.'

A morning of meetings about results. Liam emerged, confused and weary, into sunlight. There was a uniformed officer by the main gate. 'They said it would rain, Sir. Always wrong, aren't they?'

'Um, yes, well…' Was that her? Of course. That light step, low heels, navy blue trousers, a loose cardigan-ish thing, God, how could she be so sexy even in that?

'… Chap on the wireless this morning saying that it wasn't that the instruments were too basic, it was that the weather had got more complicated…'

'Yes, of course, Officer.'

'You agree with that? A clever bloke like you?'

Liam stared at him, blankly. 'Um… no. Of course not.'

'Good thing too. If you lot in there are talking bollocks too, there's no hope for the rest of us. Now who's this? A lady friend of yours?'

Liam nodded. 'Yes, officer. A lady friend of mine.'

'Liam.' She brushed her finger against his arm. 'Shall we go?'

'Ma'am.' The policeman touched his hat.

Liam linked his arm in hers with a sense of pride. Sinead would have views, but he'd think about that later.

Chapter Twenty

Iain turned the pages of the book as if looking for something.

'I haven't seen this for years,' he said, at last.

'And why is it relevant?' Berenice said.

'"And how should it be, that a particle of light is at the same time subject to the forces of gravity?"' he read. He tapped the page. 'This is what they were working on, over the wall from our lab now.' He passed it back to Berenice. 'Gabriel Voake.'

Berenice touched the leather cover. 'And Clem?'

'Clem's from a different branch. Gabriel's lot moved away. Gabriel's wife Amelia was the daughter of Johann van Mielen who wrote this.'

'What happened to Gabriel, then?'

'That's the whole dispute. About the old house over the wall from the lab. It was the van Mielen's house, Amelia lived in it, Gabriel married her. But then she disappeared, no one knows why. And he left too, people say he went to Germany, but this was the late twenties, early thirties, it would be an odd thing to do. And the house was empty for a while. Digby was some kind of great-nephew and he took it over, but he had no money. You've seen the state of it. So, I guess, when Alan put in an offer, Digby jumped at it. The Voakes might have thought they'd inherit it, but it seems he'd already sold it to Alan without telling them. You should also know that I put in an offer, but it was declined. I didn't care that much, Moffatt was welcome to it.'

'Why did Professor Moffatt want it?'

Iain stared at his hands. Berenice noticed the neat, clean cuffs of his shirt. He looked up at her. 'The first, obvious reason, is that the lab needs more space. If he bought that plot of land, with the old house, we could expand into it.'

'And the next reason?'

He chewed at his lip. 'I'm a scientist,' he began. 'I'm a rational person. But…'

Berenice waited.

'There's something weird going on. Our results are off the scale…' His hands were twisted together in his lap. 'There's a ghost, even…' He threw her a smile, but it was thin, empty. 'That book – ' He pointed at it. 'It's connected to all this.'

Berenice drew a breath, collected her thoughts. 'This book belonged to Elizabeth Merletti.'

He flinched at the name. Even Mary noticed it, Berenice sensed.

'She inherited it,' he said.

'She gave it to Murdo,' Berenice went on.

'Of course she would,' he said. 'She loved him.'

Berenice waited.

'We all knew that,' he said. 'Of course she'd give it to him. But I imagine his wife has had enough of it. Which is why she gave it away.'

'Tell me,' Berenice said. 'Do you know when it stopped being the Scallop Tower?'

He gave a thin smile. 'Hank's Tower? No one knows. Not even Neil and he knows everything. It must have just changed. No one even knows who Hank was.' He seemed cold, wrapping his arms across his chest. 'There were rumours of another tunnel, an older one, from the time of the book, you see, some kind of experiment. That was supposed to be near Hank's Tower, but no one has found anything.'

'Rumours from where?' Berenice glanced at Mary, who was still writing.

'People in the village. You've seen the hate mail. That's what it means, about ours being the second tunnel, and how the first one came to no good, bringing curses on the land itself.'

There was a silence in the room. Mary stopped writing, looked up.

'You ask me why I came here today.' He looked at Mary, then back at Berenice. 'It's about all of it. The book, the Voakes, Elizabeth… There's been so much pain. I want it to stop.' He breathed, then said, 'I became a physicist because I was drawn to all that order, explanation, rationality. Some kind of truth that you can rely on. But then, if you have hatred, and rage, a child who dies, like Amelia in the book, all that terrible loss… And her brother, of course, walking the landings in the old house and now – ' He stopped, abruptly. He stared at his fingers in his lap.

'And now with you?' she finished.

He met her eyes. 'I'm sorry, I'm not making any kind of sense… I'm really speaking out of turn. I should go.'

'Hank's Tower - '

'We used to go there. Murdo, Virginia and me. In the old days. We were friends, good friends, all of us… The sunsets from there… we saw the green ray once, you know, a kind of flash when the sun sets across the sea?' He smiled to himself.

'And then, Elizabeth…' Berenice prompted.

'Ah.' He seemed to wince. 'Elizabeth.'

'She told me. About Murdo. And about you.'

He stared at her. 'She told you?'

Berenice smiled. 'We're more broadminded than you'd think. If one woman falls in love with two men…'

He smiled too. 'Yes. Of course.' His arms unwrapped themselves. 'Of course,' he said.

'And now there's just you. And her.' Berenice wondered if she'd said too much.

He flashed her a look. 'I can't imagine she said that.'

'No,' Berenice conceded.

'She loved Murdo more than anyone. More than anything.' His gaze drifted towards the window, unseeing. 'There are no winners. Not now. We're all the poorer. All three of us. Four of us. The question is, how to carry on at all?' He had grown pale, and his fingers began to drum against the table's edge. 'How to keep going, in this chaos, where there is only uncertainty. And ghosts…'

Berenice wondered what to say.

His gaze turned to Mary, as if surprised to see her there. 'Well…' He looked at Berenice. 'I ought to go. I don't want to waste your time. I thought I could make things better, but I'm no help, really, just going on about the past like this…' He got to his feet. 'I suppose I just thought the answer lay in the past, that somehow it all made sense, the book and the strange results and the old tunnel and the land dispute…' He gave an empty smile. 'But of course, it's not like that in your world, is it. You're looking for evidence. For straightforward examples of human behaviour. And you're probably right.'

He held out a hand, let it fall to his side. He ambled out of the door. His footsteps faded away along the corridor.

Berenice looked at Mary. 'What do you make of that, then?'

Mary shrugged. 'Dunno Boss, but I'm sure as hell missing Chapeltown.'

'Oh my God - ' Helen put her hand across her mouth. 'How did it get so late?'

Liam laughed.

'Look, everyone's gone home. There's only us.'

The café was deserted. They'd had lunch, and then tea, and now the light outside the windows was fading to a dusky blue.

'Are you going to tell me you're supposed to be doing Grade Four pliés with a load of eight year olds?'

She smiled, shook her head. 'No classes today, thank goodness. But we ought to get back.'

'And we've concluded nothing.'

'Other than that we must make a proper statement to the police.'

'Yes. In the morning.'

They began to walk towards town. The sky was clearing, darkening into dots of stars. There was a fresh sea breeze.

'Your car – ' Helen said.

'At the lab,' he said. 'I can give you a lift…'

She fell into step beside him, her head bowed, aware of the movement of his legs, the rhythm of his body next to hers, aware, too, that they'd passed the road back to the lab and were now walking in the wrong direction.

She stopped and faced him. 'This isn't – '

'No,' he agreed. 'It isn't.'

'I ought to – '

'Yes,' he said. 'Of course. Let's go back.'

He didn't move. Behind him she could see the flicker of the distant road, the tall white lights of the industrial estate, the anonymous fluorescence of a business hotel.

'Unless…'

One word. He'd uttered one word, but they both knew.

He took her arm and she shivered at his touch. They began to cross the wide road, the expanse of car park. Near the gate he stopped. 'Sinead says…'

'Who?' she said, looking up at him, her eyes dark with desire. He could hardly speak for wanting her.

'My sister,' he said.

'What does she say?' Helen gazed up at him.

He looked down at her. 'Oh,' he said, 'you know the kind of thing. Disapproval, mostly.'

She laughed. She took hold of his arm again, and together they walked towards the rhythmic gleam of the revolving door.

Chapter Twenty-One

The evening air had sharpened into frost as Chad walked up to the cottage.

Tobias. The name had been on his mind, all day. A background worry, the danger he was in, the way he did nothing to protect himself, the thought that he'd been at the scene of Alan's death.

His knock was answered almost immediately. She reached out and grasped his hand, and led him inside.

Once again he was struck by the chill of the place. He looked at the stove, a black square with a chimney snaking upwards behind. It sat, half open, revealing a thin pyramid of ash.

'How are you?' he said.

She sank into a chair. She sighed. 'All these years I've been fighting for him. Health people, school people. And now the law. So, nothing's changed.' She shrugged.

'Where's Tobias now?'

She flicked her head towards the ceiling. 'In his room,' she said.

'You look tired,' he said.

She smoothed a lock of hair from her forehead.

Chad settled into his chair. 'I hope she looks after the book,' he said.

'Oh, you'll get it back.' Virginia placed her hands on the arms of the chair. 'Tea, perhaps.' She pushed herself to standing, went into the kitchen.

Chad listened to the opening of cupboards, the clink of mugs.

'It's nice of you to visit,' she said.

He turned towards her, about to speak. But what would I say, he thought. That it's better than being at home?

'I'm not even a proper parishioner,' she said, with a thin smile.

'You'll do,' he said.

'A broad church, is it?' She stirred milk into two mugs and carried them through, placing them carefully on the small table.

'Do you think they're any further on?' Chad picked up a mug of tea.

'Not really. But while Tom is in the frame, she's not going to tell me much more.' She sat down heavily.

'But Murdo's death?'

Virginia held her mug between both hands. 'She has nothing to say.'

'They came to our house last night, these young people.' Chad turned to her. 'And that man from the lab too. He was already there, my wife said. I couldn't quite get to the bottom of it. Anyway, Finn, is it? And that girl. Lisa Voake. She was in a bad way.'

'The Voakes.' She sighed. 'Not well thought of round here. They used to own the big house, as you know, but they went to the bad - '

A loud thump on the stairs, and Tobias appeared in the doorway.

'You know them, don't you, Tom,' she said. 'The Voakes. Lisa was at the vicarage last night.'

'Is she all right?' His gaze was intense as he took a step towards Chad.

'Um - ' Chad glanced at Virginia. 'Her father was… she had to stay with us last night. Finn brought her…'

'Is she all right?' He was shouting now, his fists clenched at his sides.

'Hush, dear…' Virginia's voice was firm. 'Chad's looking after her, aren't you? And his wife…'

My wife. 'Yes,' he said. 'Yes, we are.'

Tobias threw himself into a chair. 'She shouldn't live with him,' he said. 'She shouldn't. He's not a good father. Not good. The police,' he said. 'That woman. They should tell her. The black one. She's kind.'

Virginia looked up in surprise. 'Is she?'

'I like her,' Tobias said.

'You hardly spoke to her.'

He shook his head. 'No,' he agreed. It was the other one. The Mary one. The white one. She was all right too. But I didn't tell her about the men on the beach. I tried to tell her about the ghost, but I could tell she didn't believe me so I stopped. The soldier, you know, the one with all the blood who walks near the old house. But when I was on the beach I saw a man carrying another man over his shoulder. I thought it was the soldier doing something new, but then I thought the man he was carrying looked like Uncle Murdo and I thought the soldier wouldn't do that, and anyway the soldier is very thin, sort of see-through, he wouldn't be strong like that, to lift up another person, would he Auntie Ginny?'

His gaze was open, almost amused.

She was staring at him, white-faced. 'Tom... When did you see this?'

'It was when Uncle Murdo was still alive. It was the day before it all went wrong.'

'The day before he died?' She clapped one hand to her lips. 'Tom – were you there?' Her voice was hushed, appalled.

He studied her. 'I didn't tell them, Auntie Ginny. Was that the right thing to do?'

She leaned back against her chair. 'Yes,' she said. 'Yes, it was the right thing to do.' She sipped at her tea. Chad noticed the tremor in her hands as she placed the mug down on the table.

'Virginia... surely, evidence like that...?'

She met his eyes. 'You don't understand. What will they do with information like that? They'll say it puts Tom here at the scene of the crime. It's bad enough these images they claim they have of him being there when Moffatt died - '

'But I was, Aunty, I was - '

'Yes, dear, I know.'

'That doesn't mean I killed him, does it?'

She reached across and patted his hand. 'No. It doesn't mean you killed him.'

He gave a long sigh. Then he got up and left the room.

She turned to Chad. 'You must understand. I cannot risk them putting anything on to him.' She leaned back in her chair and closed her eyes. 'I am so tired,' she said.

From upstairs came a bang, a crash.

She opened her eyes. 'It's just Tom,' she said. 'He'll be looking for something in the old cupboard.' She gave a weary smile. 'You see, I have had to fight for everything. Everything,' she repeated. 'My marriage. My motherhood. And before that. Even this…' She flicked a hand towards the space around them. 'I ran away from home with nothing. I took every job I could find. I ended up as a secretary at the university here, that's when I met Murdo…' Her eyes clouded. 'I've had to fight for all of it. And I've still ended up with nothing…'

Another series of thumping noises, and Tobias reappeared. He was carrying a box, an old, square mahogany box. He settled on the sofa, the box on his knee, and opened it. He began to arrange the things within it.

Another thin smile. 'Not nothing.' She turned to Chad. 'But now you understand why I'll fight for him.'

He nodded. 'I understand.'

'The Green Lion and the Red - ' Tobias waved a small figure. 'I found them, didn't I, Auntie? But now I've only got the red one.' He replaced it in the box. 'And here's the fifth essence - '

He waved a bottle at Chad. 'It's my collection. I don't show everyone. Lisa knows about it. When I've got everything, then I'll put it all together like in the book. I've got the lead, but I still need some mercury, it's difficult because it's a liquid you see, even though it's a metal. And a prism. And some hydrogen, I don't know where I'll get that – Oh.' He was staring into the box. 'Pictures.' He produced two photographs.

'Where did you get those, Tom?' She reached out a hand.

'You don't mind, do you Auntie?'

She shook her head. She stared at the images, then passed them to Chad.

He saw a photograph of a boy, blond-curled, blue eyes, a wide, gap-toothed smile.

'Jacob,' she said.

The other was a park of some kind, a garden, filled with people – no, of course, a graveyard, a funeral, a small white coffin, a single arrangement of roses.

He studied it for a long minute, then handed it back to her.

She gazed at the image of the boy. She went over to the fireplace and placed it carefully on the mantelpiece, next to a dusty old vase and a plastic bowl filled with old buttons.

Tobias had taken some pages out of his box and was furiously writing on them.

'Time,' he said. 'If things can be and not be, maybe what it is, is that it's time that's different. Like anti-matter and matter, right?' He looked up at Chad. 'It's like we're going backwards and forwards, all the time, between matter and anti-matter, but when we look we think we're seeing just matter. Because it's all so fast.'

Chad smiled at him. 'I'm trying to write something about that too. For a sermon.'

'What's it about?'

'It's about the question of truth, of reality. How human beings always need evidence for things, which is why we've made the advances we've made, in science, for example, because we're good at asking questions and finding the evidence for the answers. But then you look at the wider question, about why, why we're here, is there a reason for it, is it just random, and our tendency to look for evidence doesn't really help us.'

Tobias was nodding. 'Yes,' he said. He bent to his paper and began to write again. 'Evidence,' he said.

Virginia watched Tobias. She turned to Chad. 'What does your wife think?'

'Of what?' He looked at her blankly.

'Of your sermon, of course.'

'Oh. I don't know.'

They sat in silence, with only the loud scratch of Tobias's pencil. Then Tobias got up. 'Thirsty,' he said. 'What am I allowed?'

'Whatever you like, dear.'

He placed his box carefully on his chair, and headed out to the kitchen.

Chad stared at the floor. My wife, he thought. It's so long since I asked her anything at all.

'What are you thinking?' Virginia broke the silence.

He didn't know what to say. The true answer would have been, Liam Phelps, but he didn't want to say that.

'Loss,' she said. 'That seems to be why I've been put on this earth. To have everything taken away from me.' Her voice cracked with feeling. She stared straight ahead, her lips working.

He reached across and placed his hand on her arm. She touched his hand with her own.

'I don't know how to help you,' he said.

She shook her head. 'It's enough you're here,' she said. 'Though I don't suppose I should keep you here much longer. You must be expected back home.'

Home.

He looked at the low damp walls and dusty unused stove. It felt warmer than the vicarage.

'I can stay for a while,' he said.

It was Helen who let herself into the empty house, surprised by the darkness. She switched on lights, called her husband's name, hearing nothing in reply.

She went up to the bedroom, reached for the lamp beside the bed, lay down on the covers.

I wonder where he is.

Liam had brought her home. A taxi from the hotel to the lab, to get his car, and then he'd driven as far as the end of the lane and stopped. A silent agreement had passed between them, that they didn't want the car to be seen. And now he'd gone.

A tumble of memories. His soft kisses, his taut muscularity. A tangle of sheets, white in the slash of street light from the window. Breathlessness, wetness, pleasure, oh God such pleasure…

She thought, with a tightening sensation that was, perhaps, guilt, that must never happen again.

She thought, with a tightening sensation that was definitely desire, I can't wait to see him again.

And then she thought, I wonder where Chad is.

She had been silent on the drive home, imagining how it would be, facing her husband, explaining her lateness, she'd worked it all out, 'oh, I had to drive one of the ballet kids home, these negligent parents, and of course it's always the wealthy ones, one of those great big townhouses on the other side of the hill…'

And now here she was in an empty house. No need to explain. No need to account for herself at all.

She got up from the bed and went to have a shower.

When Chad did appear, an hour or so later, Helen was standing at the stove with a sizzling pan in front of her.

'Omelette?' she said. 'You're just in time.'

The kitchen was brightly lit and warm. He smiled, went to her, wrapped his arms around her waist. 'Yes please,' he said.

Her face was against his chest. 'Where have you been?' she said, into his shirt.

'I was with Virginia. I told you I was going there…'

'Yes,' she said. 'Of course.'

He let go of her, and she went back to the frying pan. She heard the pop of a cork from a wine bottle, the distant chiming of the clock in the living room. Calm, quiet sounds, the bubbling of the eggs in the pan in front of her.

'Tobias saw something odd, the night that Murdo died. One man, carrying another up Hank's Tower.'

'Oh.' She looked up from her cooking. 'How extraordinary.'

'She's adamant that the police shouldn't know.'

'Oh,' she said again. She reached for the cheese grater.

'She's exhausted, poor woman. I don't really know what to do. I don't want to bring Tobias even further into the frame. It was all tied up with tales of ghosts, too.'

She watched him pour two glasses of wine. The kitchen was bright and light and warm, and already, it seemed to her, Liam had become something faded and thin, drifting away beyond the steamed-up windows, into the night.

She lifted the pan from the heat and placed it on the table mat. 'Let's eat,' she said.

Liam unlocked the door to his empty flat. He felt light-hearted, awash with delight. 'Like a man,' he said to himself, wondering at the same time whether that is, truly, what it is to be a man, thinking of her body, her breasts, the deep, urgent possession of her. He recognizes this lightness of spirit as familiar, and temporary, and destined to fade.

But while the feeling lasts, he pours himself a whisky, opens kitchen cupboards in search of food, finds some spaghetti, boils the kettle, even humming to himself, humming, me, he thinks, I never hum, enjoy it while it lasts, he thinks, pouring water into the saucepan, searching for a jar of sauce, and so fails to see the three missed calls from Neil on his mobile.

It's only much much later, when he's back at his computer, poring over the results from the lab, wondering about these results, still so inexplicable, that he glances at his phone, and thinks, well I'll see him in the morning.

"My husband believes that all will be well. He does not see the chaos that surrounds us, the whirls and the eddies, the warning signs of the flood that is readying to rush in over our heads. For me, it is too late. I do not care. I have no reason to live or die. I follow my husband, because what God has joined together, no man must put asunder."

Helen held the pages in her hand.

There was a ticking of central heating. Chad had gone to bed some time ago.

They'd eaten, exchanging bits of conversation, the budget figures for the Parish Council, the changes to the syllabus from the Associated Board.

It had been normal life, she thought.

And yet, so far from normal.

She'd come in here to delay the moment of sliding into bed next to him.

Let no man put asunder.

Had she imagined Chad's distance, some hesitation as he bent and kissed the top of her head, 'don't stay up too late, will you?'

She leaned back among the cushions.

She thought about the warnings of the flood to come, the chaos that would 'rush in over our heads…'

This is what I've brought about. This loneliness. I can't ask him what he's thinking. I can't hold him to account, even though he came back late and distracted, and he'd been at Virginia's all that time…

She looked down at the pages in her hand. Had they stayed together, this troubled couple? And what of these Van Mielens that link them to Elizabeth at the lab, that are connected to that poor injured girl?

Helen got up, smoothed the sofa, tidied the cushions. Something is still buried, she thought. The warnings are still there, whirling and eddying, ready to rush in as a flood over our heads.

She walked up the stairs in stockinged feet. A few minutes later she crept into bed beside her sleeping husband.

Chapter Twenty-Two

'What did you tell them?' Clem Voake turned to face his daughter, stooping against the low caravan ceiling.

'I said, Dad. I didn't tell them nothing.'

Tazer sat by Lisa's feet, her eyes fixed on Clem.

'Why did you go running to them, then?'

'I didn't go to the feds. I told you.'

Clem slumped onto a seat. Tazer winced as he moved.

'I've got a plan, girl. You know I have. I ain't going to let you down.' He reached for a can of beer and snapped it open.

'Yes, Dad. I know.' She sat down, wearily.

'It's nearly all in place now. They can try and take it away from me, but they ain't going to win. Not now. I've had enough, see.'

'Yes, Dad.' There was a packet of crisps open on the table, and she reached for it.

'All my life, I've been waiting. That's how I got by, when I were a kid. Whatever they were doing to me, I would hold it here, in my heart - ' he bashed his fist against his chest. 'A dream. The old house, right, the old tunnel… that bloke, that scientist, he made dreams come true… before the flood. And when I found out he was family, right, I knew it would come to me…'

She took two more crisps, passed one to the dog who was still at her feet.

'… it was like he'd passed it on to me. That knowledge. I just had to keep the dream close to my heart. Whatever they were doing, however angry it made me, I knew they couldn't take it away from me. So when I heard that Moffatt was trying to get it away from me…'

'Yes, Dad. You've told me all this.' Her voice was tired.

He looked at her. 'So why did you go telling them?'

'I've told you. It was Finn, innit. He said I needed help - '

'I won't have you seeing that boy? You hear me? I'm all you need, you're my little girl, I'm going to take care of you - '

'Yes, Dad. I know.'

'When I get that house. A big house, it is, you've seen it. You'll have the best of everything, I'll show that whore of a mother and her pimp - '

His phone trilled in his pocket. He snatched it up. 'Manny - ' He listened. The flush of his cheeks faded. 'OK,' he said. 'Ta for the warning.' He clicked off his phone. He stared ahead of him.

'Dad – what's happened?'

'It's coming true,' he said. 'What they always said, that the flood would come and wash it all clean. That lab – that new tunnel - ' He was clenching his fists in front of him, and his breathing was uneven.

Tazer gave a quiet snarl.

' – they should never have made a new tunnel. The truth is in the old tunnel…'

'Dad - '

He looked at her, his eyes blank. 'There's more trouble for us. They've found… at the lab… that other one who was out to get it…' He stared around the caravan as if unsure of where he was. 'We've got to go. We've got to get out of here.' He stumbled to his feet, drained his can of beer. 'We've got to go.'

'Where, Dad – what's happening - '

He grabbed her arm. 'If you hadn't gone telling that vicar - '

'I didn't tell anyone, Dad - '

'And now they'll think - ' He was pushing her out of the caravan.

'Where are we going? – Dad – '

Lisa was shouting but he didn't seem to hear.

'There'll be more than just the feds after us - '

She was fighting him, struggling against the grip of his big hands on her wrists.

'It's time,' he said. 'This is it. This is when we make a new life. This is when the dream comes true.'

They were out in the field, now, and he was dragging her towards his van. Tazer growled and jumped at his legs.

'Where?' Lisa shouted at him. 'Where are we gonna make a new life?' She broke away from him, but he grabbed her shoulders, one arm round her neck.

'It'll still be you, Dad. You and me. You ain't gonna get away from you, are you? Whatever your shit, you're stuck with it - '

'I won't let them get us. I won't have your mother trying to get you back – I won't let them win – '

She twisted away from him, but he grabbed her hair.

'Ow, Dad – ' He pushed Lisa into the van, slammed the doors, started the engine.

The tyres spun as he turned the van round, spattering mud across the site.

Tazer, sat, whimpering, watching them go.

Amelia sat by the window. She knew where her husband was. 'The new experiment,' he called it. 'The tunnel.' He'd leave his laboratory, his workbench, and he'd walk towards the sea, towards the Scallop Tower. Once she'd followed him, some of the way, until she sensed his awareness of her, and turned back. All she knew was that there was another laboratory, somewhere near the Tower, perhaps even at the Tower.

She wished Guy were here to ask, or her father. 'What kind of experiment is it, that needs a tunnel? What is he looking for?'

But she knew, as she sat, staring out into dusk, that if Guy were still alive, Gabriel would have no need for this. There would be no tunnel, no new experiment, no obsession with the aether, the quintessence, the force that defeats the great Nothing. Instead we would be as we were, the three of us. We would be unburdened and joyful, and Gabriel would learn, at last, how to be a father to Grace.

And a husband to me.

Gabriel lifted the heavy oak beam that sealed the door, and entered the tunnel. He carried two candles, which he placed either side of his makeshift workbench. He had stumbled upon this tunnel, a smugglers' hideout, some weeks ago, and had made it his own. He knew it was ideal for his experiment, which needed darkness, away from the forces above ground, away from the particles of light.

The bench was covered with wires, with mirrors. In the middle of the wires sat Guy's watch. It seemed to glow in the candlelight.

As it was in the beginning, he thought. Is now, and ever shall be, world without end.

Time is the key to it all.

Sometimes, even here, he glimpsed him, his blonde hair, his torn shirt.

Is now and ever shall be, he thought.

The tide was coming in. He could hear the water, lapping beyond the old brick wall. He stared at the pretty red bricks in their herring-bone pattern, and wondered what they used to store here. Contraband. Barrels of whisky. Firearms, perhaps.

But now it was his, and he was ready to work.

All these months, he'd been circling the truth of the fifth element, the quintessence, the aether. 'You and me, Guy – ' he spoke out loud, his voice muffled by the thick clay walls. 'I did not desert you. Our work will live on.'

Behind the wall, the sea murmured. In the darkness, the candles flickered.

Clem shone a torch into the darkness. His other arm was linked with Lisa's, his hand clamped onto her wrist.

'Where are we, Dad?'

'The old tunnel.'

She could hear the sea, as if close by. As her eyes adjusted to the darkness, she could see the mud walls, dripping with water, the wet floor. In the middle of the space was a wooden structure, a kind of bench.

'What's that?' Her voice shook.

'It's from the old ones, the science ones.'

'It's fucking soaking wet in here.'

'We'll wait here, Girl. They won't find us here.' He spread his coat across a puddle and sat down on it.

'Dad – you're crazy - '

His eyes were blank in the darkness. 'I won't let them take you away, Girl. We belong together. When I get the house, when we're living the dream…' He gave a brief, empty smile.

The sea seemed louder. At the far end of the space, by the wall, the water level rose.

'Dad – it ain't safe – when the tide comes in - '

'The wall will keep it out.'

'What fucking wall? It's half collapsed.'

He turned, slowly, and stared at it. 'No. It's fine. Look.'

The bricks, where they stood, were small, herring-boned. The wall was riven in two, one side still standing, the other side a heap of brick dust and stone.

'How's that going to keep out the tide, Dad?'

As she stared, another wave of seawater lapped at the broken stones.

'The flood,' he said. 'It's what they always said. The new tunnel would be cursed.'

'Who said, Dad?' She tried to calm her voice. She looked towards the entrance, the thick oak door.

'It's what I tried to tell them. Ghosts, walking the corridors. And then the flood will come and wash all clean…'

She began to move towards the door.

'Where are you going?' His voice was sharp.

'I ain't staying here, Dad. We're going to drown - '

He was on his feet, ahead of her. He reached the door, lifted the old oak beam with both hands, and dropped it across the door. He stood, breathing. 'A third one dead,' he said. 'We can't go back.'

She stared at the door. She went to the beam, tried to lift it. 'I can't… ' Tears pricked her eyes.

He went to his coat, sank back down, leaning against the side of the tunnel. He was blank-faced, clenching and unclenching his fists.

'Dad – if we stay here, we'll – we'll drown.'

He looked at her, as if seeing something beyond her. 'The old house,' he said. 'When I went there, as a child. It had roses round the door. White roses.'

'Dad – you're going to kill us both.'

He didn't answer. He stared straight ahead, a thin smile on his lips.

She moved away from the door. She sat against the opposite wall, hugging her knees.

Chapter Twenty-Three

Liam pulled out onto the dual carriageway, screwing up his eyes against the morning sun.

A press conference. Short notice. The announcement of the results, the Director had said.

What results, was the question. How is Richard going to make any kind of sense at all, when we don't even know what these particles are, these charges, whatever they are, and anyway, the press camped outside the lab may, just, be more interested in the two dead physicists rather than a ten to the minus eight-six charge possibility...

Who's next? one journalist had said to him as he had passed the other day, a guy in a crumpled leather jacket with matching face - and Liam had been rather short with him, 'it's not a field sport, you know...' But now, turning off towards the lab, Liam remembered Neil's missed calls and was aware of a background hum of anxiety.

It didn't help that some of the local press had picked up on the fragments of rumours surrounding the setting up of the lab thirty odd years ago, the ruined house, the land being cursed. Liam found himself musing on the tension between science and superstition, wondering whether it had always been this way, the stories we tell ourselves, a hint of guilt, ever-present, the inevitable come-uppance.

And there it was, beyond the intersection of the road into town, the industrial estate, the car park, the hotel. He could even pick out the window of their room, a tiny square in the pure white of the façade, innocent in the morning sun. But in his mind Liam saw them both, saw her raw nakedness arching in pleasure, felt a stiffening ache of desire.

He would call her. Later today. He'd call her.

Helen, too, tidying away the breakfast things in a blaze of sunlight, felt a lightness of mood that had been absent the night before. A phrase of music circled in her mind, what was it, a waltz, perhaps, Tchaikovsky, two bars, over and over. She put down the teapot, leaned one hand on a chair as if at the barre and tried out a plié sequence, and one and two, and rise… No, not a waltz, a Mazurka, perhaps…

She picked up the teapot and placed it in the dishwasher.

He'll call me today, she thought.

Or I might call him. A text, even. Just to say, I'm thinking of you.

This morning, Chad had said goodbye, squeezed her shoulder. In a brief moment, their eyes had met, and she had seen there – what? A doubt? A question of some kind?

Whatever it was, it had gone unasked. A few moments later the front door had slammed shut.

Now she sat at the table, pulled the newspaper towards her, gazed at it unseeing.

The thought of Liam was a hum of music, of joy, an urge to dance. It had been so long since she had felt this way, with this lightness of spirit, this aliveness. Her marriage had become something heavy, it seemed to her now, something that she carried with her, dutiful, loyal and weighed down. And now, here was a man who made her feel beautiful, made her want to dance.

She pushed the paper way, and got up from the table. There is work to be done, she thought. I must go up to the Centre, I promised we'd have a chat about the new music system there…

And as for Lisa…

The sunlight seemed to fade.

She is still in danger. Still in fear. Like poor Amelia. Someone must honour her, she thought. Someone must tell her story.

But Amelia died long ago. Whereas Lisa - Lisa is very much alive. She checked her watch, wondered whether to call in at the police station on her way to the Centre.

'Missing? Iain?' Liam looked from the Director to Roger. Roger went over to the wide windows of the meeting room, flicked at the slatted blinds.

'No sign of him,' he said. 'He was supposed to be early, to set up the kit…'

'It's not like Iain,' the Director said.

'No sign of Elizabeth either,' Roger said. 'And Neil- '

'Neil tried to call me,' Liam began. 'Last night - '

'Didn't you answer?'

Liam shook his head. He put his paper cup down on the table.

Richard stepped across the cables that trailed across the floor. 'It's no time to disappear,' he said. 'As it is I've got my work cut out trying to get the press to concentrate on our results and not on our recent ghastly events – '

Liam's phone broke the silence. He snatched it from his pocket, clicked it on, listened, replied, 'OK,' twice, clicked it off. He looked at the two men. 'Police. Downstairs. Asking for you, Richard.'

Richard sighed. 'That's all we need. Perhaps they're researching cold dark matter too.'

He left the room. In the silence, Liam found he was staring at his phone, and put it back in his pocket.

'Fuck.' Roger sank into a chair. 'How many more? Are we all going to need fucking bodyguards?' He waved an arm towards the power point screen. 'We're about to announce the kind of results that will get the whole world talking, and all eyes are on some kind of weird murder mystery instead.'

Liam fiddled with the cable across the desk. There was the approach of heavy footsteps. The door opened and Neil stood there. He looked hunched, blotchy with exhaustion.

'Neil - ' Liam stared at him.

'You look bloody awful, mate.' Roger got up, moved a chair across to him.

Neil sat down, heavily. He picked up Liam's paper cup. 'Is this coffee?'

'Help yourself,' Liam said. 'Sugared, though.'

'All the better.' Neil took a large mouthful of coffee, replaced the cup on the table.

'So – ' Roger prompted.

'It's very bad news.' He turned to Liam. 'Didn't you get my calls?'

'Um…'

'Is it Iain?' Roger's voice was loud.

Neil nodded. 'He's dead. Same thing. Hank's Tower. Found at low tide late last night. He'd fallen. Like the others.'

'Chief Super.' Berenice pushed at his open door. 'You asked to see me.'

'Ah. Yes. Miss Killick.'

There was a stress on the Miss, she thought.

'Bad times,' he was saying. 'Three of them now. I assume you've heard?'

She bowed her head. She remembered Iain's sweet face, his nervous, intense conversation. The phone call, early this morning, had made her feel sick.

'Have you seen today's papers?' He pushed a stack of newspaper across the desk to her. 'Do sit down,' he added.

She glanced at the headlines. "Murder Plot Triggered by Laws of Physics?" she read. "Hate Mail Mystery."

'We can't afford for this to go on any longer,' he said.

'No,' she said.

He leaned back in his chair. He swept a hand across his thinning grey hair. He was pink-faced, sweaty, in a shiny navy suit, which was buttoned tight across his paunch.

'Fletcher has offered his boys,' he said.

'The Met?'

He nodded. 'A kind offer. He and I go back some way, of course.'

Of course, she thought. She raised her head. 'Sir, I've cancelled all leave. I've put a watch on every gate, every doorway of the lab. I've got cars assigned to track all potential victims. I've got forensics on the case with the hate mail. I've got Imaging sending me every CCTV trace they can find, from the Tower, the Lab, everywhere. We're keeping an eye on the boy, our main suspect. And we've got a shout out for Clem Voake.'

'Who has so far evaded you, hasn't he?'

She nodded.

'That's precisely the point, Miss Killick. This boy you're calling your main suspect…'

'Yes?' She waited.

'I don't share your conviction.'

'We've got CCTV – '

'The first body we found was his stepfather. He has no motive.' His puffy gaze was fixed on her. 'Has he?'

She shook her head. 'No, Sir.'

'And this Tobias lad, is nowhere in the third killing, is he?'

'No, Sir.'

'Whereas this Clem Voake seems to be very clearly in the frame.'

'I haven't ruled him out. We were back at his caravan as soon as we heard, but he's vanished. As has his daughter,' she added.

'Is she a suspect?' His lips were raised in an almost smile.

'No, Sir. But Voake is a dangerous man, and she's –'

'It's not enough, Miss Killick.' He'd ceased to listen. 'I don't think you understood what I said. It has got to stop.' He got up, suddenly, lurched clumsily to the window. He stood, looking out. 'Miss Killick, would you say that police work is about evidence? Painstaking gathering of evidence?'

'That's exactly what I'd say, Sir.'

'And yet, here we have, one after another, three men who work at the same place, killed in similar ways… we have one suspect with a very substantial grudge against the place and a certain amount of superstitious rage against science…' He turned back to face her. 'It seems a cut and dried case.'

'Yes, Sir,' she agreed.

'So why did you say that it's as likely to be about chaos as about order?'

Berenice blinked at him. 'I'm not sure that's – '

'Notes, here.' He strutted back to the desk, waved an e-mail printout at her. 'Minutes of a Department Briefing – ' He screwed up his eyes to read the date. 'Three, no, four days ago…'

'Sir, with all due respect, I'm following every protocol – '

'We can't afford to have another homicide, Miss Killick,' he interrupted.

'No, Sir. Of course not.'

'So, you'll understand, if I allow Fletcher and his boys full rein.'

She stared at him. 'But – the chain of command…'

'I'm glad you understand.'

'You're saying I'm off the case?' She felt her face grow warm.

'We all appreciate everything you've done so far, Miss Killick, but I'm sure you too realize that something like this, a case of this extraordinary nature, it requires someone with greater experience than you can bring to it.' He waved his hand towards the door. 'Any questions?'

She got to her feet. She hesitated, then said, 'No Sir.'

She glanced back from the doorway, but he'd picked up his Blackberry and was tapping away at it.

Chaos. Order. The words echoed with her footsteps along the orange lino of the corridor.

She thought about what van Mielen said. That it is in the Chaos that order is restored. That we have to face the Chaos in order to reveal the truth.

Liam picked up his empty coffee cup and put it down again. 'Well,' he said. 'Maybe this clears Tobias.'

Roger looked at him. 'Or maybe it doesn't,' he said.

Liam put his head in his hands.

Neil sighed. 'It can't be Tom. The implication is, there really is someone out there who's after us.'

Loud footsteps signalled the reappearance of the Director. 'If anyone had set out to destroy the whole damn experiment – ' the door swung behind him as he strode into the room – 'they couldn't have done it better. These incredible new results, and now we've got a serial attacker of physicists to contend with. And not just any physicist, but specifically in our area of research. I said to those coppers, have they called CERN – maybe they're all being bumped off too?' He aimed a kick at the power point screen. 'This might as well come down again. I've got another army of reporters outside, but not the science correspondents, oh no, just yet more blasted crime hounds. The police want to meet us all to talk about security - '

A ring tone. He pulled out his mobile. 'Elizabeth? Yes. You've heard too… No. Of course. I understand…. OK. Elizabeth – be careful.' He rang off. 'She's heard. A policewoman called on her at home. She's not coming in.' He looked at his watch. 'I've got to go and give a statement downstairs to those reporters.'

The door swung shut behind him.

The three men exchanged glances.

'The curse of the second tunnel,' Neil said. 'It's not funny anymore.'

'The ghost,' Liam said.

'Oh, God, that too.'

'Do you think Iain really saw it?' Roger said.

'He said he had.'

'A First World War Soldier,' Neil said.

Roger shook his head. 'I'm a scientist,' he said. 'I work with evidence. With proof. When did it become…?' His words tailed away.

Neil looked from one to the other. 'Up till now, I haven't been scared,' he said.

'And now?' Liam said.

'I guess, now – yes,' he said. 'Yes, I'm scared.'

'But what can we do?' Roger said. 'Hide? Suspend the experiment? What does this bastard want? Revenge? Revenge for what? Money? Is he just crazy? And how come they all end up at Hank's Tower?'

Neil shrugged. Liam stared at the floor. Roger tapped his foot against the carpet.

'He's a racist jerk.' Mary put two cups of coffee down on the table.

'Shh.' Berenice glanced around the canteen.

'Don't shush me. And anyway, no one here is going to argue.' She stirred sugar into her cup. 'You should be angrier, Boss.'

'Oh, I'm angry. Sure. But I learned a long time ago, you have to be careful with that kind of anger.' She sipped her coffee. 'Thing is – ' Berenice waved her spoon. There are people, right, who have to divide people into types. And he's one of them. So, like, he divides everyone up. People who are black, people who are white. People who are girls, people who are boys. People who look for the truth on the surface of things, people who go underneath the surface, in the hope that order will appear from chaos…'

Mary was frowning at her. 'Sorry, Boss, I'm lost. Are the chaos people the same as the black ones?'

Berenice gave a brief smile. 'Or, to put it another way - he's a racist jerk.' Her eyes suddenly welled with tears. Mary leaned across the table in concern.

'Bernie – ' Mary took hold of her hand. 'Babe… '

Berenice shook her head. 'Oh, it ain't nothing.' She looked up at her. 'All my life, right, I've wanted this. I love the Job, you know I do. All that flack, from my mates, what you go wanting to join Babylon for, from my Uncle, "what kind of daughter are you, can't you see your Mam needs you" – and I turned my back on all of it. I always knew I'd do this. And now…' She dabbed tears from her eyes. 'And it's not even that he's a jerk. It's that he's wrong.'

'He is?'

'I've been thinking about this. He can round up Clem Voake, but I'm not sure that'll solve anything.'

'But – all the evidence so far…'

Berenice traced a coffee ring on the table in front of her. She sighed. 'Maybe. Maybe I'm just going crazy. That book. That old physics stuff. About the gaps and the nothing and all that… There's something about it…'

'That's the chaos bit, then?'

Berenice nodded.

Mary sipped her coffee. 'It's shit, life, innit. All this and cystitis too.'

'What?' Berenice looked blank.

Mary smiled. 'It went, then?'

'Oh. Yeah. Seems to have.'

'Proves you can only have one thing go wrong at a time.'

'Is that your philosophy, then?'

Mary shrugged. 'If I have to have one, Boss, then, yeah.'

Berenice looked at her phone. 'I'm still on a shift, technically. Though God knows what I'm going to do.' She got to her feet. 'The boys from the Met can track down Voake and he'll admit to it all, and I can go back to traffic offences.'

'All that paperwork you can catch up on, Boss.'

Berenice didn't smile. 'If that's a joke - '

Mary had focused across the canteen, as Ben approached.

'Ma'am – there's someone downstairs asking for you. The Chief tried to talk to him, but he said he'd only talk to you. The vicar, you know, Rev Meyrick.'

'Ah well.' Berenice reached for her coat. 'Maybe he's applying for a parking permit.'

Helen paced the living room, her phone in her hand. She stopped by the window, gazed out on to the drive, the hedge, the bright blue strip of sea beyond. Then she clicked on Liam's number.

'Hi – '

'Oh,' he breathed. 'You. I was going to call – '

'I've been meaning to call you all morning,' she said. 'I want to go to the caravan, Lisa's place, I feel we should be doing more to help her…'

'Oh.' He said nothing else.

'Are you all right?' she said.

'It's all going off here,' he said.

He was there, of course. Far away, surrounded by colleagues, computer screens, a click away from action, power points, particle collisions - what on earth made me think he'd be pleased to hear from me…

I can ring you later, she was about to say, but then he was talking again.

'Iain's dead.'

'What?'

'Hank's Tower again. Same day as our huge press announcement, the director's fuming… paradigm-shifting discoveries of the behaviour of B mesons, if that's what they are…'

'Iain,' she said.

'I don't think I can bear it. My sister's telling me to get out, go into hiding, it just feels so weird. When did being a science nerd get to be a high-risk profession?'

She couldn't think of anything to say.

'Richard's talking to the police about upping our security. Personal bodyguard stuff… Any of us could be next.'

She was aware she was gripping the phone tight against her ear. 'Yes,' she breathed. 'Please – please be careful…'

'Lisa,' he said. 'Visiting her?'

'I thought – ' she began. 'I thought we might…'

She heard his distance. 'I mean,' she went on, unable to stop herself, 'just to see if she's OK…'

'Helen - '

'What?'

'It's stopped being fun,' he said.

She took a deep breath. 'Sure,' she said. 'I can see that.'

His voice sounded faint. 'You don't know what it's like here… police everywhere… we're in shock. The secretaries all weeping…'

'Right.'

'I'll call you later,' he said.

'Will you?' she said.

'Of course,' he said, but his voice was thin, the off-click of his phone too loud.

The room seemed cold. She stood, her phone in her hand, her throat tight with shock, with tearfulness.

Another death. Hank's Tower. Iain. Of course he wouldn't want to see me.

I don't know what to do, she thought. I could call Anton, she thought. But no, he's the last person I should call, he'd just commiserate about the need to stray, 'oh Hon, it gets to us all in the end…' 'But I've made a complete fool of myself,' I'll wail to him, and all he'll say is, join the club…

She went to the fireplace, gazed at herself in the mirror that hung above the mantelpiece.

I'm on my own, then.

Her reflection gazed back at her.

Was it really about Lisa? Or was it just an excuse to see him, to have some kind of stupid adventure?

She turned away from the mirror, trying to keep at bay a convulsion of desire, of need, of the memory of their bodies intertwined.

She found her coat. She looked at the car keys in the palm of her hand.

Chad would tell me not to go. Chad would say, three physicists dead – it's not a game.

She thought about Lisa, standing, bleeding, on her doorstep.

I have no choice, she thought.

'I have no choice.' Amelia, standing in the empty parlour, spoke the words out loud.

She crossed the room, ran through the hall, out to the kitchen, arriving breathless in Gabriel's workshop.

He looked up with that now familiar expression, a frown of irritation, a distant, distracted look.

'Our child is still unwell,' she said.

'Worse since this morning?' He returned to his machine, his fingers tracing the line of light across the bench.

'No,' she conceded. 'But she's listless, and sleepy.'

'Dr Keppler said we were doing all the right things.'

'What if it's not a chill?' Her voice was fierce.

He glanced up at her. 'Do we have any reason not to believe Dr. Keppler?'

I have no choice. The words kept a pulse with her heartbeat.

'Gabriel - '

'What is it?'

'She cannot thrive.'

Again, the absent frown. He checked his notes.

'My brother,' she began. 'We – we miss him so. Guy…'

'Guy.' Gabriel breathed the name. 'Yes,' he said. 'We miss him so.'

'If he were here…'

'He would have known. This, for example, this trace here… It seems to have no mass.' He was talking to himself, fingering a punched print-out that unfurled from the machine. 'I would ask him, how can these charges, A and B and C, how can they add up to more than their sum…'

'Gabriel - '

He looked up at her tone.

'That's not what I meant.'

'And what did you mean?' He leaned on the bench, waiting.

'There is a gap. Where there was love…' She stopped.

'You mean us?' His voice was sharp. 'Nothing has changed, my dear.'

'A nothingness,' she said. 'It is as if Love has died for you.'

A flicker of confusion in his eyes. 'Our love?' he tried.

'Or another love,' she began. 'A love that died on the battlefields.'

He found himself silenced, his throat constricted. He stared at her. 'Your brother…' he could barely say the words.'

'I don't want to know anymore.' Her eyes burned with rage. 'How can our child thrive?'

'I don't accept - ' he began. 'Our Grace… She is my salvation. She will live. She must live.'

'How can you ask that? A mere child, and you ask that she saves you?' Her eyes filled with tears, and she turned away.

'Amelia…' He lifted a hand towards her.

She went to the door, un-clicked the latch. The door closed behind her.

He stared into the silence. 'Amelia,' he said, to emptiness.

He turned back to the machine, switched on the coil, watched the growing green glow of the aether waves.

Chapter Twenty-Four

The caravan seemed to have sunk further into the mud. Helen tried the door, which was locked. At the windows, a curtain had come unhooked. Inside she could see an unmade bed, empty beer cans.

The heavy sky threatened more rain. She wished she'd eaten lunch. She wondered what to do.

Then, footsteps approaching, hurried. She turned, fearful, saw no one, then heard a snuffling, growling noise.

'Tazer – ' she called. And there she was, bouncing towards her.

'What are you doing here?' She bent to pat her, and she jumped up, tail wagging, sniffing at her hand. 'Where's Lisa?' she was saying, 'Where's she gone?' realising as she spoke that she had an unfed, unkempt look. Realising, too, that if Lisa had had any choice in the matter, she would keep her dog with her.

She looked around the muddy site.

I don't know what to do, she thought.

A flash of colour, at the edge of the field. A figure, approaching – Lisa? She wondered, but this was older, thinner, a woman, she realized, as she drew nearer, as the dog barked, ran to greet her. The woman bent to pet the dog, called her by name, then looked up at Helen.

'You're – '

'Helen. We've met.'

The woman put out her hand. 'Elizabeth. Merletti. Of course, we met at the lab. You're the vicar's – '

Helen accepted the oddly formal handshake.

'Sorry. Not the vicar's anything,' Elizabeth was saying.

'I'm looking for Lisa,' Helen said.

'So am I.'

'I think she's in danger,' Helen said.

'I think so too.'

Elizabeth was in a short tailored wool coat, and smart brogue shoes. Helen felt rather underdressed in her jeans and sheepskin boots. They sat on the damp caravan steps.

'I'd light a cigarette,' Elizabeth said. 'If I still smoked.' She turned to Helen. 'How do you know her?'

'I – I teach her.' It sounded rather thin. 'I don't know her very well, but she was injured, she turned up on my doorstep the other night, with Tazer here, and her friend Finn, then she left. I wanted her to stay,' she added.

'Injured?' Elizabeth stared at her. 'Her horrible father?'

Helen nodded.

'Her mother's so hopeless. She gets passed from one to the other, and neither of them are any good for her at all. Actually… actually Clem is probably better for her than Andrea. Which isn't saying much. But all she's ever known is running away, that kid.'

'How do you know her?'

Elizabeth fiddled with a button on her coat. 'We're kind of related. That house over there – ' She tilted her head towards the wall. 'The Voake house. One of my distant ancestors lived there.'

'The van Mielens - ' Helen stared at her.

Elizabeth nodded. 'I met Lisa through Tobias, you know, that sweet kid who worked at the lab, Murdo's kind of ward. Anyway, we established the link. I've tried to keep in touch with her.'

A whining made them both turn, as Tazer appeared, carrying something in her mouth. It was red fabric, and she shook it from side to side.

'Here…' Elizabeth bent and took it from her.

'Lisa's – ' Helen said. 'Lisa's hairband. She was wearing it when…'

Elizabeth passed it to Helen.

'… when her father went for her.'

Elizabeth looked at Helen. 'Oh God.' She glanced up at the sky. 'Look, it's raining again. There's no point us getting wet here. Let's go and look for her at the house. She may have gone there.'

'The house?'

Elizabeth got to her feet, smoothed raindrops from her coat. 'The old Voake house. It's just over the wall there, Lisa might well be hiding there. Come on Tayze… It's a silly name for a dog, isn't it? And a girl dog at that. Lisa spells it with a 'y', like T-A-Y-Z-A but no one else does.'

Tazer jumped to her feet too. She trotted at their side along the leaf-strewn path.

'He saw what?' Berenice stared at Chad. He looked tired, or perhaps it was just the flat strip lighting of the interview room.

'One man carrying another. Towards Hank's Tower.'

'I thought that's what you said.'

'The impression Tobias gave was of a limp body being carried towards the steps by a much stronger man. He said it was difficult to tell, and he thought maybe it was a ghost, so he fled.'

'A ghost.' Berenice nodded. 'Easily done.'

'Don't mock him.' Chad was thin-lipped and tense.

'I wasn't. Believe me. My brother…' She stopped.

'Your brother - '

She interrupted. 'So, Reverend Meyrick. What do we do?'

'We?' He met her eyes. 'All I know is, Virginia didn't want anyone to know. She's worried enough about him, so if this causes any further trouble for him, she'll be upset…'

'Of course. It will go no further.'

'Promise?' He looked doubtful.

She nodded. 'For reasons I don't yet wish to share, I have no reason to discuss this information with anyone else at all.'

'Will you go and see him?'

'Yes. I think so. But I'll go alone. Informally. No powers of arrest or anything like that.'

He seemed to breathe more easily. 'Good. Good.' He got to his feet. 'I appreciate it. I just couldn't have lived with myself if I didn't tell anyone…' He paused, his hand on the door. 'Thank you, Inspector,' he said.

Inspector, she thought, as the door closed behind him. I'll think about that later. For now, there's work to do.

She pulled out her lap-top, tapped at the keyboard. There were some results from the Imaging Department, a series of car number plates, tracked along the coastal road. A fuzzy image from the sea front, time-matched. A tall-ish, male figure.

Could be anyone, she thought.

The TV news had gone mad. At lunchtime they'd had local reporters camped outside. Now, getting on for four o'clock, there were vans, OB units, reporters three deep on the doorstep… Can you tell us anymore? Why do you think the lab has been singled out? What measures are you taking to prevent a fourth killing…?

Berenice scrolled through her e-mails. And what do we tell them? Every patrol car is out, combing the streets. Door-to-door officers, although the nearest door to the lab is about four miles away, and the only report we've got so far from the neighbours is from an elderly couple who reckons 'they kept themselves to themselves…' The Chief's sent everyone back to the lab, interviewing every physicist again. And every time, the same answer. 'What can anyone have against us? We're doing sums, that's all.'

An e-mail from the Chief. She scanned it, leaned back in her chair.

'Yeah, yeah,' she said to her screen. 'I get the picture. "Assigned to Ashford for the next month". Sure, whatever you think best…'

"We can't afford another death," she read.

Rain hammered against the window. She switched on the desk lamp.

No, she thought. We can't.

She bent to her briefcase, pulled out the book. She flicked through the pages, catching at words. "For if gravity can be said to be the force that acts upon all matter, we must assert that it is put in motion by the Lord…"

She went to her screen, clicked on the photos, the threat letters that had been sent to the lab.

'The infinite circles of Satan,' she read. 'Your days are numbered…' Clumsy handwriting, threatening the end of the world. Not the same as the elegant faded script of the book in her hands.

Johann van Mielen, and his daughter. And his son-in-law Gabriel Voake.

And now, a hundred odd years later, another Voake has camped on the edge of the Lab, with his vulnerable daughter, peddling guns or drugs or both. And has been seen round Hank's Tower. The Scallop Tower.

She got up, went over to the window, fingered a gap in the blinds.

Where is the connection? she wondered. How do I get from three dead physicists to a low-life dealer and his mouthy and possibly-at-risk daughter, via a weird old book of quasi-religious writings?

I'm not used to this, she thought, sitting back at the desk, scrolling through e-mails. I'm used to straightforward criminality, greed or fraud or theft or murderous rage, where the motivation is obvious, the outcomes are clear. Not this, this life-threatening danger, so acute, so dark, so frightening – and so completely hidden from view.

She picked up the book, fingered the yellowing pages. Then she switched off her machine, packed everything into her briefcase, grabbed her coat and left.

The daylight was already fading, and the headlamps of her car cut through the falling rain as she pulled away from the exit barrier and headed towards town.

Chapter Twenty-Five

'Oh. It's you.' Virginia stood at her door. 'I've got nothing more to say to you.'

'I assume you've heard the awful news.' Berenice took a step nearer the threshold.

'You mean, poor Iain.' Virginia gazed out beyond her at the rain.

'Auntie, who is it?' Tobias jostled behind Virginia. 'Oh,' he said, 'it's you. Come in, come in, we've got lots to talk about. Haven't we Auntie, it's got very bad, very very bad.'

Virginia, reluctantly, stepped aside. Berenice went into the cottage, shaking rain from her coat. 'This isn't an official questioning,' she said.

'Good.' Virginia indicated a chair, and they all three sat down. The cat appeared, eyed Berenice, slunk away again.

Berenice put the book down on the table, which was cluttered with old coffee mugs, newspapers, a tweed hat, a wooden box. Virginia eyed the book. She appeared to shudder at the sight of it, although, Berenice thought, it might just be the chill of the room, with its unlit fire, its single lamp against the dark outside.

'This Aether,' Berenice went on. 'Is it something in the air? Is it a real thing?'

'He doesn't mean aether the way we do,' Virginia said. Her tone implied there was nothing more to say.

'Oh. Right.' Berenice looked at Tobias. He'd picked up the book and was weighing it, gently, in his hand.

'So,' she went on, 'some other kind of thing. Like, some magic thing. The way he talks about it, it's like it could unlock all the secrets of the universe. Gravity, heaviness. Emptiness…'

Virginia gave no reply, sitting with her hands in her lap. The pale lamplight sculpted the worn corduroy of her skirt, lightened the rough strands of her hair.

'Well, it must have mattered at the time,' Berenice went on. 'And perhaps it matters even now. How did it end up at your house, then?'

Virginia raised her head. 'I don't know what this has got to do with Iain,' she said. 'Or with any of them, for that matter, Murdo, Alan…'

Berenice shrugged. 'You tell me.'

Virginia's gaze was unblinking. 'That book is nothing but trouble.'

'Is that why you gave it to the vicar?'

'Something like that, yes.'

Berenice wished she had someone with her, just to break the silence, the scratch of a pen of a DC taking notes. Tobias was breathing, hard, and suddenly he slammed the book down on the table.

'Alan,' he said. 'The Professor. Not the same as Murdo and Iain. Oh, no, not the same at all.' He was shaking his head from side to side. 'Murdo and Iain knew things properly, they knew about the cold darkness out of which light comes. But Alan…'

Virginia reached across and took his hand.

'And the book isn't trouble, Auntie. Not in the right hands. I love that book, I want to have it back, it's got the whole story in it, the tunnel and everything. And Uncle Murdo liked it too. And the Professor kept asking me for it but I didn't give it to him and then he told me not to go and work there anymore. And Dr. Iain didn't like him, either, when they both wanted to buy the old house the Prof was shouting at him, going on about the ghost and the dead child, and how he'd get the house, you'll see, and Dr. Iain was very angry with the Prof after that, very very angry. Uncle Murdo had to take him for a walk to calm him down.' He got to his feet. 'And now it's all gone wrong, and I can't find Lisa either, she's not even in our special places, I'm frightened that she's next even though she's not colliding things, not like the others…' He had been pacing to and fro and now he stopped, in front of Berenice.

Their eyes met. She was about to speak, to ask about what he'd seen at Hank's Tower, but there was something about him, something restless and fearful, and she remained silent. He turned and left the room, and they heard him clomp up the stairs.

Virginia faced her, tight-lipped. 'I won't have you upsetting that boy,' she said. 'You can see what he's like. Obsessive.' The cat had reappeared, and she bent to stroke her. 'Things that the rest of us take for granted, he has to think about it. And some things capture him, his thinking gets snagged on them. It's mixtures, now, his mercuries he calls them. It was stones on the beach for a while, always bringing them back, only certain kinds, particular shapes, particular marks, it all had meaning. And then after that it was Kings and Queens, firstly the historical ones, and then after a bit any country. We became experts. Even now, there are kingdoms in the world you'd never know about without Tom telling you, Andorra, Tuvalu… Their rulers still come and have tea at Buckingham Palace, says Tom.' She allowed herself a small smile.

'So the book…?' Berenice retrieved it, held it on her lap.

The smile faded. 'Can you imagine what that did to a boy like Tom? Not only rules, but hidden rules. Not only structures, but secret ones. He became obsessed. And then he got that job. Murdo thought it would be good for him, harness all that chaos into something more orderly.' She shook her head. 'Murdo was wrong.'

The rain pattered against the thick glass of the window panes. Virginia seemed to shrink once more, her eyes downcast.

Berenice thought about Dr. Merletti, with her mistress's manifesto, the 'drooping wife', 'it was over long before I met him,' 'well, if you neglect a man like that….'

The van Mielen name in the book, too. The jealousy between Murdo and Iain. And then of course, the child, the tragic drowning.

'Mrs. Maguire,' she began. Virginia didn't move. 'Would you say your husband was troubled?'

Virginia looked up at her. She shook her head.

'There were these threats to the laboratory,' Berenice said.

'I thought at first it was just Moffatt's attention-seeking again. He likes to think he's pushing at the frontiers of science. At first I thought no one could be that bothered about Bosons and Muons, not really. But, then, of course, with these new events, I suppose one has to accept that there are indeed dangers…'

'And in your marriage?' Berenice said.

Virginia met her eyes. 'What do you mean?'

Berenice took a breath, then said, 'On Murdo's team, and Iain's…

'Is this relevant?' Her gaze was piercing now.

'I'm simply asking - ' Berenice said.

Virginia's voice was suddenly loud. 'I only let you into my home out of politeness. That's all. No doubt you've heard all sorts of rumours from the lab, from one person in particular. I will say this to you. If you believe anything that person says, you're more of a fool than I thought. There will always be the woman who imagines herself loved by a man, who enjoys the challenge of being irresistible. But what does she know of love, such a woman? Murdo and I knew a different kind of love, one which was capable of carrying us through the worst that can befall a couple, the death of a child. A woman like that can toss her hair and talk of love, but she knows nothing. There is a kind of love that is a fragment of a whole, a note in the vibration of the universe. That's what I have known, and what I have lost. What does she know of that?' She stared, unseeing, illumined by the pale lamplight.

Berenice watched her, gathering her thoughts. 'Mrs. Maguire – I have one other question. What was Tobias doing at the scene of three very serious crimes?'

They made their way under dripping trees as far as the wall. Elizabeth pushed at a gate, and then they were on an overground path. At the end stood the house, still somehow solid and elegant despite the gaps in the room, the broken, empty windows.

Amelia's house, Helen thought.

Elizabeth pushed at the front door, and then they were inside. Tazer began to nose around, sniffing her way down the corridor towards what must have been the kitchen.

'Amelia's house,' Helen said.

'You know her? Amelia Voake?'

'I've read her writings.'

'You have?' Elizabeth turned to her.

'The book – it ended up with my husband.'

'Heavens.' Elizabeth shook raindrops from her coat. 'This'll be a lovely history lesson for you, then.'

'It was yours.' Helen leaned her hand on the bannisters. She looked upwards, towards the first floor.

'Are you all right?' Elizabeth glanced at her. 'They say this place is haunted,' she added. 'Old Digby Voake said it used to scare him as a child.' She turned to follow Tazer, who was snuffling at the kitchen door.

The kitchen was drier. The table was old and wooden, and littered with several empty beer cans.

'Ah,' Elizabeth said. 'Signs of life. I wouldn't be at all surprised if Clem was hanging out here.' She pulled out a chair and inspected it. 'He always thought he'd end up with this place. But I fear Digby had other ideas.'

Helen sat down at the table. 'Did he own this?'

She nodded. 'Old Digby Voake was the last survivor of the Gabriel Voake line, indirectly, of course. But he's a roofer by trade, he could never afford to do anything with this place. Just before he died, he sold it. To the lab. Alan was desperate to get hold of it, for the land. Iain was interested too, but Alan outbid him. I think Digby got quite a good price.' She sat down opposite Helen.

'Do the police know?'

'I assume they do, yes. But…' She looked at Helen. 'Clem as – as a killer? I hadn't thought…'

Helen bent to her bag and pulled out the pink folder. She passed it across.

'What's this – '

'It's part of the book,' Helen said. 'Your book.'

Elizabeth flicked through the pages. 'Amelia's writings.' She looked up at Helen. 'She died, their child. That's what I'd heard.'

'Grace?'

Elizabeth nodded.

Helen stared at the pages in front of her. 'That explains… that explains a lot. I've read through them, loads of times, this sense of dread, this fearfulness…' She looked at Elizabeth. 'How do you know?'

'The van Mielens, my father's side. They talked about her. How she married into this Kentish family and then disappeared. It was her cousin who came to the States, he was my great-great Uncle or something… No one knows how we ended up with this book. Perhaps someone found it here in the house and shipped it over to New Jersey with the other stuff.' She shivered in the chill of the half-ruins. She touched the red hair-band that lay on the table. 'Well,' she said. 'What are we going to do?'

Virginia sat, stiff and upright. 'Tobias is incapable of harming anyone,' she said.

'How long has he been with you? Did he come to you before or after your son died?'

'Just after,' she said. 'A few months after.' She fell silent again.

'Dead children,' Berenice said. 'This whole case seems haunted by them.'

Virginia softened slightly. 'It was bad for Tobias,' she said. 'It was a bad house for him to be in. We were grief-stricken. And he'd already lost his mother, that's why he was with us. But you see-' she looked up at Berenice, 'he was a Godsend to us. We had to get on with our lives, for him. If he hadn't been there…'

'Does Tobias…' Berenice began. 'Does he think about death a lot?'

A flush of pink touched her face. She nodded. 'Yes,' she said. 'It figures in his thinking. That's another reason Murdo was so keen on the lab for him, because he thought it would be abstract, another way to think about things, not just life and death, but something eternal, universal…' She sighed. 'It didn't work.' She flashed a glance at Berenice. 'But you'll still haul him in, won't you? None of this makes any difference.'

'Virginia,' Berenice said. 'We're trying to help.'

'How does this help? Getting me to share these memories like this?' Her voice was harsh once more.

'I need to talk to him. If he's innocent – '

'There you go again. If, you say. When I know, as sure as I know anything, that he's innocent. For all these years, I've fought for that boy. And I won't stop now.' She sat there, breathing hard.

'My brother was disabled,' Berenice said. 'My mother fought for him, too.'

Virginia met her gaze, blank-faced. 'You have to,' she said. She seemed about to speak again, but Tobias was coming down the stairs. He ambled back to his seat. The cat jumped on to his lap, and he sat there, stroking her, calmly.

Virginia turned to him. 'This lady here – '

'Berenice – ' she said.

Virginia gave a small shrug. 'She says you saw something happen. At Hank's Tower. The night that Murdo… The night that he…'

Tobias looked up. He considered Berenice for a moment. Then he said, 'One man. One man carrying another. The one being carried, he looked like Uncle Murdo, he looked dead or asleep or something, his arm was swinging, like that – ' He swung his arm clumsily across the table, catching one of the mugs, tipping cold coffee across the clutter. 'My box – ' he shouted, as the sticky liquid trickled towards it. He scooped it up in his arms.

Berenice looked at it. 'What's that?' she said.

'My things. Special things.'

Berenice glanced at it. 'What kind of things?'

He settled back into his chair. 'Well,' he said, 'things to do with the Aether. From the book,' he added. He pushed the box into her arms. 'Like the lion that you took.'

Berenice looked at Virginia, who inclined her head in permission. She lifted the objects, one by one, a red plastic lion, tiny glass bottles, perfume, she thought. Sheaves of paper, covered in scribbled numbers, diagrams. A pink hair-band – '

'Lisa kept the red one,' he said, and smiled. 'She let me have that one. I like pink,' he said.

A postcard of an old painting… a tree with apples, a man, a serpent -

'Adam in the Garden,' Tobias said. 'It's old.'

Two photographs. One seemed to be a cemetery, people standing near a grave. The other, a photo of a little boy. Berenice held them, one in each hand.

Virginia began to speak, but Berenice stopped her. 'I know what these are,' she said. 'You don't have to explain.' She gazed at them for a minute. 'My brother…' she said. 'I was nine when he died. He was two years older than me. His funeral… Such terrible grief. And at that age, you don't understand, do you…' She fingered the photographs. 'He was a beautiful child,' she said.

'Yes,' Virginia said. She reached out a hand and Berenice passed her the photo of the child.

Virginia gazed at the blond hair, the open, smiling face. 'Yes. He was a beautiful child.'

Elizabeth paced the kitchen.

'I can't think where he'd have taken her,' she said. 'Where he's been hiding out. He claims to be a devoted dad, that's the problem, it's all tied up with him wanting to be something he's not…'

'The police are looking for him – ' Helen said.

'And failing to find him.' She sat down again at the table. 'Oh, God, they could be anywhere. I should have got involved earlier, I'm a relative of the poor kid, after all…'

'A very distant one,' Helen said.

'She's got no one to care for her, that's the problem.'

'There's Finn, her friend. And Tobias.'

'Yeah. Finn's probably been hauled in for dealing again. And Tobias…' Elizabeth shook her head.

Outside it had grown dark. The silence of the house was punctuated by rustlings, mice, perhaps, birds in the rafters. Tazer snuffled from her place by the back door.

'Well, no point staying here,' Elizabeth said. 'I guess you've got a home to go to.'

Helen shook her head. 'Not really, no.'

'No? That makes two of us.' Elizabeth hesitated, then said, 'When I first saw you, I thought, you don't look like a vicar's wife. You look like a dancer.'

'A dancer.' Helen looked at her. 'I am. At least I was…'

'Was?'

They faced each other across the shadows of the kitchen. Helen wondered what to say, how to begin.

'God, it's bloody dark in here,' Elizabeth said suddenly. She got to her feet, gathering candles from the old kitchen range, matches. Soon there was light, flickering across the room. 'Or maybe I've made it worse,' she said, surveying the room. 'Even more spooky.' She sat down again.

Helen gazed at the candle flame.

'Giving things up,' Elizabeth said. 'For you, it's your dancing so that you can be a vicar's wife. For me, it's any kind of life so that I can do my work.'

'Is it like that?'

'Not for every woman, no. But I guess I have standards. The kind of physics I want to do. I don't want to stop what I'm doing just to go home and cook some man's dinner.'

'Are you happy with that?' Helen hadn't meant to ask, but there was something about the house, the sense that there was only a thin crumbling wall between this room and the wild night outside.

'At this moment?' Elizabeth shook her head. 'No. I'm not happy at all. I loved two men and both of them…' Her voice cracked. 'Both of them are dead. And the worst of it is, I feel I'm to blame. I feel I'm at the heart of it all.'

'But – Elizabeth – '

'What?'

'It's someone dangerous. It's some kind of crazy, murderous vengeful person. Your lab is just the focus of a madness, surely…?'

Elizabeth traced lines on the old oak table. 'I guess I'm not thinking straight. Alan, the director, he was obsessed with this house. He got the idea he'd buy it, with the land around it. He'd go on about extending the lab. Just before he died, he'd completed the sale. It was uncomplicated – Digby Voake, apparently, he owned all this. He was quite happy to get rid of it. But Alan was nervous about it, anxious. He seemed to think I was an obstacle to it all. I don't know why. He'd use my van Mielen name, even though I shed it years ago. I don't even like it. My father's name…' She shrugged. 'Not one I want to carry.'

'So – surely, whoever is angry with the lab – it's about this house. This land. Surely the police know all that…?'

'Oh, yes. Everyone's told them. They're pursuing Clem for just that reason. That, and the fact he's a low-life criminal… which is presumably why he's gone into hiding and taken his poor kid with him.'

'Oh God.' Helen shivered. 'I should have kept her with me.'

'Would she have let you?'

'No.'

'It's not your fault,' Elizabeth said. 'And I guess it's not mine. It's just, everyone sees me as some kind of femme fatale. And that isn't me at all. I loved Murdo. I loved him very very much. When I came back here, from Italy… God, I was so moral. So bloody *good*. I kept my distance, I left him to his drippy wife… and Iain was funny and sweet and supportive, he knew the whole story, he and I had been… well, I guess we'd sort of been lovers in the past… who would blame me for turning to him?'

'No one,' Helen murmured.

'I mean, if the man you love makes himself unavailable in some way, it's just human nature to find love elsewhere, isn't it?'

Helen met her eyes. 'Yes,' she said. 'I suppose it is.'

Berenice sat in her car in a layby on the dual carriageway. The rain poured down, blurring the headlights of the oncoming cars. It was late, she realized, and she was hungry.

On the seat next to her, sat Tobias's box. Virginia had softened, somehow, had even offered her something to eat, which Berenice had declined. When she'd asked Virginia, and Tobias, if she could keep the box for a few days, they'd agreed, 'As long as you look after it, and don't do any of the experiments, promise…' he'd said. She'd promised. Now it was all there, in her car, apart from the photo of Jacob, which Virginia had placed on her mantelpiece, 'Where it belongs,' she'd said.

The other photo was tucked amongst the objects, the plastic animals, a toy yellow tractor, she saw now.

I am going crazy, she thought. What made me ask to take this stuff away?

It's madness. Like mentioning Danny, I've never done that, never in all my years in the job…

She was about to start the engine again, when her phone rang.

'Mary – wassup?'

'DNA matching. At last. There's a match between Clem Voake and Moffatt's SOC. And the path labs say that Hendrickson has significant toxicity, probably sedatives.'

'Oh.'

'I thought you'd like to know. I'm just leaving the office, though the Chief has put me on earlies from tomorrow, with

Kevin, it'll be hell, it's all right for you. Or, maybe, it isn't. Anyway, proper evidence, at last, the Chief's delighted.'

'I can imagine.'

Mary was silent for a moment. 'Sorry. Guess I said the wrong thing.'

'It's cool.'

'It is?'

'Sure. See you around.'

Mary sounded uncertain. 'OK. See you soon.'

Berenice put her phone back in her bag.

Evidence, she thought. Every case I've been on, there's been evidence. There's been imaging, forensics, fingerprints, witness statements. And here I am, getting caught up in a weird old book, a muddle of local history; the grief of a bereaved mother.

She glanced at Tobias's collection on the seat beside her. She thought about Virginia, iron-willed, deflecting anything that would harm Tobias. She'd looked so like my mother. Weary, steadfast, determined...

Perhaps that's why I'd talked about my brother. Letting down my guard...

At her door, as she'd said goodbye, Virginia had half-shaken her hand, a brief touch of her fingertips.

Berenice started her car engine. She thought about a tailored raincoat, a toss of pale hair, smart court shoes.

She turned off on the road back into town. She remembered there was a pizza in the freezer. A boring, cheese and tomato thing, but there were some olives in the fridge, and she'd stop off at the corner shop and see if he had a drinkable red.

'I guess we should go,' Elizabeth said.
Helen sighed.
'Dinners to cook for husbands…'
Helen nodded.
'You don't have children,' Elizabeth said.
'No. We – we tried. We lost one… miscarriage, you know… Since then…'
'Oh. I'm sorry. I didn't mean to pry.' She fiddled with some loose candlewax.
'You don't either?' Helen said.
Elizabeth looked up. 'What? Oh, children. No. Not part of my plan. I saw what it did to my mother.'
'Your mother?'
'She was depressive. It killed her in the end. Or, rather, she killed herself.'
The silence held them for a moment.
'I was twelve. Raised a Catholic. Everyone told me she was in Heaven,' she went on. 'But I knew they were lying. So, I made a few decisions. No God, no motherhood. No fairy tales. It worked very well, until… all this.' She shivered. 'We'd better go. We'll either die of cold or hunger at this rate.'
Helen gathered her coat around her. 'Amelia's child,' she began.

'Grace,' Elizabeth said.

'Do you know what happened?'

'Not really. They said the child died. There were rumours of a grave, out on the marshes, there's a ruined church, Neil took me to see it once. St. Bruin's I think it's called. I remember the name, because in all the lists of Saints I was supposed to remember as a child, I'd never heard of that one...' She gave a brief smile. 'It explains the tone of her writings, don't you think? Amelia?'

'It does?'

Elizabeth gathered her coat around her. 'Her rage. Such a terrible loss, and there's her husband taking refuge in his work. Not listening to her. You would be angry, wouldn't you?'

Helen watched the candle flames flickering in the draught. 'Yes,' she said. 'Yes, I would.'

'It's getting colder.' Elizabeth looked out at the night. 'Creepy place, this. Probably haunted.'

'Ghosts,' Helen said. 'Liam said there'd been sightings at the lab...'

'You know Liam?'

'Oh,' Helen said, 'Just a bit. Through Tobias, you know...'

'Yes, of course. He's a nice man. A great help to Tobias.' Her face shadowed. 'Yes, people have talked of ghosts. Even Iain...' Her voice faltered. 'That poor, poor man. All of them... I really don't know how we're going to carry on...' Her gaze went to the darkened windows. 'Neil said that people always thought this land was cursed. He said, all the crops would fail, and they'd blame the salt from the marshes, or say it was too wet. Yet all the fields round about always thrived...' She wrapped her scarf round her neck. 'We should go.'

Helen buttoned her coat. 'And what shall we do about Lisa?'

'I know what I'm going to do. I'm going to take that red hair band to the police. First thing tomorrow.'

'And Tazer?'

'I'll take her too,' Elizabeth said. 'If she'll come with me.'

They made their way back towards the caravan. The half-moon was low and bright in the clear cold sky. Tazer trotted next to Elizabeth, glancing back at the house from time to time.

'I've got my car,' Helen began, but Elizabeth indicated her own, parked some distance away. It shone in the darkness, sleek and luxurious.

Elizabeth looked at the caravan, its darkened windows, its tattered curtains. 'I have a very bad feeling,' she said. 'Very bad.'

'Well, you've been through terrible things...'

Elizabeth shook her head. 'No, worse than that. Even worse. The shadow of the past, that house...' She shuddered. 'Amelia's pain, the land being cursed... The hate mail notes talked about a second tunnel, and how the first was the true tunnel...' She gave a thin smile. 'All those years ago, I promised my child-self, to deal with the rational, with what we can prove, and here I am caught up in a terror of the supernatural…' Her eyes welled with tears. 'Well, I'll go to the police. I'll tell them all I can. I'll try not to talk about ghosts.'

'Perhaps they've seen it too.'

Elizabeth nodded. 'Perhaps they have. They can get their forensic people on to it.'

Helen smiled. Elizabeth reached out, and again, they shook hands. Then there were two car doors opened, two engines starting, two sets of headlights cutting through the frosty night.

Chad glanced at the clock that sat on his desk. It was time to go home, he thought.

He stared at his computer screen, scrolled through the text for Sunday's sermon.

This is no good, he thought. What I want to talk about is Sin. Danger. A murderer in our midst. Three men having died at the hands of someone else. I should address this, I should face this head on, this problem of evil. But this…

He scanned the words in front of him.

Clichés, he thought. Empty words of hope, that there might be meaning in it all, that out of the terrible actions of a human being we might still find reason to believe in our redemption.

And anyway, he thought, exiting the document, switching off his machine, I haven't really nailed the argument. I'm circling something just beyond my reach.

He locked up his office, switched off all the lights.

Outside it was dark and chilly, and he buttoned up his coat. The lights on the sea front were blurred by mist. The streets were deserted.

Evil, and danger. He wondered whether to be more afraid.

A distant siren sounded through the damp air. He thought about the police, that nice woman and her team, out and about.

She must think I'm mad, he thought, going on about God, questioning whether the universe has any meaning at all, when there's a real killer at large.

As it was in the beginning, is now and ever shall be, world without end…

Perhaps that's what I should have said. That God is constantly bringing the universe into being, and allowing it to go out of being. Which means we, as mere humans, have an illusion of a continuum. It might even explain cold dark matter, and the fact that we're in a matter dominated universe rather than there being symmetry between matter and anti-matter, as that physicist was trying to explain to me…

Is that really what I think? More to the point, he thought, as he walked up the hill towards the vicarage, is that the right viewpoint for a clergyman to express in an interview with the police?

A nice woman, that Berenice, he thought. He'd felt scrutinized by her, but not in an unpleasant way.

Even when he'd mentioned Helen, he'd felt she was weighing him up, as if she was going to say, what sort of marriage is that then?

A good question.

There was something about the way Helen was last night, standing there by the stove making an omelette. Something about the way she'd turned to him, a distance, as if she was elsewhere…

What sort of marriage is that, then?

A fractured marriage. One with gaping great holes, like thin ice on a lake, around which we circle, hapless, incapable.

Perhaps it can't heal. Perhaps it's too late. Perhaps when that physicist appeared in our lives it was already too late, that blasted physicist, I could kill him…

Her car was in the drive. He walked up to the house, round to the side door. Even now, he thought, I could just walk into the kitchen, she'll be sitting at the table, I can see the lights on, the steamed up windows…

I could just walk in and say it. I could say, 'I'm thinking of killing that physicist, shooting probably, cleanest way after all, can't be too difficult to get hold of a gun in these parts…'

I could say, 'You're having an affair, aren't you?'

His hand on the door.

She looked up, sitting at the table in the light, warm kitchen.

Their eyes met.

He walked in, shook the rain off his shoes, took off his coat. He heard himself begin to speak, heard himself suggest that they could have a Chinese take-away as it's a Friday night, watched her breathe again, watched as the gaps in the ice seemed to widen.

There is always, he thought, the risk of falling in and freezing to death.

Chapter Twenty-Six

Finn Brady walked along the beach, dragging a huge lump of driftwood behind him. It left a trail in the sand, next to the light prints of his trainers.

It was a wet morning, but he barely noticed the driving rain, almost horizontal in the wind, the white foam of the waves.

What am I going to do, he thought.

I ain't going to leave her. If her bad-ass father has done something…

I've got to do something.

I thought Tom would help. Went up his yard last night, and there he is telling me he ain't allowed near Hank's Tower, Feds will pick him up if they see him there…

He paused, looked out to sea. The waves were high, brown-churned.

Tom went on about the flood they said would happen. He said that's what these deaths are, 'cos there was an old tunnel and the second tunnel was cursed or something…

I thought he'd help me, Tobias. And all he did was sit there with his jars and his mixtures, and his step-Mum saying he's not allowed out and certainly not to help that Voake girl…

Finn set off again, dragging the driftwood behind him.

To Gabriel, it seemed that two things were happening at once. One was a shriek, rippling out of the windows of the house, shaking the walls. The other was a hammering at the door of the laboratory –

'Mr Voake, please Sir, please come quickly, the doctor wants you – '

The shrieking continued from somewhere in the house. The door flew open. The maid was standing there, and behind her, Doctor Knox.

He was grey-faced, silent. 'Gabriel,' he said. 'It's over.'

Gabriel faced him. 'It's over?'

'She's dead.'

'Amelia?'

'Grace.' The tone was questioning. 'Your daughter, Gabriel. The fever has claimed her.'

'But – '

The green light from the machine seemed to glow darker, seemed to fill the space around him. He tried to speak, to say, it cannot be, Grace is my salvation, Grace is the order imposed on disorder, Grace is the reason that emerges from chaos, she's the goodness that has come from bad...

'No,' he said.

'Your wife needs you,' the doctor said, and then Gabriel realized.

'That noise… Amelia – that weeping…?'

'Please go to her, Sir.' Alice touched his sleeve. He stood, unmoving, until Doctor Knox took his arm, steered him out of the laboratory, into the house.

He found himself pushed into the nursery. Amelia's wailing had settled to a quiet sobbing. She was kneeling on the floor, her arms around their daughter. He could see the child's curls, the folds of her nightdress.

'Tell me it's not true,' he said.

She looked up. Her expression was vacant, as if she could barely see him.

'Amelia…' he tried.

She began to sob again, bent over the body of their child. He knelt down beside her. Grace looked oddly limp, the fabric of her nightdress lying in strange twisted folds.

'No, no, no…' Amelia cried, her mouth buried in her daughter's curls.

His wife. His daughter. This was to be the future. This light, this cleanliness, these golden curls, leaving behind the chaos and the bleeding, the screams of pain, the choking mustard smog. There was to be order, and rays of energy, the experiment that would control chaos, that would channel the light at the heart of things, that would keep the darkness at bay.

But now all is revealed. There is no escape. The truth lies in the darkness and the chaos. When they led me, limping and resistant, *out of that ditch, I left the truth behind, in the broken body of the man I loved.*

Amelia had stopped weeping. She raised her eyes to his. He saw, in her odd expression of polite restraint, a gap too wide to breach, the beam broken, the particles too weak to jump across.

'It is too late,' she said.

'But – ' He put out a hand, touched her arm.

She shook her head. 'Grace is dead. It is too late.'

Elizabeth drove fast. Tazer shuffled and whiffled in the back seat. 'Soon be there,' she cooed at her. 'We'll get a nice police officer to look after you.' Although he probably won't give you best beef steak like you had for dinner last night, she thought to herself. 'And then you'll be reunited with your mistress,' she added. That was the most important thing, she thought, glancing at the red hair band on the seat next to her.

'No dogs, Madam,' the duty sergeant said.

'But - '

He gestured to a tattered notice on the wall behind the reception desk.

'This dog is evidence. The missing girl, daughter of the main suspect in the physics case…' She spoke loudly, and people turned to look.

'Ah. Well, in that case, Ma'am…'

He left his post, went through a security door and came back a minute later with a tall, suited man with slicked back grey hair and an unfriendly expression.

'Stuart Coles.' He offered her a hand, unsmiling, then ushered her into a tiny, windowless room.

'So,' he said. 'What's all this about?' He glanced at the dog, who was sitting close to Elizabeth's knees. The dog eyed him.

'The missing girl's dog?' He placed his phone on the desk in front of him.

She nodded. She placed the hair band on the desk. 'We found both at the caravan where she lives.'

'We?'

'Her ballet teacher. We were looking for her.'

He glanced at his mobile.

'Is Berenice here?' she said. 'DI Killick?'

His gaze seemed more distant. 'She's on another case,' he said. He looked at the hairband. 'Did you do that? Wrap it up like that?'

'I thought it was best – contamination, you know…'

He gave a small smile. 'Sure. Well…' He put his phone in his jacket pocket. 'Hand them both in at the desk.'

'The dog as well? But do you - ?'

'Sure. We'll look after him.'

'Her,' she said.

Tazer trotted at her ankles as she went back down the corridor. The duty sergeant at the desk had changed, a woman now. She barely looked up.

'I've been told to hand in this dog - '

'We don't take lost dogs.'

'But - '

She had straggling blonde hair. She peered at Elizabeth.

'I was told you'd - '

'Don't like dogs, me.'

'No.' Elizabeth tightened her grip on the lead. 'I can see that.'

She opened the car door, and Tazer jumped happily back in. More muddy footprints, Elizabeth thought. 'Just don't expect more steak, OK?'

Tazer wagged her tail.

'We'll wait for DI Killick,' Elizabeth said to her.

Ashford, Berenice thought. I wonder if the Chief has told them to expect me. I wonder how long it'll take until they call me in.

The kettle had boiled. She poured more coffee.

She flicked through the book, again.

Perhaps I've brought this on myself, she thought.

This God, that van Mielen believes in, his daughter too. Those physicists… they don't seem to need God.

And that nice vicar…

And me?

My God is a loud, angry God, the one I was raised with. The one who took my brother up to Heaven because I wasn't good enough, because I didn't deserve a brother…

Did they say that? Did I just think it? Did my mother make it clear, without putting it into words?

Is that my God now?

She reached for the plastic folders that contained the hate mail.

I wonder how long it'll take before the Chief misses these, she thought.

She read them, again, holding the plastic covers flat.

There were six, all saying roughly the same thing. That the lab was bringing evil upon us. That it had to be stopped.

Whoever's writing these notes believes that the lab is dangerous. Whoever killed these physicists believes that murder is the lesser harm.

The most recent looked slightly different. Same red pen, but the writing a bit neater, the wording more correct.

She stared at it. It was Liam Phelps who'd reported it. It had come from Iain Hendrickson. And then Iain…

The last note. The last death.

And the notes had stopped.

Perhaps the killer believes they've done their job.

Or, he's done a runner, and taken the poor kid with him.

She gazed at the red ink scrawls.

It doesn't add up. Clem Voake is a small-time crook. A dealer in firearms. These notes are impassioned, steeped in righteousness.

Perhaps the Chief was right to move me. I'm used to order. I'm used to criminals being criminal, and leaving traces, and being caught. The courts, well that's up to them, but I'm used to doing my job well. But this… this is chaos. This is like smashing atoms and trying to see stuff in the mess, muons, mesons…

Tobias's box was sitting on the kitchen table. She pulled it towards her. She fingered the tiny bottles, the plastic lion, the postcard of the painting, Adam in the Garden, he'd said… She thought about Tobias's orderly world where things could be grouped, managed, catalogued.

I am out of my depth.

What has any of this got to do with physics, or collisions? What makes three intelligent men all want to go to Hank's Tower, one after the other, all meeting their death there?

She bent to her case, and pulled out a plastic bag, in which was wrapped the green plastic lion. She took the lion out of the bag, and placed it carefully in Tobias's collection.

She clicked on her laptop. She pulled up a map, and traced lines on the screen; from the lab to the old Voake house; from the old house to Hank's Tower; from Hank's Tower to the Lab.

Liam wandered through his flat, his hair still wet from the shower. There were papers in heaps here and there, on the landing by his bedroom door, on a spare chair outside the bathroom. He pulled on a sweater, went to the kettle, opened cupboards in search of coffee.

'Breakfast, Jonas,' he said.

The dog sat at his feet, nosing at a packet of dry dog food.

'Paw, Jonas,' and the dog offered him a paw to shake.

'Good dog.' He put down the bowl of food. 'The problem is, Jonas – ' He went to the fridge, poured a glass of orange juice – 'Women. Closed book. You're lucky you don't have to bother with all that…' He glanced down at Jonas, who was watching him, one ear cocked. 'Or perhaps you don't see it that way. Impudent of me to presume, old chap…' He sipped his juice. 'I mean, I could call her. But then what? Last time I did that with a woman, got involved like that, it all went wrong, didn't it, boy? Do you remember all that dumping of possessions outside my window? And it's pouring with rain, and there's me, running around trying to save the books, and half those chemicals were radioactive. Just as well she decided to run off to Almeria with a piano tuner.'

Jonas returned to eating. 'Oh, you've heard it all before, boy.' Liam poured coffee, carried a mug over to the kitchen table. He shifted a pile of papers to clear a space, wiped some crumbs from the surface with the side of his hand, reached for his laptop. He sipped coffee, staring at the screen, idly scrolling.

'Recorded luminosity of a hundred and sixty-three point two. But you see, Jonas, at one inverse femtobarn…' He scrolled some more. 'These are weird. If these aren't strong WW bosons…' He flicked through some papers at his side, pulled out a sheet of figures. 'I'd show these to you, but you chewed the last lot.' He rang his finger along the paper. 'It's the generation of the W Boson mass. Perhaps Murdo was right about the Higgs mechanism… It still doesn't explain all this.'

It doesn't explain three killings either.

He'd had sister on the phone, 'For Christ's sake Liam, who's next? Just get away from there, it's all very well that bloke on the news going on about round-the-clock policing, you're my only living relative, well, apart from Jake but he's just my husband…'

And Lisa. And Tobias.

I ought to find out what's happened.

Helen would know.

He stood up and refilled his mug. Jonas had finished eating, and was looking at him. 'If I call her, what then? And if I don't…?' He went back to his computer and stared at the screen. 'A married woman,' he said. 'Typical of me. It's never straightforward, is it boy?'

Jonas's tail thumped loudly on the kitchen floor. Liam scrolled down his screen, scribbling numbers on the papers at his side.

Helen watched her husband. She sat with a cup of tea in front of her, her chin resting on her hands. He was spreading butter on a piece of toast.

'Elizabeth said she'd go to the police this morning.'

He looked up. 'Why?'

'I told you,' she said. 'We found the hair band. And the dog.'

'Why?' he said. He laid his knife down beside his place. 'Why are you getting so involved in all this?'

He was paper pale, the window bright behind him.

She might have said, Because I care. She might have said, Because I've got nothing else to do, nothing else to live for…

'You're just the same,' she said.

'Virginia's a parishioner,' he said, and she wondered how he knew that's what she meant. 'I didn't spend all that time with the police for fun,' he said. 'She has to have someone on her side.'

'What's she got to hide?' Helen stood up, bent to put her plate in the dishwasher.

'Hide?' His voice was sharp behind her.

'Yes. She had the book. She was dead keen to pass it on to you. Why?'

'Her husband,' he began.

'Her husband was in love with Elizabeth.'

'Your new best friend,' he said.

She stacked mugs, plates, loudly into cupboards. 'Wasn't he?' she said.

'Yes.' He stared at the table. 'Yes, he was.'

She turned to him. 'See what I mean? Too much to hide.'

'Why is that hiding anything?' The chair scraped the floor as he stood up. 'She's struggling, surely you can see that? Her husband killed, that poor boy she cares for under suspicion, all these rumours of her husband's infidelity – '

'More than rumours,' she said.

'Well you'd know all about that,' he said. 'Who went with you?'

'When?'

'When you visited the caravan and bumped into the Merletti woman.'

She breathed. 'I went alone,' she said.

A mutual pause. They stared at each other. Then he turned, picked up his jacket from the back of the chair. 'I have to see the archdeacon,' he said. 'Insurance renewal. And then…'

'And then?'

He turned back to her. 'Virginia…' he began. 'Just a short visit… after that Detective woman yesterday, Tobias is still in danger of being arrested…'

'Yes, of course,' she said.

His eyes held hers. 'I…'

She waited.

He fiddled his keys into a pocket. 'I'll be back for dinner.'

She heard the front door slam.

The house was cold. Even her studio was cold. She stood in the silence, one hand on the barre, immobile, staring at the sea, at the gathering rainclouds.

Berenice's mobile rang loudly on the table.

'Mary - ' she snatched it up.

'Are you hiding?'

'Something like that, yeah. Any news?'

'Nada. Though, what do I know, the Chief's been in hiding with his homies from the Met all morning. Nah, I just thought I'd wish you a nice weekend. Seeing as we're off the case.'

'Weekend?' Berenice looked at the rain-spattered window.

'Oh, Boss, don't tell me – '

'I just thought I'd call into the lab. They're clever guys, I can ask them all about everything.'

'Even though – '

'Yes.' Her voice was firm.

'You mean, they can take the case off the girl but they can't take the girl off the case?'

Berenice laughed. 'Something like that. What about you?'

'London, since you ask. Hen night. Remember Issy from college?'

'She's never getting married.'

'To a girl.'

'Ah.' Berenice said. 'Lucky her.'

'See you Monday. Or, tomorrow. If they cancel all leave again.'

Her phone clicked off. The kitchen seemed even quieter. Berenice put the Book into her bag, picked up her car keys and left.

I need him to save me from myself.

Helen crossed the room and sat down at the table.

I need Chad to see…

She stared into a cup of cold tea.

He's the last person I can ask. My own husband…

How has it come to this? The man I love, taking refuge in that weird cottage…

If only… if only he'd reach out to me instead.

She saw him, wind-blown, coat flapping, striding along the cliffs towards that woman's fireside. She recalled Elizabeth's words about Amelia, how she was angry with Gabriel…

A car engine approached. Perhaps he'd come back, perhaps he, too, had realized that all that was left to them was to cling together, hold fast, wait for this tide of chaos to wash back out and leave them alone once more…

The car engine faded away to silence.

The silence was shattered by the ringing of her mobile phone.

Liam, she saw, answering it.

'Hi,' she said.

His voice was low, warm, apologetic.

'Sure,' she said. 'The lab. I'll see you then.'

One tiny decision, Helen thought, accelerating away from the lights. Should I, shouldn't I… So, you say yes. And then everything follows from there, and then the decisions aren't small any more, they're huge great big things…

She turned on to the ring road out of town.

Life is too short to turn away from love. Or, life is too short to do the wrong thing.

Not a decision at all, in fact. Just fumbling my way through the chaos. Knowing that I have to see him again. Wanting so much to see him again that I can hardly breathe.

In the fields around her, the grass glinted wetly, the frost thawing in the sunlight.

Chapter Twenty-Seven

'It was you I wanted to see.' Berenice thumped her briefcase down on Liam's desk.

'Me?' He looked up at her. 'What do I know?'

Berenice pulled up a chair next to him. 'This case. It's about physics. And it's about men. And you're an expert in both.'

He laughed. 'Not me, lady. I'm an expert in neither. The truth of my work is elusive. And as for being a man… completely in the dark about that. But fire ahead.'

She smiled. 'OK. What we know is, there's something about the experiment you guys are working on. There's something that's drawn three physicists to Hank's Tower. And then, between Iain and Murdo, this Elizabeth – '

Liam held up his hand. 'That was years ago. From what I've heard, there was gossip, sure. But then Elizabeth was in Italy.'

'And then she came back.'

Liam adjusted his desk chair.

'This experiment,' Berenice pursued. 'There've been odd results.'

He nodded. 'Yes.'

'Do you want to tell me?'

He eyed her, as if making a judgement. 'It's dynamical symmetry breaking, strong WW Boson scattering.'

'Right,' she said.

'The force that arrests the growth of the collision rate is also responsible for generation of the W boson mass. That's what we're looking at.'

'Go on,' she said.

He hesitated. 'Well,' he said. 'It's all about the three generations of spin-half particles, measured in units of Planck's quantum. What we're looking at is asymmetry, where matter dominates. At the point where you're colliding protons at ten giga electronvolts, B-mesons are visible.'

'Visible how?'

'By the patterns of the particles in the collisions.'

Berenice nodded. 'Right,' she said.

There was a small silence. 'I told you I wasn't an expert,' he said.

'Sounds pretty clever to me,' she said.

He shook his head. 'If I was really clever, I'd be able to explain it in a way you'd understand. You see, however many equations you do, it can only explain a tiny part. It's like the Buddha's handful of leaves.'

'It is?'

'The Buddha, with his disciples in the forest, he holds out a handful of leaves, and he says in terms of what they could know, there are all the leaves in the forest, but they only need that. Just the handful he's offering them.'

'A scientist and a hippy too,' she said.

'You'd be surprised.'

'I thought you scientists were supposed to be finding the answer.'

'To everything?'

'Isn't that what we're paying you for?'

He laughed. 'That's what I love about all this.' He waved his arm, as if to take in the grey office walls, the piles of papers on the floor, the thin strip of light across the ceiling, the plastic blinds on the window.

'You do?' she said.

'Over at CERN,' he said, 'they're replicating the conditions of the universe when it was less than a trillionth of a second old.'

'And you're telling me they don't know why they're doing that?'

'What I'm saying is, we know what questions to ask. And we have the technology to set up the experiment to ask those questions. But no, we don't know the answer. And if we did…' He flicked at the plastic blinds, glanced outside. 'If we did, we wouldn't bother with the experiment, would we. It's a huge act of faith.'

'Oh. And there's me thinking that science was about evidence, not faith.'

'But you can't have one without the other. That's what I love about it. We're a tiny planet on the edge of a minor solar system. We're tiny life forms, on a tiny planet. We're investigating the smallest possible components of matter, smaller than anyone's ever seen. When we look outwards, we see stars, solar systems so far away they don't even exist by now. And we ask questions. We investigate it, get to know it, get to know more about it… But we can't do that without accepting, first and foremost, how little we know. We're adrift in the chaos. You have to start from that. You can call it God if you want, and then it has meaning, it has a story, a reason… but if you don't have God, if you trust in Science, as I do…' He looked up at her. 'That's what science is. Being brave in the chaos.'

'And is there still a story?'

He glanced towards the window, then back at her. 'Yes,' he said. 'There's a story. But you have to be careful about who's doing the telling of it. If it's God, you see, then you have the True Story, already written, In the beginning was the Word, all that… If it's just us, here, now, then you have to be careful. You can't just make it up. You have to be clear about what you can say about it.'

'Hence the very expensive tunnel,' she said.

'Yeah,' he said. 'Exactly.'

'And you don't mind the chaos?'

He smiled. 'I don't need my life to make sense.'

Again, the glance towards the car park.

Berenice smoothed her jacket. 'Well, that's physics covered. What about men? Murdo Maguire and Iain, and the Professor…'

His laugh faded. 'We've lost three very good scientists,' he said. 'Two of them more than very good. Irreplaceable. And in such circumstances… we're all very jumpy here, you know. Did you send those heavies to man the front gates?'

'Um…' She hesitated. 'Not me personally, no.'

'My sister thinks I need a personal body guard, not bouncers,' he went on. 'Tell me honestly…' He fixed her with a clear gaze. 'Do you think we're all in danger here?'

'Do you?' she countered.

'You're the expert,' he said.

She got up, went over to the window. She turned and faced him. 'Like you, my job involves seeing patterns in things. Seeing order in chaos. Murdo, Iain, Alan. They're all connected. There's the land sale, from the Voakes, which has got the wrong side of Clem, the old house on the edge of the lab. There's Tobias, and his connection with the book, the van Mielen thing. And…' She returned to her seat, looked up at him. 'There's the relationship between Elizabeth, Murdo and Iain.'

'They were friends,' he said.

'How much would you have known, you and the rest of the lab?'

'Good scientists are team players. They don't keep secrets.'

'Even from each other?'

His reply was measured. 'We knew, you see. Those three. We just accepted it. And then Elizabeth left, and the other two went back to normal.'

'Is that normal?' Berenice was gazing out of the window.

He didn't reply.

'"… the man who has the power to turn lead into gold,"' she said. '"Purified by one drop of baptismal water…"'

'Oh, the Book.' He sighed.

'You don't approve?'

'My view on the Book is that it's seventeenth century alchemical rubbish re-written by a nineteenth century obsessive. And that wouldn't matter, if it wasn't that poor Tobias got far too caught up in it. Murdo's wife should have kept it away from him.'

'It belonged to Elizabeth.'

'It was in her family. So what?'

Berenice shrugged. 'Sure,' she said. 'So what.'

'You want me to say it was some kind of love token? The way the men were both after it – and the Professor…' He stopped, looked at her. 'That doesn't make it true,' he said.

'No,' she agreed.

His attention had drifted away from her towards the corridor.

'However,' she went on. 'Like you, the author of the book is struggling with faith, and evidence. And like you, he's finding another way to ask questions of the chaos.'

Liam seemed to be about to say something, but then the door clicked open behind Berenice, and all she could see was the change to his face as he jumped to his feet.

'Helen.' His voice shook slightly. 'You knew where to find me?'

'Neil walked me through reception. They gave me a pass,' she said.

'You know DI – um – '

'We spoke on the phone.' Helen offered her hand.

'So we did.' Berenice got to her feet. 'We were just discussing chaos,' she said.

Virginia poked at the ash in the grate. The early frost had given way to grey cloud and the room was dull and cold.

'Love gone wrong,' she said.

Chad, still in his coat, sat on one edge of the sofa.

'Hate,' she went on. 'Hate is love gone wrong.'

He listened to the scraping of the ash.

'A few sticks of wood,' she said. 'At least they're dry. I don't usually bother, but today…'

'Not on my account,' he said.

'No,' she said. 'Not on your account.'

She laid the fire, struck a match. The flames struggled in the damp chimney, then flared into a feeble fire. She came to sit next to him. 'His birthday,' she said. 'He'd have been fourteen.'

She sat, dry-eyed, next to him. After a while, he placed one arm around her shoulders.

'Your husband, Mrs. Meyrick - ' Berenice watched the glance between Liam and Helen and wondered why she felt as if she'd said the wrong thing. 'He's been a great help to that family.'

'Tobias.' Helen was unbuttoning her coat. 'Poor kid.' She turned to Liam. 'I met Elizabeth. At the caravan. She was so helpful.'

He was gazing at her as she stood in her jeans, her pastel pink cashmere, her coat slung over one arm, her hair loose around her shoulders. Tall, and poised. Like a fashion model, Berenice thought. No wonder he's looking at her like that.

Helen turned to Berenice. 'She was going to come and see you. We found Lisa's hair band at the old house, she's disappeared from the caravan but her dog was there, looking terrible - did she tell you? She said she'd call at your offices - '

'I – um – I haven't been there.'

'Perhaps she handed them into someone else. One of your team – '

Berenice could see the question in Helen's eyes.

'We were really worried about her,' Helen said.

'A dog – she was going to hand it in?'

Helen shrugged. 'She wasn't that keen on keeping him, I don't think. Mud all over her flash car…'

Liam was smiling at her.

'I'll go to HQ and see what they say.' Berenice seemed reluctant to move.

Beyond the slatted blinds, the sky was growing dark.

'It's going to rain,' Liam said.

'This land dispute – ' Berenice turned to him. 'How much of a dispute was it?'

'All I know is,' Liam began, 'Alan was very keen to get the land from whoever owned it – the Voakes, you say? I don't know much about it. And the sale was agreed just before he died.'

Berenice picked up her bag. 'I should be going,' she said. At the door she turned to Liam. 'These recent results – they're not what you were expecting?'

'They're odd, sure.'

'WW Boson scattering sort of odd?'

'Yeah.' He smiled. 'That sort of thing.'

'Not bad for a handful of leaves,' she said. 'Thanks for the teachings.'

'And you call me a hippy?' he said.

She returned his smile. 'See you around.'

It was as if the tension in the room drifted out into the corridor with her. Her last glance backwards, as the door shut, took in the two of them, Helen taking a step towards him as he reached out his arms to her.

The flames crackled in the grate.

'There is nothing,' Virginia said. 'In the gaps. There's silence. And nothing. Murdo knew that too.'

Chad withdrew his hand from her shoulder. He sat, motionless, next to her.

'He knew it the way a scientist knows it,' she went on. 'Matter. Anti-matter. The nothing in the gaps between the smallest smallest particles. The silence of space. That was how he knew it. As a scientist.'

'Whereas you – '

She turned to him. 'When there's life, and breathing, and you're listening to the in breath and the out breath, and in between... in between there's a gap. And you listen, the breath in, the breath out... and they get slower and slower, and the gaps get longer and longer... and in those gaps there's silence and nothingness. And terror, I suppose...' She turned back to face the fire. 'When he stopped breathing, I listened to the silence. And I knew it would always be with me.'

The sticks of wood shifted, settled. Chad moved his hand so it was touching hers.

'Perhaps that's what you'd call God?' She turned, slightly.

'I'm not sure,' he said. 'The God beyond words, perhaps.'

'The gaps are still there,' she said. 'The nothing. Your God can't fill those gaps.'

'No,' he agreed.

They stared at the fire. The tired plaster of the walls seemed to brighten in the firelight.

'But in the gaps,' he said. 'Where God is. There is love.'

'Love?' Her voice was harsh. 'Do you really think that?'

He turned to face her. 'I don't mean easy love. I don't mean happiness, or joy, or comfort… I mean the love where in our suffering God walks by our side.'

She shook her head. 'It's not something I know. Does he walk next to you?'

He met her eyes. 'No,' he said. 'I wouldn't say he does.'

She went to the grate. 'Your wife – '

'Yes?'

She picked up a log from the basket.

'She must be in mourning too.'

'Not like yours.'

'No,' she agreed. She placed the log on the fire. 'Murdo and I, we didn't survive, you see. The silence. The nothing.'

'No.'

She came and sat next to him again. 'She's far away from you.'

He wasn't sure if it was a question or a statement. 'Yes,' he said. 'Yes, she is.'

She turned to him. She seemed full of life, her features softened by the firelight, her eyes bright as she gazed at him. Once again, he reached out and took her hand.

After a moment she withdrew from him. She stood up, brushing ash from her skirt. 'He'll be back soon. Tobias. He said the bus would be late, repairs on the main road. We need to consider him.'

'We do?'

'Of course.' She looked down at him. 'He's still a suspect, he's taken refuge in all that magic. He's still afraid.'

'The police must know that he can't possibly have done these things.'

'I keep telling him that,' she said. 'I've told him that we'll keep him safe.'

'We?' He gazed up at her.

She smoothed at her skirt. She looked towards the window. 'It's getting dark,' she said.

Falling. Helen stared at the darkened hotel window as the word touched her thoughts.

Falling.

His breathing, next to her. The tangle of white sheets, the white floodlights of the car park softening the darkness of the room.

How had this happened?

She could trace their path, of course. The walk to his car, the ring road, twilight, car park, the swish of doors, the awkwardness, his joke - something about a loyalty card - the cool blank look from the receptionist. And then no words, no jokes, just clothes ripped off, just the aching gasping breathing of desire, the play of limbs, the hot, sweating, timeless hours of pleasure and possession.

And here I am, she thought. Here, in darkness, in these clean white sheets. And next to me, his breathing. Rising. And falling.

He rolled sleepily towards her. 'I love you,' he murmured.

'No you don't,' she said, into his chest.

'Do.' He raised himself on an elbow, looked down at her. She saw the curves of his jaw, the stubble on his chin, the downy hair of his chest, his smooth muscularity, the dark yearning of his gaze, and felt once more a convulsion of desire.

'Prove it,' she said.

The flames were dying down. The fire made a dim glow in the twilight. 'Shall I put on another log?' he asked.

'Are you staying?' She went over to the table, switched on the lamp.

'Do you want me to?'

She gave a small shrug.

'I mean,' he went on, 'as it's his birthday.'

She turned to him. 'All these years, I've done this day alone. It makes no difference to me.'

The light lent her a kind of grace, her hair in soft curls, her skirt in smooth folds.

'And if I want to stay?' he said. 'If I don't want you to be alone?'

'You have a home to go to.' Her voice was flat.

'It'll be empty,' he said, and as he spoke he knew, with a pit-of-the-stomach certainty, that it was true.

She watched him. 'If that's the case,' she said at last, 'then the answer doesn't lie in staying here. Does it?'

'You and Murdo,' he began, wondering where his words would lead him. 'And – '

'Elizabeth van Mielen?' she said.

'Yes.'

'No one loved that man as I did,' she said. 'Our child's death was the ending of us.' She sat down heavily on the sofa again. 'Jacob's death was sudden, of course. One minute here, the next gone. But what I didn't realize was, death is also a slow, slow thing. And we died with him.'

She was sitting very close to him. It occurred to him that he was waiting for her to speak again, waiting for her to fill in a gap, as if there was more to the story, and her silence now seemed like a deliberate withholding.

The fire was turning to ash, with wisps of smoke.

'Perhaps I should go,' he said. He stood up. Then, looking down at her, he said, 'Is there more you want to say?'

She met his eyes. 'No', she said. 'Should there be?'

He shook his head.

'It'll take you longer,' she said. 'Main road closed for repairs.'

The room had grown cold. He reached for his coat. 'I'll call you tomorrow,' he said. 'Check you're OK.'

She nodded.

On the doorstep he touched her arm. 'I'll pray for you,' he said. 'In the gaps, and the silences.'

She reached up, then, and all of a sudden, kissed his cheek. 'Thank you,' she said.

The door shut, and he was out in the cold evening air.

The headlights cut across dark lanes. Chad drove slowly, not wanting to go home, not wanting to face the empty silence of the vicarage. At the roundabout the signs said 'Diversion.' The road was unfamiliar, but signs still said Town Centre, so he followed them, until he found himself heading away from the town, somehow, and the signs were saying Canterbury.

Whether he knew the church was there, or whether it was chance, a random event, or even the Lord's will, but there it was, a steeple in the headlights, a flash of gothic windows… He parked, got out, his breath making mist in the cold night.

He tried the doorway. Locked, of course. A funny sort of church. An archway in thick grey stone. The gravestones too seemed old, with odd carvings, though he couldn't read the dates.

The half-moon had risen above the trees. He stood in the graveyard. He thought about how Virginia had hesitated, there on her doorstep. He wondered what she was hiding from him. He wondered why he didn't want to go home. He wondered what he was afraid of finding there.

He walked slowly back along the overgrown path.

A man's face emerged from the branches. Chad stopped, stared, his heart racing. The face stared back.

Chad wondered whether to speak. He breathed, took a step forward.

The face was empty-eyed and still, and made of stone, Chad realized as he approached. A carving of a man's head emerging from a tree. Chad put out his hand and touched the rough jaw, the tangles of hair entwined with leaves.

There were other carvings, Chad saw. Another tree, a snaked wrapped round its trunk, a man and a woman carved on each side. The fall, of course, Adam and Eve. And then the third, the Holy Cross itself, and Jesus crucified. All in rough stone, but the details stood out, the patterns on the leaves, the apple in the woman's hand, the almost friendly smile of the snake, the wounds in the body of Our Lord.

Was it a progression? he wondered. From something ancient and Pagan, through the Fall, to our redemption of sin by Christ's death. Or, just a commentary, a series of stories. Or even, a commission, and the sculptor just doing as he was told…

In every case, a tree. A tree of life. He looked back towards the church, and in the moonlight it looked squat and ancient, as if it had been here forever, long before the Christian story, bearing witness to other tales, far older, even, than our own.

Life, it's beginning and its end.

And it still goes on, he thought, in the circle of the tunnel down the road, telling the story of the first few moments of the universe itself.

For Newton, it was still the work of God. In the discovery of the vacuum, the Great Nothing, God's starting point. For those chaps down the road, they don't need God. In their great, silent, colder-than-cold Nothing where the truth will be revealed, they have no need of God. I don't suppose that friend of my wife's believes in God.

Perhaps that's what she needs.

It was a sudden, jolting thought. Chad sat down, breathless, on a gravestone.

That scientist, sitting in my house, all warmth and smiles. While my wife and I, living in emptiness, struggling with childlessness, and all I preach is God and love...

I've driven her away.

The Green Man seemed to watch him in the darkness. A story too ancient to be told.

He stared back at the stone face. He thought about the sculptor, echoing some ancient truth, now lost. He gazed at the crucifix, another version of man emerging from a tree, but in this case a tale of humanity divine, a God in human form.

A promise of redemption.

Chad stood up, stamping his feet against the cold.

And what if it, too, is an empty promise? What if this God, who so loved the world that he gave us his Son, is no more or less true than the hurtling particles in the gleaming tunnel, or this savage ancient face that stares me out, telling me a story that I cannot understand.

He fished in his pocket for the car keys. The graveyard had a pale sheen in the moonlight, in the frosty air, as he walked back down the drive.

He started the car engine, picturing his home. One version, cold and dark; the other, warm, illumined, his wife seated at the kitchen table.

He turned back towards the lane. Whether present or absent, he thought – the truth is, that she's left me.

Helen sat in her living room, watching the slow tick of the carriage clock.

He is with Virginia, she thought.

I'm back home, showered, changed, it's now nearly eleven, and my husband is not here.

He is with that woman.

Which of us has done this?

She went to the window, stared out into the night.

Then she rushed to the pages, snatched them up, read Amelia's words, seeing a new sense in them.

'It is over, my husband said to me. It is the ending. And now I write these words, a woman alone, with no husband and no child. And I say to him again, though he is far away, which of us is to blame? Which of us has brought about this destruction, this catastrophe? Were I to blame him, then he could turn to me and place the blame on me. Yet am I blameless.'

Helen held the pages in her hands. She placed them back in the folder.

A car engine, a distant hum, approaching.

I am to blame, she thought. Whatever he has done… I am to blame.

The gravel on the drive. The engine stops. My husband, coming home.

I will never make love with Liam again.

And my marriage is over.

Berenice drove fast through the dark lanes.

'Bastard – Stuart fucking Coles – Bastard…'

The brakes screeched on a corner.

'Bastard – to take me off the case and then do that…'

She'd gone from the lab to HQ. She'd gone to the Chief's office, asking to see him. He'd refused to meet her. Ben, in the corridor, stopped her, told her that the woman from the lab had come in with evidence, Lisa's dog, of all things, he'd sent her away…

'Sent her away?'

She'd gone straight to his office then, asked him straight out, Lisa's our main witness, her dog is a gift, the best way to find her, if she's still in the country –

He'd laughed. 'You can take on a missing person's case if you want, Miss Killick.'

'Her father is our main suspect.'

'We're doing all we can.'

'Why didn't you impound the dog?'

He'd sat, a silent sneer on his lips.

And then she'd realized. 'She asked for me, didn't she? And you wouldn't admit I was off the case.'

The sneer had stayed, unchanged. He'd said nothing more, just waved towards the door.

Her car juddered to a halt outside her house.

She slammed her front door, threw down her bag on the shabby sofa.

Saturday night, she thought. A girl should be out partying.

Berenice twitched back the grey-ish net curtains and stared out at the street. The city lights seemed to vibrate with beats of music, the shrieks of girlish laughter.

And here I am, she thought, with only a book, a folder full of hate mail and a box of weird toys for company.

"The Philosopher's stone is a fixed, subtle, concentrated fire which does these things. Men greater than I have explored its power. But what I know to be true, is that Fallen Man must rise again. He must be united to the Divine Light, from which by disobedience he was separated. A flash or tincture of this must come or he can no more discern things spiritually than he can distinguish colours naturally without the light of the sun."

She closed the book.

No way, she thought. No way those guys at the lab would take this stuff seriously.

So, what were they fighting over? What was it about the sale of the Voake house, that led them one by one to Hank's Tower?

And as for the way that boy today was looking at the vicar's wife…

I nearly said to her, Don't do it girlfriend. I've seen enough in my time, not scientists, mind you, crime reporters, but still, I can tell a cheat when I see one.

Although, that Liam, maybe not a cheat exactly. Just a man.

She plumped the tired velvet cushions on the worn sofa.

But what do I know? A cheating hack might be better than nothing.

But then she remembered. She remembered the silences, the unanswered texts, phone calls going to voice mail. The sudden flights from her flat, pulling on of clothes, mumbled excuses, parents evenings, 'got to be there, she'll be suspicious otherwise'… Hopes raised, hopes dashed. Hopes so trampled underfoot that they turned to – what? To rage, certainly. Hatred, perhaps. Cynicism too.

And in the end, came that day on the doorstep, refusing to let him in, telling him his wife was welcome to him, throwing all his clothes out into the street, into the rain, a cliché, sure, but God it was fun…

The affair, once the solid core of her life, had drifted to the edges, had become as easy to discard as bubble wrap.

And now here I am, with only long dead madmen for company. In the hope that they'll lead me to a killer.

She yawned, went to the kitchen, put on a kettle, opened cupboards in search of peppermint tea.

Chapter Twenty-Eight

Sunday lunch, Helen thought. Cooking for my husband. Normal life.

Perhaps everything's going to be all right.

The night before, Chad had come back late. 'The road was up,' he'd said. 'Had to drive around the long way.' He'd talked about stone carvings in a church, a Green Man. 'I know that church,' she'd said. 'Out on the marshes? St Bruin's. I passed it once…' but he'd hardly looked at her.

After a while she'd gone to bed. She had lain awake, sleepless, hearing him typing downstairs.

She tossed potatoes with salt and rosemary. If this is normal life, she thought, why do I feel so afraid?

Berenice checked the address again. She knocked on the brass lion's head on the red-painted door.

The door opened and Elizabeth stood there.

'Detective Inspector Killick,' Berenice said.

'Oh,' Elizabeth said. 'Thank goodness.'

She led the way through the black-and-white tiled hall.

'Please take her away,' she said.

The dog was curled up on a newly-upholstered antique chair.

'I don't know why I agreed to keep her,' Elizabeth was saying, 'but your underling was so reluctant… Do sit down.'

'My underling,' Berenice said, and smiled.

The room had pale walls, white window blinds. In the stripped, clean fireplace stood an abstract bronze sculpture.

Elizabeth took a seat on the sofa, which was large and maroon and matched the thick rug that almost covered the polished wooden floor. She eyed the dog again.

Berenice saw the well-cut trousers, the camel cashmere sweater, the slick of lipstick.

The droopy wife, she thought.

She settled on another antique chair. 'So, you found the dog – '

'Yes. And this.' Elizabeth held out the hair band in its plastic bag. 'It's Lisa's. Helen was sure of it.'

Berenice noticed the odd mixed accent, the hint of American with a slight Italian lilt.

'We were at the old house. The Voake house. We were looking for Lisa.'

'But she wasn't there. Just the dog.'

Elizabeth nodded.

'So - ' Berenice leaned back on her chair. 'What do you know about Clem Voake? Apart from the fact he seems to be running a gun racket from the edge of your lab?'

'Very little. His family and mine are distantly connected.'

'Would he have a grudge against the lab?'

Elizabeth frowned. 'He seems to have. If we assume it was him writing those notes. And Alan, our chief, bought the Voake land from under him. But it was never his, he just thought that Digby would leave it to him. God knows why he wanted it, you've seen the house, it's a wreck.'

Berenice nodded at her. 'And the book?'

Elizabeth sighed. 'The book.'

'It has your surname in it. Johann van Mielen, it says. Your maiden name.'

Elizabeth smiled at her. 'It turns out, I came home. Without even realizing it. Or maybe, there aren't that many places to do physics. Johann's cousin came over to the States, before the First World War, and his offspring produced my father.'

'How did you end up with the book?'

'Amelia must have passed it on to our lot, somehow.'

'And the Voakes? Gabriel, in the book? And Clem?'

Elizabeth sighed. 'I wish I knew more. Ask Neil, he knows more about my family history than I do.'

Berenice met her eyes. 'Why did the book end up with Virginia?'

'It was of no interest to me,' Elizabeth said. 'Some weird pseudo-scientific ramblings from a distant ancestor.'

'And it was interesting to her?'

'To Murdo,' Elizabeth said. 'A gift,' she added. 'From me to him. He loved that book.' She gave a brief, soft smile.

'She was keen to get rid of it, Chad said.'

Elizabeth's gaze was even. 'I'm not at all surprised.'

On her luxury chair, the dog stirred, stretched, settled again.

'Dr Merletti,' Berenice began. 'Your relationship with Murdo… and Iain…'

'We were friends. The three of us.'

'You used to go to Hank's Tower.'

Elizabeth smiled. 'We did, yes. We'd take wine, look out to sea, watch the sunset…'

'Why Hank's Tower?'

'Why not? And anyway, we had a joke, about the old tunnel there, how we could set up our own private collider.'

'What old tunnel?'

Elizabeth looked at her. 'It's mentioned in the book, those pages at the back, Amelia's ones.'

'I haven't seen those.'

'Ah.'

'Am I missing anything?' Berenice threw her a look.

'Just the pain of an unhappy woman. And maybe a map, though I think that was lost.'

'A map?'

'Amelia's husband made this tunnel, supposedly. And he left a map. It was said to have an entrance underneath Hank's Tower. We never found it. I guess it was flooded years ago.'

Berenice glanced at the bronze shape in the fireplace. It looked vaguely humanoid. A skull? she wondered. 'Dr Merletti – these terrible events at the lab… do you have any idea what might be the cause?'

Elizabeth shook her head. 'Alan Moffatt was an angry man. He'd take dislikes to people. Me, for example. There were grudges, certainly. But the others…' Her face clouded. She shook her head.

'Do you feel endangered?'

'No more than anyone else. In fact, probably less. Whoever's doing this, if he's going for physicists, he might think they're all men. It's a common mistake.'

'Yes, like Detective Inspectors. They're always men too.'

Elizabeth gave a thin smile.

'Was Murdo happy, in those days?' Berenice asked.

Elizabeth gazed towards the windows. 'We were happy, yes.'

'But he was married. With a son – '

'No. No son. Not in those days. Jacob came along later. Murdo was so sure he was infertile…' Her words tailed away.

A miracle child. Berenice remembered what Virginia had said.

'Ghosts,' Elizabeth said, suddenly. 'This case is full of them. Peppered with them.' She looked at Berenice. 'Although, I expect you police, with your rationality, your quest for evidence…'

'Ghosts?' Berenice said.

'There's an old soldier. A wounded soldier. He walks the lab. Loads of people have seen him.'

'Aren't you rational too, you physicists?'

Elizabeth sighed. 'We're going through terrible times,' she said. 'The Voake family… Amelia had great loss in her life. She had a daughter who died too, a little girl. Neil says there's a grave in a funny old church, up on the marshes.' She sighed. 'It's the past, you see. The shadows it casts. It's like the book. For Johann, it's about purity, but spiritual purity. If you're aiming to turn lead into gold, you have to be a certain kind of person. But then later, for Gabriel, it's still about purity. The Aether, the fifth essence,' she said. 'The truth beyond which there is nothing more to say. And even for us, trying to balance matter with anti-matter…' She gazed, unseeing, at the floor.

'This ghost,' Berenice prompted.

Elizabeth met her eyes. 'I think he's Amelia's brother, Guy. He was best friends with her husband, Gabriel. He was a physicist too, involved with the aether experiment. Until he died in the War.'

'And why should he be an unquiet spirit?' Berenice asked.

Elizabeth shook her head. 'I don't know.

She looked up at Berenice. 'You must think I'm mad.'

'No,' Berenice said. 'I had a brother who died. I know about hauntings.'

A quiet drizzle spattered the windows.

Elizabeth's eyes welled with tears. 'I loved them both, you see. Can you understand that?'

Berenice gave a small nod.

'For many women… I might seem unnatural…' Elizabeth twisted her manicured fingers together.

'I wouldn't dream of judging – '

' - but Murdo was the love of my life. And yet, in the end, I lost him.' She stretched out her legs, re-crossed them. 'What I've learned in this, is that it's always the Wife who wins. Always. Anyone who thinks otherwise is deluding herself.' She smiled, wearily. 'When you people allow us a funeral, she will be his widow. She will have the rightful place.' She dabbed at her eyes.

The dog began to whimper.

'You'd better take her away,' Elizabeth said. 'I've run out of steak.'

His feet on the pulpit steps seemed to echo through the church. Chad, ordering the notes for his sermon, took in the sparse congregation. Joyce Benfield, with her sister - Lilian, was it, he had been told once… And Mrs. Lynch, arms folded, as if already anticipating a point of theology with which she was bound to disagree.

Chad glanced down at his typed-out words. This had all made sense, very late last night, as he'd worked through his ideas.

'" And Jesus took the Blind Man by the hand and led him out of the town; and when he had spit on his eyes, and put his hands up on him, he asked him if he saw anything. And the blind man looked up and said, 'I see men like trees, walking.'"

He'd sat downstairs, at the kitchen table, in the silent house, his wife, sleepless, he knew, upstairs, and he'd trawled the sacred texts for healing, for a miracle.

'In Biblical times,' he began, facing the congregation, 'being ill was also about being unclean, being spiritually exiled in some way. Not something that can be cured by a couple of aspirin…'

The arms folded themselves more tightly.

'When we hear these ancient tales, we have to remember that this is a different way of telling a story. The distinction about what's true, and what's false, falls away. There is a blurring of fact and fiction.'

The two Benfield sisters glanced at each other.

'A man with leprosy can be cured with the right words. A woman troubled by demons can have them dismissed. It's important – ' he raised his head, surveyed them all – 'it's important to be open to the possibility of these stories.'

His words filled the church. The thoughts of the congregation too, whispered between the pillars of stone… if it's a three pound bird it better be put in the oven as soon as I get back… Perhaps it should have been an each-way bet on the Kempton Park two-thirty… Mother does hate lunch being late… Look at that damp wall, I don't suppose we'll ever get the funds to fix it now Robinson's gone…

Chad came to the last page. A brief burst of sunlight through the stained glass. His audience seemed to fade beyond the wash of colour. He spoke again.

'…and to finish, I would say, that whatever the story is, it is nothing, without Love. That is the message of the Gospels, and it is as true now as it was then.'

Chad folded up his notes, and descended the pulpit steps.

'Dad – ' Lisa's voice shook with fear.

'What is it?' He was hunched over a pistol, polishing it.

'Dad – you've got to let us out of here.'

'We'll be OK, you and me. We'll be OK.' His fingers moved feverishly to and fro.

'Dad – you've been doing that for hours.'

He looked up, blankly. He went back to the polishing.

'We've run out of water.'

'There's lots of water.'

She looked at the rising puddles of sea water at their feet.'

'I'm hungry, Dad.'

'When it's safe, we'll go. When it's safe…'

'And when's that, Dad?'

Again, the blank look.

She could hear the wind rattling the rotten wood above them. She could hear the rhythmic swishing of the waves.

And the faint barking of a dog.

She strained to listen. Was that really her?

No. No dog. A moment of hope faded to despair. Lisa imagined her dog, circling, barking, sniffing at the blocked door.

And even if she did come back, what good is that? She'd be out there, loyally standing at her post, waiting for her mistress.

When we drown, she'll drown with us.

Berenice allowed her car to roll to a stop. Rain hammered on the roof, on the windscreen. The ruined tower was black against the dark grey sea.

'… that the great flood will wash all clean…'

Was that what he'd said, the author of the book. Water, the purifier, and yet also the destroyer.

And here I am, she thought, looking out to sea, facing the flood. With a missing girl, a father who's killed. And with only a dog to help me.

What am I doing?

Elizabeth had been effusive in her thanks, 'I so appreciate you taking her, she's called Tazer, by the way, yes I know, that's Lisa for you…'

An odd woman. Something so detached about her. Perhaps that's what you need if you're smashing particles for a living.

An outsider, in a way.

Perhaps they say the same of me.

Certainly now. I used to head a team. I used to have Mary at my side. And now…

She turned to look at the dog, who sat, waiting, breathing.

'Now there's just me and you, kid.'

The dog eyed her.

The book was on the seat next to her. She brushed the leather cover with her fingertips.

'There's something about all this, you see, Tazer. What a crap name for a dog. And a girl dog at that...' The dog panted, her head on one side. 'Something that woman wasn't saying. Or am I going mad? Does this book drive you mad, maybe? So that you end up chasing the book. And in the end, you're here, at Hank's Tower. And dead.' She stared out at the tower, blurred by the rain.

A need for revenge, she thought. Like the hate mail, with its determination that the flood would come and wash us from our sins...

Something buried, some deep wrong, emerging into the light.

Murdo ended up with the book, because of Elizabeth.

And Alan...

Alan bought the land.

She flicked through the pages.

'...the Tree of Life, the Lord emerging from the Tree, the first Adam and the last. Who can say, I am worthy of this knowledge....' 'Entelechia... whereby matter comes to be the thing in itself...' 'One drop of baptismal water may be equal to the flood of Noah in washing clean our sins. At that moment does the man stand on the threshold, where there is no time, no God, where the moment endures forever.'

She closed the book. She stared at the angry sea, the driving rain. She turned to the dog.

'Come on, kid, let's get wet.'

She got out of the car. She picked the hair-band out of its wrapper, and gave it to Tazer.

Tazer sniffed at it. She jumped down from the car, still sniffing. She began to circle, her nose in the sand, then, barking loudly, headed for Hank's Tower.

Lisa heard it first, the barking of a dog.

It's Taze, she thought. They've found us.

'What the fuck is that - ' Her father stared through the darkness. 'Your fucking dog - ?' He looked at his phone. 'It's morning. Were we asleep?'

'You were,' she said. He had gradually slumped sideways, until he'd ended up asleep and snoring. She had stayed awake all night, watching him, hearing the sea encroach, hearing it withdraw again. The water levels had risen with the tide, lapping in the mud only feet away from them. There'd been sirens, police cars, and she'd thought at first they'd come to rescue her, but they too had faded with the dawn.

The barking drew nearer.

Clem stumbled to his feet. 'That's it, girl - ' He moved towards the door, and for a moment, a brief moment of relief, she thought he'd changed his mind, that he was going to let her go. But all he did was kick the beam to check it was still there. Then he went to the bench and began to drag it, too, towards the door.

'Dad – what you doing?'

'Your fucking dog. She'll bring the feds, won't she?'

'If we stay here, Dad – '

'We'll be safe,' he said. The bench left thick gouges in the mud. In the thin torch light Lisa could see wires, dials, churned to the surface.

'Dad – if we stay here we'll die.'

'I'm not having them stealing from me.' He stood back, panting with effort. The bench, too, was blocking the door. 'All my life they took my dreams away. They won't do it now. Not now.'

Lisa began to cry. Cold, wet, hungry, she crouched down in the mud, among the old wires. At her feet something glittered in the torchlight. She dug into the mud, picked it up. A watch. An old one, with a chain.

She held it in her hand and gazed at it. She wondered how it had come to be here, who had owned it before. She wondered if he, too, had died in the mud, and his watch was all that was left of him.

Tazer was standing by Hank's Tower, barking at an ancient strip of wood. Berenice approached. 'Here?'

The dog barked in reply.

She approached the wood, saw that it was a door. 'Holy crap, Taze,' she said. 'If they're in there, they're in trouble.'

Tazer barked and jumped, running to and fro.

Berenice grabbed her collar. 'More to the point – if we go in alone, given his passion for firearms – we'll be in trouble too.'

She dragged the protesting dog back towards the car, grabbed her phone, clicked on Mary's number, heard it go to voicemail.

'Mary – I've found the missing kid. Holed up with her Dad. Call me.'

Helen heard Chad's car on the drive as she was putting the roast potatoes back into the oven. She heard his key in the door, looked up, 'They're not quite ready,' she smiled.

He gazed at her blankly.

'Are you all right?' she said.

He leaned one hand on the kitchen table, standing stiff and awkward in his coat.

'Your sermon…?' she began.

He shook his head. 'I don't suppose they heard it. It was about truth, and stories, and how we all hear the stories that we need to hear.'

'It sounds very interesting,' she said.

He was still staring at her. 'You're having an affair, aren't you?' he said.

Chapter Twenty-Nine

'I have no husband. I have no child. I, Amelia van Mielen, am once more alone. With these pages I finish my story.' Amelia lay down her pen next to the bottle of ink.

The pages lay on the mahogany desk in front of her. At her side, a vase of white roses caught a shaft of sunlight from the open window. From the garden there wafted the scent of rosemary.

Rosemary for remembrance, she thought.

There is nothing more to say.

I wanted so little in life. A home in which to raise my child. The love of my husband.

All of it is gone. My child, my home. And the love of my husband was never mine.

'I look around at this place I have called my home, and I know that soon it will no longer be mine. I shall turn my back on this plate and these cloths, the candles, the silverware. I shall take my leave of it all. I have no husband. I have no child. I, Amelia van Mielen, am once more alone. With these pages I finish my story.'

Helen closed the rose-covered folder.

I have no husband.

He had been hushed and pale, his voice tight with rage, standing at the kitchen table. 'That smarmy physicist,' he'd said.

And Helen, sunk onto a chair, her guts twisting with misery.

'How often? Where? In this house – '

'No,' she said. 'Not here.'

'His place? Or hotels, perhaps? How sordid.' He stared at her, as if at a stranger. 'How did you become such a person?'

He appeared to be wanting an answer. She shook her head, staring at the table.

'I suppose you'll say I'm to blame – '

'No,' she said.

'Good. Because I'm not. It was your choice. Was it his cute dog? Is that what I'm lacking?'

'Chad, please…'

'Please what?'

She raised her eyes to his.

His gaze was fiery. 'At the risk of sounding like a clergyman,' he said, 'I must remind you, we made vows. In church. To love, honour, to renounce all others… Didn't we?'

Again, waiting for an answer. She nodded.

'So, there is nowhere to go from here. Is there?'

'Chad – '

'Is there?' he repeated, his voice loud.

'If you say so,' she murmured.

'I do say so.'

After that, there had been no more words. Just sounds, coat buttoned up, briefcase gathered up, front door slamming, car revving, fading away.

And now here she sat, in the debris, with the dishes of a burnt Sunday roast cooling around her.

Tazer sat in the back of the car, whimpering. Berenice surveyed the empty, rain-soaked beach. She dialled Mary's number again, left another message.

'Not a soul here. I saw a kid, a lad, dragging a piece of driftwood, but he took one look at me and legged it. The girl's here, and her dad, I reckon. I need back-up. Ring me – '

The sound of a car. A sleek, black sports car appeared at her side. A woman got out of it, her tailored raincoat flapping in the wind.

Berenice wound down her window.

'Dr Merletti - ?'

'I thought you might need a hand,' she said.

Lisa held the watch in her hand. The dog had gone away. The torchlight was fading as the batteries began to die.

Her father was digging in the mud, scrabbling through the puddles with his bare hands, while the sea lapped under the brick wall. The tide must be coming in again, Lisa thought.

She wondered how high it would come up this time.

Clem was murmuring… 'if the other stuff was there, then they'd be there too…' He dug deeper, found something, pulled at it. A ragged piece of something… leather. 'This is it,' he said. 'Well done, girl. Of course he'd have put it with his other stuff. Under his bench… I should have dug here before.' He grabbed the torch, shone it at the square of leather in his hand. 'The deeds,' he said. 'The deeds to the house. That's why everyone came here. Moffatt knew they were here, but he didn't know about the tunnel, did he? Only I know this place.' His voice was raised, jubilant. 'They can't take it away from me now, can they?' He slipped one finger inside the folder. Pieces of rotten leather fell into the mud. 'The deeds…' he was murmuring. He pulled out a scrap of paper, a fragment, held between finger and thumb. 'They've… but…' He opened the folder and peered into it, shining the torch towards it. 'But…'

'Dad… the sea…'

The torch fell from his hand. She picked it up. He was holding the folder open, shaking out tiny pieces of paper. They scattered like leaves on to the wet ground.

He stared at them. 'They can't take it away from me. I fought them for this…'

'Dad – we've got to get out of here.'

He shook his head.

'Dad – even if you've killed – '

His face was shadowed in the dim light. 'I had to,' he said. 'He weren't expecting it, see. Fist into his face, he were gone then.

And then up there…' He jerked his head in the direction of the tower above them. 'They fall,' he said. 'You watch them. Tip them over the edge, them bricks at the top. At first they look like a man, a big heavy lump of human being. But then, falling, they get smaller and smaller. And then there's the splash, long time after. They're just a black speck after that. Just the sea and the rocks. You have to get the tide right…'

He fell silent.

Lisa clutched the watch in her hand. She sat, dry-eyed with despair. She watched the scraps of paper floating in the rising water, and wondered what it felt like to drown.

'I was at home, you see, picking dog hairs off my sofa…' Elizabeth was sitting in the passenger seat of Berenice's car. 'And I thought, that poor girl. And here's me, her closest relative after her god-awful father.'

'What made you come here?' Berenice watched the rain through the misted-up windscreen.

'I don't know. I was just driving around wondering what to do, and I saw your car, and I thought… I don't know what I thought. When I saw your car, well, I thought that was odd. I thought you'd have back-up, you know, a whole police force, a team…'

'It's complicated,' Berenice said.

'Being an outsider?' Elizabeth said.

Berenice nodded.

There were voices, shouts. Berenice opened the car door. 'It's OK,' she said to Elizabeth. 'Here's the cavalry. And he's still got his driftwood with him.'

Finn was walking towards the car. Next to him, walked Tobias. 'I brought him, Miss. I made him come. I said, Lise is there and she needs you.'

Berenice got out of her car. 'It's kind of you – but this is dangerous. You have to understand. The man is armed. I'm waiting for my team to arrive – '

Tazer jumped out of the car, and ran down to the tower, to the old wooden door. She barked and growled and jumped at the door.

Tobias turned to Berenice. 'I don't think there's time to wait any more.' He began to walk, stride across the stones, towards the tower.

'Stop – ' Berenice called after him. 'I can't have this – what if he gets shot – what if – '

Finn put up his hand to silence her. 'Ain't no one going to sit on the sidelines no more, Miss.'

Barking. Loud barking. 'Taze,' Lisa said. She stumbled to her feet. 'Tayza,' she began to shout.

'What - ?' Clem was on his feet too.

'We're here,' Lisa was shouting.

'Shut it, girl – '

'Tayze – ' Clem's hand was clamped across her mouth.

Lisa struggled in his grip. He kicked the torch and the light died.

'I won't let them take it away,' Clem was saying. 'Not now. No one's going to take what's mine…'

A crash. Shouting, footsteps. A rattling of the heavy door. The beam wedged fast across it, the bench alongside.

Another crash. The tearing of rotten wood, as the door was beaten down. In the shaft of pale light, a pair of hands appeared, large hands. A blond head bent down, and through the gap that had appeared in the wood, the hands went to the beam. Slowly, they lifted it away from the door.

'Tobias,' Lisa breathed. Clem's grip loosened as he stared too.

Tobias stood, holding the beam. The workbench was still in the doorway. He put the beam down, leaning it against the wall. Then he put his weight against the bench and pushed.

A moment of stillness. Then chaos. Shouting, barking, seawater, Tobias's voice, 'Run, run for it – '

But Lisa was still trapped in her father's grip, and even though Tazer was growling at her feet, splashing through the waves, she couldn't move.

Clem began to walk, holding Lisa in front of him. He moved slowly, through the doorway, emerging blinking into the rain, one arm still locked round his daughter's neck, the other holding his pistol.

Lisa was blue-lipped and shivering.

Tobias stared. Finn stared.

Berenice too, was staring. What she saw was the gun, levelled, aiming at them all.

Clem spoke. 'Ain't no one going to beat me this time. Me and my kid, we're going – '

'No, you're not.' It was Elizabeth. She stepped forward and faced him. 'You're going to let Lisa go,' she said.

Clem shook his head. 'You of all people…'

'My name is nothing to do with it – '

'I found them, bitch. I found them papers… buried there… If I can't have that house, ain't no one else going to have it.'

'It's over, Clem.'

Then, two things happened. The first was that Tobias lunged at Clem. The second, was that Clem fired.

A shot, two shots.

A flash of pale coat, then searing red.

Rain, blood, screaming, barking.

Berenice saw the pistol arcing through the air. It landed at her feet. She saw Clem, on the ground, pinned there by Tobias. Finn, holding Lisa, who seemed uninjured. Elizabeth, lying on her side, bleeding, panting, empty-eyed. And through the rain, flashing blue lights, sirens. The slam of car doors, people shouting, uniforms, stretchers, blankets, oxygen. Clem, handcuffed, bundled into a van.

The tower loomed, black against the stormy sky. At its feet the sea crashed across the rocks.

Chapter Thirty

'Is she still in hospital, the kid?' Berenice looked up as Mary came into her office.

Mary nodded. 'They're keeping her in overnight. Shock, mostly. She seems OK.' She put two paper cups down on Berenice's desk.

'And Elizabeth?'

'It could have been much worse, the medics are saying. One bullet missed, the other grazed her ribs. She'll be fine.'

'Thanks to Tobias.'

Mary nodded.

'Not thanks to me.' Berenice gazed at the darkness outside, the flood lights of the car park. 'No way they'll let me keep my job. Not even traffic offences.'

'I wouldn't be too sure.' Mary sat down.

'What about Clem. Is he talking?' Berenice picked up her coffee.

Mary shrugged. 'Not much. Stuff about destiny and flood and tunnels, and the deeds to the house. They want you down there.'

'Me? But I'm – I mean… where's the Chief?'

'Stuart? Oh, Ashford I think.'

Berenice stared at her. Then smiled. She got to her feet. 'Thanks for picking up the call.'

'Duty, Boss.'

'How was the hen night?'

Mary sighed.

'Disappointing?'

'I just was expecting something a bit less…'

'Oh. You mean it was all – '

'Yes. Pink. Loud. Tinsel. Whistles. Too much Tequila…'

'Oh dear.'

'Nice that she's happy though.'

The night gave way to dawn. Clem refused to speak. Reminded of the charges against him, the killing of three men, wounding with intent, possession of firearms, kidnap, he stared straight ahead of him. From time to time he shook his head, or murmured something. Once he fixed his gaze on Berenice and said, 'My little girl…? She's OK?'

'Yes, Berenice replied. 'She's fine.'

He nodded, and returned to silence.

By morning they decided to give it a rest. Berenice went to get some sleep, driving home through the rain. The flood, she wondered, yawning. The ending of it all.

At the lab, people arrived, gathering in corners, in coffee bars, 'have you heard… they've got him… Dr. Merletti shot, yes, really… We're safe, it seems… Elizabeth was really brave… Someone's organised a card for her… out of hospital in a day or two, they said…' People settled at their desks, stared at their screens.

'There's still the little matter of our weird results,' Roger said to Neil.

'Perhaps this Voake chap caused those too. Perhaps it'll all go back to normal now.'

Roger gave a thin smile. 'Whatever normal is.'

'I look around at this place I have called my home, and I know that soon it will no longer be mine. I shall turn my back on this plate and these cloths, the candles, the silverware. I shall take my leave of it all.'

Helen put down the yellowing pages on her kitchen table.

This place I have called my home.

I wonder how the church views the re-housing of divorced vicar's wives, she thought.

Knowing the church, not at all.

Perhaps if children are involved…

If children were involved… would I have done the same? Liam, with his care, his concern, his sexiness, his laughter - would I have fallen just the same?

In her mind, the picture of Chad, leaving. Not a shuffling, defeated, half-man, but tall and broad and strong, and striding away from her. Forever, she supposed.

I wonder where people live when they only live half a life. Wherever it is, that's where I'm headed…

A loud knocking at the kitchen door. A breath of relief, he's back, of course he is, he's not going to let our marriage go –

'Oh,' she said. 'Liam.'

He'd been talking to his sister, in his head, all the way there, driving along the coastal road, the rain against the windscreen.

She listens, he'd told Sinead. When I talk about my work, she understands. Not all of it, obviously, but she likes to hear about it. It's the way she speaks, the way she laughs. It's the way she moves. When she moves it's always in the right way. When she throws an old cardigan over a pair of jeans, it hangs in the right way, as if there was no other way that it could hang. And when we're in bed…

Oh God.

I have to have her. Not just for now. Forever…

And now here she was, standing in her kitchen doorway, staring up at him.

'Are you alone?' he said.

She was still staring, as the trees dripped rain behind him.

'I need you,' he said.

She noticed the sparkle of raindrops in his hair.

He took a step towards her, and she put her hand up to stop him, her fingers against the soft linen of his shirt.

'Helen – '

'You know what I'm going to say,' she said.

He shook his head, gazing at her.

'It was never possible,' she said.

'What? You're wrong – I've come here to tell you – '

'Liam.' Her eyes on his.

'No.' His voice was loud. 'This is different. For the first time in my life - Oh, God. Helen. Surely you can see – '

She was shaking her head.

'I love you,' he said. 'I know you're married, I know there's your husband – '

'There isn't,' she said.

He looked at her. 'What?'

'He's gone. Chad.'

'He found out?'

She stared at him, at his wide-eyed surprise, and she wanted to laugh. 'Found out?' she echoed. 'Oh, God, Liam, how little you know. Chad… he's my life. He's the man I chose. And I know everything was so right with you, and you made me laugh like no one else and you're so clever and sexy and… and sexy,' she finished. 'But Chad's my husband. Or was, anyway.'

And then she burst into tears, real sobbing, standing there in the rain on her doorstep, and Liam reached out and took hold of her, clumsily, and as she didn't move, he found himself gripping her elbow as she sobbed, her other hand dashing tears from her face. Aren't you going to ask me in, he was about to say, but it was quite clear she wasn't.

'I'm sorry,' he said. 'I didn't want it to be like this. I didn't want to harm your life…'

She shook her head. 'It's me,' she said, through tears. 'I harmed my life. Not you.'

He moved to hug her then. She stood, stiff and awkward in his arms. And then, soaked with rain, he faced her. 'We'll be friends,' he said. 'Won't we?'

She almost smiled, through tears. 'Who knows,' she said.

He turned away, took a few steps towards his car. She saw him dab at his eyes, at his wet face. She watched him get into the car and drive away.

The voice in Liam's head was silent. Just the windscreen wipers, slicing through the grey day.

He drove, waiting for the words to start, his sister's voice.

There was still silence.

Just as well, he thought.

What Sinead will say, when she gets to hear, is that it's typical of me. Same old Liam, falling in love with the unattainable. Perhaps I always knew she loved her husband. Perhaps that's what made her so desirable…

A sudden braking, a scuttle of paws across his path, a rabbit, badger, maybe.

No. This is not the same old Liam.

I love her. Helen.

I don't think I can bear it.

Helen stared unseeing at Amelia's pages.

I don't think I can bear it.

It was for fun, wasn't it? To be desired, to make love without thought of anything else, to push to one side all those hopes of conception.

And now it's not fun. I've lost the man I love most of all. And I've hurt poor Liam…

Poor Liam. He had walked away into the rain, his coat flapping at his shins.

If there's one thing I know in all this, she thought, it's that Liam will be all right.

She picked up Amelia's pages and began to read.

Chapter Thirty-One

The day wore on. Berenice reappeared at work. Four hours sleep, it's enough, she thought.

'Any news?'

DS Conway looked up from his files. 'He's still quiet. We've told him about the DNA match, the CCTV from near the Tower.'

'We've told him that no one else could have killed Moffatt,' Mary added.

'What does he say?'

Ben shrugged. 'Nothing much. He goes on about the house, the old Voake house. Told me he's going to plant white roses round the door. He said there used to be roses there when he was a kid.'

'Has he asked about Elizabeth?'

Ben shook his head. 'Not once.'

'I'll go back in and have a word.'

'He said – ' Ben glanced at Mary, shuffled his notes.

'He said,' Mary finished for him, 'that if we sent that mare in to see him, he wouldn't say a word.'

Berenice smiled. 'I expect there was another word before the mare one, wasn't there?'

Ben chewed his lip.

'If references to my colour were any bar...' Berenice picked up the file.

'... you wouldn't be where you are today.' Mary finished.

'Wherever that is.' Berenice went to the door. 'I'll have a lovely chat and nice cup of tea with our friend. Those attitudes are very easy to shift, trust me.'

At the lab, Richard the director consulted Tricia in the Press Office.

'Ooh, I don't know, Director. I mean I know these new particles are all very exciting, but hadn't we better wait until the fuss has died down...'

At the lab, Neil wondered, quietly, to Liam, when the funerals would be. 'More to the point, who will be at them? Do you think Elizabeth will go to Murdo's – or maybe she can use her injury as an excuse to absent herself. Liam?' But Liam, gazing at his screen, seemed not to be listening.

In her hospital bed, Lisa slept. Sometimes she would stir, aware of whispering anxieties, about where she would live, where they might put her, wishing she were older and could decide for herself... but then she'd settle back to sleep, the dreamless sleep of someone warm, dry, fed and safe. For now, at least.

On the floor above, Elizabeth dozed. There were wires, and drips, and beeping. Sometimes she heard rushing water, like the sea. Sometimes she'd hear deafening loud bangs, and the beeping would shift rhythm, and a passing nurse would come and soothe her. 'You'll be well enough for visitors soon,' one of them said.

Visitors. Will they come to blame or praise? Will they talk to me of courage or foolhardiness?

It was neither, of course. At the point where I walked into the firing line, it was because I didn't care whether I lived or died.

And now…

The beeping settled into evenness. The rushing tidal noise retreated. She could hear the quiet busyness of the hospital ward. Elizabeth breathed, and thought, I am still here.

At the end of that day, Clem Voake appeared in court charged with murder, kidnap, wounding and firearms offences. In the absence of any response, a not guilty plea was entered. He was remanded in custody.

Outside Police HQ the reporters began to drift away. The rain, too, had stopped, and the evening air was cold.

'It's late, Boss.'

Berenice looked up from her desk. 'I'm thinking,' she said.

Mary laughed. 'The DS better get further away than Ashford, then.' She glanced at Berenice's desk.

'What's that photo?'

Berenice sighed. 'It's a funeral.'

Mary took it from her. 'A baby? That little white coffin…'

'It belongs to the Maguires. I should give it back to them.' Berenice placed it on her desk. 'Do you think the case stands up?'

'The Voake case? Sure. DNA everywhere on the Moffatt killing. He's admitted to a grudge against Henrickson, as he wanted the house too. It's all about the house. All about his entitlement. He would have killed Dr. Merletti, as she was a Van Mielen once.'

'How's she doing?'

'OK. The hospital want to discharge her tomorrow.'

'Good.'

'It's amazing what she did. She saved that kid's life, I reckon. Do you think it makes you brave like that, being The Other Woman?'

Berenice smiled. 'I'm not sure it extends to walking into a firing line. Not in my case, anyway.'

'Not yet, Boss.' Mary closed the door behind her, wishing her a good night.

Outside the beams of departing cars cut through the darkness.

She picked up Tobias's lions, the green and the red. The coloured paint was flecking away from the brown plastic underneath.

Dear Tobias, she thought. An ordinary toy plastic lion becomes something greater, endowed with meaning, with magic…

She looked at his mixtures. Perhaps he'll do it, she thought. Perhaps he'll make gold out of lead. Perhaps all you need is faith...

As if we thought he was capable of killing. Just because he was angry with the Prof. But then, it's quite clear Alan was capable of shouting at everyone, like his rage with Iain over the land sale, what was it Tobias said, that he was shouting at Iain about the ghost and the dead child, and how Iain was very angry with the Prof after that, very very angry. Uncle Murdo had to take him for a walk to calm him down, Tobias had said.

Berenice put the lions back in their box. She stared at the photograph on her desk. That small white coffin...

What she remembered was the flowers. Cascades of them, draped in piles, over the coffin, filling the church. She remembered thinking that perhaps he was hiding behind them, perhaps he'd jump out, smiling, laughing, and their mother would look up and see him. She'd imagined, perhaps, how her mother would give him a clip round the ear, giving him what for, getting everyone to make this fuss...

But there'd been nothing like that. Her mother, when she glanced at her, as she did all through the service, was tight-faced with grief, unashamed of the tears which soaked her face.

We didn't recover. My mother and I. We never managed to negotiate the gap that lay between us. As soon as I could, I joined the Job, fled to Leeds.

Berenice fingered the edge of the photograph, then slipped it into the file. Her fingers brushed against the van Mielen book, and she pulled it out.

She scanned the words in front of her, about light and rays and transformations, about particles and aether and the flood that will cleanse us all.

And yet, in the end, it was an ordinary crime.

That man downstairs is hard, ruthless, greedy. Damaged, maybe, but in the end just an ordinary criminal.

She stared at the photograph again. Jacob, she thought. She imagined the tiny body lying in its coffin. That mother, the van Mielen one. Amelia. Burying her child. And then, years later, Virginia has to do the same…

She remembered her mother saying, over and over, I loved him more than my own life. She remembered Virginia's words, I couldn't have loved that child more.

I couldn't have loved that child more. If… if what?

She stared, unseeing at the plastic lions. A thought, just beyond her reach. The white coffin, the flowers…

Oh My God, she thought. It's so bloody obvious. No wonder Clem Voake is denying everything.

She picked up her coat, grabbed her bag, and raced for her car.

Helen set the table for dinner. One plate, one glass. She picked up her phone, dialled Chad's number again, heard it click to answer, left yet another message.

'It's me. Please just tell me where you are.'

He could be anywhere, she thought. When does he become a missing person? When do I tell the police? Tomorrow? Now?

The saucepan of pasta was boiling over, dripping sticky water over the hob. She switched off the gas. Then she poured a large glass of wine. The pasta congealed, uneaten, in the pan.

Berenice drove slowly through the darkness. The sea glittered in the distance.

If I'm right, she thought, Elizabeth lied. But why? Why would she lie?

And if Iain and Murdo were best friends…

If I'm right…

Ghosts. Like Amelia's brother. And Amelia's daughter, buried in an old church.

What if they're just stories, just fairy tales?

In the beginning, she thought…

She drove up the hill to Virginia's cottage, slowed to a halt. A single light glowed pale in the window.

She switched off the engine. Then she walked up the path to Virginia's door.

Chapter Thirty-Two

Virginia stood in her doorway.

'What do you want?'

'I'd like a word, Mrs. Maguire.'

'You've arrested him.'

'Yes.'

'Has he admitted it all?'

'I'm afraid I can't go into that.'

Virginia gave a shrug of her shoulders. She turned, unsmiling, and led the way inside. She indicated a chair, and Berenice sat down.

'I'm not sure I can help you any further,' Virginia said.

'Are you alone?'

Virginia nodded. 'Tobias will be back soon. He's out at the pub, with his friend Finn.' She looked up, nervously. 'This isn't about him, is it? He's a changed boy with all that suspicion lifted –'

'No,' Berenice said. 'This isn't about him.'

'Oh. Good.'

Berenice fished in her bag and drew out the photograph. She showed it to Virginia.

Virginia looked down at it. 'Did I give you that?'

'It was in Tobias's things.'

'Oh. Yes.' She glanced at the mantelpiece. 'We can have it back now, can't we?' She spoke fast.

'Soon, yes.'

Virginia reached for the photo, but Berenice moved it out of reach.

'Mrs. Maguire,' she said. 'Why is Elizabeth at Jacob's funeral?'

'Was she?' Virginia stared at Berenice's hands. 'I can't remember.'

Berenice held it out again. 'There. And she looks terrible.'

'It's not a good picture – '

'You can see she's crying…'

Again Virginia grabbed at it. Berenice tucked it back into her briefcase.

'You shouldn't have it,' Virginia said. 'It's not yours…'

'You and Elizabeth… You've not been entirely honest, have you? About your relationship…' Berenice watched her.

Virginia shrugged. 'You can understand why, surely. After she and Murdo…'

'After she and Murdo what?' Berenice waited.

'Do I have to spell it out to you? You know all there is to know about that woman tempting my husband away from me…' She got to her feet. 'Do you have anything else to say to me?'

Berenice returned her gaze. She shook her head.

Virginia went to the door and held it open for her.

Berenice gathered up her things.

'I'd like my photograph back too.'

Berenice shook her head. 'Evidence, I'm afraid.'

At the door she offered her hand to Virginia. 'Thanks so much for seeing me.'

Virginia's arms stayed at her side. The door slammed behind her.

She drove fast, back to the police station. No point going home, she thought.

The duty sergeant nodded at her in greeting. 'Someone to see you, Ma'am,' he said. 'In reception. A woman. Bit of a state, I'd say.'

She walked round, glanced through the glass.

The vicar's wife. Helen, wasn't it?

She opened the door. 'Hello.'

Helen looked up. She was ashen-white, red-eyed. She got to her feet. 'I want you to have these,' she said.

She was holding out some sheets of paper in trembling fingers.

'Amelia,' she said. 'Van Mielen's daughter. Gabriel's wife. Her child died…'

'Are you all right?' Berenice said.

'No,' Helen said. 'I'm not all right at all.'

They sat in the canteen. Berenice placed a large mug of tea in front of her.

'Missing?' she said.

'I bet he's with Virginia,' Helen said.

Berenice shook her head. 'I've just come from there. She was alone. Unless he was hiding.'

'He doesn't need to hide.'

'Do you think he's in danger?' Berenice asked.

Helen shook her head. 'Not in physical danger, no.'

Berenice felt suddenly weary. It must be about midnight, she thought. I have work to do –

'… it's all connected,' Helen said, suddenly. 'The physics and the lab and the aether in the writings, and the dead child and the poor ghost of a soldier who died in the war. And now Chad has gone.'

'I have a murder enquiry on my hands.'

Helen looked at her. 'That's what I mean. It's all the same.'

'In what sense is it all the same?' Berenice stifled a yawn.

Helen began to speak, stopped. She shook her head. 'Perhaps I'm wrong. I'm not really thinking straight at the moment.'

'Marriages often have their troubles.' Berenice stirred her spoon around in her mug.

'This isn't troubles.' Helen's voice was loud. 'Oh no. This is entirely my fault. This is me wrecking something that was good, just because I – I wanted…' She looked up. 'I'm not even sure I want children. I mean, yes, of course, I do, but to wreck my marriage, to run off with someone else out of some kind of rage or pain or something, when I could have just said to Chad, we need to talk about this – '

'Perhaps you did say all that. Perhaps he just didn't listen.'

Helen looked at her.

'Mind you,' Berenice was saying, 'what do I know? All I've learned about marriage I learned from being the Other Woman.' She glanced at Helen. 'I don't imagine that's your problem with him, is it?'

Helen shrugged. 'Who knows?'

'Even vicars, yeah?'

'They're only human.'

Berenice smiled. 'Aren't we all.'

Helen pushed the yellowed pages across the table to her. 'Keep these. Please.'

'You don't want them?'

She shook her head. 'They're bad for me. All that pain and heartbreak and grief about children. I can't do it anymore.' She got to her feet.

'What will you do?' Berenice walked beside her through the canteen.

Helen shrugged. 'What can I do? Hope he comes back, I guess.'

'He'll probably try to tell you he's safe. People usually do that.'

'And if he doesn't?'

Berenice held the door open for her. 'I'll put out a shout if you like. At least we can try to find out where he's hiding. But we don't extend to marriage guidance.'

Helen gave her a thin smile.

'And even if we did – ' Berenice held out her hand. ' – I'm not the person to ask.'

She saw Helen out to her car, returned to her office. She sat in the silence, in the pool of light from her anglepoise lamp.

The notes of hate mail were spread out in front of her, all with their clumsy red words predicting disaster. She picked up the last one. The handwriting was different. Neater.

Found by Iain Hendrickson, she thought. And what if he'd written it himself? What if he'd thought of a way to keep the heat off him. After Murdo's death.

In her mind, she saw the beach. Two men, shouting, fighting. One blow, two blows to the head. And then one carries the other, his arm swinging, as Tobias said. And he carries him, somehow, all the way up Hank's Tower.

She picked up the book. And if I'm right, she thought, the answer is here.

'Amelia Voake,' she said, out loud, poring over the writings. She flicked to the last few pages.

'I have no husband. I have no child. I, Amelia van Mielen, am once more alone. With these pages I finish my story.'

'I have no child…'

Berenice held the funeral photograph in the palm of her hand. She recalled Virginia's words, all those days ago, sitting in the interrogation room downstairs, 'I couldn't have loved that child more...'

The unbearable pain of the loss of a child. The destructive force of a mother's grief.

Her desk phone shrilled. 'Killick,' she said, hearing the duty sergeant ask if she'd be sleeping at HQ that night.

'No,' she said. 'I'm off home. Don't suppose I'll sleep, but I'm off home anyway. Yeah. Ta. Night.'

She gathered up her coat, her bag, her car keys.

I know I'm right, she thought.

The night was cold and clear, and gave way to a crisp bright dawn. At nine o'clock, Berenice drove through the gates of the lab and parked in the visitor's car park.

'DI Killick,' she said to the young woman on reception. 'I want to speak to Dr. Merletti. The hospital said she'd come straight back to work.'

She was shown into a waiting area. A young man appeared. 'Dr. Merletti is in the engineering sheds. She said would you mind joining her there.'

'I don't mind where I go.' Berenice followed him along the sunlit corridor, out of a door, through a yard, then through a huge industrial doorway.

They were standing in something like an aircraft hangar. Huge steel trolleys wheeled past. She saw workbenches, shining metal.

From the groups of white-coated people, Elizabeth emerged. Even with one arm in a sling, she looked groomed and smart. She smiled at Berenice. 'Glad it's over, are you? Has he confessed?'

'You look well,' Berenice said.

'I was lucky.' She shrugged.

'And brave.'

Elizabeth glanced at her. 'That too. Perhaps. At the time I didn't think. I just saw that poor child in danger and I – ' she shuddered. 'Well, it turned out OK. Let's go somewhere we can talk.

'Back at work.' Berenice glanced around the huge space as they walked through the hangar. 'I thought it was all about the maths.'

Elizabeth smiled. 'You can't prove the maths without the right kit.'

'And this is the kit?'

They passed two white-coated men, bent over a bench on which was placed a huge metallic hexagonal shaped tube.

'Electro-magnets,' Elizabeth said. 'You can't just buy them in Homebase.' She pushed at two swing doors. It was a quieter space, stacked with bits of furniture, and clear plastic boxes that seemed to hold nuts and bolts. 'So.' Elizabeth leaned against the table. 'How can I help?'

Berenice took the funeral photo from her pocket and held it out to her.

Elizabeth glanced at it. 'What's – Oh. Oh God.'

Berenice watched her. 'You're there. In the corner there.'

'Of course… Jacob's funeral…' Her voice was shaking. The colour had drained from her face. 'Of course I'm there.'

'He was your son.'

The words hung in the air.

'Yes,' Elizabeth said. 'He was my son.' She sank down onto a plastic chair.

'Why did you lie?'

Elizabeth looked up at her. She was empty-eyed, grey-faced. Her lips moved, but no words came.

Berenice tried again. 'You didn't tell - '

Elizabeth's eyes blazed sudden fury. 'Is there any reason why I should? Is it the kind of thing you go around telling people you hardly know?'

Berenice sat down next to her. 'Why did you give your baby away?'

Elizabeth raised her head. 'Are you a mother?' Her voice was oddly sharp.

Berenice shook her head.

'Have you ever loved a man? I mean, really loved a man?'

Berenice hesitated. She shook her head.

'When I saw the situation clearly – when I looked at it for what it was…' Her voice was firmer now. 'When I realized that

Murdo was never going to leave her… I thought to myself, what do I want? And I realized that it was all wrong, to have the child but – but not to have him…' She met her gaze. 'It was all wrong,' she repeated.

Berenice was silent.

'Do you think I'm unnatural? Not a proper woman… to give away one's child?'

Berenice spoke quietly. 'As you say – I know nothing about it.'

'I got used to it, of course,' Elizabeth went on. 'That look in people's eyes, that flicker of judgement, as if I'd been weighed up and found wanting…'

'Was it - ?' Berenice hesitated.

'What?'

'Was it your idea or his?'

The poise faltered slightly. 'We were as one,' she said.

'You and Murdo?'

'We adored each other. We had to find a solution…'

'But you weren't going to raise him, this baby?'

Elizabeth smoothed her skirt on her knees. 'Murdo made it clear…'

Berenice waited.

Elizabeth met her eyes. 'We needed a solution. And he came up with one.'

'To adopt the baby? To raise it with his wife?'

'She'd always wanted children. She was an excellent mother, too.'

'But why…?'

'Why what?' Elizabeth was upright, now, her tone matter-of-fact. 'You mean, why didn't he leave? Why didn't he and I run away, raise the child together?'

'If he loved you as you say…'

Elizabeth shook her head. 'It wasn't just Murdo. If you knew about my upbringing, the pain I saw my mother bear…' She breathed. 'It killed her in the end.'

'And you felt as if you were to blame?'

Elizabeth threw her a cold, blank look. 'I'd always known I wasn't cut out for motherhood, that's all.'

Berenice nodded. 'I know the feeling,' she said.

A burst of distant noise, electrical, drilling of some kind.

'So - ?'

Elizabeth sighed. 'Murdo talked to his wife. She accepted it. More than that, she was happy, I think. It solved a lot of problems. And she won, after all.'

'You mean, she ended up with Murdo?'

'That's winning, isn't it?'

'And you went to Italy.'

Elizabeth nodded. 'Yes.'

'Did you ever come back – I mean, in between - '

'No.'

'Apart from for the funeral.' Berenice flicked the photograph between her fingers.

'Apart from that. I caught the next flight back to Rome.'

Berenice gazed at the image, the tiny coffin, the white flowers. 'Jacob,' she said.

Elizabeth's gaze was unblinking. 'Jacob,' she said.

'So – what happened next?'

'It was the end of Murdo and me. We were both heartbroken, of course.'

'And Iain?'

Elizabeth flashed her a glance. 'Iain?'

'You'd had an affair with him.'

She shrugged. 'Sort of. On and off.'

'But nothing serious? Not like you and Murdo?'

'Oh, no.' Her tone was emphatic. 'Nothing like me and Murdo. Iain had hopes of me. But I went to the new lab, started a new life.'

'Met your husband,' Berenice said.

'Yes.'

'Until…'

Elizabeth crossed one neat shoe over the other. 'You know the rest. A job came up here. My marriage was over. So I came back.'

'And you and Murdo?'

Elizabeth fixed her with a look. 'You say you've been in love? Can you imagine, after all those years, of silence, of nothing… to set eyes on each other again? It was wonderful.'

'Until he died.'

A nod of her head. 'Yes,' she said.

The drilling noise erupted, briefly, then faded away.

Berenice shifted on the hard plastic chair. 'Going back some years… what did Murdo think about you and Iain?'

A brief smile, a shrug.

'He knew you were sleeping with Iain?'

'He didn't care. He knew I loved him more than life itself.'

'Do you remember telling me, about Murdo? About their difficulties in conceiving?'

Elizabeth raised her eyes, slowly. She stared at her.

'Was it, perhaps, more than difficulties? More like, impossibility?'

Elizabeth's gaze didn't falter.

'You did know, didn't you,' Berenice went on. 'And Murdo knew too. So this baby, this miraculous baby – '

'No.' It was almost a shout.

'This child - '

'He was our child.' Her voice was loud. 'I wasn't going to have it any other way…'

'He was Iain's son.'

Elizabeth clapped her hand across her mouth. She stared, mutely, at Berenice.

'You knew. And Murdo knew. But Iain trusted you… he trusted you to tell him the truth.'

Elizabeth was shaking her head, her hand still covering her lips.

'And then came the day, not that long ago, when Virginia found out, that the child she'd accepted as her husband's, her beloved husband's - and raised, and mourned for all these years, was the child of another man.'

Elizabeth took her hand away from her mouth. She sat, her breathing shallow, staring at her lap. At length, she spoke. 'I wished it was his,' she said. 'The baby. I wanted it to be Murdo's.'

'But Iain must have had suspicions… the timing….?'

'He asked me. I said no. We all signed… we all signed documents.' Her voice was small. 'They were similar men. The baby… he looked like both of them.' Elizabeth glanced up at her. 'I loved Murdo. I loved him more than I've ever loved anyone, before or since. But – but he was never mine. When I found I was pregnant… I so wanted it to be his.' She was almost whispering.

'And Iain?'

Elizabeth gave a dismissive wave of her manicured fingers.

Berenice was silent. Then she said, 'When did Virginia find out?'

'I don't know.' Elizabeth's voice was small.

'She had raised your child, believing it was her husband's. And now she'd found out that you had deceived her. And deceived her so cruelly. And all that rage, the rage of the wronged wife, multiplied by – by the sort of numbers you deal with here, must have come to the fore.'

Another brief nod.

'So – ' Berenice leaned against the hard back of her chair. 'Three weeks ago, Alan and Iain are having a shouting match about the land sale, the Voake house. And in the heat of the moment, Alan suggests to Iain that he's been misled, by you and Murdo. He talks of ghosts, and dead children. Is that what happened?'

Elizabeth was shaking her head.

'And Murdo, attempting to calm things down, takes Iain for a walk on the beach…'

'I wasn't there.' She stared, sullenly, at her lap.

'And something that had been gathering, some truth lurking at the back of his mind, fell into focus.'

'I told you - '

'I know. You weren't there. But let's just say, you're Iain. And you've discovered that you were deceived by people who claimed to love you. And that as a result you'd been made to sign away your paternal rights to a child that was yours, a son.'

A silence. Elizabeth stared at the floor.

Berenice sighed. 'Ghosts,' she said. 'As you said the other day. The shadow of the past.'

Elizabeth raised her eyes to her. 'I don't know what you mean.'

'You know the truth, Elizabeth. You know who killed Murdo.'

'So why ask me?' Elizabeth flashed back. 'Sure. I know who killed Murdo. What good does that do anyone?'

Berenice got to her feet. She looked down at Elizabeth. 'And who killed Iain?'

Elizabeth too, stood up. In her heels she was taller than Berenice. 'If you know so much, you know the answer to that too. Like I said, Lady, we do the same job, you and me. We define our questions. We sift through the evidence until we find the right answer. And now may I go?'

She stepped past Berenice and opened the door. Berenice watched her go, watched her glide through the sun-lit shed, flanked by towering tunnel pieces and half-built magnets.

Chapter Thirty-Three

The sun was shining when Berenice's car pulled out of the lab car park. It was still shining when she drove up the track to Virginia's cottage and parked.

The slam of the car door. The twitch of the curtains.

She knocked on the door.

Virginia opened it.

'What now?' She blinked at the brightness beyond. 'I'd heard you weren't even on the case anymore.'

'It's complicated.'

'I don't have to ask you in.'

'No,' Berenice agreed. 'You don't.'

The two women stood there on the doorstep.

'However,' Berenice went on, 'I wanted to ask you a question.'

'Another one? Do I have to answer it?'

Berenice hesitated. Then she said, 'Who would have wanted your husband dead?'

'He's been arrested – charged - '

Berenice shook her head. 'Not Clem. I'm not talking about him.'

Virginia gave a small shrug. She moved as if to shut the door.

'More to the point,' Berenice said, her foot against the edge of the door, 'Who would have wanted Iain dead?'

Virginia's gaze hardened. She stood, unmoving.

'You blamed him,' Berenice went on.

'Why shouldn't I?' Her eyes flashed with sudden rage. 'It was all his fault. Everything. It all came down to him.'

'Not Murdo's fault, then?' Berenice said. 'The affair with Elizabeth. The child who wasn't yours? They lied to you, didn't they – Elizabeth and Murdo – '

'How dare you?' Her eyes were black with anger. 'How dare you… He was blameless. Blameless, I tell you. Hoodwinked by that man…. That man…' She gulped, as if more speech might choke her.

'So Iain…'

'Murdo was the only man I ever loved. A worthy, brave, stalwart man.'

'And Iain killed him,' Berenice said.

'Yes,' she said. 'Iain killed him.' Berenice heard her vengefulness, wondered at her rage. This tiny woman, wringing her apron between her bony hands, and that bluff, towering scientist… it seemed impossible.

Berenice faced her. 'And who killed Iain?'

Virginia was motionless.

'You were angry,' Berenice said. 'With Elizabeth – '

'No.' The word was a shout. 'I don't even think about her, I don't care about her, as far as I'm concerned she's nothing, nothing...'

'And you were angry with Iain. Very angry.'

Virginia swayed, put one hand against the door frame.

Berenice waited.

Virginia was breathing, fast, her eyes darting. Suddenly, she spoke. 'He didn't believe I'd kill him. I knew he'd be there, up at the Tower, he was there every night after Murdo... after he left us... Guilt, maybe... re-visiting things... And so, one night, I was there too. Offered him a drink. He was surprised. Let bygones be bygones, he said, he thought that's what I was doing, sitting there with my bottle of brandy, my two glasses.'

'The sedative...'

'Exactly.' She gave a small smile.

'And then, when he was stumbling anyway...'

'I lured him to the edge. I wanted him to know, I wanted him to understand... It was only a slight push after that...'

'What did you say to him?'

Virginia looked at her. Her eyes were wide now, a new vulnerability... 'Don't you understand? I raised that child as if he were my own, because of Murdo, because I loved him. I didn't care about her, I didn't care how that child came to be. It was my husband's child and that was enough for me. And then to find out he was – ' She clapped her hand across her mouth.

'...it was Iain's?' Berenice finished for her.

She waved her other hand frantically across her face. 'No,' she mumbled, behind her fingers. 'No, no…'

'When did you find out?' Berenice asked.

She was shaking her head now, her hands clasped to the side of her face, still murmuring refusal.

'It was then, wasn't it?' Berenice prompted. 'On the tower.'

'He wouldn't tell me.' She stared downwards. 'He wouldn't say. Whose was he, I was asking, tell me, and he said nothing, sipping on his glass, but in the end he looked me in the eyes and said, you know, Virginia. You've always known. And I said, did he know? Did Murdo know that it was your son? And he was looking straight at me, and he said, you know Murdo couldn't have children, you know that Virginia… And by then his speech was slurring, and he said he felt unwell, he got up, and I said, come and look at the sea, like we used to, in the old days, and we went under the barrier and stood on the old bricks and we watched the sea crash against the rocks beneath us, and he turned to me and said, I had to do it, Ginny, believe me, I loved her so…' She sat there, breathing, silenced.

'Murdo knew the baby wasn't his. He must have known. I mean, long before…'

Virginia looked up at her. Her voice was flat. 'A miracle child. That's how I thought of it. Why shouldn't I believe in miracles? Why shouldn't it be true that you can have light in the darkness?'

Berenice was silent.

'It wasn't difficult, after that,' Virginia said.

'Did Iain know what you'd done?'

'Oh yes.' Virginia gave a nod. 'He was unsteady, complaining of dizziness. His last words were, 'Have you done this? And as I put my hand on his arm, I said, Yes, I said. Yes, I have done this.'

Now, she looked at her. A direct, clear gaze.

Berenice gazed back. 'And then what?' she asked.

Virginia blinked, chewing at her lip. She shook her head. 'After that... it only took a little push.' Her gaze faltered again. 'I heard him fall. It was very loud... I don't know... I didn't know a man falling can make that kind of noise.' She fell silent, staring at her hands.

They listened to the sea, the distant crashing of the stormy waves. After a while Virginia said, 'Will they charge me with murder?'

She held out her hands, as if waiting for handcuffs.

Berenice leaned forward and grasped the two cold hands in her own. The movement took them both by surprise.

Chapter Thirty-Four

Three days. Helen sat by the window of the lounge and looked out to sea.

Three days. One text, two days ago, saying, 'I am still here'. Then nothing, his phone switched off.

She'd told the police, of course. Berenice herself had tried to help, but she was so busy with the case, such an extraordinary outcome, it was all over the press, photographs of Virginia, photographs of the lab, Liam, even...

She wondered what Chad made of it. She wondered if he knew. Presumably he'd heard somewhere, seen a television or a newspaper, wherever he was...

Her heart clenched at the thought.

And Virginia, capable of that. Berenice had said to Helen, over a cup of tea, that she'd seemed almost relieved when she'd challenged her, as if something had come to an end, something burdensome and terrible, and now over.

Poor woman, Helen. Thought. Poor poor woman.

Murdo was the love of her life, she'd said.

Perhaps it drives you mad. Perhaps I'll be the same, as the years pass, sitting here by the window waiting for my husband, becoming more and more shrivelled with rage until one day, I too...

Except, the difference is, the only person I'm angry with – is myself.

Funny how things change, Berenice thought, as she walked through reception and along the sunlit corridor. Two days ago I had to creep through the car park entrance, in the hope of not seeing anyone, in the hope of avoiding the Chief Super with his snide comments. And today –

' - Morning Ma'am,' said a passing sergeant, a boy she hardly knew.

'Morning,' she replied.

His hand briefly touched his forehead.

A salute, she thought. They'll be doffing hats next.

She rounded the corridor into the foyer area.

'Ah – Berenice – '

'Morning, Sir,' she said.

He faced her. 'Well…' He stood there, pink-faced against the orange lino. 'Well… carry on, eh? Good work.'

'Thank you, Sir,' she said.

'You should have called him Stuart,' Mary said, later, as they sat in her office.

'I thought of it. Then I thought, I don't care.' She pulled the papers on her desk towards her. 'So – wassup?'

'These are the new files. Clem to be charged with the murder of Alan Moffatt. And the other stuff still stands, of course. Iain

Hendrickson, deceased, is named as the person responsible for the murder of Murdo Maguire, by assault and drowning. And Virginia's been remanded in custody, charged with the murder of Iain Hendrickson.'

Berenice scanned the paperwork. 'Tobias,' she said. 'He's on his own in that cottage.'

'I've talked to social services. They said he's technically an adult. I said he still needs looking after. They said last time they'd called he wasn't there.'

'Great. And Lisa?'

Mary inspected her nails. 'She's gone again.'

'Gone?'

'The hospital were supposed to keep her until children's services could find a place for her. But in the meantime, she discharged herself.'

'Fuck.' Berenice reached to her computer. 'I'm not having that kid going missing. Can't we find her?'

'We've tried everyone. Finn Brady. Tobias. The caravan.'

'And Tazer?'

'The dog? No sign either.'

'Keep a shout out, OK?'

'Will do. One other thing.' Mary checked her notebook. 'There was a sighting of a man at Hank's Tower. Sleeping rough.'

Helen clicked off her phone. 'Could be anyone,' Berenice had said. 'Be careful.'

Helen, still curled on her sofa, watched the distant waves, blue like the sky. She felt cold. She stretched her legs out, shifted her shoulders. It was time to take action.

She went out to the hall, found boots, coat, keys. Five minutes later she was driving along the track towards the coastal road.

It was a high tide, a spring tide. A sharp wind buffeted the waves. Foam crashed onto the stones beneath, as Helen parked the car.

The sky had clouded over. The tower, Hank's tower, rose darkly in front of her. She thought of the men spiralling to their deaths. She shuddered.

The stone staircase was narrow and worn with age. She leaned on the curved brickwork as she climbed. She found herself out on a platform, half sheltered from the wind by a wooden roof.

She screwed up her eyes, adjusted to the flat grey light. She saw the cold stone of the floor. In one corner, a pile of blankets. A figure, seated, his back to her. He turned.

The sea quietened as they looked at each other.

She took a step towards him. He got to his feet, stumbled towards her. He took her hands and stared at her.

'You look awful,' she said, her fingers touching his cheek, which was rough with three days' beard.

He was still holding her gaze, blank-eyed, vacant.

'I'm so sorry,' she said, and burst into tears.

Later they would stand, arm in arm, looking out to sea. Later he would turn to her, nuzzle at her hair, murmur her name. Later still, much later, they will make love, and she will find, in his rough familiarity, the glimpse of a future, the promise of forgiveness.

But that is yet to come. For now, he faces her, his skin wind-blown, his eyes steel-bright with sleeplessness. She is still crying, and he reaches out a chilled hand and touches the tears.

'I was very angry,' he says. 'Very very angry.'

'I know,' she whispers, staring at the ground.

He touches her chin, tilts her face upwards. 'Sitting in the wreckage,' he says.

'It's my fault – '

'No. No blame. Not now.'

'But – '

'I didn't listen to you. You wanting a child… I didn't hear what you were saying.'

She meets his eyes. 'Sitting in the wreckage,' she says.

He takes hold of her hands. 'It's as good as any place to start.'

Chapter Thirty-Five

It was a moonlit night. Tobias squeezed through the gap in the fence. He saw the flicker of candlelight in the broken windows.

He opened the door. A smell of wood smoke, cigarette smoke.

'Chips,' he said. 'And ketchup.'

A loud bark greeted him.

'I got enough for Taze,' he said.

'They ain't no good for her,' came Lisa's voice from the darkness. 'Tomorrow I'll go thief some dog food.'

She was sitting by the fire, which blazed brightly. Tobias joined her, and they ate the chips, passing one or two to the dog from time to time.

'Tom – we can't stay here, y'know.'

'Yes we can,' he said.

'They'll find us.'

'Where are they going to send us?' he said. 'Auntie Ginny's not there anymore…' A catch in his voice. He sniffed, ate another chip.

Lisa patted his arm.

'She's all right, though,' he went on. 'She's happy where she is. That's what she told me last time.'

'She can look after herself, that one,' Lisa said.

'Yes,' he agreed. 'She can.'

'But we still have to find somewhere else,' Lisa said. 'I'm fed up with the rain coming in.'

'And the ghost,' Tobias said.

'I ain't seen no ghost,' Lisa said. 'Never have.'

'I don't mind him,' Tobias said. 'He's a friendly ghost.'

Lisa finished her chips. She got out papers and tobacco and began to roll a joint.

Rain dripped from the corner of the ceiling.

'Weird thing is,' she said, 'it probably belongs to me, this house. If Dad found them deeds and now he's banged up… Funny he knew the papers were there all along. And they're still there. When he opened the thing what he'd dug up, they just fell out in tiny bits.' She took a long drag on the joint.

Tobias licked ketchup from his finger. 'We can grow white roses round the door,' Tobias said, and Lisa laughed.

The moon shone through the wide windows, as Liam walked along the corridor. Through the glass screens he could see the curves of the machine, hunched in semi-darkness, humming quietly.

He reached his office, switched on his computer, stared at the screen. He thought about Helen. Again.

I don't suppose I'll ever see her again.

He'd glimpsed her in town, the day before, he was sure it was her, her light step, her ballet-dancer's walk, her coat swinging at her legs… He'd imagined running towards her, grabbing her hand, 'Helen, it's me…'

It was impossible.

Sinead was right.

He clicked on the keyboard. He looked at the two lines, one red, one blue. He looked again. Something had changed.

His door swung open. Roger was standing there.

'Have you seen – ' Roger said.

'It's different – '

'It's a regular pattern again. B-mesons. Don't you think?'

Liam gazed at the screen. He clicked through a series of graphs, then back to the beam.

'I've just seen Neil,' Roger said. 'He reckons that whatever we were seeing, it was just a B-D asymmetry. That's all. I'm going to put in a call to Richard. Get him to call off the press hounds.'

Liam, alone, stared at the screen. Patterns, he thought. We scan the evidence to find a pattern, to find meaning.

Three physicists dead looked like a pattern.

But in the end, there was no meaning. There was just chaos. Messy, human, murderous chaos.

He clicked on a graph. 'B-D asymmetry,' he said out loud. In that case, he thought… if we've got these charges here… a co-sign of that…

He turned to the notebook at his side and began to scribble numbers.

In the moonlight, a car drew up outside the Voake house.

Berenice got out. A thin column of smoke rose from the chimney.

She walked up the overgrown drive, and pushed at the door.

Candlelight. The smell of cannabis, of chips, of dog. Two warm faces turned to her.

Lisa spoke. 'You can't make us leave.'

'It's her house,' Tobias said. 'We live here.'

Tazer eyed her, growling.

Berenice looked at the rain dripping from the ceiling.

'Well,' she said, 'at least let me recommend you some decent builders.'

Chapter Thirty-Six

The reception area of the lab was thronged with people. There was a hubbub of chatter, the clink of glasses. Richard circulated, greeting people.

'... results still very significant, of course, not quite what we thought at first, but even so...'

'... terrible events, terrible, I know, sorely missed, we feel their absence...'

Liam watched the staircase. He remembered the last time, the way she'd descended the polished steps, her grace, her shyness...

She won't be here. They were invited, but they won't come. Of course.

'Ghosts?' Elizabeth handed him a glass of champagne.

'Ghosts.' He smiled at her.

'All we can see are the gaps. The people who should be here.' She surveyed the room. 'I don't know why he bothered. No Alan. No Iain. No Murdo. These so-called significant results he's announcing, and the people who made them aren't here.'

'You're here,' he said.

She looked up at him. She looked older, and weary, in spite of the hair pinned up, the heels, the black dress. 'Not really,' she said.

'What will you do?'

'Do you remember Bruno, at CERN? He's asked me if I want to join the LHCb experiment there. I've said yes.' Again her gaze scanned the room, the be-suited people, funding bodies, the press. 'There's nothing for me here.'

'Will you keep in touch?'

'There's one person here… one person I care about…' She was still surveying the crowd, and suddenly her face lit up. 'Ah. Good. I invited them – '

Tobias was standing at the top of the steps, with Lisa on his arm. He was wearing a suit. She was in a skirt and low heels, with newly-straightened hair.

They smiled at Elizabeth as they came to join her.

'You look like man and wife,' she said.

'Don't be stupid,' Lisa said. 'Brother and sister, more like.'

'Forever,' Tobias said.

Lisa reached up to Elizabeth and hugged her. 'No sling, then?'

'Doesn't match my dress,' she said. 'And anyway, it only hurts at night these days. How are things?'

'Fine,' Lisa said.

'I heard you were living at the old house,' Elizabeth said.

Lisa looked at Tobias and giggled. 'We were, weren't we, Tom? Thought we was going to stay there forever, didn't we.'

Tobias smiled. 'But then they made it so we can go back home. So we're both there. And Taze, she's there too.'

'His Aunty Ginny's house,' Lisa added. 'That copper came and sorted it for us.'

'We even have a social worker,' Tobias said. 'She drinks all our tea and complains about our food.'

'Too many chips, she says,' Lisa said.

'Says the dog should be vegetarian,' Tobias said.

'She hates cheese, Taze does. We tried it, didn't we, Tom?'

Liam smiled. 'It sounds like she isn't much use.'

'But we do,' Lisa said. 'We really need her. Taze and the cat can't stand each other, fighting and that, she comes and sorts them out.'

Tobias turned to Liam. 'Is this about the results, then?' He waved an arm towards the crowd.

'Yes,' Liam said.

'Is it a new particle?' Tobias said.

Liam shook his head. 'No,' he said. 'It's just a new pattern, perhaps. It just confirms something we suspected about B and D Mesons.'

Tobias nodded. 'I'm looking for a new particle. I've set up my lab in Aunty Ginny's room as she won't need it for a while.'

'Your lab?'

Tobias nodded. 'I've got it all working. I'm looking for aether rays.'

'How – ' Liam stared at him. 'How does that work?'

'I've got batteries, because you need a beam. And in the middle of it all I've got Lisa's magic watch.'

'Lisa's magic watch?'

Tobias nodded. 'From the old tunnel. She found it in the mud. I've wired it into the machine. It works off the cogs, see.'

'I see,' Liam said.

'You could try it here,' Tobias said. 'Only you'd need a very big watch. A very very big one.'

'I hope he's OK. Tobias.' Virginia faced Berenice across the table in the visitors' room.

'They're doing fine,' Berenice said.

'How long has it been?'

'A month. Since they moved back into your house.'

'Is he happy?'

Berenice nodded.

'Does he miss me?'

Berenice hesitated. 'Yes,' she said. 'I'm sure he does.'

'I bet Lisa lets him eat chips the whole time.'

'They've got a social worker – '

'What good will that do?' Virginia shifted on the hard plastic seat. 'They offered me counselling here, you know. I said, what's the point of that? I know what I did and I know why I did it. Then they went on about mitigating circumstances.' She frowned. 'What do they know, these people?'

'It's about sentencing. That's what they mean.'

'What, diminished responsibility? I'm not pleading that.' She leaned back on her chair. The room was high ceilinged, with dim fluorescent lighting and blank, pale walls. 'I was completely responsible,' Virginia went on. 'I've told my solicitor. She says I might feel differently when the case comes up. But I won't. I know I won't.' Her face clouded. 'I killed a man. Iain... he didn't deserve to die.' Her eyes seemed to focus on a distant scene. 'He should be here. And now – now he isn't. And it's because of me.' She looked up at Berenice. 'All I can say is, that anger would have killed me. I would have died of it. And instead... ' Again, that faraway look. 'Instead, I'm here. And he isn't.' She reached for one of the biscuits that Berenice had brought. Around them there was the murmur of other visits, the occasional squawk of a child.

'Chad was here yesterday,' Virginia said.

'The vicar?'

'He pops in from time to time.'

'Does he think he'll convert you?'

Virginia smiled, shook her head. 'He knows me better than that. I wanted to apologise to him. I deceived him, you see, I almost told him, two or three times I was on the point of telling him, but it was too big a story, I didn't know where to start... And the strange thing is, he doesn't seem to mind. It's like he doesn't judge me. I said to him, doesn't it say in the Bible, an eye for an eye. Shouldn't it be a life for a life?'

'And what did he say?'

She smiled. 'He said that what his faith allows him, is a kind of trust – that justice will be done without a human being having to make that kind of judgment.'

'However crap the courts are,' Berenice said, 'I'd rather have their judgments in this life, not the next. When I was a kid, they'd tell me about hell. I don't want no dealings with the devil now I'm grown.'

Virginia shook her head. 'I can't imagine he means hell. He's so jolly these days. There's a lightness of step about him, you wouldn't recognize him. And you know what it is? He told me his wife's expecting, he said. A miracle baby. He said he wasn't sure it was his to start with, but it is, apparently, definitely. Early days, I told him he should wait for three months, before he tells people that kind of news…'

Berenice stared at her.

Virginia bent to her pockets. 'I showed him these. The ones you gave me back, the pages from the back of Murdo's book. He told me his wife took them out, she was crazy, you see, but now she's not.'

'The stuff that Amelia wrote…'

Virginia nodded. 'Her daughter, little Grace, she's buried up at the old church on the marshes, you can see the grave if you know where to look. Anyway, then Amelia disappeared. No one knows what happened to her after that. These pages end with her terrible sorrow, but maybe that's not the end of the story.'

The bell rang for the end of visiting hours. Berenice reached across and touched Virginia's arm. 'I'll come and see you again.'

'Thank you. That would be nice.' Virginia was calm, composed, as if she'd just invited her to tea. She folded Amelia's pages back into her bag, and allowed the warder to lead her back to her cell.

Amelia put down her pen. She blew on the paper to let the ink dry. Then she re-read her words.

'This is not the end,' she'd written. 'I will not say, this is the ending of my story. Dear Gabriel,' the letter went on, 'as you well know, when I left you, I had no idea where I was going. I couldn't see beyond my grief. Our grief, I should say. Now, all this time later, I can acknowledge that you too were in pain, the pain of a father whose child has died.

'I do hope you get this letter. I'm concerned not to have heard from you for so long. I hope you got my last letter, thanking you for sending my brother's crucifix. I am so very grateful for it, the more so in that I know it to be yours. Guy would have wanted you to have it, but in turn, I must thank you for making it a gift to me. I was glad to get your news from Berlin. I'm glad your science is going so well, and that you have found happiness. If Ernst is also a scientist, you and he must have much in common. As I have said before, who would have imagined these chapters of our stories? Who would have thought that I would find such happiness with my dear William?

Yet even now, we cannot know the ending of our stories. Distant as it is from Philadelphia, we are all concerned to hear that Europe is on the brink of another war.

'I do hope we meet again. Germany seems so far away. I was concerned at the fear you expressed in your last letter, that people such as you are no longer welcome there. I hope I hear from you soon, dear Gabriel. Guy would have been so happy to know that we are friends.

'Well, I must go now. And here's my darling daughter, Clara, coming to tell her Mother to put down her pen and to ask Cook if there's cake for tea.

'With every good wish,

'Your loving friend, Amelia.'

Piano notes. Sunlight pours through the studio windows. Helen, alone, is practicing. *Jetée, coupé, pas de bourée…*

He opens the door, almost silently. He begins to follow her, watching her feet, a step here, a step there, an attempt at a pirouette. He almost falls, and she reaches out to steady him, and starts to laugh, and Chad laughs too, holding her, her crimson dancewear bright against the pale walls. She clings to him, still laughing, and he places a hand on her rounded belly, in wonderment at the new life growing there.

In her cell, Virginia sits, alone. She holds a photograph. It shows a boy, blond and sweet-smiling. She smiles too, gazing on his face.

His story, she thinks. His conception, his adoption, the web of lies that entrapped us all, that cost two men their lives, that cost me my freedom. But he is free, this child. He is beyond this realm, the ties that bind us here.

She gazes upwards, at the tiny square of light with bars across it. I brought this on myself, she thinks. There was chaos, and disorder. There was a father, ousted from the truth, who met his end…

Who met his end at my hands.

I deserve my fate.

In her mind he's falling, falling, turning, spinning, the splash of the sea loud against the stones, deafeningly loud.

Chaos and disorder.

She thinks of the lab, the particles colliding, turning, spinning, smashing, falling.

Falling.

She breathes, in, out. But now, there is peace. It is over. Out of the collidings, there is meaning. Out of the chaos, there is truth.

As it was in the beginning, is now, and ever shall be…

She stares again at the photograph. She smiles, at his beauty, at his innocence.

It is enough, that he lived.

She breathes his name. 'Jacob...' However it was you came into this world - I was the woman you called mother. I raised you. I had that place. You loved me as your mother. And I loved you.

A whisper, again, of his name.

I love you still.

It is enough.

Acknowledgments

Many people have helped me with this novel. My visit to the Large Hadron Collider at CERN was compellingly fascinating, and I would like to thank Steven Goldfarb of the ATLAS experiment there, and also Ariane Koek and Renilde Vanden Broeck for making me so welcome. I would also like to thank Steve Lloyd and Adrian Bevan of the School of Physics and Astronomy at Queen Mary, University of London.

I also wish to thank Detective Chief Superintendent David Gaylor, retired, formerly of Sussex Police, and Glenn and Liz Stone of Kent Police.

Thanks are also owed to The Royal Literary Fund Fellowship Scheme, and to my agent, Vivien Green, for her unwavering support.

Over the time of writing this novel, I have had various physicists explain their work to me in great detail. I fear they will shake their heads at just how little I really understood. Were this a work of physics, my mistakes would be unforgivable, but this is a novel, and in my defence I would say that my aim was always to describe the poetry of physics as much as its mathematics.

Lastly, I wish to add that without the faith and encouragement of my husband, Tim Boon, this book would never have been written. I dedicate this book to him with gratitude and love.

Printed in Germany
by Amazon Distribution
GmbH, Leipzig